The Best Man

Dianne Blacklock

First published by Macmillan Australia in 2013
This edition published in 2017 by Dianne Blacklock

Copyright © Dianne Blacklock 2013

dianneblacklock.com

The Best Man

EPUB format: 9781925579604
Print on Demand format: 9781925579611

Cover design by Red Tally Studios

Publishing services provided by Critical Mass
www.critmassconsulting.com

Dianne Blacklock has been a teacher, trainer, counsellor, check-out chick, and even one of those annoying market researchers you avoid in shopping malls. Nowadays she tries not to annoy anyone by staying home and writing.

Also by Dianne Blacklock

Call Waiting
Wife for Hire
Almost Perfect
False Advertising
Crossing Paths
Three's a Crowd
The Right Time
The Secret Ingredient

To the readers who never stopped asking when my next book would be out, who cajoled, flattered, badgered and begged. You're the reason I keep writing, so this book is dedicated to all of you, with much love and gratitude.

Happy 80th Birthday, Dad!

Madeleine

Finally, LANDED flickered over on the arrivals board for United flight 839 from LAX. Madeleine let out a little squeal. She looked up at Henry's impassive face, her eyes shining.

'Well, aren't you excited?' she said.

'Of course,' he said calmly.

'You'd never know it. If I were you I'd be jumping out of my skin.'

'I am, just on the inside.'

She grinned. 'You can't jump *out* of your skin on the *in*side. That's not possible.'

He leant closer. 'Just between you and me, it's not possible to jump out of your skin at all.'

Madeleine screwed up her nose at him. 'Anything's possible in a metaphor.'

It didn't matter, she was excited enough for the both of them. She was finally going to meet Henry's lifelong best friend, Aiden Carmichael. Well, not entirely *life*long – they had been roommates in college back in the States, so it was more like half a lifetime. But Madeleine had never met anyone from Henry's past. And from all accounts Aiden was going to be a lot more forthcoming than Henry, which wouldn't be hard, given that Henry was one of the most *un*forthcoming people Madeleine had ever known. No, that wasn't fair, that made him sound cold or aloof, and he was neither. He was always calm and supremely patient, while she was generally excitable and terribly *im*patient, which often provoked the observation 'You two are so different!', to which Madeleine wanted to retort, 'Haven't you heard that opposites attract?' But she generally held her tongue these days; she didn't need to have a comeback for everything, better to let some things just slide. Being with Henry had taught her that. He was the yin to her yang, or the yang to her yin, whichever way it went. All she knew was that Henry centred her, providing much-needed balance in her life, and now she couldn't imagine a life without him. And that's why she was going to marry him, in just a few short weeks.

Her phone suddenly started to ring inside her handbag. She used to have the old-fashioned telephone ring, to differentiate it from all the pop tunes everyone else had. But then everyone must have had the same idea, and Madeleine was forever diving into her bag until she realised it wasn't her phone ringing. So she'd changed her ringtone to a rumba, or a tango, or the Macarena, something like that. And now she felt mortified every time it rang.

'It's not work, is it?' Henry sighed and returned his gaze to the arrivals board as Madeleine rooted around for her phone. Henry hated the thing, and she could hardly blame him; it did go off an awful lot, and the rumba-tango did get pretty annoying. Henry's phone rarely went off, seeing as she was about the only person who had his number.

She finally plucked it out of her bag and checked the screen. 'Nope, not work – Mum.' She flashed Henry a quick, appeasing smile before answering the phone, covering her other ear to block out the surrounding hubbub. 'Hi, Mum?'

'Yes, it's me. How did you know?'

Madeleine had to go over this every second time her mother rang. She really should just answer with her stock greeting, 'Madeleine Pepper's phone', but that usually elicited the response, 'No need to be so formal, it's only your mum.'

'Your name comes up on my phone, remember?' Madeleine explained now.

'Oh, that's clever,' Margaret said. 'How does it know?'

This was going to turn into one of those conversations if Madeleine didn't rein it in now. 'Listen, Mum, I can't hear you very well, so I better not stay on long. What were you ringing about?'

'Why can't you hear me? Are you in the shower?'

'No, Mum, you can't take a phone into the shower.' Madeleine thought it prudent to mention that little safety tip. 'We're at the airport, to pick up Henry's best man, remember?'

'Yes, I think I remember him. Pleasant-looking fellow, with the wavy brown hair?'

She was describing Henry. 'No, Mum, you haven't met Aiden.'

'Who's Aiden?'

'Henry's best man. His plane just landed. I haven't even met him yet.'

'Well, you'd better get off the phone and go and say hello or else it will look rude.'

'It's okay, he's not through Customs yet.'

'What was that?'

Madeleine had to put an end to this. 'You're right, Mum, I better go say hello. What were you calling about?'

'I wasn't calling you, I was calling your sister.'

'Oh, did you ring my number by mistake?'

'No, when Genevieve didn't answer I tried you instead. I thought you might know where she is.'

Madeleine glanced at her watch. It was just before nine. 'At this time of the morning she'll be in a mad panic trying to get the kids out the door for school. I think she'd likely ignore the phone.'

'But doesn't she have one of those phones like yours, that tells her who's calling?'

Of course she did, which explained why she didn't pick up. 'Was it important, Mum?'

'Oh, no, not important . . . I didn't mean to bother anyone . . .'

'You're not bothering anyone,' Madeleine tried to reassure her. 'It's just that Gen's usually pretty frantic before school. She probably thought she'd let it go to voicemail and then ring back later.'

'But I didn't leave a message. How will she know it was me?'

'The phone will know it was you.'

'Goodness, it's a little creepy, isn't it?'

'I guess.'

'Oh, I just realised . . . Is that why they call them smartphones?'

'It's probably one of the reasons,' said Madeleine. 'Anyway, if that's everything, Mum, I better go.'

'Say goodbye to Henry's friend for me,' Margaret said. 'We'll see him next time.'

Madeleine decided it wasn't worth trying to clarify things over again, so she said goodbye and hung up, turning off her phone this time before slipping it back into her bag.

'Is everything all right?' Henry asked.

She just gave him a shrug in reply.

Her mother had been like this ever since Madeleine's dad died. Well, not immediately after; at first she was grief-stricken and wandered around the house in a daze. Madeleine had had to cook and clean, and basically pick up after her as though she was a child. Eventually the fog lifted, but after that she was easily confused, her thoughts scattered, her memory patchy. At Genevieve's insistence, Madeleine finally took her for tests, but apparently there was nothing wrong with her, she didn't have Alzheimer's or dementia. The doctor had explained to Madeleine that as Margaret had always let her husband do the talking, make the decisions and generally deal with everything, she was probably just a little overwhelmed at having to do it for herself. Jonathan Pepper wasn't authoritarian, not in the least. He was kind and articulate and wise, and they had all deferred to him to varying degrees. So really, Margaret just had to find her own voice. She would be her old self again in time, the doctor assured Madeleine. But nearly ten years had passed, and she was still not her old self. How could she be, when she'd lost her other half?

'Any sign of him yet?' Madeleine asked Henry, craning to see between the heads blocking her view.

'The plane only landed five minutes ago,' he reminded her. 'He'll be a while yet. Do you want to go get a coffee?'

'No I do not,' she said, horrified. 'You can't say for sure how long it'll take. What if he was to come down the ramp, searching hopefully among the faces in the crowd, and we weren't here? It's unthinkable. We're not budging from this spot!'

'All right,' Henry said, looking bemused. 'Are you always this anxious waiting at airports?'

She glanced at him sideways. 'You should see me when I'm waiting for you.'

He smiled, leaning closer to press his lips against her forehead. 'We have had some significant moments in airports, haven't we?'

'Yes we have.' Madeleine tucked her arm into his. 'And this is going to be another. I'm just excited to finally meet someone from your side. It's a big deal, like meeting family for the first time.'

'But Aiden's not family.'

She scanned his face for a hint of sadness, but as usual, Henry wasn't giving anything away. It was only when they'd started to plan the wedding that Madeleine discovered there was no family on Henry's side to invite. He'd never talked about his early life much. She knew that he was born in Columbus, Ohio, the only child of older parents who hadn't been expecting a baby at that stage of their lives. Henry said they didn't really know what to do with a kid. He was fed and clothed and schooled, but left to his own devices the rest of the time. So from a very young age he'd learnt to occupy himself, which was how his passion for drawing, and later painting, had developed. Madeleine liked to imagine a Robert Louis Stevenson–type scenario, a small, sensitive boy tucked away in his bedroom creating stories – or, in Henry's case, pictures – and later becoming a renowned author and illustrator of children's books. She wondered why some clever marketing executive hadn't exploited that image ages ago, but Henry didn't need it now, his books sold on his name alone.

Sadly, his parents were never to know of his success. His mother died of kidney failure in Henry's first year away at college, and his father died some time after. Although Henry didn't say much about it, Madeleine gathered that he and his father hadn't had a great deal to do with each other in the intervening years. He'd had a grandmother, his mother's mother, who'd sent him a birthday card every year, with a five-dollar note inside. And each summer he'd made the trek back out to the Midwest to visit her, until she'd died too. He had no other family that he was aware of.

'Aiden's the closest thing you've got to family,' Madeleine pointed out. 'You said he's like a brother to you.'

'Yes, but I also told you he's nothing like me.'

'Still, he knew you way back, longer than anyone else I've met.'

Henry looked at her. 'Are you hoping to dig up some dirt on me?'

'I won't be holding my breath,' she said drolly. She couldn't imagine there being any dirt to dig up on Henry, though for some reason he did seem to have mixed feelings about Aiden coming to stay. Madeleine just put that down to the fact that Henry was an intensely private man, but she couldn't help being curious to meet someone who had shared a little of his past.

'Look,' she said, 'you know all my family, my friends, the people I work with. Don't you think that gives you a greater understanding of me?'

'I don't know,' he said. 'You're not much like your mother or Genevieve.'

'Oh yes I am,' she begged to differ.

'All due respect,' he said, dropping his voice, 'but they're both a little crazy.'

Madeleine smiled up at him. 'Don't you remember what I was like when we met?'

She often wondered now if she'd been on the verge of some kind of breakdown. Perhaps that was overstating it, but it would certainly not be an overstatement to say that her life had been spiralling out of control. And it had probably been heading that way ever since her dad died. It was a devastating loss for their family, really for anyone who knew Jon Pepper, and there were an awful lot of people who knew and loved him. He'd been a high school English teacher for nearly thirty years, and he should have had many more years ahead of him. The good really do die young – and it wasn't a cliché if it was true. Madeleine was always being pulled up for her overuse of clichés and metaphors; it was one of the drawbacks of spending your working life surrounded by authors and editors . . .

Anyway, where was she? (She was also frequently accused of losing track of what she was saying. Her mind just went into overdrive sometimes. Okay, often.) After her beloved father died, they'd all had to somehow find a way to go on without him. But Margaret had struggled, so even though Madeleine was twenty-five years old with two degrees under her belt and really should have been off finding her own feet, instead she had to stay around and help her mother find hers. By then Genevieve was already living out of home, and as far as she was concerned, Margaret was primarily Madeleine's responsibility. Especially with the wedding coming up. Genevieve had promptly become engaged to her boyfriend after their father's death, in a rather impulsive attempt to re-create the family she felt she'd lost, at least that's how Madeleine read it. What else could explain the sheer madness of organising a wedding when everyone was still in the throes of grief? Madeleine was appointed maid of honour, of course – a dubious honour which apparently gave Genevieve the right to treat her like an indentured servant, but indentured servant of honour didn't have quite the same ring to it.

Needless to say, the first year was tough. But with Genevieve safely delivered into matrimony, and Margaret becoming a smidge more independent, Madeleine was finally able to start thinking about her own future. Jonathan had instilled a love of literature in both his daughters, and so Madeleine found herself with both a BA and a master's in English literature and no idea what to do with either of them. After finishing her bachelor's degree she had only intended to take honours, but then her father got sick and she was incapable of thinking of life beyond his next treatment, his next test result, his dwindling options. So Madeleine stayed at uni, where it was familiar and comfortable, and her honours thesis developed into a master's. If her father had lived longer, she may well have ended up with a doctorate.

Jonathan had probably assumed she would follow the family tradition and become a teacher, just as Genevieve had, but the idea left Madeleine cold; the sheer patience required was beyond her. But what else was she going to do? The practical applications of her qualifications were limited, to say the least. Despite her obsession with books, she had no desire to write. Well, the truth was she couldn't write. She could barely manage a page of so-so, derivative prose before she got bored. What she did love to do was read, and she read fast and prolifically, always impatient to get to the end of the story and start on the next on her to-be-read pile. She didn't know of any jobs that paid you to do that.

But she had to do something. Eventually she registered with a temp agency so that she could gain some office skills, and after three excruciatingly dull and, frankly, mystifying placements in finance companies, she was sent to Amblin Press, a publishing house! Why hadn't she thought of this before? Although at her level the work was tiresome and seemed to consist almost entirely of photocopying, she was surrounded by books and manuscripts – so many pages, so many words, so much to read! She was in heaven, and she was in an ideal position to figure out where she could possibly slot into such an establishment.

The role of publisher appealed, naturally – getting to read manuscripts and take authors to lunch, while delegating all the boring stuff. Plus they seemed to be the only ones who had offices with windows. But the other thing Madeleine soon learnt was that to be a publisher you had to work your way up the editorial ladder and earn that office with a window. She could think of nothing more tedious or thankless than combing the pages of manuscripts searching for typos and errors and making corrections and writing tiny little notes on tiny little post-its. Good for them, salt of the earth and all that, books wouldn't be readable without editors . . . but it just wasn't for Madeleine. She knew her limitations: she simply did not possess the patience gene, or the focus gene, or the attention-to-detail gene, for that matter. The more senior editors wielded a broader brush, but to get to that level you still had to do the tedious jobs first. There seemed to be no way to bypass that painstaking route.

Then one day, on another floor, Madeleine discovered the publicity department and had an epiphany. It was just like in the movies when they play that angel-chorus sound effect. That's what Madeleine heard when she stepped into the big open-plan office, buzzing with activity. The women – and they were all women – were glamorous and confident and totally out there, and Madeleine was immediately in awe of them. She was seconded a few times to help out in the section, and although the work was boring there too – she was only temping, so it was mostly clipping reviews, answering phones, running errands – Madeleine was entranced just watching the publicists do their thing. It was like being in one of those old Hollywood screwball comedies with smart, sassy, fast-talking women in tight suits and high heels. If they weren't on the phone, they were rushing off to lunches or launches, or meeting planes and ferrying authors around to 'it' restaurants and being on a first-name basis with *everyone* in the media. And to top it all off, they got to read books – they *had* to read books, it was part of the job! Madeleine had found her calling, now she just had to find a way in.

She began by dressing the part, transforming her look from 'student on work experience' to proper, fully fledged working adult. Considering she had been an adult for some time, that transformation was long overdue. From then on, she put up her hand to work in publicity at every opportunity. If she was working in another section, she would drop by after she was finished to see if they needed a hand with anything, like one of those goody two-shoes, schoolgirl teacher's pets. Liv, the head publicist, started to notice her, and a kind of informal mentorship evolved. They often got to talking, late in the afternoon when no one else was around. Liv was going through a hard time since her marriage had broken down, leaving her holding not one but two babies – twins. They were school age by then and Liv was trying to juggle a demanding full-time job, which she loved, with raising her young sons, whom she loved much more. She constantly worried that she was a bad mother, and then she worried that she wasn't giving her all to her job. She adored her boys, but she wondered when she would ever get her life back, and then she worried that she was being selfish even having that thought.

Madeleine was horrified that someone as accomplished and amazing and awesome as Liv should be second guessing herself that way. So she told Liv she wasn't a bad mother at all, that her own sister was a married, stay-at-home mum and yet she, too, was constantly plagued with guilt that she wasn't a good mother. That it seemed to Madeleine that guilt was the default position for all mothers, and she pondered the now rapidly becoming age-old question of why men didn't have any guilt about juggling children and work. The two of them became fast friends, and the next time a position came up in the department Liv decided to give Madeleine the opportunity.

There was no way she was going to let Liv down, so Madeleine had literally thrown herself into the job – okay, not *literally*, she wouldn't hear the end of it if she dared to utter *that* in front of an editor. One could not literally throw oneself into a job, that wasn't physically possible, she got it. *Anyway* . . . the job, it consumed her life. It was more than nine to five, more than five days a week. She was on call nights, weekends, for days at a time at festivals, or weeks at a time on author tours, flying around the country, living in hotel rooms. There was one memorable stretch when she didn't sleep a single night in her own bed for eight weeks. But it was exhilarating and Madeleine thrived on it. She didn't have time any more to miss her dad, or feel guilty that she wasn't spending enough time with her mum, or listen to Genevieve telling her that she ought to feel guilty that she wasn't spending enough time with their mum . . . truth was she didn't have time to stop and think about much of anything. Certainly not what all of this was doing to her health and general wellbeing. After a few years in the job she was drinking way too much, way too often, but it was difficult to avoid. It was a rare author who didn't like a drink, and if you were accompanying them to events you had to be sociable. She even took up smoking for a while there; again, a fair proportion of authors liked a smoke, and with all the regulations they could only smoke outside, and Madeleine couldn't let them stand out there by themselves. She had to go with them, and it was easier just to join them – it made them feel more comfortable, and that was her job, after all.

'To get lung cancer?' Margaret cried, the first time she smelt it on Madeleine's clothes. Her mother was constantly worried about her. But her mother was constantly worried about everything: global warming, boat people, the Greens, bacteria on kitchen benchtops, you name it. She no longer had her husband's voice of reason to calm her fears, and so they proliferated unchecked, a little like bacteria on kitchen benchtops. Ever since she'd taken to listening to talkback radio – she said it kept her company – Margaret Pepper was frightened of everything.

Madeleine's lifestyle also provided her sister with endless opportunities to tell her what she was doing wrong with her life. Genevieve had the typical married-with-children mindset: everyone was supposed to *settle down*, because that's what adults did, even if it made them miserable. Madeleine had no business at her age to be out partying and travelling and generally having a good time.

'How are you ever going to settle down?' Genevieve would commonly ask.

'Who said I want to settle down?' Madeleine would commonly answer.

To which Genevieve would commonly take offence.

Madeleine could never understand why people reacted that way. If you lived your life differently to them it didn't mean you were casting aspersions on their choices. The logical conclusion of that line of thought would have everyone making the same choices, living the same lives. What a boring place the world would be then.

'You can't keep living like this, Mad,' Genevieve would declare loudly down the phone, so that she could be heard over the cacophony produced by three little boys running amok.

'It's my job,' Madeleine would reply.

'It's a young person's job,' Genevieve would counter. 'You're over thirty now, Mad, you're going to burn out at this rate. You have to start thinking about slowing down, getting into some other line of work.'

Though Madeleine would never have admitted it to Genevieve, she'd started to suspect she might be heading for burnout. She felt as though she was suffering from a perpetual hangover, she had to buy concealer in bulk to hide the dark shadows under her eyes, and she was becoming forgetful and sloppy. She had arrived late for a number of early meetings, wearing clothes she had fished out of a pile on the floor. Liv had started to make the odd pointed comment, and she was a seasoned party girl herself. However, there was an unwritten code in publicity: party as hard as you like, but you must never let it affect your work the next day. Despite having twins to organise, Liv was never late for morning meetings, Madeleine had never noticed dark circles under her eyes, and she would never have been caught dead in the same clothes two days running. Liv had told Madeleine that she had to start looking after herself or she wouldn't be any use to anyone. Then, with the Sydney Writers' Festival fast approaching, she was assigned just one, solitary children's author. Madeleine was dismayed; usually she handled three or four authors, depending on how big they were, if they had come from overseas, and how many sessions they were booked for. But Liv was adamant. Henry Darrow was very important, she explained, he made more money for them than most of the other authors at the festival put together. It was an absolute coup that he was coming at all – he was known to be a bit of a recluse, rarely attending festivals, and yet he was travelling all the way from the States for this.

Yay. A reclusive children's book author. This'll be fun, Madeleine had thought wryly.

'I still remember the expression on your face when you were waiting for me at the airport that first time, holding the placard with my name,' Henry said now. 'You didn't look very excited.'

'I was just having a pout because I was going to miss the festival opening-night party, and I'd *never* missed a festival opening-night party,' said Madeleine.

'Just because I didn't want to go didn't mean you couldn't.'

'Yes it did. See, it wasn't just the party, there was the afterparty as well, and they go all night, and I had to pick you up at, like, eight in the morning.'

'I'm sorry I ruined your fun.'

Madeleine grinned up at him. 'I know, the sacrifices I've made.'

She'd had to remain on her best behaviour for the entire festival, which wasn't too difficult – children's authors were not exactly party animals, and Henry's sessions were all scheduled in the morning. Madeleine offered to take him to lunch the first day, but he politely declined, saying he preferred to go for a walk, explore the city a little. The expression on her face must have given her away, because he quickly added, 'It's okay, you don't have to come with me.'

'But I do,' she said. 'It's my job.'

'You're not really dressed for walking,' he said with a glance at her pencil-thin skirt and matching pencil-thin heels. 'Seriously, Ms Pepper, I don't need a minder. And I can make my way back to the hotel myself, there's no need for you to wait around.'

Madeleine was perplexed. Liv would not be happy about this – she should be doing far more to promote him. 'What if I set up drinks later, after you've come back from your walk?' she suggested.

'I'm not much of a drinker, I'm afraid.'

'But there are lots of influential people here, I can arrange for you to meet some of them.'

'Why?'

'Well, so you can network, make contacts.'

He took his time to answer, and he seemed self-conscious when he finally did. 'I don't know if you're aware, Ms Pepper, but I'm doing all right. I don't really need to make "contacts".'

Madeleine cringed inside. Of course he didn't. He would be the star attraction at any meet and greet she could throw together, and she could totally understand why he didn't want to be put through that, considering his shyness.

Though Madeleine wasn't so sure she would call him shy. He was reserved, or maybe contained was a better word, but he seemed comfortable enough in his own skin. He led his sessions confidently, in a quiet but commanding voice that had his young audiences leaning forward in their seats to catch his every word. Even Madeleine had found herself mesmerised, and she was clearly not the only grown-up who was. The mothers lining up at the signings afterwards behaved like schoolgirls, giggling and flirting; one woman even leant right over the signing table to flash her cleavage at him, and she had a four year old with her! Madeleine had felt quite affronted, and then protective, and then outright possessive. *Back off, ladies*, she felt like saying, *he's mine. Um, as in, he's my charge . . . my responsibility . . . Oh, just back off!*

And it wasn't like he was all smooth and flirty back at them; on the contrary, he often looked abashed, and a little overwhelmed by it all. There was something in that diffidence, in the slight, tentative smiles, that Madeleine found endearing. Or maybe it was his eyes, soft brown eyes you could get quite lost in. Or his dark hair that looked like it was overdue for a cut, and was always a little tousled, which made you want to run your fingers through it to straighten it up, or at least Madeleine did.

Whatever it was, by week's end she'd decided she could not leave Henry Darrow to wander the streets again all day on his own. It was impolite, if nothing else, and he had shown himself to be polite to a fault. She felt he deserved the same consideration in return – indeed, it was her duty as his publicist.

So when she picked him up on the morning of his final session she was dressed in jeans and walking shoes. She noticed a faint flicker of surprise pass across his eyes.

'I figured you must have walked the entire length and breadth of the city by now and you might want to go further afield,' she said, oddly nervous. 'So after your session this morning, I'll be at your disposal for the rest of the day. I'll take you wherever you want to go.'

She was rewarded with a smile for that. Score. 'That's very thoughtful of you,' he said. 'I appreciate it.'

Of course, not knowing the country, he couldn't really say where he wanted to go, just that he wanted to go somewhere, anywhere, away from the city, and Madeleine knew just the place. Her father had been a keen bushwalker, and one of his favourite haunts was the Sydney Harbour National Park at North Head. It was just out of Manly, so it wouldn't take them too long to get there. But it was surprisingly secluded and unspoilt, even rugged in patches, and as a bonus it had fabulous views to the city across the water. Henry was suitably impressed, and he seemed to be more at ease out there in the open.

Madeleine would later tell people that this was the day she started to fall in love with Henry Darrow, even though nothing particularly remarkable happened. Mostly they'd just walked and talked. She learnt that he lived in New York, but that he also had a place in the Hamptons – he needed to get out of the city to be able to get inside his head to work. He craved open spaces, which was partly what had prompted him to accept the invitation to Australia, but he was a little disappointed to find that the outback was a long way out back and that Sydney was as bustling and busy as any international city.

As they walked, Madeleine found herself telling him about her life, her family, and especially her dad, something she wasn't in the habit of doing. Publicists were not particularly prone to talking about themselves, their job was to talk up other people, yet here she was, pouring out her life story to a stranger. But Henry didn't feel like a stranger. She didn't know exactly why; maybe it was because he reminded her a little of her dad, especially in that setting.

Perhaps the most surprising part for Madeleine was that they also walked for long stretches and didn't talk at all, which was a whole new experience for her. But it was okay, she didn't feel the need to fill up the silence with mindless chatter. And the silence, the stillness, was a revelation, clearing her head, giving her a sense of peace she hadn't felt in a long time.

That night Madeleine had poured herself a glass of wine and opened the box of Henry's books she'd brought home from the office. They had won awards in almost every language they had been translated into, but it wasn't really about the words – the pictures were universal. His books were bought by new parents to be the first books they read to their babies, and they were cherished by those same babies as they grew up. You were unlikely to find Henry Darrow books in secondhand stores – they were kept, destined to become heirlooms.

Madeleine had flicked through them before, of course, but they were picture books, with barely more than a line of text to a page. They could be read in a couple of minutes, so she'd never taken the time to examine them closely. Now she saw that the pictures were exquisite, simple and sophisticated at the same time. Clean, elegant lines and smudges of colour – dappled pink for a child's cheek, a blot of blue, and there was a baby with wonder in her eyes, so real that Madeleine could almost feel her breathing. On another page was a menacing sky in shades of grey and, unexpectedly, a splash of yellow. Again the colours were smudged on the page, with only a line and a couple of strokes to suggest the land below, or tufts of grass on the horizon. The colours darkened over the page, a storm was brewing, and Madeleine felt cold.

An hour passed, maybe two, and she hadn't touched her wine. She usually rushed through books, gobbling up the words greedily, but here the words were sparse, every syllable intentional. Madeleine slowed down, savouring the images. They held stories too; she just had to be still and give them time to sink in.

On second thoughts, maybe that was when she fell in love with Henry Darrow.

The following day, Madeleine took Henry to the airport for his flight home. He tried to insist that she drop him off at Departures, but Madeleine wouldn't hear of it. 'They make you check in so early for overseas flights, I don't want you to have to wait on your own all that time.'

'It's really okay.'

Madeleine didn't want to push it. Actually, yes she did. 'The thing is, I was going to ask you to sign some of your books for me.'

He glanced at the pile on the back seat, then gave her a faint smile. 'Of course.'

So after he'd checked in, they went to get coffee, and Henry signed the books, and Madeleine waited with him right up until his flight was called. They talked, or they didn't, either way was fine – she had never felt so comfortable just sitting in silence with another person. Finally, when they stood facing each other at the departure gate, she was overwhelmed by an urge to grab him and hold him close to her, to keep a part of him with her. There was something he had that she wanted to hold on to. Although she had met him only a few days ago, she knew she was going to feel bereft without him. But she had no idea what to do about it; nothing remotely like this had ever happened to her before.

Henry was first to speak. 'It was good to meet you.'

'It was?'

He smiled. That smile. 'Yes,' he assured her, 'it was very good to meet you, Madeleine.'

She loved the way he said her name in his soft Midwestern accent. Who knew Americans could be so soft-spoken?

'Thank you,' she said. 'Because I don't know if I come across all that well.'

'Why would you say that about yourself?' he asked kindly.

'What I mean is,' Madeleine quickly tried to explain, 'I talk too much, like I'm going to talk too much now. I'm sure someone like me must grate on someone like you. I mean, you choose your words carefully, and you don't need to yabber on all the time, whereas I don't seem to know when to stop – you might have noticed. But I hope I didn't grate on you, not too much anyway. Because I think . . . I think you're nice, you're very nice, and I've really enjoyed being your publicist, and getting to know you . . . and I really hope I see you again . . . sometime.'

As soon as she managed to get the words out, tears welled up in her eyes. She could *not* believe this was happening! He was going to think she was no better than a moony adolescent, and she would have to agree. But instead, to her surprise, he took both her hands in his, and Madeleine didn't feel the jolt of electricity you read about in romance novels, but rather a sense of calm, travelling right up her arms and through her whole body, engulfing her. It was like being wrapped in a warm blanket.

'I hope I see you again too,' he said.

Madeleine decided she had to do something to make sure of that. She had no idea what, but she couldn't let go of the first real connection she had felt to another person since her father had died.

The best she could come up with for now was to send an email, straightaway, so that it would be waiting for him when he arrived home. But when she sat down to write it, she had no idea what to say. They'd only just parted, she had no news to share, and there were only so many ways to ask him if he'd had a good flight home. After discarding too many attempts to count, Madeleine finally decided to be upfront.

> When I said I hope to see you again, I wasn't just being polite. I realise we live on opposite sides of the world, and I don't even know how it would be possible, but I really do want to see you again.
>
> There, I said it. If you think I'm nuts, just don't respond to this email.

But he did respond. *Anything's possible*, he assured her, *if you want it badly enough*.

The email conversation continued, and they became virtual best friends over cyberspace. Madeleine babbled about anything and everything. When she had a prickly author to deal with, or a stressful meeting coming up, Henry would always remember to ask her about it afterwards. He wrote to her when he hadn't talked to anyone else in days. She knew when he'd had a good day working, or a bad day, what the weather was like in the Hamptons, how beautiful the beach was in front of his cottage. She said she would love to see it. He said she should come over.

Madeleine said yes without hesitation. She was prepared to go halfway across the world to be with him even though they had never so much as kissed. It felt romantic and exciting . . . and bloody terrifying. What if she was reading more into it than Henry intended? What if he was only inviting her as a friend? She had gone on and on about New York and the Hamptons, how much she'd always wanted to go – perhaps he'd felt harangued into asking her?

'Are you kidding me?' Liv had said in response to Madeleine's litany of hypotheticals. 'He didn't ask you to come to New York – *and stay with him* – because he wants to give you a cheap holiday and show you the sights. Wake up and smell the bagels, girl.'

She had a point. 'Okay, but what if it all goes horribly wrong?' said Madeleine. 'We haven't even kissed. What if he's a terrible kisser? What if *I* am? You know, at least to him. What I mean is, what if there's just no chemistry?'

Liv groaned. 'So far there's been nothing *but* chemistry between you two. I don't think you have to worry about that. You should be more worried you might both spontaneously self-combust on contact, there's so much bloody chemistry.'

She was probably right, but still there was more turbulence going on inside Madeleine's head than on the flight over. But she knew what she had to do. She couldn't stand the uncertainty for a moment longer, and she had to leave no room for misinterpretation. So she marched through the barrier at JFK and right up to Henry, threw her arms around him and kissed him soundly. Although he couldn't have been expecting it, it took him only seconds to catch up, and as he brought his arms around her and held her close, Madeleine had the most overwhelming sensation that she was home – not in America, but with Henry.

They made love as soon as they got back to his apartment, but not urgently or frantically; Madeleine could never imagine Henry doing anything urgently. And she soon discovered to her delight that there was something to be said for non-urgent lovemaking. In fact, a lot to be said.

There followed almost a year of going back and forth between New York and Sydney – Madeleine only the once, she didn't have the leave or the funds to repeat it, but Henry came out four times.

Madeleine had never felt so grounded, and calm, and just happy. Except whenever he had to leave.

The morning of his last flight home, she was lying on the bed watching him pack, already missing him. 'I wish you didn't have to go.'

'Me too.'

She jumped up onto her knees. 'Then don't.'

'What?'

'I'll marry you,' she said. 'Then you won't have to go.'

He looked taken aback for a moment, and then he gave her an indulgent smile. 'That's not how it works, Madeleine.'

'Yes it is, you'll become a citizen automatically.'

'No, I won't.'

She looked blankly at him. 'You won't?'

'Citizenship isn't automatically granted on marriage,' he said. 'You still have to go through the whole process of proving your relationship.'

'Oh. Well, we can do that, can't we?'

'It hasn't been long enough.'

Madeleine's stomach lurched. She'd put him on the spot. She shouldn't have said anything about marrying him. What was she thinking? Worse, what was he?

'So you think it's too soon?' she said in a small voice.

'Not me, the Department of Immigration,' he said.

'Oh.' How should she take that? And how did he know all this? 'How do you know all this?' she asked out loud.

'I've looked into it.'

She blinked. 'You have?'

'I have.' Henry closed his suitcase, zipped it all the way around, then lifted it off the bed and set it down on the floor.

'And?' Madeleine said impatiently.

'What?'

'What did you find out?'

He took a breath. 'As I'm self-supporting and wouldn't be expecting to draw any kind of government benefits, and would certainly not be taking anyone else's job, I can apply for a long-stay visa and simply wait it out a couple of years. Then, on fulfilling a few other conditions, like a health check, I'll most likely be granted permanent residency. So we can get married any time we like.'

Madeleine's eyes widened. 'Oh . . . So, um, have you . . . have you thought about what you might want to do?'

'I've already applied for the visa.'

'Henry!' She lunged at him from the bed, throwing her arms around his neck. 'Why didn't you tell me?'

'I was going to surprise you,' he said. 'But now you've stolen all my thunder.'

'I'm sorry.'

'It's okay.' He gave her a quick kiss on the lips. 'But I'll have to cancel the skywriter.'

She drew back to look at him. 'What are you talking about?'

'It's just part of the whole big proposal thing I had planned.'

'There's no need to tease,' she said. 'I was only trying to find a way that you could stay.'

'So you don't want me to propose?'

Now she was confused. 'I didn't say that . . . I just wasn't trying to force your hand.'

'Well,' he said, 'it's ruined now anyway. Shame really, it was going to be pretty amazing.'

Madeleine caught the glint in his eye. She dropped back onto the bed, propping herself on her elbows and looking up at him. 'Well, a skywriter's okay, I guess. Is that all you got?'

'No,' he said, sitting down beside her. 'I'll have to call it off with the zoo as well.'

'The zoo?' She raised an eyebrow.

Henry nodded. 'They've been training a seal to balance the ring on his nose and present it to you during the seal show. It would have brought the house down.'

'Stop it.'

'You think I'm making this up?'

'I think this is what I get for falling in love with a children's author,' said Madeleine. 'Fantastical stories about seals delivering rings.'

'It's not all "fantastical", and I'm not even sure that's a word.'

'It is so a word. It perfectly describes ridiculous stories made up by boyfriends to tease their girlfriends.'

'I'm not teasing you.'

'About the seal?'

'No, about the ring.'

'Enough!'

'You don't believe me?'

'I'll believe it when I see it.'

'It's locked in a safety deposit box back home,' said Henry. 'I'll bring it with me next time.'

Madeleine's heart was racing, but she still didn't want to fall for it. Though she couldn't recall Henry ever being such a tease before. She sat up straight, facing him. 'When did you get it?'

'Six months ago.'

'That long?'

'I've known longer than that, but I bought it six months ago.'

Her eyes teared up. 'You did? You really did? You're not teasing?'

Henry smiled. 'I wouldn't tease you about this.'

'So what have you been waiting for?'

'These things take a lot of planning, the seal had to be trained . . .'

'Henry!'

He took hold of her hands. 'I've been waiting,' he said, 'to have the long-stay visa approved, and to come back here and tell you that I love you, and that I want to be with you every day, all the days of my life, for as long as we both shall live. And that's when I was going to give you the ring.'

Which was exactly what he did, two months later, in the arrivals hall, not far from where they were standing now. He didn't get down on one knee or anything – Henry wouldn't want to attract attention – but Madeleine liked it that way anyway. This momentous thing was happening in the middle of all the hubbub, and no one even knew.

'We have had a lot of significant moments in airports,' she sighed happily, leaning her head on Henry's shoulder.

'Ah, there he is,' Henry said calmly. 'Oh, sorry, what did you say?'

Madeleine jerked her head up. 'No, what did *you* say?'

'Aiden,' he said. 'He's walking down the ramp.'

She gasped. 'Where?'

Henry leaned in close to her and raised his arm to point through the mass of people congregating at the base of the ramp. Madeleine's eyes followed, and the face she had previously seen only in photographs suddenly came into focus. She wondered how she could have missed him; tall and bronzed, with golden-blond hair, he looked like a movie star in the midst of all the rumpled travellers.

'I don't think he can see us,' said Henry.

Madeleine sprang into action. 'Aiden!' she cried, waving furiously, before launching herself headlong into the throng. Henry had to grab hold of the back of her jacket to keep up with her. Soon they all arrived at the clearing at the end of the ramp, and there was a moment's hesitation as they stood smiling expectantly at one another. Someone had to say something.

'Man, you've gotten old, Darrow.'

Henry's face broke into a wider-than-usual-for-Henry smile. 'And you haven't changed at all, Aid.'

Aiden laughed loudly as he shoved his luggage trolley aside and threw his arms around Henry with such exuberance that Madeleine thought Henry's feet might have left the ground. Aiden eventually released him, turning his sights on her.

'Madeleine, I presume?' he said, before sweeping her up in an equally enthusiastic hug, and because she was shorter and lighter than Henry, her feet actually did leave the ground before he set her down again.

'You didn't tell me your wife-to-be was such a knockout,' he declared.

'He didn't?' said Madeleine. 'You didn't?' She turned to Henry with mock indignation.

Of course Henry didn't, that wasn't his way. Aiden was clearly a charmer. Madeleine scrubbed up all right, but she knew she was nothing out of the ordinary. She had never been too hung up on her looks – her dad had always made both her and Genevieve feel like they were the most beautiful girls in the world. But he also used to say that looks were a gift you were given, character was a gift you gave to others. Her eyes were her best feature, mostly because they were an unusual shade of green. She had her dad's eyes, so she was happy to accept compliments for them.

'I had a feeling you two were going to gang up on me,' Henry was saying. 'I just didn't expect it to start two minutes after you arrived, Aid.'

'Have you forgotten what a fast worker I am?' Aiden joked, offering Madeleine his arm. 'Grab the trolley, would you, Darrow?'

Henry trailed behind them out of the airport as Aiden and Madeleine got acquainted, exchanging all the usual pleasantries: How was his flight? Did he manage to get any sleep? How were the wedding preparations coming along? Did she know it wasn't too late to ditch Henry and run away with him?

'You know I can hear you, right?' Henry said from the rear.

It occurred to Madeleine that Henry had also failed to mention quite how breathtakingly good-looking his friend was. But she supposed that was something guys didn't do. She had seen pictures of Aiden in their college yearbook, but that was a long time ago, when they were both still very boyish-looking – handsome, but with decidedly bad haircuts, and yet to fully grow into their features. Henry didn't have any other albums, or boxes of old photos; she supposed that was something guys didn't do either. So Madeleine had had no choice but to google Aiden. That always made her feel a bit like a stalker, but Liv told her that was nonsense, as she grabbed the keyboard from Madeleine and typed in his name. Unsurprisingly, given his résumé, there was no shortage of images. Aiden set up relief programs across the third world on behalf of a major multinational, so there were pictures of him standing among groups of shiny black children in Africa, outside humpies with toothless old men in Vietnam, surveying the slums of Mexico and India. In the photos he always had a smile on his face, his eyes bright with hope despite the apparent hopelessness of his surroundings. But the energy of the man in the flesh was a whole other thing.

'Well, gentlemen,' Madeleine said as they exited the terminal, 'this is where I must love you and leave you.'

Aiden's face dropped. 'What are you talking about? I just got here.'

'I'm afraid some of us have to work.'

'I'm crushed!' he said, holding a hand to his heart. 'I thought your lives would revolve around me from the moment I deigned to grace you with my presence.'

Madeleine grinned up at him. 'That's what you get for arriving on a weekday.'

Aiden turned to Henry. 'Looks like it's just you and me, bud,' he said as he slapped Henry on the back.

'I'll be home for dinner, we'll catch up properly then,' Madeleine promised. She reached up to give him a hug. 'I'm so glad you're here, Aiden.'

'And I'm glad to be here.'

9.30 am

Madeleine had left her car at work the night before so they would only have to bring one car to the airport today. Now in the cab on the way to the office, she had the chance to check her messages. There was already a screenful of missed calls, texts and voicemails, and it was barely half an hour into the working day.

Since Henry had moved to Australia, Madeleine had gradually taken on more responsibility in the office so she wouldn't have to do so much travelling. She'd kept the authors she had at the time, but she didn't take on any more, nor did she look after any of the one-off blockbusters – celebrity autobiographies, memoirs of sporting stars, or exposés by journalists with an inside scoop and often a grudge. As it happened, Liv had been itching to get back on the road ever since the twins had started high school and she didn't have to be quite so hands-on with them, so the change in roles suited them both. Though it didn't take long for Madeleine to see why Liv had wanted a break: these days, the buck stopped right at her feet with a resounding thud. Every mistake, misquote, missing author, even flight delays, were either blamed on her or she was expected to fix them somehow. It was an entirely different world of stress, she just got to go home at night. Most of the time.

Madeleine called Stacey first. Stacey was the publicity assistant and Madeleine's right-hand girl. She was efficient, organised and completely indispensable.

'Hey, how's the best man?' she chirped. 'Did he arrive in one piece?'

'He did,' Madeleine confirmed. 'He and Henry are off having some quality time together, and I'm on my way in now.'

'I've got about a bazillion messages. What order do you want them in?'

'From bad to worse, I guess.'

'Okay, the library called about Emily Tanner's event, they've only had four bookings so far and they think they should cancel. What shall I tell them?'

Madeleine sighed. Emily's self-esteem was wafer thin as it was. 'Leave it with me. I'll give the library a call, see if there isn't something we can do. And I'll handle Emily myself. Next?'

'Lydia Carlyle rang about the marketing for her literary lunch.'

'But that's being handled by the events manager at the venue.'

'I know, but she wants us to fix it. She's angry that they called her book a romance.'

'They called it "a romance in the tradition of *Jane Eyre*",' said Madeleine. Though God knows why. 'How can she have a problem with that?'

'Maybe she's never read *Jane Eyre*?'

'Well it's about time she did. Leave it with me. Next?'

'Peter Norris rang, upset about the review in the weekend paper.'

Madeleine groaned. 'Did you remind him that we don't write the reviews?'

'Of course.'

'Okay, I'll talk to him. Anything else?'

'Let me see . . . The books haven't been delivered for the *Taste* launch . . . Um, Michael Kelly wasn't home, or at least he wasn't answering his phone at the appointed time for his radio interview –'

'Get Amy onto that. He's her author.'

'She's on tour with Brad Mackie.'

The footballer. 'Damn, I forgot.'

These were the times Madeleine missed only having to worry about her own stable of authors. At least then if something went wrong it was her fault or her problem and her direct responsibility. Now she was forever cleaning up other people's messes.

'Anything else?' she said, less than enthusiastically.

'Oh, you know, the usual. I can deal with most of this.' Stacey was very good at picking up on tone. 'Have you had coffee yet?'

'No.'

'What's your ETA?'

Madeleine peered out the windscreen to the road ahead. 'Ten, maybe fifteen?'

'Okay, I'm onto it.'

Bless her. Madeleine loved Stacey so much she would have married her if she wasn't already marrying Henry. And if she wasn't heterosexual. And if Stacey wasn't.

Madeleine rang the library first, and had a chat to the event coordinator. In situations like these they could sometimes dig up relatives and friends to flesh out the numbers, but the woman said they'd already tried everything. They agreed it would be worse to go ahead, but Madeleine discovered that there had been one other author event cancelled in the last couple of months. That would help her to put an acceptable spin on it to Emily, to reassure her that this happened all the time. And in fact, it did happen all the time. But Emily would take it badly. On the other hand, Madeleine knew she'd be relieved that she didn't have to get up and talk in front of all those people. The problem was, this would make it doubly difficult to convince her to do it next time.

Madeleine put a reminder in her phone to email her – it was preferable to calling her: Emily wasn't good on the phone, she would only be awkward and embarrassed. This way, Madeleine could carefully word an email, and Emily could take her time to digest it. And within a day or two, Madeleine knew she would receive a thoughtfully crafted response. Emily always wrote beautiful, lyrical prose that broke your heart. Her books just didn't sell all that well, and that broke everyone's hearts at Amblin Press.

Lydia Carlyle was another story. Real name Lina Hammoud, she had taken a pseudonym that she considered would be more marketable in the current climate. Certainly no one at Amblin had put that on her, and Madeleine was pretty sure it had more to do with ensuring her books sat in a prominent position on the shelves. She sold well, but she was what was known in the trade as a 'difficult' author. Her writing was perfunctory, as were her storylines, so why her books were so popular was anybody's guess. If publishers knew what made a bestseller, or even a respectable seller, obviously that was all they would publish. But nobody knew. The longer Madeleine worked in publishing, the surer she was that there was no such thing as a sure thing. Beautiful books failed, dreadful dross prospered, it might as well be on the roll of a dice. And once in a while an author came along who didn't consider themselves lucky at all, but perfectly entitled, and everyone was forced to cajole and flatter and generally pander to them. The confounding nature of fate and success never ceased to bewilder Madeleine.

Lydia was crisp when she first answered the phone, until Madeleine had performed the requisite amount of sucking up. Once Lydia had relaxed, Madeleine started to work through the 'issue'. As predicted, she had not read *Jane Eyre*, though she didn't exactly admit to that, instead brushing off the question with a vague, 'Of course I did . . . I must have . . . years ago.' Madeleine certainly had no idea why the events manager had made the comparison. She could only guess she hadn't read more than the blurb of Lydia's book and her imagination had taken flight with the reference to a male protagonist tortured by memories of a wife driven to suicide. But *Chasing Butterflies* was no *Jane Eyre*. It was a tired romance between a lepidopterist and an environmentalist, with pretensions to something more weighty indicated by a liberal sprinkling of pseudo-scientific 'facts' throughout.

Madeleine proposed that Lydia read the classic novel again – she would even send her a copy – and then, if she still didn't like the comparison, Madeleine promised she'd do something about the offending quote. But Lydia would have to be quick, she urged – the luncheon was only weeks away and the advertising copy had to go to press ASAP. Madeleine knew that Lydia wouldn't read the book, but she would probably google *Jane Eyre* and read some critiques, and hopefully that would be enough to silence her. She'd had her fifteen minutes of attention, which was mostly what this was about. Lydia liked to remind her underlings on a regular basis that she was Important and they'd better not forget it.

As her cab pulled up outside the offices of Amblin Press, Madeleine was just wrapping up her standard spiel to Peter Norris re the bad review – in essence, all publicity was good publicity (even though that had never actually been proven with hard data). She told him that his name and the name of his book would stick in people's minds, so that when they saw it in a store they would think, 'Oh yes, I've heard of him,' and not remember the details of what they had actually heard, or rather read.

'Sorry, Peter, I'm heading for the elevator, so I'll probably lose you. Would you like me to call you back?'

'Oh no, don't worry about it any further, Madeleine,' he assured her, in a tone far less vexed than when they'd started the conversation. 'It was good of you to call me back so promptly.'

'Well, of course, you're very important to us. Anything I can do, ever, you only have to call. I hope you know that.'

'I do. Thank you, Madeleine.'

Peter was all right, he was just insecure. He was an author; that was their default position.

As Madeleine rode the lift to her floor, she remembered an interview with a director who made the remark that filmmaking would be a lot easier without actors. It could be a little like that in publishing.

'Morning!' Stacey greeted Madeleine with a coffee as she came around the corner into the bustling publicity department. Whatever problems she knew she had waiting for her, Madeleine still got a buzz whenever she walked into the open-plan office.

'Thank you, thank you,' she said, taking a sip of the coffee and experiencing instant relief. She knew the caffeine couldn't have hit her bloodstream that quickly, so it had to be some kind of Pavlov's dog effect – the aroma and taste were enough to produce the physiological response. Whatever it was, Madeleine was grateful. It was really too late in the morning for her first coffee.

'I sorted out the delivery for the *Taste* launch,' Stacey said, following Madeleine to her desk.

'Great, and I've more or less dealt with the others,' said Madeleine. 'Have any more catastrophes occurred in the last ten minutes?'

Stacey smiled. 'No, you should have time to drink your coffee.'

Madeleine dumped her bag on the desk and dropped down into her chair.

'So, what's he like?' Ren popped her head around the wall. Madeleine didn't have an office, as such. She was tucked into the space created by a nib wall, providing an annexure of sorts.

'What's who like?' Madeleine asked blithely.

'The best man, of course!' Sarah exclaimed, wheeling her chair over.

'He has a name,' Madeleine reminded them.

'Aiden.' Natalie pretended to swoon as she did a kind of pirouette across the floor.

Seriously?

'Is he like Aiden from *Sex and the City*?' asked Sarah, almost bursting from the very idea.

'Yes,' Madeleine said, deadpan. 'Because all babies who are named Aiden grow up to look the same. Even fictitious ones. That's how it works.'

Stacey smiled.

'Oh, come on, give us something!' Natalie stamped her foot. 'Did you take a photo of him?'

Madeleine hadn't shown them Aiden's picture online, or mentioned his surname, so they couldn't google him themselves. She had intentionally kept as many Aiden-related details to herself for now. It was enough for these girls that he was a single male; they'd become rabid once they actually got a glimpse of him.

'Did I take a photo?' Madeleine pondered. 'Sure, as he came through the arrivals hall, I said, "Hi, Aiden, nice to meet you. Now would you mind posing for a photo so I can show you off to my desperate colleagues?" '

'You know sarcasm is the refuge of the . . .' Natalie bit her lip. 'What is it again?'

'The smart-arse,' Ren finished for her. 'Why are you being so secretive, Mad? We're going to meet him soon enough at the wedding.'

'And you can't keep him for yourself anyway,' Sarah pointed out. 'You've already got Henry.'

'Gosh, thanks for reminding me,' said Madeleine, 'or I might have accidentally married Aiden as well.'

'What's with all the snark?' said Ren. 'We're just interested.'

'All right,' Madeleine relented. 'For the five minutes I got to spend with him walking through the terminal, he seemed very nice.'

'Is he good-looking?' Natalie asked.

'Yes.'

'How good-looking?'

'Very.'

That was met with a collective gasp.

'What part of the States is he from?' said Ren. 'I love a Boston accent. What's his accent like?'

Madeleine thought about it. She hadn't really noticed an accent, maybe because she was so used to Henry. Or perhaps with all the travelling he did Aiden had developed one of those neutral, transatlantic accents. 'It's not that strong,' she said finally. 'I know he's originally from New York state – Long Island, I think. But he travels a lot.'

Natalie's eyes lit up. 'What does he do?'

Okay, this had gone far enough. 'Listen, what's with the twenty questions?'

'He's a single man,' Ren said flatly. 'We work in publishing. We don't come across many of his kind.'

This was true. The publishing industry was dominated by women, until you got to the upper echelons of management, and then there were suddenly men everywhere. No one knew where they came from, but they were usually older and mostly married, so it was not a workplace where one was likely to find a husband. Or even a boyfriend. Or even a date. Aiden was going to be fair game at the wedding. Poor man, what had she dragged him into?

'Right, girls, can we just get on with it?' said Madeleine. 'I have not one but *two* gorgeous men waiting at home for me, so I want to get out of here at a reasonable time.'

'You don't have to brag,' Ren muttered, as they all turned back towards their desks and work.

Liv

The plane trip home was one of Liv's favourite parts of any book tour. On the final leg she never travelled with the author, usually able to concoct an excuse that there was business to wrap up at their last port of call and she would have to catch a later plane. This was as much for the author's sake as hers. The publicist–author relationship was a funny one – it involved spending an inordinate amount of time together, but in short, intense bursts, which led to a level of intimacy that could be trying, especially if you weren't a natural fit. As head of publicity, Liv did her darndest to match the author to the right publicist, and she generally took on the more difficult contenders. However, for her troubles, she also kept one or two of the best for herself. Cameron West was adorable, easygoing, a sheer delight to tour with, and Liv genuinely enjoyed his books. Maybe because she had boys she had developed an appreciation of the action-adventure genre. Over the last year she had introduced Cameron's books to the twins and they were now hooked – even Lachie, who was a reluctant reader at best.

As things had turned out, Cameron was taking a couple more days in Melbourne to catch up with friends, so there was no need for any kind of ruse on her part. Liv boarded the plane as soon as it was called, took her seat by the window and set about organising herself for the flight. She took out her e-reader, though unfortunately, due to somewhat draconian airline rules, she couldn't turn it on until after take-off, and that was a pain in the backside. It wasn't that she couldn't cope without being plugged into an electronic device for twenty minutes – she loved that she had a legitimate reason to turn off her phone, for example. No, it was that she wanted to look like she was occupied, so that whoever sat in the adjacent seat didn't think they had an invitation to chat. For the entire flight. Liv had worked out long ago that she must just have one of those faces: people were always striking up conversations with her, mistaking her for a salesperson in shops, asking for complicated help or directions in the street, talking to her from the next table in cafés. Crazy people seemed particularly drawn to her, all the more so in confined spaces where she had no means of escape. So on planes she always made sure she had her head buried in a book. But these days she only carried a Kindle or an iPad, largely to keep up with her reading for work. Liv needed to read books before they were printed, and she could carry a veritable truckload of manuscripts in one slim little device.

So the rule about e-readers was just plain annoying. The flight home was Liv's last chance to be alone for a while. No more nights in hotel rooms on her own, with no washing or homework, or meals to cook. She missed the boys when she was away on tour, desperately at times, but once she was home it didn't take long for her to crave solitude, and room service.

Just when she was thinking she might have been lucky enough to have scored an empty row, she became aware of someone rummaging in the overhead locker. Damn, she should have grabbed the inflight magazine and pretended to be absorbed in it; not that anyone would believe that. Instead she turned away and stared resolutely out the window as the guilty party dropped heavily into the aisle seat. Without moving her head, Liv peered out of the corner of her eye and glimpsed a pair of men's shoes. At least there was still a seat between them. That usually provided enough of a buffer.

'You use an e-reader too,' said the owner of the shoes.

Not so much of a buffer after all.

Liv shifted a little to better see what he was doing. He was sliding his device into the seat pocket in front of him, as Liv had done with hers; he'd obviously noticed her Kindle protruding.

'Crazy how they don't let you turn them on till after take-off,' he continued. 'They're completely innocuous, especially with wi-fi turned off.'

Liv offered a faint murmur of agreement. While she valued her privacy, she was incapable of being rude. Years as a publicist had trained her to be assiduously polite; maybe that's why the crazies always talked to her. She stole a quick furtive glance at her neighbour. He seemed normal enough – he was a reader, so he couldn't be all bad – and she knew now that he had something to occupy him for the trip. So she decided it was safe to engage, for the moment.

'I heard it's because flight attendants can't be expected to check everyone's device individually, to make sure the wi-fi is turned off,' she said. 'So they have to institute a blanket rule.'

'How much longer do you reckon they'll get away with that?' he said. 'People can barely go five minutes without checking their smartphones. I foresee an uprising: "You can take away our freedom to move around the cabin, but you'll never take away our right to be plugged in twenty-four/seven."'

Liv smiled. 'I'm more than happy to have an excuse to turn off my phone.'

'I take your point,' he said, turning to face her fully for the first time. He was actually not bad-looking for an old bloke. 'Old bloke' being anyone in her general age group. Though blokes over forty did get out of it so much better than women. The salt and pepper hair looked great on him; the creases around his blue-grey eyes as he smiled, damned attractive.

Liv suddenly realised she was staring. She cleared her throat. 'Anyway, could you imagine a flight where everyone was taking calls the whole time?' she said. 'That would do my head in. A plane trip is respite for me.'

'I take it your work involves a lot of time on the phone?'

'Doesn't everyone's?' she said, and left it at that. Liv tried to avoid revealing what she did for a living, at least with strangers. Everyone believed they had a book in them, and as soon as they discovered she worked in publishing they wanted to tell her all about their fabulous idea. And a plane was the perfect place to do just that: she was a captive audience.

They were conveniently interrupted by the pre-flight announcements over the PA.

'I hope you'll excuse me,' her neighbour said, his voice lowered. 'But I always try to pay attention to the safety demonstration.'

'Oh, do you have a fear of crashing?'

'Well, yeah,' he said. 'Does anybody like the idea of crashing?'

Good point.

'Actually, I try not to listen too closely,' he said. 'It does kind of freak me out when they show you the light and whistle in case you end up in water in the dark. No one really wants that image in their head when the plane's about to take off.'

'Yet now I do,' said Liv.

'Sorry,' he said with a self-conscious smile.

'It's fine,' she assured him.

'Anyway,' he went on, 'I feel a little sorry for the flight attendant, standing up there doing her act and being ignored. I just like to show some respect.'

Liv was oddly touched by that.

'Besides, I reckon if I make eye contact, she'll be more likely to come to my aid in the event of an accident, when everyone else who ignored her has no idea.'

That made her smile. 'So there's method in your madness?'

'Always,' he said, returning her smile. 'I'm David, by the way.'

Were names really necessary? But it would be rude if she didn't respond now; it was a slippery slope once you decided to engage. 'Liv,' she said finally.

He nodded. 'Is that short for anything?'

'No, my mother named me after the actress Liv Ullmann. She's Norwegian.'

'Your mother?'

'No, Liv Ullmann. I guess Norwegians don't feel the need to have longer names.'

'Maybe because it's so cold they don't want to have to open their mouths for more syllables than absolutely necessary.'

'That could be it.'

'Your mother must have really loved that actress,' he mused.

'Not particularly, she just liked the name.'

The flight attendant began her spiel, and David turned dutifully towards the front. Liv wasn't named after any actress; her mother wouldn't have even heard of Liv Ullmann, let alone seen one of her films. The truth was that Liv was short for Olive, but she never told anyone that. Most people assumed her name was Olivia, and she didn't correct them. Funny how one syllable could make such a difference. Olivia was such a pretty name, you expected an Olivia to be attractive, whereas Olive was the dowdy sister, scowling in the corner. Apparently the name was enjoying some kind of hipster resurgence now, but Liv didn't care what heights of cooldom it achieved – she had dropped it as a girl, and she didn't even consider it her name anymore. Despite the fact that her mother persisted in using it, in all its drab green glory.

The attendant finished her demonstration, and they were taxiing to the runway.

'Can't say I enjoy take-off,' said David, almost to himself.

Liv glanced across at him. He was sitting quite stiffly in his seat, his hands clasped in his lap. 'I fly so much I don't even notice any more,' she said, she hoped reassuringly. 'It's over so quickly.'

'I know. I just don't like that bit after the ascent when it feels like the engines cut out.' He grimaced. 'After that I'm okay.'

Liv found it a little endearing that he would admit to something like that, it was nothing like the macho crap she was used to. Rick would consider it a weakness. But some people just weren't good flyers, and needed distracting; Liv had had to do it for enough authors over the years. 'So, are you coming or going?' she asked.

He looked at her. 'I'm sorry?'

'Well, I mean are you coming home to Sydney, or visiting from Melbourne?'

'Going home to Sydney,' he said. 'What about you?'

'Home to Sydney too.' She noticed that he unclasped his hands and took hold of the armrests instead. 'Were you in Melbourne for work?' she asked.

He shook his head. 'No, my daughter's graduation, actually.'

'Oh, that's special,' said Liv. She should be able to keep him talking now. 'What was she graduating from?'

'Medicine.'

Liv didn't expect that; he didn't look old enough to have a doctor for a daughter. 'You must be very proud.'

'I am,' he said. 'And broke. She's going on to do a specialty now, so that'll be another six years, but at least she'll start getting paid.'

'You must have had her very young,' said Liv.

He smiled. 'I'll take that as a compliment,' he said. 'But it's true, we were very young, and it didn't last. But I've got Scarlett, so I'm not complaining.'

'Her name's Scarlett?'

'Like I said, we were very young.'

'No, I think it's a lovely name.'

'She doesn't, not for a doctor anyway. It's true what they say – when you're naming your child you should think about how it will sound if they want to be a doctor or a lawyer, or a politician.'

'I was told to try yelling the names out the back door, see how they sounded.'

He laughed. 'So you have kids too?'

Liv nodded. 'Two boys.'

'How old are they?'

'Just turned fourteen.'

'And?' David prompted.

She looked at him.

'You said you had two?' he said. 'One's just turned fourteen . . .'

'Oh,' Liv said. 'Didn't I say they were twins?'

'No you didn't, but now it all makes sense.' He grinned. 'Wow, twins, that must be fascinating.'

'It has its moments,' said Liv.

'Are they identical?'

'They are.'

He was shaking his head with an expression of awe. 'I've always wondered what it must be like to look at another person like you're looking into a mirror.'

'Well, they're not mirror image,' said Liv. 'That only happens in about a quarter of identical twins.'

'Oh. There you go.'

'I'm a regular fount of fun twin facts.'

David smiled. 'Do twins run in your family?'

'No.'

'Your husband's?'

She wondered if that was a veiled attempt to find out if she was married. 'Identical twins aren't hereditary,' she answered, sidestepping the husband issue altogether. 'They're just an accident of birth. Did you know that the rate of identical twins is the same across all races, wherever you live, no matter what the conditions?'

'You *are* a fount of twin facts.'

'Told you so.' She paused. 'And we're up and away.'

David glanced past her out the window. 'So we are.' He gave her a slightly bashful look. 'Thank you for taking my mind off it. It was nice talking to you. You're off the hook now, I don't want to keep you from your reading.'

Liv realised she wouldn't mind continuing the conversation, but he was reaching for his e-reader, so she reached for hers as well, with a vague feeling of disappointment, and she wasn't sure why. She had all but ceased to think about men as romantic prospects. It had just been too long. In the beginning, another relationship was the last thing she wanted. Rick had hurt her badly, over and over. The coming and going, the admissions of wrongdoing, the professions of undying love, the abject pleas to take him back. And then he'd go out and do it all over again. When Liv thought of herself back then, it made her cringe. She'd always considered herself a strong woman, fiercely independent. She'd made Rick work very hard to win her over in the first place. They'd met when they were both working for the same PR firm; Liv was ambitious, and marriage wasn't part of her game plan. As the product of an ultra-conservative marriage, she had vowed never to find herself trapped in a loveless – or at least stagnant – union, unable to move out of it because of inertia, because of the kids, because you simply didn't know any other way of being. But Rick convinced her they'd be different.

'Then why get married?' she had protested at the time. 'It's only a piece of paper.'

'If it's only a piece of paper, why are you so against it?'

He was persistent. He wore her down, even bought a ring and did the whole romantic proposal thing, which only served to make Liv feel awkward and guilty for saying no. But it didn't faze Rick one bit; he took it as a challenge, not a rejection. He talked about it all the time, always referring to '*when* we get married', as if it was a foregone conclusion. He especially loved it when the topic came up around their friends, who were all dropping like flies into the marital pond. 'When are you two going to tie the knot?' they would ask, or worse, 'When are you going to make an honest woman out of her?' Ugh. And each time Rick would give the same forlorn answer: 'I would marry her in a heartbeat, but she keeps turning me down.' Everyone would sympathise with 'poor Rick', wanting to know if Liv realised how lucky she was to have a man who wasn't afraid of commitment, telling her she ought to snap him up while she could, and offering a lot of other opinions that she hadn't asked for.

Liv often wondered what it would be like the other way around – if it was Rick who didn't want to marry her and she moped about, complaining loudly to her friends in front of him, would they all be siding with her and giving Rick a hard time? Of course not; she'd probably be hustled out of sight and admonished by her girlfriends to stop embarrassing herself, it was only making her look pathetic.

Liv had finally said yes, to shut him up as much as anything. But it wasn't going to change a thing, she warned him.

Of course it did, subtly, insidiously. The first time Rick called her his wife, Liv felt like a possession. Sure, he was her husband, but for some reason it felt more like a label of subjugation the other way around. Maybe it was all in her head, she didn't know. They got on with their lives, bought a house, bickered over the equitable division of chores, split Christmas Day between both sets of parents . . . basically did all the things a married couple do. Then Rick started talking about kids. She wasn't ready, Liv told him firmly. Nobody's ever really ready, Rick pointed out, you just have to jump in and do it. Liv didn't think that sounded like a very wise approach to parenting. Then Rick began sharing articles he found online, citing studies about the perils of having a baby over thirty. When their friends started to breed, it came from all quarters. 'When are you two going to get pregnant?', and Rick was ready with the same forlorn responses, 'I can't wait, but Liv's not keen.' This put her in the position of having to assure her affronted friends that she thought their offspring were wonderful, and of course she wanted babies, just not yet. 'Well, you don't want to leave it too long,' they would caution, before launching into the same studies and statistics Rick had already thrown at her, while he nodded sagely in the background. She finally gave in; it wasn't that she didn't want kids, so if it meant that much to Rick . . .

Liv was pregnant two months later, much to his delight and her surprise. She thought it would take a lot longer, she'd been on the pill for over a decade. Surprise turned to shock, however, when her first ultrasound revealed twins. Everyone was thrilled, except Liv. She'd watched her friends barely coping with one child, and she was going to have two at once. It was all twice as bad from then on – the morning sickness, fluid retention, stretch marks, fatigue. She had to leave work earlier than planned to have a caesarean before her due date, and then stay in hospital longer because of something called placental asymmetry, which had left Dylan underweight and needing a little closer attention. Put simply, his brother had hogged the placenta, which, knowing Lachie now, was hardly surprising. But he also took to the breast as ravenously, keeping her supply up enough to express milk for Dylan. And that was how it went on. Dylan never developed an adequate sucking reflex, and so Lachie breastfed, Liv pumped, and Dylan was bottle-fed on expressed milk. It was a nightmare, and she would have considered giving up and sticking them both on formula, except she knew that Dylan needed the breastmilk even more than Lachie, and there was something about their little three-way team effort that tugged at her heartstrings. It was almost as though she and Lachie were looking out for Dylan together, and in many ways that was how it had continued to this day.

Needless to say, Liv's life changed dramatically, but Rick's not so much. His career carried on unimpeded, with promotions and pay rises, and increased status and responsibility, while Liv ultimately had to give up her job. She had originally only planned to take six months' maternity leave, but Rick kept harping on that it just wasn't possible with twins. Liv didn't appear to have a say in it, but nor did she have the energy to fight about it. So she extended her leave to a year. That took them into winter, and Dylan suffered from such chronic ear infections the doctor was contemplating surgery to insert grommets. Rick declared it was impossible for her to consider returning to work right then, so Liv suggested that he take some leave from his job, while she settled back into hers. He just scoffed at that. 'And how do you propose we pay the mortgage on your salary?'

In the end, Liv had had no choice but to resign her position; the company couldn't hold it open any longer, and she couldn't return to work full-time with twins and an unsupportive husband. She was pissed off, but arguing about it didn't achieve anything except hostility, and that wasn't good for the boys. So she bided her time. After the twins turned two, she started putting out feelers for freelance work she could do from home, without telling Rick. The jobs came trickling in, so she placed the boys into day care a couple of days a week, for just a few hours at a time. Lachie flourished, and Dylan eventually settled in okay. Rick wasn't happy, complaining that life was too stressed, that it just wasn't workable. But this time Liv was ready. She stood her ground, stating that she had every right to pick up her career again, that he'd had everything his way until now but things were going to change. And they did, though not in the way she'd anticipated. A year later, Liv discovered Rick's first affair. It was downhill from then on.

Three times he talked her into taking him back before she refused to take him back again. But no sooner had the divorce papers been lodged than her friends starting urging Liv to find someone. She thought they had rocks in their heads. It was hard enough looking after two kids on her own and holding down a job, without thinking about a relationship.

'But what about sex?' they would ask furtively. 'Don't you miss it?' She had to work hard to contain her laughter at that. Liv didn't know of any mother of toddlers, let alone twins, who would miss sex; most would consider it a blessed relief not to get the midnight poke.

Once the boys started school, the pressure was really on. All everyone wanted to know was if she was seeing someone, and if not, why wasn't she doing something about that. Liv maintained that she was happier single, that she didn't want to go through all that crap again, thank you very much.

'But maybe the next one will be a good guy?' Madeleine had suggested.

'And maybe pigs will start flying 747s,' Liv had said right back. 'Look, I'm perfectly happy, except for one thing: the way everyone feels so sorry for me. I'm just like Jennifer Aniston – well, except for the looks, the fame and the money. But the point is, she's a successful, gorgeous, independent woman, but everyone pitied her until she found a husband. What's that about? No one pitied George Clooney before he finally got married.'

*

'Your book isn't grabbing you?'

Liv stirred, turning her head and blinking at David, slightly dazed.

'I just couldn't help noticing you were still on the screensaver,' he said.

She glanced down at the Kindle in her lap. 'I guess I must have been daydreaming.'

'I didn't mean to disturb.'

'No, it's fine.' Liv shifted in her seat and stretched as best she could to rouse herself. She looked over at David, who was returning his reader to the seat pocket. 'What about your book? Not grabbing you either?'

'Oh, it's grabbing me all right,' he said. 'It's so full-on I need to take a breather every now and then.'

'Wow, what is it?'

'Cameron West's latest.'

Liv blinked. 'Oh.'

He looked at her. 'You've heard of him?'

'Sure. Actually, I've read all his books.'

'No kidding?'

'That surprises you?'

'I just wouldn't have thought they'd be of any interest to a woman.'

'Whoa, sexist much?'

'Sorry,' he said sheepishly. 'Scarlett wouldn't have let me get away with that either. It's only that – in my experience – women don't seem so interested in the action-adventure genre, that's all I'm saying. Not that they can't be, or that they shouldn't be.'

Liv shrugged. 'Depends on the book, and the woman. It's not sexist to say that women are more likely to be drawn to character, and you have to admit, Cameron West writes some pretty hunky characters.'

'I don't have to admit that,' said David. 'In fact it might be a bit gay for me to admit such a thing. Not that there's anything wrong with that.'

Liv grinned then. 'Look, the truth is, women are the greatest readers by far, across all genres – action, adventure, thrillers, crime, biographies . . . All the books you might assume are written for men are probably read by more women.'

David was nodding thoughtfully. 'You seem to know an awful lot about this. Do you work in publishing or something?'

Damn. She really should keep her opinions to herself. She glanced at him sideways. She didn't figure him for the pestering wannabe-writer type. Wouldn't hurt to check though. She turned to him. 'I'll answer that question only if you tell me something first.'

'Sure.'

'Are you writing a book or planning to write a book, or have you always wanted to write a book?'

He laughed. 'No, no fear of that. I promise.'

'Okay, so guilty as charged,' Liv said. 'I do work for a publishing company, as a publicist.'

'Is that as cool as it sounds? Because that sounds pretty cool to me.'

'It can be fun, but it's also a job,' she said. 'And a pretty demanding one at times.'

'I'd believe it,' said David. 'But still, working with books and writers must be . . . Sorry, I can't think of another word but "cool". I've been hanging around my daughter too much this past week.'

'It is cool working with writers.'

'Anyone I might have heard of?' he asked.

Liv shot him a sly look. 'Actually, I've just finished a tour with Cameron West.'

His face lit up. 'You're kidding me.'

'I'm not.'

'So that makes me, like, two degrees of separation from the guy who wrote this book,' he said, tapping his reader.

Liv was always amused by the general population's fascination with writers, who were pretty much on the bottom rung of the celebrity ladder. And most of the writers Liv knew were just as amused.

'What's he like?' David asked.

'Cameron? He's lovely. And hardworking, super-smart, polite to a fault. He's one of my favourites.'

He smiled. 'Well, it's nice to hear success doesn't make people wankers.'

'Oh, I assure you, it does. Just not Cameron.'

'So you must have to do a lot of travelling, I suppose?'

She nodded. 'Yeah, book tours, festivals, that kind of thing.'

'Is that hard with kids?'

'It is a juggle, but I love it so much, I think it's worth it.'

'Your husband must be very supportive.'

There it was again. She supposed she should give him points for effort. 'Not so much,' she said. 'And not so much my husband any more, either.'

'Sorry, didn't mean to pry.'

Oh yes you did. 'When the boys were little I couldn't really go away,' said Liv. 'But once they started high school, I decided they could cope. Their father "minds" them part of the time I'm away – that's his term. It annoys me: they're his kids too, he's not minding them for me.'

David gave half a laugh. 'I know what you mean. After Scarlett came to live with me, I couldn't get over the offers of help that streamed in, endlessly. I mean, it was lovely, and I appreciated it, but I started to wonder if people didn't think I was capable of looking after my own child. Her mum had raised her solo for eight years, and no one ever ran to her aid. It's a strange double standard.'

The PA crackled into life with the announcement that they were soon going to land.

'Well, time has literally flown,' said David.

Liv decided not to correct him on the use of 'literally'. Besides, that was kind of poetic, so she could allow him some licence. The time had passed very quickly indeed, darn it; she would have liked to hear the rest of that story. Why had the daughter come to live with him after eight years with her mother? Were they overseas, or interstate maybe? It was so intriguing. From what age did she go to live with him? What had changed? Liv was dying of curiosity, but she could hardly start grilling him now: it wasn't exactly a conversation to be had as they disembarked.

When the plane came to a stop at the terminal, and the fasten seatbelts light went out, David stood to open the overhead locker. 'Have you got anything up here, Liv?' he asked. 'I'll grab it for you.'

She shook her head. 'Thanks, but I had to check my baggage.'

'I never check baggage if I can help it.'

'Me either,' she assured him. 'But being away for over a week I can't get away with packing light.'

He nodded before lifting his bag out of the locker. 'Would you like to go ahead?'

Liv thought it best to sever the relationship now, make it swift and painless, no standing around awkwardly out in the arrival hall. 'No thanks,' she said. 'I usually wait for the line to dwindle.'

He glanced over his shoulder: the queue was advancing on him, he would have to move on. He looked back at her with an expression that was almost regretful. 'Well, it was nice meeting you, Liv.'

'You too, David.'

And that was that.

Liv wasn't making an excuse. She did usually wait in her seat until everyone else had shuffled past, especially when she had luggage to collect. What was the point in rushing – you only had to stand around waiting at the carousel. After she eventually made her way off the plane, she stopped at the ladies room to freshen up, and then walked down to the baggage claims area. As she approached the carousel for her flight, she was surprised to see David standing at the periphery, watching her, his wheelie bag propped beside him.

Liv spoke first. 'I thought you said you didn't have any baggage?'

'Oh, I have plenty of baggage,' he said with a wry grin. 'Look, I don't want you to think I'm weird or a stalker or anything, but you see, I made a promise to myself when I turned forty, and I don't like to break promises, especially to myself.'

Liv was intrigued. 'What was the promise?'

'To try to avoid having regrets,' he said plainly. 'Now, I don't want it to sound like I've been plagued by regrets all my life, but there have been a few . . .'

This was starting to sound like that Frank Sinatra song.

'Mostly there's just been too many times that I've regretted not acting on something when I could have, or should have.'

She was listening.

'The thing is, Liv, I enjoyed talking to you, a lot. And in the past I would have left it at that. And for a few days, maybe longer, I would have kicked myself for not plucking up the courage to ask for your number. I don't want to have that regret this time.'

'Look, David, I'm flattered, I really am . . .'

He dropped his gaze to the floor. 'I see.'

'It's just that I have kids, I'm not really looking for anything.'

'I'm only talking about coffee.'

Liv wondered if her face had turned red. 'Sorry, I didn't mean to imply –'

'It's fine, I understand, I really do,' he said. 'I don't know what it's like for you, but I get constant pressure from my friends, my daughter, that I should be putting myself out there.'

'Tell me about it.'

'I don't know how I'm supposed to do that. I'm not interested in internet dating, I don't go to places to pick up. I certainly didn't get on that plane looking to pick up. I guess I like the idea that good things just might happen when you least expect it.'

She nodded, thinking. It was a nice idea, but . . .

'Tell you what,' he said, reaching into his pocket and pulling out his wallet. He drew out a docket, and quickly checked both sides. 'What if I give you my number . . .' He took a pen out of his breast pocket and jotted something down. 'And then it's entirely up to you.'

Liv hesitated as he held out the slip of paper to her.

'Take it as a favour to me,' he persisted. 'That way I have no regrets, and next time she asks I can tell Scarlett that I have put myself out there. And you can throw it in the bin after I walk away, I'll never know. So it's a win-win.'

Liv frowned. 'For you maybe. Can't see any win in there for me.'

He smiled. 'I guess it all depends on what you do with the number.'

She couldn't help smiling back as she finally accepted the slip of paper.

'Thanks.' He returned his wallet to his pocket and grabbed the handle of his wheelie bag. 'Maybe I'll see you around, Liv.' And then he walked away out of the terminal.

Liv stood there, still holding the slip of paper. She really was flattered, but she wasn't going to call him, of course. She shoved it into her pocket as she looked over to the carousel. The other passengers had all dispersed, and there was her bag, all on its own, about to complete the loop. She had to make a dash to grab it before it disappeared again.

4 pm

Madeleine glanced at the time on her computer. She had told Henry she'd be home as early as she could manage, and if she wanted to beat the traffic she'd have to leave soon to get across the Spit Bridge before it turned into a carpark. She had managed to put out all the fires for today; there were a few embers still smouldering, but hopefully they wouldn't catch alight overnight.

Simone's head suddenly appeared around the wall, seemingly disembodied. 'See you in five,' she chirped, before disappearing again.

'Wait – Simone?' Madeleine called after her.

She reappeared around the wall, in full body form this time.

'See me in five for what?' Madeleine asked.

'The special editorial meeting Jane called.'

'When?'

'In five minutes.'

'No, I mean when did she call it?'

'First thing this morning.'

'I wasn't here first thing.'

'It was sent around by email.'

Madeleine generally skipped over emails from their fearless leader when they had the word 'editorial' in the subject line. 'Yeah well, lucky for me I'm not an editor,' she reminded Simone with a hopeful smile.

'I'm aware of that, but Jane wants publicity in the meeting, and Liv's away on tour.'

Madeleine sighed inwardly. 'Gosh, I don't think I'm going to be able to wait around, actually. You wouldn't even have caught me in another minute. I was just about to walk out . . .'

'Oh, well of course. If you have to be somewhere, I'll make your excuses to Jane. What do you want me to tell her?'

Madeleine liked Simone, she really did, but she could be a bit officious. She supposed being gatekeeper assistant to the director might incline you that way. So now she was stuck. The excuse of 'dinner with Henry Darrow' wasn't going to cut it – she couldn't get away with invoking his name in a professional capacity any more. And it was still inside normal working hours, as much as there were normal working hours in this job.

'Never mind,' she said finally. 'I'll be there.'

'Very good.' Simone disappeared again, and Madeleine groaned, slowly lowering her forehead to the desk. She wanted to go *home*. There was nothing for it but to get in there and get it over with. Move the meeting along, keep it snappy, and keep everyone on track. She sat up straight and reached for her phone to call Henry, but it started to ring first. She peered at the screen. It was Genevieve. What did she want? Madeleine knew from experience that her sister only rang when she wanted something.

'Hey Gen,' she said, mustering her clipped, rushed-at-work voice. 'You've just caught me before I have to go into a meeting, sorry.'

'I'll be quick,' Genevieve said. 'Actually, best if you just come to my place after work and I'll explain everything then.'

'I can't come to your place after work,' Madeleine said bluntly.

'Why not?'

'Aiden arrived today.'

'Aiden, Henry's best man?'

'What other Aiden would I be talking about, Gen?'

'I'm aware of who Aiden is,' Genevieve retorted. 'The point I was making is that he's Henry's friend – can't Henry look after him?'

Madeleine steeled herself. 'I only got to say hello to him for five minutes this morning,' she explained, 'and now I have a meeting, so I'm going to be home late as it is. What's so important anyway?'

The sigh down the phone line reeked of frustration. 'Archie's sick, and I have to take Gabe to Kajukenbo.'

'So I gather Mark's away?'

'Of course he's away, where else would he be?' Genevieve echoed Madeleine's sarcastic tone. She didn't much like it coming back at her.

Mark was the Asia Pacific – or was it Australasian? – manager for an international firm of property developers. He travelled constantly, and consequently Genevieve was constantly stressed. She really didn't seem very happy, and Madeleine did feel for her – Gen was her sister and she loved her, but surely there was only so much she could be expected to do. She did have a life of her own these days, not that Genevieve seemed to notice.

'Can't Gabe just miss . . . whatever that is, for a night?' Madeleine suggested.

'Ka-ju-ken-bo,' Genevieve enunciated the word for her, like that was going to help. 'And no, he can't "just miss it", he's being graded tonight. It's only preliminary, but Gabe would have a royal fit if I said we couldn't go. Why should he care that his baby brother has a head cold, and is prone to ear infections, and so taking him out in the night air is the worst possible thing I could do to him? No, none of that matters, because the world revolves around Gabriel Ryan after all . . . just like his father . . . Bloody eldest children, they're all the same . . . Sense of bloody privilege like they're all heirs to a throne . . .'

Genevieve was conveniently forgetting, for the sake of her argument, that she was also an eldest child. As her sister ranted on, Madeleine glanced at the time and reached down to retrieve her bag from the floor beside her desk. 'Why don't you call Mum?' she eventually said, interrupting.

'Mum? Are you kidding?'

'No.'

'She's beyond useless.'

'She is not,' Madeleine chided.

'Okay, she's nuts.'

'Gen, our mother is not "nuts", and we have the test results to prove it. Did you call her back this morning?'

'How do you know she called me this morning?'

'Because she called me when you didn't answer to see if I knew where you were.'

'And she's not nuts?'

Madeleine got to her feet. 'Gen, that doesn't make her nuts. It makes her caring, and interested, and concerned about you. Call her, I'm sure she'd be happy to sit with Archie while you go to . . . Kick-a-poo-pa. It'll only be for a couple of hours, won't it?'

'Ka-ju-ken-bo!' Genevieve repeated. 'And I'd never be able to relax.'

'You relax at Cajun-Ken-doll?'

'You know what I mean. I can't trust her with the boys, she's hopeless.'

'You do realise she raised us?'

'With Dad, a schoolteacher who was home pretty much whenever we were. Can you imagine how she would have coped if Dad had worked the kind of hours Mark does?'

Madeleine picked up her jacket. 'Look, I have to go to my meeting, Gen. And I'm sorry, but I just can't help you out today.'

Her sister's sigh this time was loud and recriminatory. 'Fine.' And she hung up.

Madeleine rushed out of the office, calling over her shoulder, 'I'll be in a meeting' to anyone who was still around and within earshot. While she waited for an elevator she phoned Henry.

'Hi,' he answered. 'Are you on your way?'

'No, sorry, I have a meeting. I couldn't get out of it.'

'You're going to hit traffic.'

'I know, I'll do my best to get away as quickly as I can. Apologise to Aiden.'

'Okay. Drive safe.'

By the time Madeleine made it to the boardroom two floors above, it looked as though all of the key staff had assembled – all the publishers and commissioning editors, the head of marketing and his second-in-charge, the national sales manager, even Jordan, the head designer. Madeleine wondered what this was about. It wasn't the best of times for the industry: bookshops were collapsing like dominoes around the country, and publishing houses were definitely shrinking. Madeleine hadn't heard of any lay-offs as such, though the printing sector had taken a hit since the rise of ebooks. Staff members who left were not replaced, and more and more work was being done by fewer and fewer people. It was only a matter of time before actual retrenchments started, and an extraordinary meeting at the arse-end of the day made Madeleine a little nervous. Looking around at the faces of her colleagues, she could tell she wasn't the only one.

Bridget caught her eye across the table. She was the most senior publisher, and deservedly so. She was smart and insightful and professional to a fault. Madeleine had a lot of time for Bridget.

'I haven't had a chance to thank you for the publicity you did for *Tigers in the Mist*. It was really exceptional.'

'It's an exceptional book,' Madeleine said graciously. 'It could sell itself.'

'If only that were true,' said Bridget. 'Seriously, you put together a great campaign. Thank you.'

'You're welcome,' said Madeleine. 'I saw that it hit the bestseller list on the weekend. Congratulations.'

Bridget gave her a wan smile. 'Hmm, bestsellers aren't quite what they used to be.'

It didn't take as many sales to make the list these days, because sales of books were declining overall. Madeleine knew Bridget had paid a lot of money for that book, after a pretty fierce bidding war. Every time a publisher took a risk like that she was putting her reputation, and hence her job, on the line. Bridget was probably feeling particularly vulnerable right now.

'Thanks, everyone,' Jane said as she strode into the room and took her place at the head of the boardroom table. She was a diminutive woman with doe eyes set in a pixie face, all of which belied her indomitable toughness. 'Let's get down to it immediately,' she began.

Good. Madeleine sat up to attention.

'The erotica bubble has burst,' Jane announced.

There was a general look of bemusement around the table.

'By which I mean it appears that, based on our most recent sales figures, erotica has finally peaked.'

'Shouldn't you say climaxed?' said Emma, one of the commissioning editors.

Jane lifted an eyebrow at the barely suppressed snickers. 'What I probably should have said is it's actually on the downward slide. I'm not even sure there's going to be any afterglow.'

That garnered a nervous laugh. 'Should we be lighting a cigarette?' someone offered from the end of the table.

'All right,' said Jane, 'joke all you like, but this is a real problem, and we can't afford to be complacent about it, given the current climate.'

That silenced everyone, and an air of solemnity laced with fear descended once more upon the room.

'So I gather you don't want us commissioning anything in the genre?' Bridget asked.

'That goes without saying,' said Jane. 'And I'm afraid anything you currently have under consideration is going to have to be passed on. And,' she continued over some muttered protests, 'it doesn't matter how good it is. I don't care if you think you've found the erotic answer to *Harry Potter* and *The Da Vinci Code* rolled into one, the market is so saturated, it just wouldn't get noticed.'

'So what should we be looking for?' asked Emma.

'Anything that's not erotica,' Jane replied simply. 'Except for that, nothing's changed. Good writing, great characters – I don't have to tell you how to do your jobs.'

'Well, I for one am glad I don't have to wade through any more of the stuff,' said Emma. 'It's like eating too much chocolate, makes you queasy after a while.'

'The acquisition stage isn't my greatest concern,' Jane went on. 'That's easily fixed by just applying the brakes. And we can't do much about books that are already going through the editing stage, but if there's any opportunity to tone things down at all, cut the odd sex scene, then go for it.'

'Some that I'm working on barely have a plot to hold the sex scenes together,' muttered Beth, another editor.

'I know, you're right,' said Jane. 'It's only a suggestion, we certainly can't completely change a book at this point. But unfortunately, some are going to get lost in such a crowded market. If there are any changes you can make, any wiggle room at all, present it to the author as an opportunity to stand out from the masses. Something's got to be the next big thing, after all.'

'If only we knew what it was going to be,' Emma mused.

'In the absence of a crystal ball, we just have to push on,' said Jane. 'Jordan, cover designs are going to have to go through a major overhaul. You'll have to brief your freelancers: no more blacks, reds, greys. And no more ties, blindfolds, cuffs, in fact any suggestion of restraints on the covers. Bridget, Emma, Beth, all of the publishers,' Jane went on, getting their attention, 'you have to get to work on cover blurbs, even change titles if possible, especially if they're suggestive.'

'What tone should we aim for?' asked Bridget.

'I don't know,' Jane said frankly. 'I only know what we're not aiming for. Maybe try to reimagine the book as though you're telling your grandmother about it.'

'My grandmother read every book in the *Nine Kinds of Pain* series,' Beth pointed out.

'Okay, then your great-grandmother,' said Jane. 'Same goes for your team, Madeleine. You'll have to review the promotional angle for any erotica that's already printed and waiting in the warehouses for distribution. Press releases will need to be rewritten, you might have to rethink where you're sending review copies and scheduling interviews. Have all the publicists meet with the relevant authors and talk them through this. Get them to think about higher-level themes, ways of talking about their books without mentioning sex, or at least without emphasising it.'

Madeleine nodded as she scribbled down some notes, but inside she was groaning. This was going to be huge. If it wasn't for Aiden, she would be staying back tonight to assess just how much work it was going to involve, so that she could be ready to brief everyone first thing tomorrow morning. But bad luck, she was leaving straight after the meeting. It wasn't her fault they'd overdone the erotica; it was no surprise to Madeleine that the market was saturated. The same thing had happened with teenage vampires before this wave, and it would happen again with the next publishing phenomenon. Madeleine didn't blame anyone, though:

this was a business, after all. If you didn't get on the bandwagon, you risked being left behind in a trail of dust.

'We all have to do our best to salvage whatever we can,' said Jane. 'Or else we'll be remaindering books in their tens of thousands, and we just can't afford that right now.'

Oatley

Liv had barely managed to deposit her bag in her room, kick off her shoes and put on the kettle before she heard the boys burst through the front door. They must have caught the early train. She thought she'd have time to drink a cup of tea while she checked her emails. But no matter. She'd rather see her boys than catch up on office work any day. When she'd first started travelling again, she felt like she'd lost an arm, or two arms. Until then she had rarely been apart from her boys: Rick had taken ages to agree to have them overnight, claiming he wouldn't be able to manage. When Liv pushed it, he started taking them for one night at a time, no more. But things had to change once she went back on the road; everyone had to adapt, Liv probably the most. She had to give up a lot of control, she had to accept that the boys might not get the same level – or at least style – of care when they were with their father, she had to accept that she would miss out on a lot. It was a myth that you could have it all. Nobody had it all; at best you got bits and pieces that you could stitch together to form the patchwork of your life. And you just had to make every square count.

'Hey,' she called from the kitchen as they thundered down the hall. Sometimes she wished she and Rick had never stripped the floors back to timber when they first bought the house. If not for the aesthetics, Liv would have considered carpeting not only the floors but the walls as well, if it would help muffle the din produced by two teenage boys.

'Heya, Ma.' Lachie threw his arms around her with a force that might have knocked her over had she not been buttressed by the kitchen cabinets. He was already taller than her, and likely to be taller than his father as well before he was through. He turned directly to the fridge. 'How's it going?' he said, opening the door and gazing inside.

'Good, thanks.' It really wouldn't have mattered what she said, he was no longer paying attention to anything that wasn't edible.

'Hi, Mum.' Dylan had materialised in front of her.

'Hi, sweet boy,' she said, bringing her arms around him.

He really was a sweet boy. The twins were identical, but people often doubted her. 'Are you sure?' they would question. 'There are actual tests to prove it, you know, you can't just go on looks.' Did they think Liv wasn't aware of this? And if she was only going on looks, as they obviously were, wouldn't she doubt it too? Dylan had always been smaller, even though he was technically the big brother, born six minutes ahead of Lachie. The placental issue, and subsequent minor but chronic complaints throughout his childhood, had left him not as robust. But they both had exactly the same blond hair, the same vivid blue eyes and, uncannily, the same voices. The only time she couldn't tell them apart was over the phone, or if they were calling to her from another room and she couldn't see them.

'I missed you,' Liv said, ruffling Dylan's hair now.

'Missed you too,' he said, as he stepped back to lean against the kitchen bench beside her.

'I didn't think you guys could make the early train on Wednesdays?'

'Nah,' said Lachie, 'Dad drove us.'

As if on cue, Liv heard the front door closing. She sighed inwardly; that meant Rick was coming in to say hi. He really didn't need to bother. When the boys were younger, she and Rick generally had to debrief at handover, but now the twins could speak for themselves. If she needed to know anything, or Rick needed to tell her anything, it could be communicated later, by phone.

'Ma, there's nothing to eat,' Lachie complained as he bit into an apple.

'Give me a chance, Lach, I only just got in the door five minutes before you.'

'So I see,' Rick declared, stepping into the kitchen from the hall. 'What are you doing back so early?'

'I'm not early,' Liv countered. 'I said I'd be home by the end of school today, so the boys could've just come home by themselves.' Subtext: you actually don't have to be here.

He shrugged. 'I couldn't remember.'

Typical. Liv always prepared a complicated roster for Rick and her mother whenever she was away, largely because Rick made everything so complicated. He couldn't possibly just take over – no, that would be too easy. His life had to proceed with as little disruption as possible, so her mother had to be auxiliary caregiver, which brought with it a whole other swathe of problems.

'Well, I'm here,' said Liv, as evenly as she could manage. 'So, thanks . . .'

'It's okay.' Rick seemed oblivious to the hint. 'I promised the boys pizza for dinner.'

'Yesss!' Lachie exclaimed, pumping his fist.

'But I like to cook for them when I get home from a trip,' Liv objected. More to the point, she liked to feed them vegetables and some kind of non-fried protein. She knew the boys would have eaten okay at their grandmother's, but Rick nearly always bought them takeaway. He didn't cook, and nor did his other half, apparently.

'There's no food here, Ma,' Lachie was saying, 'so you'll have to go up the shops. You don't wanna do that, do you?'

Of course she didn't. But she wasn't going to admit it. 'I don't mind . . .'

'Hey, no need, Liv, I'm here anyway,' said Rick. 'You won't get to catch up with the boys if you're running around shopping and cooking. Why don't we just chill, order in some food, have some family time?'

The only chill was the one running up her spine. This was all sounding too familiar. Rick was onto his third girlfriend since their split, and Liv remembered him behaving this way when he broke up with the other two. Each time he'd started hanging around more, wanting to do things together as a 'family'. Sure enough, both times the relationship had ended, and he wormed his way in further, lamenting mistakes made, talking about being lonely . . . The first time, Liv had found herself feeling sorry for him, wondering if they could make a go of it again, for the sake of the boys. Fortunately, before she did anything stupid, he was off again. Then Liv knew she finally had to do something permanent, and although Rick didn't like it, she'd filed for divorce.

So now Liv suspected trouble on the home front again, and she was hardly surprised. She knew Rick better than he did himself, and each time he'd chosen women as selfish as he was, so the relationships were doomed from the start. But she didn't care, and she certainly didn't want to know about it. And furthermore, she really didn't want him here tonight. She wanted the boys to herself; they needed the whole night to catch up properly, in their own time. They always had plenty of phone contact while she was away, even a Skype call here and there, when Dylan set it up. But it wasn't the same as physically being together. Liv had always subscribed to the theory that ninety percent of parenting was just being there. When she was home, the boys would drift off and do their own thing throughout the evening, but at different times they would each seek her out. Lachie would talk nonsense half the time, but he would talk, and in the midst of the nonsense Liv would pick up the trail of crumbs – a teacher who was bugging him or a subject he was having trouble with, a girl he had his eye on. Lachie was a bit of a lad, a lot like his father, but Liv liked to think he had the best of Rick: the big, sparkling personality without the self-centredness. Perhaps having a twin had made Lachie more empathetic; he was certainly fiercely protective of his brother, even a bit affectionate, or as affectionate as a fourteen-year-old male could be expected to be. Dylan was a quieter, more sensitive soul. He was a deep thinker, and a worrier, and at some point during the evening he would usually seek Liv out, curl up on the sofa beside her, and have a heart-to-heart about whatever was on his mind.

But not tonight. Tonight Rick would be the centre of attention, because Rick always managed to be the centre of attention. It wasn't long before all three of them were lined up on the sofa playing a video game. Liv knew she wasn't going to get any sense from them until the hunger pangs struck, so she went ahead and made her cup of tea and took herself off to her bedroom to check her emails. She quickly discarded the morning's missive from Jane about a meeting this afternoon, but another email had been sent not long ago with notes from the meeting. Liv sighed as she read through them: this was going to be a lot of work. So much for her plan to take the rest of the week off in lieu.

She closed the laptop. If she was going to have to work tomorrow she refused to do any work now. Instead she would take a quick shower and change into her house trackies; there was no one to impress here. She slipped off her jeans and went to toss them in the hamper when she felt the slip of paper in the pocket. She pulled it out and read it properly this time: David Lessing, and a mobile number. His handwriting was a bit messy – was that a five or a three?

What did it matter? Liv scrunched it up and dropped it into the wastepaper basket beside her desk.

6 pm

Because of the meeting, Madeleine had left work at the worst possible time for traffic, bang on five, along with every other commuter in the CBD. She had only just made it across the Spit Bridge, and there was still up to another hour's drive to go. She would never have chosen to live at Pittwater herself, but Henry had fallen in love with the place, so what could she do?

Madeleine had finally moved out of the family home during the year of their long-distance courtship. She could hardly expect Henry to stay at her mother's when he came out to visit, and besides, her emancipation was well overdue. Having blown a good chunk of her savings on her own trip to New York, she could only manage the bond for a compact one-bedder, but as she was still away a lot it was really all she needed. Not so when Henry moved out to Australia and in with her: for one it was cosy, for two it was hopelessly cramped. Henry had ended up renting a studio to work in, but that was only a temporary solution at best. He had always worked from home, and he sometimes liked to work late at night if the inspiration took him, or an hour here or there, and he couldn't do that so easily if his workspace was located elsewhere. He understood that the apartment was convenient for Madeleine's job, but he said he just wasn't going to be able to work so close to the city long-term. In New York he'd had an apartment in an old brownstone in the East Village, but he usually moved up to his place in the Hamptons more or less full-time when he was working on a book. As he had grown more successful and could be selective about promotional commitments, Henry found he was spending the vast majority of his time in the Hamptons, which was how he'd earned the 'reclusive' tag. It was true that he was quite content in his own company, but he still had friends in New York, and apparently he often had visitors to stay at the house in the Hamptons – at least when he wasn't working.

So Madeleine had agreed they could look for a place away from the city. Henry had researched locations online even before he moved over, and he had his heart set on Pittwater. When he told her, Madeleine tried to be philosophical. It was a little further out than she had envisaged, and the commute was going to be a bitch, but she totally understood why Henry wanted to live there. It was beautiful and peaceful and remote, the perfect setting for an artist, and she wanted him to be happy. He had moved across the world to be with her; she could hardly complain about moving out of the city.

However, when Henry insisted on buying, Madeleine finally baulked. She wasn't at all sure she wanted the move to be so permanent or binding, but mostly she just felt extremely uncomfortable that she didn't have any capital to contribute. Henry said he didn't care about that. He could afford it, and it was silly for them to rent somewhere that wasn't quite what they wanted when they could remodel a house of their own to suit their needs. Besides, rentals were so scarce up that way, it would take ages for them to find something. In that case Madeleine didn't want her name to go on the title deed, but as it turned out, they didn't have a choice. As a non-resident, Henry wasn't permitted to buy property, so the deed had to be solely in her name. That made her even more uncomfortable, but Henry waved away her concerns. It was going to be their home, he insisted; everything else was just paperwork.

They held on to the apartment during the period of the renovations; it was the practical thing to do, and Henry mastered driving on the left side of the road during all the trips back and forth supervising the renovation. He even did some of the work himself. They had chosen a house with solid bones and a good layout. It really only needed a new kitchen and bathrooms, and a reworking of the downstairs space for Henry's studio and office.

The plan was to let go of the apartment once they had moved into the house, but Madeleine still hadn't got around to it. Every time she went to give notice to the property manager, something came up. She liked having the alternative if she had to work late, or if she had to be at the airport early. But in reality she rarely stayed at the flat these days, especially if she worked back: she would look at the time and realise that she could spend the night alone, or in one short hour – even less if it was late at night – she could be home with Henry. The second option nearly always won out. But still she couldn't bring herself to give up the flat.

It was going on seven when Madeleine finally pulled into their street. Their block was typical for the area, a steep embankment off a winding section of road, with the garage suspended on a concrete slab at street level and the house perched on the side of the hill below, giving them sweeping views across Salt Pan Cove.

There wasn't a lot even an architect could do about the precipitous site, and the house could only be accessed via a flight of steep stairs. Madeleine kept a pair of Crocs in the garage so she could change out of her heels and navigate the stairs safely. Now she kicked them off again at the front door and let herself in. The house was in virtual darkness, and she couldn't hear any signs of life. She didn't think they would have gone out, especially as Henry knew she was on her way home; she had sent him a text when she'd finally left the office. Perhaps Aiden was resting and Henry had decided to do some work. His studio was on the level underneath, all by itself except for the laundry and a storage area. Henry loved it: he had uninterrupted views and absolute privacy. It was his sanctuary.

As Madeleine walked barefoot through to the main living area, she was hit by the aroma of dinner cooking, which meant the boys couldn't be far away. She peered out to the deck, and could just make out their silhouettes in the rapidly fading twilight. They must have been too busy catching up to notice they were sitting in the dark. That was a good sign.

'Hey, the working girl returns!' Aiden exclaimed, jumping to his feet as Madeleine switched on a light inside.

She stepped out onto the deck to join them. 'Hi, boys.'

She was suddenly and unexpectedly scooped up into Aiden's arms with the same enthusiasm he had displayed this morning. Not that she was complaining – a big, exuberant hug was a very nice welcome to come home to.

'I'll get you a drink, Madeleine,' Henry said, standing up.

Aiden released her. 'No, let me,' he insisted. 'I'll let you have a moment with your beautiful fiancée, Henry, but after that you have to share.' He paused in the doorway. 'What will you have, Madeleine?'

'Ah, mineral water, thanks.'

Aiden frowned. 'You're not going to drink with us?'

'Well, the thing is, I don't normally drink during the week –'

'But surely this isn't a normal weekday,' Aiden declared. 'It's a special occasion! Besides, we have to make a toast, so you have to have a drink or it's bad luck. What'll it be?'

She shot Henry a wary glance. 'Okay, white wine. There should be some in the fridge.'

'White wine it is,' said Aiden, walking inside.

'Do you know where the glasses are?' she called after him.

'I'll find them.'

Madeleine turned to face Henry. 'I'll just have the one.'

'Whatever you think,' he said, leaning close to give her a soft but lingering kiss on the lips. Aiden obviously knew Henry well enough to know that he was unlikely to show overt physical affection in front of his friend. That was just how Henry was. It didn't bother Madeleine – he gave her plenty of affection in private.

'How was your day?' he asked.

'The best thing I can say about it is that it's over.'

'That bad, huh?'

'Oh, just the usual,' she said, sagging against him.

He held her snug, planting a kiss on the top of her head. 'Well, go easy on the wine, you know how it hits you when you're stressed.'

Madeleine could feel her hackles rising. Jeez, it's not as though she couldn't control herself, and like Aiden said, it was a special occasion. His footsteps sounded on the polished boards as he crossed the living room towards them, and Henry quickly released her, taking a step back.

'Here you are, my lady,' Aiden said as he came out onto the deck and passed Madeleine a very full glass of wine. 'Now we can toast,' he added, picking up his beer.

'Absolutely.' Madeleine raised her glass. 'To our best man.'

'And to my best friend and one hell of a lucky man, and his beautiful bride-to-be. Every happiness to you both.'

Aiden and Henry clinked their bottles against Madeleine's glass. She noticed that Henry's was almost empty; he'd probably been nursing the same beer all afternoon. Well, she'd show him; she would do the same, make this glass last all night. But as she took her first sip, the Pavlov's dog effect kicked in, just as it had with the coffee this morning, and immediately Madeleine felt the hit she could only get from a glass of chilled wine after a busy day. She quickly took another, larger sip, before placing the glass down on the table.

'Before anything else,' Aiden said, as they all sat down, 'I want to know, are you always called Madeleine? Or is Maddie permissible?'

She smiled. 'You can call me anything you like.'

'No, no,' he said, with a firm shake of his head. 'Some people are particular about these things, and I notice Henry only ever refers to you as Madeleine.'

'He does, like my dad,' she said, with a pang of nostalgia. Jonathan had always been insistent about calling both her and Genevieve by their full names, not out of any sense of pompous formality, but because he loved the way they sounded – like tiny arias, he used to say.

'Mum sometimes calls me Maddie,' she went on, 'and I often get "Mad", though there could be another reason for that.' She grinned. 'Seriously, I get all kinds of variations, I'm not precious about it . . . Oh, except "Maz".' She turned up her nose. 'I don't like that.'

'Why would I call you Maz?' Aiden looked baffled.

'Well, it is a nickname for Madeleine.'

'Is it?'

'You haven't heard of that?'

'Nope.'

'I guess it must be an Australian thing then,' she said. 'Carolines get "Caz", Harrys get "Haz" . . .'

'So does Henry get "Hez"?' asked Aiden.

'No, probably not,' she said, thinking about it. 'He might get "Daz", from Darrow.'

Aiden was clearly trying to keep up. 'What's the rule, then? Does it only come after an *a*?'

'No, I know of Kerries who get Kez,' said Madeleine. 'Maybe it's the *r* that gets replaced with the *z*?'

'But that doesn't apply to Madeleine,' Aiden pointed out.

'Huh, so it doesn't.' She nodded, realising.

'Well, how am I supposed to figure it out?'

She shrugged. 'I can't help you. I guess it's just one of those things you had to grow up with.'

'I can see it's not going to be that easy to blend in here,' said Aiden.

'Take it from me,' said Henry, 'you'll never blend in with that accent.'

'I don't think his accent is very strong,' Madeleine protested.

'That's because you're used to mine,' said Henry. 'I've been here over a year, and visiting for another year before that, and barely a day goes by without some remark. Or should I say slur.'

Aiden's face dropped. 'So they don't like us here?'

'Yes we do!' Madeleine cried. 'Why are you being so negative, Henry?'

'I'm only trying to prepare him.'

'It won't be the same for Aiden,' she said. 'It's just because you're so . . . reserved, Henry. Australians don't expect that from an American, so they think you're arrogant.'

'Who thinks I'm arrogant?' Henry looked dismayed.

Whoops. Genevieve for one, but Madeleine wasn't about to wade into those waters right now. 'They *probably* think you're arrogant, is what I meant,' she corrected herself. 'Anyway, this is a crazy conversation. Aiden, there's a whole gaggle of women in my office who are dying to meet you, and who are more than a little fascinated to hear your accent.'

'Are there any Cazes or Kezes or other strange nomenclature I should know about?' he asked.

'Nope.'

'Well, okay then, I'll look forward to it.'

'So,' Madeleine said, picking up her glass, 'I want to know everything. Tell me all about yourself.'

'God no,' Aiden grimaced. 'I've talked about myself all day.'

'It's true, he has,' said Henry. 'I was nodding off at one point.'

Aiden laughed. 'So was I. Please, right now I want to know all about you,' he said, looking at Madeleine. 'Your beloved tells me you're a big-shot publicist for a big-shot publishing house.'

She knew Henry would never have put it like that.

'What's a typical day in the life of Madeleine Pepper, publicist extraordinaire?'

She sipped her wine, thinking about it. 'I don't know that there is such a thing as a typical day.'

'That must keep things interesting.'

'Yeah, I suppose it does,' she agreed.

'So, come on, give me some idea. What did you do today, for example?'

'Actually, this will probably amuse you.' Madeleine glanced at Henry as well. 'We had a big meeting this afternoon to announce that the erotica bubble has finally burst.'

'What's an erotica bubble and where can I get one?' said Aiden.

Madeleine smiled. 'You're aware that erotica has become hugely popular since the rise of e-readers?'

'No, I'm afraid I know next to nothing about popular culture. I spend half my time out of internet range.'

'Now you see, *that's* a lot more interesting –'

'No, it isn't,' Aiden interrupted. 'I want to hear about this erotica bubble.'

'All right.' Madeleine took another large sip from her glass before sliding it back onto the table. 'I take it you know what an e-reader is?'

'Yes, I even have one,' said Aiden. 'Great for travelling.'

'Yes, they are.' Madeleine waited for the grunt from Henry, which came right on cue.

'You got a problem there, Darrow?' asked Aiden.

'Henry doesn't believe in ebooks.'

'I don't think you have a choice about that. They're not an existential concept like God, they're a real thing.'

'I just don't understand why you need an electronic gadget to read a book,' Henry said. 'We did all right for hundreds of years. Didn't need power to run them, could take them anywhere. And there's nothing like the smell of a real book.'

Madeleine rolled her eyes. 'Henry, tell me this, how many authors do you think slave away at the keyboard wondering how their book is going to smell? You of all people should know that it's about the content.'

'But you can get it all in a real book,' he said. 'The content, printed on pages that you can feel, and turn between your fingers, and smell . . .'

She gave an exasperated sigh. 'I'll get you some of that "smell of books" scent if it means so much to you.'

'There's no such thing!' Aiden scoffed.

'Oh yes, there is,' she said.

Aiden laughed. 'Have any of your books been turned into ebooks, Henry?' he asked.

'Some of them. Luckily, so far children's books haven't been too adversely affected by the fad.'

'It's hardly a fad,' said Madeleine.

'Seriously, Darrow, you sound like a Luddite.'

'And proud of it,' Henry said.

'So Madeleine, back to the twenty-first century. You were saying . . . ?' Aiden prompted her.

'Ah yes. Where were we?' She frowned for a moment, thinking. 'E-readers, that's it. E-readers are giving people the freedom to read whatever they want without feeling judged or embarrassed. They don't have to go into a shop and buy it, much less ask for it out loud, and no one can tell what they're reading on the bus.'

'But now we know they're all reading dirty books?' said Aiden.

'A lot of them are.' Madeleine grinned. 'Romance boomed first, though that's always been a huge market. But then things took a turn for the raunchy. There was one infamous series that was phenomenally successful, then everyone went into a mad frenzy to publish more of the same.'

'So much for literature.'

Madeleine shrugged. 'In the end, publishing is a business. If we can't sell books in large enough quantities, there'll be no "literature" published. What some of the literati don't realise, or don't like to admit, is that big blockbusters finance all the much less commercially successful literary books.'

'So this trend in erotica must have financed a whole bunch of books?'

'Definitely. But now the market's saturated we're going to end up pulping a lot of them if we don't do something about it.'

'How do you pulp an ebook?' asked Aiden.

'You don't, which is another point in their favour,' Madeleine directed at Henry. 'And they never have to go out of print,' she added. 'But anyway, contrary to the scare stories that it's the end of the world as we know it, we're still producing a lot of paper books, and if they don't sell, they end up having to be remaindered or, worse, pulped.'

'Shouldn't somebody at the reins have seen this coming?' Aiden asked.

'I guess, but while it's successful it's understandable everyone will try to get a share of the spoils. No one can predict when readers will get tired of something. The public are a mystery, let me tell you.'

'To the great unwashed,' said Aiden, raising his beer.

Madeleine laughed. She raised her glass and took a good gulp. This was fun. They didn't entertain often, generally because no one wanted to hoof it all the way up here. And she hardly drank at all – no, these days she was 'good'. But it was nice to kick back for a change and relax. She hadn't been sure what to expect with Aiden; she certainly hadn't expected to enjoy his company so much, or to feel so at ease with him right from the start. Perhaps it was because they both knew Henry so well, or perhaps it was just the wine, but she already felt like she'd known him for years.

'So anyway,' she said, 'I should warn you that I'm going to have to work back the next couple of nights, until we get this under control. Sorry.'

'Can't you delegate?' said Henry.

'Oh, don't you worry, I'll be delegating all over the place,' Madeleine assured him. 'But I write most of the press releases, and they're all going to have to be revised. I think I'll have to stay in the city tomorrow night.'

'You know we're not going to have that apartment forever,' Henry said.

'What?' said Madeleine. 'What's that got to do with anything?'

'I'm just saying, if you didn't have the apartment as a fallback, maybe you'd finish up at a decent hour and be able to make it home.'

Madeleine blinked. 'Excuse me?'

'Just sayin',' he muttered.

'Henry, I don't stay in the city because we have an apartment there, I stay because of work commitments . . . and I hardly ever stay there anyway.'

'So why are we keeping it?'

Henry had had a bee in his bonnet about this for a while, but now wasn't the time to have it out. Madeleine glanced at Aiden, who was beginning to look a little uncomfortable. She took another sip of her wine and set it down again. 'Henry,' she said, adopting a more conciliatory tone, 'if you recall, we agreed it was a good idea to keep the apartment until after the wedding, for anyone who might need a place to stay. Especially you, Aiden.'

Aiden stirred then. 'You're trying to get rid of me already?'

'No!' Madeleine rushed to assure him, and then saw that he was smiling. 'Henry said you're going to have to do some work while you're here, take some meetings? The apartment's very close to the city, it'll be a lot more convenient for you to get around.'

Madeleine thought she heard a mild grunt from Henry, but decided to ignore it. She picked up her glass and realised with a start that it was almost empty. How did that happen so fast? Oh well, she felt completely fine, and it *was* a special night. 'Now, can we please talk about you, Aiden?' she said. 'I have so many questions.'

Henry got to his feet. 'That's my cue to check on dinner.'

'Henry!' Madeleine scolded.

'What?'

'That was a little rude . . .'

'Not at all,' Aiden said. 'I told you he's had to listen to me all day.'

Henry had come around behind her, placing his hands on her shoulders. 'And we do have to eat,' he said.

Madeleine softened. She didn't know why she was getting so defensive. 'Do you want a hand?'

'No, you've been working all day. Relax.' He gave her shoulders a gentle squeeze before retreating indoors.

'The apartment's a sore point, I take it?' Aiden said carefully, once Henry was inside.

'Apparently so.' Madeleine didn't want to talk about it; as far as she was concerned the moment had already passed. That's how it was with her and Henry: they had minor flare-ups occasionally, but they never amounted to anything. She changed the subject. 'So come on, tell me everything. What's a typical day in the life of Aiden Carmichael?'

'Two words: mosquito nets and immunisation.'

'That's three words.'

'If you're going to be pedantic, it's actually four words.'

Madeleine smiled. 'I googled you, you know,' she said. 'There's a little more to the work you do than mosquito nets and immunisation. Though, as I understand it, they are your core programs, and vitally important. It's all very impressive, Aiden. It must be so rewarding.'

He nodded, though without much conviction. 'Yeah, of course it has its rewards. I don't know how impressive it is in the scheme of things.'

'What are you saying?' Madeleine was stunned. 'I read that tens of millions of dollars have already been poured into these programs.'

'Yet it's still only a drop in the ocean,' said Aiden. 'You know, when I first started out on all this, I thought I was going to change the world. It was amazing – I was being given the money and resources to go wherever the need was greatest and to do whatever had to be done.' He stared out at the river. 'I guess I was naive, but I just had no idea it would be so relentless. That no matter how much money you throw at it, it never ends. You go to a new place, a new country, and start all over again. Sometimes it feels insurmountable.'

'Nobody said saving the world was going to be easy,' said Madeleine, to lighten the mood. She watched him take a long, slow swig of his beer. 'It sounds like you just need a break,' she added quietly.

'You know what they say, no rest for the wicked.'

'But you are going to take some time off while you're here, aren't you?'

He looked at her. 'Of course. That's why I'm imposing myself on you for a whole month before your wedding.'

'You're not imposing,' she assured him. 'I'm thrilled you're here, Aiden. You realise you're the only person I've ever met from Henry's past.'

'That's because Henry doesn't have a past,' he said, becoming serious.

'I'm sure he's pure as the driven snow, but everybody has a past.'

Aiden was shaking his head. 'You're not following. You see, I found his pod when I was out walking in the woods one day. I was the one who released him.'

Henry appeared in the doorway. 'What are you saying about me?'

'Only the truth, Darrow.'

'You told her about the pod?'

Madeleine looked between them, confused.

'I thought she had a right to know,' Aiden said, deadpan.

'I'm not sure she's ready,' said Henry. 'It might be too much for her to take in.'

'What do you think, Madeleine?' Aiden turned to her. 'Can you handle it?'

'She can't handle the truth.'

'Are you quite done, fellas?' Madeleine said, while they snickered at their joke. She was relieved that Henry seemed to have recovered his sense of humour at least.

'I only came out to tell you that I'm ready to serve dinner,' he said. 'Let's bring this inside.'

*

Henry was an excellent cook, whereas Madeleine could at best be described as competent. So he did most of the cooking through the week, which made sense anyway – they would end up eating too late if they had to wait for her to get home and start. Besides, Henry claimed he enjoyed it, and Madeleine supposed it was all part of the artistic temperament, simply another avenue of creative endeavour. She clearly fell on the consumer side of the equation: books, food, wine, whatever – her appetite was voracious. Speaking of wine, there were only dregs left in her glass. It wouldn't hurt to have a refill, especially as she'd be eating.

'Aiden, would you prefer to switch to wine with dinner?' she asked on her way to the fridge.

'Why not!' he declared.

'Henry?' Madeleine prompted, holding up the bottle.

He glanced at it, and then back at her. 'Okay, but just a little.'

She wondered if that was some kind of veiled hint for her benefit. Henry turned his attention to serving the meal, and Madeleine slipped another bottle from the rack above into the fridge; the one Aiden had already opened wouldn't last long between the three of them and she had to make sure there was enough chilled wine for their guest. She busied herself fetching glasses and pouring the wine while Henry plated up dinner. It smelled divine: butterflied leg of lamb that had been marinated in one of Henry's special concoctions, no doubt, and roasted with kipfler potatoes and caramelised vegetables. Madeleine was suddenly aware of her stomach grumbling.

'Man, where did you learn to cook like this?' Aiden exclaimed, as he tucked into the meal. 'Have you been giving him lessons, Madeleine?'

'I can't take any credit,' she said. 'It's all him, and basically the main reason I'm marrying him.'

Henry smiled at that. 'I got into cooking during those long stretches up at my house in the Hamptons. In New York I often ate out, but up there I preferred to stay in. So it gave me the chance to experiment – cooking for myself it didn't matter if something didn't turn out.'

'So, returning to Henry's mysterious past,' Madeleine said, pushing her plate aside when she'd had her fill. 'You were roommates in college . . . ?'

Aiden nodded. 'From day one, freshman year.'

'I was quietly unpacking in my dorm room,' Henry took up the story, 'minding my own business, when Aiden barged in, threw his bags down in the middle of the floor and started ordering me around.'

'All I said was that we needed to go out and get our bearings.'

'In other words, find out where the girls were,' said Henry.

'Well, yeah,' Aiden said, like that was obvious.

'I died a little on the inside at that moment,' Henry went on. 'I realised I was going to have to put up with this loudmouth for at least a whole year – administration didn't take kindly to dorm changes.'

Aiden was grinning. 'It was love at first sight.'

'For you, maybe,' said Henry, but Madeleine could see the glint in his eye. 'I just learnt to tolerate you.'

She had never witnessed this side of Henry's sense of humour before, the kind of good-natured ribbing that men in particular engaged in. But of course she'd never seen him with a close male friend before.

'Funny,' said Aiden, 'the whole time we were at college you never did apply for that dorm change.'

Henry shrugged. 'I figured better the devil you know.'

'Admit it, you wouldn't have survived without me.' Aiden turned to Madeleine. 'You see, I made it my mission to pick up girls for Henry. He really couldn't be left to do it for himself.'

Henry cleared his throat.

'You going to argue with that, Darrow?'

He opened his mouth as though to protest, but then all he said was, 'No.'

'In fact, I'm surprised he managed to snare you all by himself, Madeleine.'

'Let's just say I played easy to get.'

'Some guys have all the luck.' Aiden shook his head. 'Well, I don't know what he was like when you met him, but back then Henry always had his head in a sketchpad. Friday afternoons after class I'd find him hunched over it and I'd literally have to drag him away to have some fun.'

'I *was* having fun,' said Henry.

'Sad but true,' said Aiden. 'He was obsessed, and he was brilliant – we all know that now, but I like to think I was the first one to recognise it. I kept telling him he was too talented not to do something with it, but he maintained it was just a hobby. At the same time, he was taking all these random classes with no major because he had no idea what he really wanted to do with his life. So I stole one of his sketchpads and took it to show my uncle next time I went home.'

'Your uncle?' Madeleine asked. 'Why?'

'He was a literary agent,' Aiden said. 'I thought he might be able to point me in the right direction, give me some leads. Anyway, he said the drawings were impressive, and more importantly, they were unique. He hadn't seen anything quite like them. He said if Henry could come up with stories to go with the pictures he might be able to do something with them himself, which would be way more marketable than trying to sell his pictures as straight art. So when I got back to college I eventually talked Henry into it, and we started writing the words.'

Madeleine glanced from Aiden to Henry and back again. 'You two? Together? You and Henry wrote his books together?'

'Only the first two or three,' said Aiden.

'And only the first drafts,' Henry added. 'I didn't really learn how to write until I had an editor.'

Madeleine had always known that Henry's books began with the pictures, but she didn't realise that was how he got started in the first place. Or that Aiden had been so closely involved. 'I hope you got a share of the royalties,' she said.

Aiden sighed and shook his head. 'You know, not a red cent.'

'Aid,' Henry protested.

'He did offer –'

'Tried to insist,' Henry interrupted.

'He did.' Aiden grinned. 'But I didn't do that much, seriously. I was more of a motivating force, an inspiration. His muse, you might even say.'

Henry snorted. 'If by "muse" you mean you sat in the corner making paper airplanes and flying them at me while you whined about being late for some party or other.'

'But it did make you work faster, if only to get me off your back.'

'That's true.'

'It's really Uncle Gene who deserves the credit.'

'Absolutely,' said Henry.

Aiden raised his glass, and Henry followed. 'To Uncle Gene.'

Madeleine suddenly put it all together. 'Oh God, you're talking about Gene Wallace, your agent?'

'That's right,' said Henry. 'He was more than an agent, he was my mentor. He helped me develop my work to the point where it could be submitted to publishers.'

'And before they knew it, they had a bidding war on their hands,' said Aiden.

'That's amazing,' said Madeleine. 'I had no idea.'

'Didn't he tell you any of this?' Aiden frowned.

'Most of it. I didn't know Gene Wallace was your uncle, or how much you were involved.'

'Trying to keep all the glory for yourself, Darrow?'

'Well, maybe you can motivate Henry to write his vows, Aiden. He seems to be having so much trouble with them.'

Henry stood abruptly and started to clear the table. 'I can write them myself.'

'And yet you haven't.' She could hear the nasty tone in her own voice but she couldn't seem to help herself.

'What's this, Darrow, you haven't written your vows?' said Aiden. 'Is this one of my best man duties, to see you get it done?'

'There's plenty of time,' Henry said dismissively.

He went to take the bottle of wine, and Madeleine said, 'Leave that, thanks.'

Was that a glare? He picked up their plates and walked around to the kitchen. While his back was turned, Madeleine quickly refilled her glass, draining the bottle.

'That's Henry's excuse whenever I bring it up, Aiden,' she went on. '"There's plenty of time", and I predict he'll still be saying it the night before the wedding. And then he'll get his own way.'

Henry didn't respond, pretending to be preoccupied stacking the dishwasher. But Madeleine couldn't stop herself now. They rarely had an audience – perhaps that was why Henry had brought up the apartment as well. There was someone to bear witness.

'You see,' she continued, 'Henry thinks writing your own vows is naff.'

He looked across at her then. 'I never said that.'

'But it's what you think.'

Henry sighed. 'I just don't see what's wrong with using the traditional vows. They've served their purpose for hundreds of years –'

'Oh Henry.' Aiden gave him the look a parent would give a misbehaving child. 'How could you be struggling to come up with words to describe this woman?'

'I'm not struggling,' Henry said tightly. 'I just don't think it's anyone else's business how I feel about Madeleine.'

Aiden raised an eyebrow. 'You're talking about the people at your wedding? The friends and family gathered there to witness you committing yourselves to each other? You don't think they have some idea how you feel?'

'So why do they need me to spell it out?'

'They don't, Madeleine does.'

She nodded. 'See, Aiden gets it.'

Henry held up his hands in surrender. 'I will write the vows,' he said. 'But right now, I think it's time to call it a night.' He looked pointedly at Madeleine. 'You've got an early start tomorrow.'

'We can't leave our guest sitting up on his own,' she protested.

'Now hold on right there,' said Aiden. 'This isn't going to work if you guys treat me like a guest. So thank you, Madeleine, but you don't have to sit up with me.'

'But I want to,' she said. 'And I'm not even tired.'

'You'll pay for it tomorrow,' Henry warned, coming back around to the table.

'Tomorrow is another day,' she reminded him. 'And I'm not over this one yet.'

'Whatever you think.' He leaned over to kiss her on the top of her head, but Madeleine threw her head back, presenting her lips instead. He gave her a quick peck and straightened again, walking backwards away from them. 'Goodnight then.'

'See you in the morning, buddy,' Aiden called after him.

Once Henry had disappeared up the hall, Madeleine leapt up out of her chair and headed straight for the fridge. 'Now the old man has gone to bed, we can really get this party going.' She grabbed the other bottle of wine and twirled around to face Aiden again, a glint in her eye as she nudged the fridge door shut behind her and waved the bottle in the air, dancing a kind of cha-cha back to the table.

Aiden was smiling, watching her. 'You know, you're not at all what I expected,' he said as she filled his glass.

'Oh? Why?'

'Well, you're about ten times more gorgeous.'

He was such a smooth talker. 'Well, thank you, but why wouldn't you expect that? Henry's pretty gorgeous too.'

'He's not bad, but he's punching way above his weight with you.'

'Okay, enough with the flattery, Carmichael,' said Madeleine. 'Seriously, how am I not what you expected?'

'I don't know . . . I suppose I expected someone quieter, for starters.'

She pressed her lips together. Damn, she tended to get a little loud when she drank. 'Sorry, I know I can be obnoxiously loud.'

'You're not obnoxious or loud. Far from it,' said Aiden. 'You're bubbly and . . . effervescent.'

'Don't they mean the same thing?'

'You really are a pedant.'

'Sorry.' Madeleine smiled, topping up her own glass again. 'Do go on.'

'Well, you know Henry better than me. I haven't seen him in years, though he doesn't seem to have changed much. I always thought he'd end up with somebody a little more . . . his speed, I suppose. More conservative.'

'Henry's not conservative,' she exclaimed as she plonked back down on her chair.

'I don't mean politically,' said Aiden. 'I mean . . . Never mind, what do I know?'

'Look, I understand what you're saying, and yeah, we get that a lot, that we're so different,' said Madeleine. 'But look at you and Henry, you're just as different, and you're old friends. Opposites attract.'

'So what attracted you to Henry?'

'His eyes,' she said without hesitation. Then she smiled. 'Seriously, he was just so centred, so self-contained. I mean that in a good way.'

Aiden looked dubious. 'If you say so.'

'No, really, there was something about him, I was drawn to him. He came along at the right time for me. I was going off the rails a little, and I needed someone like him, someone solid and stable. He saved me.'

'I'm losing track of the chronology here,' Aiden said, frowning. 'You guys have been together, what, two, three years?'

Madeleine nodded. 'We first met at the Sydney Writers' Festival, two and a half years ago.'

'So how old were you then?'

'Two and a half years younger than I am now,' she demurred, smiling. 'Don't you know you're not supposed to ask a lady her age?'

He grinned. 'I'm just saying, I assume you were out of your teens at least. Isn't that a little old to be going off the rails?'

'Well, I lost a few years after university,' she explained, 'so I guess I was making up for it.'

'What do you mean, lost?'

'My dad was very sick, for a long time.'

'How is he now?'

Madeleine hesitated. It never got any easier. 'Um, he died.'

'I'm so sorry . . . You mentioned him before, I didn't realise.' The look on Aiden's face was quite disconcerting. He seemed genuinely affected, and Madeleine felt a lump rise in her throat. 'What happened? Sorry,' he added quickly, 'that's if you're okay talking about it.'

She should have been okay, after all this time, but Madeleine still found it difficult. Maybe that was the problem, she needed to talk about it more. Normalise it. It was the reality of her life now – her father had died, and he wouldn't be giving her away at her wedding. It was one of the times when a father figured large in a girl's life. No matter how antiquated the tradition, no matter how feminist the daughter – even if she had been living independently for some time, most likely with the groom in question – most brides still had their fathers give them away. *Give them away*. It was quite astonishing when you thought about it. But Madeleine still wished her dad was here to do just that.

Aiden was watching her, his blue eyes intent.

'It was leukaemia,' she said finally. 'A particularly nasty strain. He didn't respond to treatment, so the only hope he had was a bone marrow transplant.' She paused. 'But we never found a match.'

Both Madeleine and Genevieve had been tested, but the chances were slim with offspring, as they only shared half his genes. Although it was no surprise, they were nonetheless shattered when neither of them was a match. Their mother insisted on being tested too, on the narrowest of off-chances. She didn't share any DNA with her husband, of course, but she argued she had the same odds as anyone on the public register. She would have gladly given her life to save him, but it didn't matter, she wasn't a match either. Their best hope was his only sister, who had married a Canadian and moved there more than twenty years ago. She had the preliminary tests in Canada, and the whole family waited with bated breath for the results, in vain, as it turned out.

It just seemed particularly unjust that this should happen to someone like her dad, a good, kind, decent man, a loving husband and devoted father, a wonderful teacher. But he took the news with the kind of equanimity with which he'd lived his life. When everyone else was ranting, 'Why you?' he would say, 'Why not me?' So with all other avenues exhausted, he was placed on the donor list, but his age, and the progress of the disease, meant that the likelihood of finding a donor while he was strong enough to endure the transplant was minimal at best.

The hardest thing Madeleine had ever done was watch her beloved dad slowly deteriorate. The disease didn't just rob them of a husband and a father, it robbed them of their entire happy family life. It was like living in a prisoner-of-war camp, with the cloud of imminent death hanging over them the whole time. And no matter how he tried, he could no longer be the dad he'd always been, the rock, the one they all depended on. So they were robbed of that as well.

'He was the centre of our family, of our lives,' said Madeleine. 'You know, he was just one of those people.'

Aiden had been listening intently. 'How old were you . . . when he . . .'

'I was twenty-five, still living at home, because I was there when it all started, when he was first diagnosed, so I couldn't leave. I didn't want to leave. I wanted to have as much time with him as he had left. Then afterwards my mum didn't do so well, so I stayed for her. By the time I got out into the real world and started a career, I guess I had a lot of catching up to do.'

'And that's when you went "off the rails"?'

She nodded.

'Well, it's not surprising,' said Aiden, 'after what you'd been through. But I'm sure you couldn't have done anything too terrible.'

Terrible enough. Madeleine couldn't bring herself to talk about it out loud, to anyone. Twice she slept with authors while on tour; one of them was married, and that was so incredibly unprofessional, not to mention of such dubious morality that she hadn't even been able to confide in Liv. Of course she was drunk at the time, but that was no excuse, it just made her actions even more unprofessional. It remained a dark, dirty secret, until she'd eventually confessed to Henry, who encouraged her to stop beating herself up about it, to put it behind her and move on.

'By the time I met Henry, I felt like I was coming apart at the edges,' said Madeleine. 'He was this rock I could anchor myself to.'

'What do you mean, coming apart?' said Aiden. 'That sounds serious.'

She shrugged. 'I was just working hard, partying hard.' She didn't want to go into details.

Aiden frowned. 'Does that mean the same thing here as it does in the States?'

'What does it mean in the States?'

'If you "party", it usually involves drugs.'

'Oh no,' said Madeleine. 'I kept to the legal stuff.' She picked up the bottle and refilled her glass. 'But I was burning the candle at both ends, and my work was suffering. Actually, that was the reason I met Henry.'

'How do you mean?'

'My boss was aware I was overdoing it, so she assigned me to Henry at a writers' festival. She figured I couldn't get into much trouble with a children's author.'

'And yet here you are, marrying him,' said Aiden. 'You can't get into much more trouble than that.'

She smiled. 'I take it you're not the marrying kind?' she said, grabbing the opportunity to steer the conversation away from her.

'I didn't say that. I have nothing against the concept, I just haven't found the right girl.'

Madeleine found that hard to believe; someone like Aiden could surely have his pick. Half the girls – no, *all* the girls from the office would be clambering over each other to get near him at the wedding.

'Maybe it's your lifestyle?' she suggested.

'I'm sorry?'

'I mean, because you travel so much. How would you even get to meet women, much less maintain a relationship?'

'Oh, I still meet them,' said Aiden. 'But you're right, maintaining a relationship is a lot harder. In fact, I met someone very special, not so long ago. Lost my heart to her, big time.'

'What happened?'

He took a breath. 'We met at a global conference on poverty. She was Irish. That accent – she only had to ask for a cup of tea and I'd go weak at the knees. Anyway, we tried to keep up a long-distance relationship . . .' He drifted off, his blue eyes looking soulful.

Why did she keep noticing what colour his eyes were? Focus, Madeleine! 'What happened?' she asked.

'She found someone else, in her own country. I guess she couldn't wait around for me.'

'Oh no, really?' she said, her heart breaking just a little for him.

Aiden looked at her. 'No, not really.'

'What?'

He flashed her a smile that was quite disarming. Madeleine was confused now. 'I'm not following. Were you in love with this woman or what?'

'I was in love with the idea of her.'

Her head was hurting. 'What are you talking about?'

'Oh Madeleine, you're not real quick on the uptake, are you?'

Her mouth dropped open. 'Did you just make all that up?'

'It got your sympathy, didn't it?'

'Why would you do that?'

'To prove a point,' said Aiden. 'You see, my "lifestyle", as you put it, really has prevented me from having a serious relationship for a very long time, and now it's like a catch-22 – girls think you're shallow if you haven't had a serious relationship, so they don't take you seriously, and you don't get the chance to develop a relationship. So I sometimes give myself a past.'

'Hmm . . . I suppose it's like trying to get a job when you have no experience,' Madeleine said finally. 'Or . . . I know, it's like how you don't have a credit rating when you've never used credit, and therefore you can't get credit. Now, that really doesn't make any sense to me. I mean, if you've never been in debt, isn't that a good thing? Wouldn't that make you a better risk? But no, they want you to be in debt, so they can tell if you'll pay it off. But isn't it better that you haven't been in debt in the first place?'

Madeleine tried to remember the point she'd been intending to make, but she had no idea what it was any more. She looked across at Aiden, who was just smiling indulgently at her, and felt a blush creep into her cheeks.

'Sorry,' she said, flustered. 'I've gone off on a tangent. It's my tragic flaw. What were we saying?'

'I believe you asked me if I was the marrying kind,' he said.

'And then you made up a story to get my sympathy,' said Madeleine, back on track.

'Well, usually I get a bit more than sympathy . . .'

Now she went into full blush mode. 'Mr Carmichael!'

He laughed. 'I wasn't implying . . . ah, whatever.' He raised his glass. 'Seriously, I'm envious of Henry – of you both,' he added quickly. 'Of what you both have, together. I really hope I'm lucky enough to have the same one day.'

Madeleine raised her glass to him, and promptly drained it. She felt the wine swimming around in her head. She hadn't drunk this much in a while, and Henry was right, she'd pay for it tomorrow, but she was having such a good time. She knew she was getting to the point of no return and that she should resist while she still could. She hadn't yet reached the level of inebriation that made rational decisions impossible. One more glass ought to do it.

'So,' she said, picking up the bottle, 'can I top you up?'

Aiden regarded her with an adorable expression of regret. 'As much as I could sit up all night with you, I'm going to get into big trouble with Henry if I don't release you from your hosting duties very soon. You do have to work tomorrow.'

She felt immediately self-conscious. She wondered if he was thinking she'd had quite enough, if he thought she was drunk, if he'd noticed her speech slurring. She hated when that happened. That was it, she'd better quit while she was ahead. 'You're right,' she agreed reluctantly.

Aiden stood up and came around the table to offer her his hand. 'You're going to need all your energy for cleaning up all that smut, aren't you?'

Madeleine took his hand and got to her feet. They were standing facing each other, just a little too close. She suddenly felt woozy, and he grabbed her arms to steady her.

'I'm really glad you're here, Aiden,' she said.

'So you keep saying.'

'Oh, sorry.' She also repeated herself when she drank too much.

'No, I'm flattered. It's been great to finally meet you, Maddie.'

'So you're going with Maddie?' she said.

'I think so.' He smiled. 'We'll see how it fits for a day or two.'

'Okay. So you know where you're sleeping?'

'I do, Henry set me up in the guestroom today.'

'Of course,' she said. 'Well, goodnight.' She looped her arms around his neck and hugged him, and he hugged her in return. It was all chaste and friendly, nothing to see here, people.

Aiden drew back first. 'Goodnight, Maddie.'

She turned up the hall and crept into the bedroom, but she didn't feel like sleeping. She felt wired. And restless. And horny. Yes, okay, she was a little tipsy, and it was late, and she should just be sensible and go to sleep. But she couldn't help the way she felt. And she had a nice warm fiancé right there in her bed, who could put her out of her misery. Madeleine stripped down to her underwear and climbed in behind Henry, snuggling into his back. He didn't budge. She planted a row of kisses along his shoulder blade as she brought her arm around him and grazed his chest with her fingertips. He stirred then, but only to clasp her hand firmly in his, effectively restraining it. Hmm. Time to move to DEFCON 4. Madeleine had no idea what that meant, just that in movies it was always when things got serious. She drew her leg over Henry's and raised herself up so she could reach around to kiss his cheek, his ear, his neck . . . Finally, a response.

'Hon,' he murmured, 'I'm sleeping.'

'And I'm waking you,' she breathed close to his ear, before teasing his lobe with her teeth.

'Madeleine,' he groaned.

'Come on,' she urged, 'you know you want to . . .'

'No, I don't.' His voice was firmer now. Properly awake, he shifted onto his back to look up at her. 'It's late, and you have an early start.'

'So? That's my problem,' she said, leaning down to press her lips against his, her tongue working its way into his mouth.

'Madeleine,' he said, holding her off, 'you're drunk.'

She leaned back on her elbow, feeling hurt and defensive. 'I'm not drunk.'

'You've had too much to drink, and it's late and I was asleep.'

'Why are you being so mean?'

She heard him sigh loudly in the darkness. 'I'm sorry,' he said. 'Hey?' He brought his arm around her, drawing her close to his side. 'It's not you, it's me, okay? I guess I just feel a bit weird with Aiden in the house.'

'Seriously? But he's going to be here for weeks, on and off. Are we not going to have sex any time he's around?'

'Of course not. I mean, of course we will,' he said. 'I just have to get used to it, that's all.' He drew her head down onto his chest and gently stroked her hair. 'You really need to get some sleep, you're going to regret this in the morning.'

Madeleine felt frustrated, in every sense of the word. What kind of man refuses sex when it's being handed to him on a platter? Obviously the same kind of man who argues sensibly about getting enough sleep when he could be getting laid. Sometimes Madeleine worried they were like an old married couple already. Maybe she should push a bit harder now, she wondered with a yawn. Henry drew the covers up over her shoulders, and they both shifted, settling into each other, her head nestling perfectly into the hollow between his neck and his shoulder. His skin was warm against her cheek, and Madeleine felt cosy. He was still stroking her hair . . . it was nice, soothing . . . she was pretty tired . . . it had been a long day . . .

Morning

'Madeleine? Madeleine, honey . . . it's time to get up.'

She opened one eye and peered out at Henry through the gloom. He was sitting on the bed, dressed already, gazing down at her.

'What time is it?' she croaked.

'It's still only early, but you said you had to meet with your staff first thing.'

'Oh God.' She brought up a hand to cover her eyes. 'What time did I come to bed last night?'

'Late,' he said. 'Here, I brought you tea. Have a shower, and I'll make you some breakfast.'

'Okay,' she said weakly. 'Thank you.'

Twenty minutes later, Madeleine joined Henry in the kitchen, dressed and ready for work. At least that was what she was trying to convince herself; in reality she wasn't at all sure she was ready for a long drive and what was bound to be a very long day. Henry poured her another cup of tea and slid a plate of toast with butter and Vegemite in front of her. Being American he didn't really get Vegemite, but he did know it was all Madeleine could stomach the morning after; she didn't subscribe to the big fry-up hangover cure.

'I'm not hung-over,' she said defensively.

Henry's face was impassive. 'Okay, you want me to make you something else?'

'No . . .' She eased herself onto the stool. 'It's fine . . . thank you.'

He nodded, turning back to the sink. Madeleine bit into the toast.

'Did we have a fight last night?' she asked Henry suddenly.

He turned around again. 'No. What makes you think that?'

As she was standing in the shower, something had niggled at Madeleine. She had a blurry image of Henry pushing her away and telling her she was drunk.

'Were you mad at me because I stayed up and had a drink with Aiden?'

Henry walked over to where she was sitting at the island bench. He took her hand in his. 'I think you had more than "a" drink,' he said, but he was smiling. 'You just came on a little strong when you came to bed –'

'And you rejected me!' Madeleine said, her eyes wide. 'I remember now.'

'I was only conscious that you had to get up early,' he said, leaning in closer. 'If you'd come to bed earlier, it would have been a different story.' He traced the line of her jaw with his fingertips and then held her face in both hands as he brought her lips to his. Madeleine melted into him; Henry was an exceptional kisser. She would even risk being late for work if he was to lift her up right now, and lay her back across the island bench, and . . . but Henry wouldn't do something like that.

She suddenly had another mental flash. 'Hold on,' she said, pulling back to look at him. 'I remember now! You didn't want to have sex with me because of Aiden, not because it was late.'

'Look, it was late . . . but I guess I do feel a little uncomfortable with Aiden in the house.'

'Henry, he's going to be here quite a lot before the wedding.' She'd long ago accepted the fact that Henry wasn't very demonstrative in front of company, but this was taking it up another notch. 'Are you not even going to touch me when he's around?' she asked, her voice breaking slightly.

'Madeleine . . .' He leaned in to kiss her again, trying to draw her closer.

But she resisted. 'You better not – what if Aiden walks in and sees us?'

'He's not here.'

She frowned. 'What do you mean? Where is he?'

'He's still on northern hemisphere time, so he didn't get much sleep. He wanted to go for an early surf, clear his head. I drove him over to Avalon, and I'll go back and meet him after you leave.'

She blinked. 'You came back just to get me off to work?'

'You said you weren't coming home tonight. I wanted to see you.'

Madeleine softened at that. Henry had this completely artless way of expressing how he felt about her; it often caught her by surprise. He wasn't one to get mushy and sentimental, he just gave it to her straight, which often turned out to be more romantic than if he'd recited a sonnet. She slipped off the stool and brought her arms around his neck, pressing herself up against him. 'I love you very much, do you know that?' she said.

'I do.' This time she didn't resist as he leaned in and his lips met hers. As they kissed, Madeleine let her mind drift, imagining just what they could get up to on the kitchen bench, until finally she couldn't stand it anymore.

'Henry,' she said, her mouth barely leaving his, 'seeing as we're alone, maybe we should take the opportunity . . .'

'You'll be late,' he murmured against her lips.

'I've still got time.'

'You're dressed already, you don't want to get your clothes all smutched.'

She broke away to look him in the eye. 'Right, come with me.' She grabbed his hand and walked determinedly back to their bedroom, pulling him behind her.

'Madeleine . . .'

She didn't say anything, releasing his hand as she walked into the room and kicked off her shoes. She slipped off her skirt and laid it carefully over the bedroom chair. Henry watched her from the doorway while she unbuttoned her blouse and hung it neatly across the back of the chair. She turned to face him as she reached around to unclasp her bra and toss it aside. He was still standing in the same spot, staring at her.

'What are you waiting for?' she asked.

'You take my breath away, do you know that?' he said in a low voice.

She smiled as she walked over to him and took hold of both his hands, drawing him into the room. As they neared the bed, Henry took over, sliding his arms around her and lowering her down in one graceful movement. Henry was always graceful in bed. Occasionally she fantasised about him ripping off her clothes and taking her fast and hard. But then again, once he got going, it was the best sex she had ever had in her life. The man had the patience of a saint. Madeleine brought her arms up over her head while Henry had his way, his hands and lips and tongue performing a kind of synchronised sweep across her body, until she was panting with need, and aching for him. They climaxed together; they nearly always did. It was perfection.

*

As she drove down the street a half an hour later, Madeleine glanced at Henry waving her off in the rearview mirror, a satisfied smile on his face. They'd both needed that. There had been a strange vibe going on last night. It wasn't like them to bicker, and Madeleine didn't like feeling disconnected from him, especially when she wouldn't see him again until tomorrow. But now they were back in step, and Madeleine felt exhilarated and deliciously free of tension all at once. This must be what they meant in that song about sexual healing; even her hangover had faded to a manageable level. Okay, so she'd had one night off the wagon – not that she was *on* a wagon, as such: that made her sound like an alcoholic or something. She just hadn't drunk as much as she had last night in a long time, and that's why it had hit her so hard.

But it was a one-off, a special occasion . . . It wasn't going to happen again.

Amblin Press

The office was quiet when Liv arrived. She was a little early – Lachie had training before school, and Dylan was happy to go early as well to work in the library. Then, miracle of miracles, the traffic gods smiled on her and she enjoyed an uneventful run into the city. It was going to be a good day, she decided. Though it was a bit of an anticlimax to walk into an empty office. Not that she expected a marching band, but it was always nice to be welcomed back after a tour.

Fortunately for her delicate ego, she didn't have to wait long. She heard the cry first: 'Liv!' And then Madeleine appeared flushed-faced in the doorway of her office. 'I didn't realise you were going to be back this week.'

'Yeah, well, I had planned to give myself a couple of days off. But then I got Jane's email last night, and I thought I better come in and help out.'

'I honestly couldn't love you more right now,' Madeleine declared.

'Stop, people will talk,' Liv said. 'I am going to knock off early, though. I want to be home for the boys this afternoon.'

'I'm just so relieved you're here at all!' Madeleine walked into the office and dropped into a chair. 'I was feeling a bit overwhelmed.'

'Oh, you could do it with your hands tied behind your back,' Liv dismissed. 'I wasn't worried about that. But you know what they say, she who wears the crown . . . something something, whatever that saying is. I just felt bad leaving you to deal with something so major.'

'And you're a control freak, so you couldn't bear it.'

'There's that too.'

Madeleine grinned. 'I wouldn't have you any other way. So where do we start?'

'With coffee,' said Liv, getting to her feet, 'and I don't mean from the plunger in the staffroom. It has to be espresso today.'

'So tell me about your trip,' Madeleine said as they walked around to the elevator.

'You know Cameron, he's a publicist's dream. Every venue was at capacity, and he owned them all. The only issue is that his sessions always run so late because of the long queues for book signings, and the fact that the darling boy has to talk to every single person in the queue for as long as they feel inclined, let them take pictures, hold their babies . . .'

'The fans do love him,' said Madeleine.

'I just wish they would love him a bit less after, say, 10 pm.'

The ping sounded and the doors slid open. As they stepped into the elevator Liv grabbed Madeleine by the arm. 'So how's the best man? Tell me all the goss. Is he as gorgeous in the flesh?'

'Oh, way more,' said Madeleine.

'And tall? He seemed tall, but a lot of the pictures were with children or Asian people, so it's hard to tell.'

'That's racist, you know.'

'It's not racist to identify people by their . . . their race,' Liv defended herself, but then saw that Madeleine was smiling. 'Okay, I took the bait. Congratulations. Now can we go back to the case of the best man? Gorgeous – tick. Tall?'

'Yep,' Madeleine confirmed. 'And funny and gregarious and wonderful company. He's so different to Henry.'

'Oh, poor Henry!'

Madeleine winced. 'I didn't mean it to come out like that. Actually, I saw a whole other side of Henry around Aiden. They had a lot of little in-jokes, it was nice. But they're very different – it made me wonder how they ever became friends in the first place. Whereas Aiden and I, well, we clicked right away. It was like we'd known each other forever.'

'Makes sense,' said Liv. 'If Aiden's nothing like Henry, and you and Henry are chalk and cheese as well, then that means you and Aiden must be more alike. That's why you got on so well. It's simple mathematics. Or maybe it's chemistry?'

The elevator arrived at the ground floor and they walked out across the lobby to the coffee shop. There was a queue; there was always a queue at this place. Coffee was the new cigarette break.

Liv glanced at Madeleine, who was frowning. 'What's furrowing your brow, girlie?'

'You think Henry and I are like chalk and cheese?' Madeleine said.

'This is the first time it's occurring to you?'

'No, of course not. I just didn't realise it was *that* obvious. Even Aiden said I was nothing like what he expected, Henry and I so different.'

Liv shrugged. 'Aren't you always the one saying opposites attract? Take it from me, if you're too much alike, it's a disaster waiting to happen. Case in point, my erstwhile husband. Rick and I were very alike on the surface, but it was *all* surface. We were both party people way back, it was all fun, fun, fun, until it wasn't. He didn't have the staying power when things got real. But your boy Henry is husband material. Aiden's type is all about the fun.'

'Well, that's the thing, he's not only about the fun,' said Madeleine. 'He's also hard at work saving the third world.'

Liv arched an eyebrow. 'Someone's got a little crush.'

Madeleine looked flustered. 'Just because you admire a person who happens to be of the opposite sex –'

'Save the speech, I'm only teasing,' Liv assured her with a wink.

They made it to the front of the queue and gave their orders, before stepping aside to wait.

'Anyway,' Liv resumed, 'I'm glad you had a good time. I got stuck with Rick for the night.'

'For the night!'

'Not overnight – God forbid,' said Liv. 'No, he brought the boys home from school even though it wasn't on the schedule. And he'd already promised them pizza, so he suggested we have some "family time".' She shook her head. 'I have a sneaking suspicion something's going on.'

Madeleine blinked. 'Like what?'

'Well, last time he started hanging around and getting all sentimental, he ended up breaking up with Bree, remember? And he did the same thing after Amber.'

'You think he's breaking up with . . . what's the latest one's name again?'

'Carly.'

Madeleine pulled a face. 'Is he making his way through the alphabet or something?'

'Probably.' Liv sighed. 'I don't know what to think. But I certainly didn't appreciate him gatecrashing my first night back with the boys. You know, there's a reason people get divorced, and it's not so they can hang out together afterwards. If you liked each other's company that much, you wouldn't have got divorced in the first place.'

'Good point,' said Madeleine. 'So even after all this time, you reckon Rick thinks he has a chance to get back with you?'

'I think if he and Carly are on the rocks, he's probably just hedging his bets. He couldn't go five minutes on his own, it's pathetic. People talk of being brave and putting yourself out there, but most men run from one woman's skirts to the next. They're not brave, they're just petrified of being alone and not having someone to look after them.' As she was speaking, it suddenly occurred to Liv that that was probably the case with David from the plane. 'Like, I got talking to this guy on the plane home –'

Madeleine's head shot up. 'Did you?'

'You can lower your eyebrows, and the pitch of your voice,' Liv said dryly. 'And probably your expectations as well. We just talked, but he gave me this line about taking risks and not having regrets.' She snorted. 'Bet you any money he's freshly divorced.'

'But what was he like?'

Liv turned to look at her directly. 'Have you been listening to anything I've said?'

'Yes, but no need to cut off your nose to spite your face,' said Madeleine. 'You might be judging him unfairly, he could be –'

'Don't you dare say it.'

'You don't know what I was going to say.'

'"He could be the love of your life, the best thing that ever happened to you."'

'I was going to say he could be a nice companion for going to the movies or having a cup of coffee with. Jeez!' Madeleine shook her head. 'So I assume there was no exchanging of phone numbers, or anything promising?'

Liv hesitated. 'He gave me his number.'

'Great. What are you going to do about it?'

'I threw it out.'

'Why did you do that?'

'Because I have no intention of using it.'

Madeleine was agog. 'But surely it couldn't hurt to give him a call.'

'Oh, but surely it could.'

Madeleine's face softened. 'Is that why, you're afraid of being hurt?'

Liv rolled her eyes. 'I didn't mean it like that. I meant hurt in the sense of . . . spoil, wreck, ruin. I like my life. I don't need the complication right now. You know how I feel about it, I'm just like –'

'Yeah, yeah, Jennifer Aniston,' said Madeleine. 'Only you're not, now she's married. You're going to have to find another patron saint.'

The barista caught Liv's eye and beckoned them over. They collected their coffees from the counter and made their way back to the elevators. Madeleine sipped hers and sighed with relief. 'God, I needed that.'

'Oh?' Liv said, watching her.

'Hm, it was a bit of a late one last night.' She glanced sideways at Liv. 'I'm feeling a touch fragile.'

Liv wondered what she meant by fragile, but she didn't know how to ask without sounding suspicious, even judgemental. It was none of her business; although, on some level, it was entirely her business. Madeleine didn't drink much these days – she had cut down substantially after she met Henry, and since he'd moved out to Australia she barely touched the stuff. Which was just as well.

Henry had saved Madeleine's skin, and certainly her job. She was heading for her first official warning before the writers' festival that year. Liv had tried to warn her, unofficially, as a friend, but it didn't seem to get through. That was the problem with being friends with your subordinates. Liv hated that word, she disliked any kind of hierarchy, but like it or not, she was the boss, and she had obligations to her employer to act like one. Finally Jane had weighed in. She had no such compunctions about doing what needed to be done, and she didn't want Madeleine anywhere near the festival. Liv worried that would only make Mad sink further into the rut she was in, and while she was well aware the workplace wasn't a treatment centre, she felt she just had to find a way to help her prove herself again. Somehow Liv managed to convince Jane to let Madeleine look after Henry Darrow. It was a risk, but a calculated one. All of Henry's sessions were in the morning, which would keep Madeleine on her toes, and Liv had got the heads-up from his publisher in New York that he was definitely not a party person.

'If she screws this up it'll be on your head, Liv,' Jane had warned.

'Don't worry, she won't.'

Liv would make sure of it. She checked in on them whenever she could manage it, even if it was just poking her head into the venue to see that Henry was where he was supposed to be and that everything seemed to be in order. It all worked out, but of course Liv could never have guessed how well.

Henry Darrow was a genuinely decent man. He was a little on the quiet side, but he was always polite – he had that old-school, gentlemanly way about him. But what struck Liv more than anything was the way he looked at Madeleine. He clearly adored her, and it tugged at Liv's heartstrings in a bittersweet way – what woman wouldn't want a man to look at her like that? Since they'd got together, Madeleine had blossomed; she was a different person. Actually, that wasn't quite true – she wasn't different, she was more herself, the young woman who had so impressed Liv as a temp: hardworking, enthusiastic, bright as a button. She had totally earned her subsequent rise in the ranks of the publicity department, and Liv didn't want to see her doing anything to jeopardise that again.

When they got back to the office, the rest of the staff had arrived for the day, and Liv called them to attention.

'Oh, hey Liv,' said Ren. 'You're back?'

'Hey Liv.'

'Hi Liv.'

'Welcome back.'

That was her marching band.

'Huddle around, everyone,' she announced, striding into the middle of the space. They didn't have a meeting room – the only walls were around Liv's office, and that was way too small to run a meeting – so they usually just wheeled their chairs into the centre.

'What's this about, boss?' asked Ren.

'Well, I'm going to leave that to Madeleine to explain. She was at the special meeting Jane called yesterday afternoon –'

'Is this about our jobs?' Sarah said, looking vaguely terrified. She was the last one employed, so Liv could understand her anxiety.

'No, it's not,' she assured them quickly. 'Mad, why don't you go ahead.'

Madeleine joined Liv in the centre of the floor. 'Okay, everyone, it's like this – in the words of our esteemed leader, the erotica bubble has burst.'

She was met with the same kind of sniggering and innuendo that Jane had probably encountered at the meeting yesterday, Liv imagined. Madeleine waited until it died down and then went on to outline the specific issues for publicity. Liv found it very revealing to watch the way the staff took on news that would mean extra work. Over the years she had seen many people come and go; some just didn't seem to get that at the end of the day, this was a bloody hard job. It wasn't enough to be sociable and outgoing, as Madeleine had discovered to her peril. To really succeed, you needed to be smart, unflappable, have an exceptional head for details, and be tireless. Literally. As for some of the girls in the office, Liv was not so sure. Sarah and Katie were still quite young, but they did show an eagerness to learn. They were both furiously scribbling notes as Madeleine spoke. Ren brought her own inimitable style – that of smart alec – but there was a place for this, and she always maintained her professionalism. She was quick-witted and more than a match for some of the blokey authors – they liked her chutzpah, especially the sportsmen. Natalie presented very well: she revelled in the glamorous side of things, but she was sloppy with her admin and, in truth, just a little lazy.

'So I need each of you to review your lists, and we'll come up with a timeline so that we can work through this in chronological order,' said Liv. 'Then you need to pass on all the relevant press material to Madeleine for rewriting. Stacey, if you can keep everything else off Mad's desk today . . . and Amy . . . Where is Amy?'

'She called in sick,' Stacey said. 'She wasn't well at all yesterday.'

Liv had no doubt it was genuine; Amy was a good kid. Fortunately for them, Stacey could handle the work of two assistants. 'Okay, later in the day we'll need to talk about how we're going to deal with the authors, but for now it's important to get that material to Madeleine as soon as possible.'

Natalie sighed. 'I have a bookstore appearance at lunchtime,' she said, as an excuse to get out of doing anything, Liv assumed.

'Well,' she said, 'you'd best get right onto it then.'

*

Rewriting the press releases meant Madeleine had to reacquaint herself with the books in question and find other elements to highlight – the characters, for example, rather than what they got up to with each other.

This proved quite a challenge with a couple of the books – as Beth had pointed out in the original meeting, some only had a plot to string together the sex scenes. Madeleine had to wade through pages and pages of locked lips and limbs, and nipples, tongues and hips, and other bits besides, thrusting here, there and everywhere. She wasn't immune to the stimuli, especially while her earlier tryst with Henry was still fresh in her mind. But after hours of it, she was beginning to feel a little queasy, like Emma had said at the meeting. It reminded her of when she worked part-time at McDonald's during high school. Back then, employees were allowed to eat as much as they liked on their breaks. You could always tell the people who had just started – they gorged themselves stupid. And they rarely touched the stuff after that. Madeleine wondered if this was what had happened to the population at large in regard to erotica. Once it became so freely available, so mainstream, perhaps it lost the very thing that made it so appealing – its forbiddenness. No doubt there was already somebody somewhere writing an academic thesis on the phenomenon.

'How's it coming along?' Liv asked, dropping by her desk in the afternoon.

'I'm nearly cross-eyed,' said Madeleine.

'I thought it made you go blind, not cross-eyed.'

Madeleine gave her a look. 'I'm not getting off on the stuff, I just never sit in front of a computer screen for so long at a stretch. But I'm getting there – I should be able to have most of it done by tonight.'

'There's no need to stay back late, Mad,' said Liv. 'Now that we've worked out a timeline, it doesn't all have to be done at once.'

'I've already said I'll stay at the flat tonight, so I'm going to make the most of it,' said Madeleine, suppressing a yawn. 'Then I might be able to go home at a normal time tomorrow, which should keep Henry happy.'

'Keep reading that stuff, and you'll know exactly how to keep Henry happy.' Liv winked.

*

Liv left for the day soon after. She would have liked to pick the boys up from school, but she really did need to stock the cupboards, so she texted them both to ask if they wanted to come shopping with her. The reply was a resounding no, as she'd expected, so Liv responded that she'd see them at home soon. With supplies. This made Lachie very happy. At least, she was pretty sure the string of incomprehensible words and symbols in his reply was an expression of happiness.

School knock-off hour wasn't the ideal time to hit the shops, but it was better than going out again later, so Liv girded her loins and pushed the trolley through the turnstile into the vast supermarket. No matter that she'd just come from her job as head of department in a large company, for some reason Liv always felt out of her depth in supermarkets. She had no authority here, and she felt it. It seemed to her that mothers with small children ran the place, especially if they were wielding those monster prams. Liv didn't recall being so pushy when the boys were babies. Then again, she didn't go out with them very often, especially during the early months of tandem feeding and pumping. She used to wait until Rick was home and the boys were asleep and then duck out on her own to do the shopping, even though this invariably caused a major panic.

'How am I supposed to take care of both of them?' Rick would ask.

'What, you mean like I do every day?'

'You've got tits.'

'Thanks for noticing.'

'What do I do if they wake up at the same time?'

'Give them both a bottle. There are two ready to go in the fridge.'

'But Lachie's on the breast.'

'The milk in the bottles is breastmilk.'

'But isn't that for Dylan?'

Liv would sigh. 'Stop worrying. I won't be gone that long, you probably won't even have to feed them.'

'Well, don't have an accident or anything, then I'll really be screwed.'

Liv was currently standing glazed-eyed in front of a wall of cereal boxes when she was roused by her phone ringing. Probably Lachie with a list of special requests. Good, she could ask him what was the cereal du jour. Every month or so Liv had to clean out the pantry of half-empty boxes, abandoned when they had moved on to something else. Those boys changed cereal as often as they changed socks; actually, from the smell of some of their socks, it was probably more often.

She looked at the screen on her phone. Oh cripes, it was her mother – Liv had forgotten to call her yesterday with Rick there.

'Hi, Mum,' she answered brightly.

'Olive,' said Joy. 'You're back, I presume, because all I can do is presume.'

'I know, Mum. I'm so sorry, I should have called you last night, but Rick ended up staying.'

'He did?' There was a marked change of tone.

'For dinner,' Liv added quickly, so as not to give her any ideas. 'He drove the boys home from school, he forgot that he didn't need to.'

'Well, that was very nice of him, very thoughtful.'

Liv gritted her teeth. 'Actually, it wasn't thoughtful at all, Mum, quite the opposite. He *didn't* think, he didn't check the schedule.'

'Come now, you'd be complaining if he forgot when he had to pick them up, so at least give him bonus points for this.'

Liv was trying to follow that logic – so the next time Rick forgot the boys and left them stranded, which had happened more times than she cared to think about over the years, she should give him a free pass because he showed up one time when he didn't need to? Her mother was always trying to find ways to emphasise Rick's good side, and sometimes that involved straining the levels of credibility to breaking point. It wasn't that she approved of Rick's infidelity, it was that she approved of divorce less. Joy Walsh was a deeply religious woman, and from her perspective, divorce was a far greater transgression. A marriage undertaken before God could never be dissolved by any court, so in her mind, Liv and Rick were still married. The right course, the *godly* course, would have been for Liv to forgive Rick and take him back, once he had got 'it' out of his system. In fact, as far as her mother was concerned, Liv wasn't giving Rick the opportunity to truly repent, so she was just as accountable – if not more so – for the tragic collapse of their marriage.

'So Rick stayed for dinner,' her mother was saying. 'What a treat for the boys.'

'Hm, they got to have pizza,' Liv muttered, reaching for a random box of cereal.

'Olive, really,' her mother admonished. 'How do you expect to make things right if you won't even cook him a meal?'

'I'm not expecting to make things right,' said Liv. 'Have you forgotten that Rick is living with someone?'

'Only because he doesn't have a choice,' Joy returned. 'You took his home away from him.'

Liv had had enough. They had the same, or a similar, circuitous argument almost every time Rick's name came up. 'Look, Mum, I'm in the supermarket, and I have to get home to the boys.'

'Well, okay then.' Joy sounded miffed. There was definitely miff in her voice.

'Thank you so much for helping while I was away, for picking up the slack.'

'If you didn't work so much, there would be no slack to pick up.'

'There'd also be no way to pay for these groceries.'

'I'm sure Rick can afford all the groceries you need.'

'Mum, lay off, all right?' Liv finally snapped. 'Rick is paying for another woman's groceries, because he made the choice to sleep around and break our marriage vows while I was knee-deep caring for two babies. How can you keep blaming this on me? It's been almost ten years.'

'I know what it's like to look after two children,' her mother said, her voice shifting slightly to a more conciliatory tone. 'It is really hard work, so you have to make an effort if you're going to keep your husband interested –'

'Oh, for Chrissakes!'

'Olive!'

'Goodbye, Mum.' Liv hung up. She should have just given her the f-bomb and been done with it, instead of taking the Lord's name in vain. Joy would be furious. And now Liv was going to have to call her back later to apologise. She didn't normally let her mother upset her these days; it was all so far in the past she usually just tuned out. But Rick showing up and hanging around yesterday had rattled her. She really couldn't go through another round with him. Lately she had felt that she was finally building her own life. She'd read a report once that claimed divorced men were unhappier than divorced women. Liv had to wonder who they'd interviewed for that. Every divorced man she'd ever known of had started a whole new life with a younger wife five minutes after the papers were filed, while the wife he left behind was literally left behind. Liv was living in the same house, still the 'primary caregiver' for the boys. Her life didn't change much when Rick left, except that she had less money, and less support.

She knew she was free of the lies and the stress, but she wasn't free. Every minute of her life had to be accountable.

But things were beginning to free up now. The boys could get themselves to and from school, they could be at home on their own for limited periods, and she had been able to get back out on the road. Most importantly, she could see a time when the boys could have their own relationship with their father and she wouldn't have to broker it. And she was counting the days. Because then Rick could finally be relegated to a minor player in her life.

Liv was so rattled by her mother's call that she forgot half of what she came to the supermarket to get, but ended up with more junk food, and way more chocolate, than was absolutely necessary. The boys certainly didn't object when she got home and they started raiding the bags.

'Please pack the groceries away,' said Liv, 'if there are any left after you've finished with them.'

'Everything okay, Mum?' Dylan asked her, ever the sensitive one.

'I'm just tired,' she assured him.

Liv was still stewing when she walked into her room to change out of her work clothes. She decided that a shower might help her cool off and calm down, so she stripped off and tossed her clothes into the hamper. And that's when the wastepaper basket caught her eye. After a moment's hesitation, Liv reached in and picked up the scrunched slip of paper. She popped it into the drawer of her desk and closed it firmly.

9.30 pm

The end was in sight. There was a little polishing left to do, but Madeleine decided to leave that until the morning when her head would be clearer. She had already eaten dinner at her desk – a microwaved Lean Cuisine followed by a Mars bar, just to provide balance – so she only had to pick up some milk on her way back to the flat, and by ten o'clock she was curled up on the sofa with a cup of tea. The flat was in Chippendale, so at this time of night it wasn't even ten minutes from the office by car. It really was ridiculously convenient, and it was a perfect little place for one – comfortable and cosy and very safe, you had to swipe one of those security cards to get into the garage or the main entrance, and again for the elevator. But maybe it was an extravagance when she used it so infrequently. Madeleine didn't know why she was having so much trouble letting it go, and every time Henry pressured her she felt herself digging her heels in all the more.

Which reminded her. She picked up the phone and called him. 'Hi,' she said when he answered.

'How are you feeling?' he asked.

What did he mean by that? 'I'm fine. A little tired, it's been a very long day. I just got back to the flat.'

'You were working until now?'

'Until about half an hour ago,' she said. Was he doubting her? 'What else do you think I'd be doing?'

'Nothing,' he said. 'I didn't mean anything, Madeleine.'

She could hear the tone of appeasement in his voice, and that was worse. She hated being handled. Why was he handling her? Just because she'd had a few drinks last night? Madeleine sighed. And why was she being so paranoid about it? 'So what did you boys get up to today?' she asked, changing the subject.

She listened while Henry proceeded to give her a recap – they'd stayed at the beach for a while this morning, then driven around to some of the sites, lookouts and such. She hoped Aiden appreciated nature, because that was mostly all the area had to offer. The small shopping villages were nice enough, but there wasn't a lot going on at the far end of the peninsula.

'Jet lag finally caught up with him this afternoon,' Henry said, 'so he had a nap while I got some work done.'

Henry was determined to clear his schedule before the wedding, or more specifically, the honeymoon. They hadn't had a real holiday together since her trip to New York, because Madeleine had always had to work during his visits to Sydney. So Henry was excited that he was finally going to get to see some of the famed outback he'd heard so much about. He'd insisted on organising everything – he said she had enough to do with the wedding, and anyway, he wanted to surprise her. Madeleine was a little worried that she was going to spend her entire honeymoon trekking in remote bushland, which didn't exactly scream romance. But she didn't feel she could say anything. At least they were having a holiday together – that was something.

She suddenly felt lonely away from him. 'I miss you,' she said.

'Miss you too.'

'You know, I really was working right up until half an hour ago. I'd much rather be home with you now.'

She heard him sigh. 'I know. And I'm glad you didn't have to drive home this late,' he said. 'I'm sorry I get cranky about it. I'm just looking forward to after the wedding, when you're not working these kinds of hours, and we won't need the apartment.'

Madeleine wondered why being married was suddenly going to reduce her hours at work. But she didn't want to get into that now; she certainly didn't want to start that unpleasant bickering again.

'Anyway, you must be tired,' said Henry. 'I better let you get some sleep.'

She thought about the long conversations they used to have over Skype, in totally disparate time zones. She never remembered finishing the call so either one of them could get some sleep.

'Henry?'

'Mm?'

'I love you.'

'Love you too. See you tomorrow.'

He hung up, and Madeleine sat staring at the phone. Of course he was right, it was late and she needed to get some sleep. But after she had changed into her pyjamas and washed her face and brushed her teeth, she felt oddly restless. She wasn't going to get off to sleep until she unwound a little.

She sat on the edge of the bed as she set the alarm on her phone. It occurred to her that her mum would definitely be awake. Margaret's habits had undergone a radical reversal since her husband died. Together they used to be early to bed and early risers, but now that she was on her own she was suddenly a night owl.

'Hi, Mum, it's me,' Madeleine said quickly when Margaret answered the phone with a wary 'Hello?'

'Oh, is anything wrong, darling?'

'No, no,' she assured her. 'I had to work late, so I'm staying at the flat. I thought it was a good chance to say hi. I haven't called too late, have I?'

'Oh no, I'll be up for ages yet.'

'Are you watching telly?'

'Yes, but it's a show I recorded, so I've paused it. I'd rather talk to you anyway.'

Madeleine smiled. 'Sorry I haven't called lately.'

'But we only spoke yesterday, didn't we?' she said.

'Well, yes,' said Madeleine. 'But I couldn't talk, we were at the airport to pick up Henry's best man, remember?'

'Oh, how exciting! Henry must be so happy to have someone from home visiting . . . He's from America as well, I take it?'

'Yes, they went to college together, he's Henry's oldest friend.' Madeleine had previously told her all of this, but never mind. She was used to having to repeat things to her mother. 'His name's Aiden, and he's very charming, Mum. I'm sure you're going to like him.'

'Of course I'll like him, any friend of Henry's . . .'

That was sweet. And Madeleine knew she meant it.

'So are we going to get to meet him?' Margaret asked.

'Well, of course, Mum. He's Henry's best man . . . for the wedding.'

'No, I mean before that.'

'Oh, sure.' She shouldn't always assume that her mother wasn't keeping up. 'Genevieve mentioned something about having a lunch. She had to check Mark's schedule.'

'Well, that will be lovely, I'll look forward to it.'

'Has Gen been in touch with you?'

'About the lunch?'

'Not specifically . . .' Madeleine hesitated over how to put this. 'I was just wondering if she got back to you when you called her yesterday.' In other words, had Genevieve asked her to mind the boys?

'I'm sure I've spoken to her . . . I think . . .'

'But you haven't seen her?'

'Not this week, no, dear. Genevieve's a busy girl . . . I wish there was some way I could help her.'

Madeleine was going to have to work on her sister some more. 'So what did you get up to today, Mum?'

'Oh, not much.'

Margaret then proceeded to give her an exhaustively detailed rundown of doing pretty much nothing for the entire day. This was why Madeleine didn't call her more often, and she felt a deep sense of guilt about it. She had despaired early on, while she was still living at home. Whenever she returned from a tour, she would have to listen to her mother debrief about doing nothing the whole time she'd been away. So Madeleine started to collect brochures for courses she might be interested in, mention groups she might like to join. Until one day, Margaret responded with a clarity and forthrightness Madeleine hadn't heard from her in a long time. 'Why would I want to join a scrapbooking group, darling?' she said. 'Don't you think I would already be scrapbooking if that was something I was interested in doing? I admit, I'm lonely, and I know you worry, but I don't want to do things just for the sake of filling in time. If your father was alive, no one would be telling me to keep myself busy – if we just wanted to sit around reading books all day, nobody would care. But now I'm supposed to keep busy, and have "interests". Why should I have to make such a constant effort at my age? It really isn't fair.'

So Madeleine listened with uncharacteristic patience to the litany of the day's non-activities, and didn't interrupt or cut the call short. By the time she hung up, she wasn't feeling so guilty, but she was feeling sleepy, so there had been something in it for her after all. She switched off the bedside lamp and lay down on her side. She missed having Henry there to nestle into. She hoped they would have a marriage like her parents', but then Madeleine wondered if it was such a good thing to be so dependent on another person for your happiness, because what happened if you lost them? She felt a shiver run up her spine, the kind her mother always said was someone walking over your grave. She really didn't want to think about that.

Saturday

'Boys, we're leaving in ten!' Liv sang out up the hall.

Like thousands of parents everywhere, Liv spent her weekends driving to sporting fields across the metropolitan area, and sometimes beyond. The boys played sport all year round – now that soccer season was over, cricket season was in full swing. Rick was firmly of the school that sport built character, whereas Liv was inclined to believe that it only revealed it. There were plenty of sports-playing people who were thugs and bullies and who hadn't learnt a thing about team spirit or fair play or any other noble virtues.

However, she certainly supported the idea of physical activity out in the fresh air. Lachie didn't have to be encouraged, if anything he needed to learn to sit still occasionally. Dylan, on the other hand, would have barely seen the light of day if not for organised sport. After one too many injuries he had dropped out of soccer, despite his father's protestations. But Liv had supported Dylan. He didn't enjoy it and he just got hurt all the time, so what was the point? However, she did agree with Rick that he had to find something else. When Lachie declared that he wanted to sign up for cricket that summer, Liv was initially aghast at the thought of spending long days out in the beating sun watching a game she had never been able to understand, let alone follow. But when Dylan decided he was interested – something about the whites and the gentlemanly code appealed to his quirky nature – Liv knew she was outnumbered.

She soon discovered the delights of having a whole day when she didn't have to do anything but sit in a fold-out chair and gaze into the middle distance. As long as she gave them a wave now and then, and brought a hamper of food, the boys were happy. As both a working and only-every-second-weekend mother, Liv wasn't very well known among the other parents, so she didn't feel obliged to sit with them. She quickly worked out that if she played shy – always polite but no eye contact, slightly awkward responses to any invitations to join them – she was left blissfully to herself. She set up camp just far enough away from the main throng to enjoy her solitude. Over time Liv acquired a sturdy, easy-to-assemble shade shelter, a deceptively comfortable sling chair, and a large esky on wheels. She made a particular effort with the food: hearty wraps or rolls for the boys, and plenty of snacks and sports drinks. As well, she always made a quick trip to the David Jones food hall in town on Fridays, treating herself to an array of gourmet finger foods for her own little private picnic. The only thing that would have made it better was if she could have had a drink without worrying about driving. But that was a small price to pay, and anyway, sometimes she packed a single bottle of imported beer, or the last glass of a bottle of white wine, or even a gin and tonic pre-mixed in a thermos, to sip slowly throughout the afternoon.

Many of the places they played had poor mobile reception, but as the boys were with her, Liv was happy to leave her phone on silent anyway. She always brought something to read, and had podcasts and music to listen to, but often she found herself drifting into an almost meditative state as she gazed out at the figures in white, blurring against the vivid green of the oval, and breathed in the scent of cut grass, the only sound the occasional thwack of ball against bat. Honestly, she was like a pig in mud.

'Liv!'

She jumped. That was Rick, she'd know his holler anywhere. She peered around the shade shelter to see him striding towards her, waving enthusiastically, a manic grin plastered across his face. Bugger. What was he doing here?

'Why are you sitting all the way over here on your own?' he said, and before she realised what he was doing, he'd swooped down to plant a kiss on her cheek. What the . . . ?

'Come over and join the others,' he went on. 'You know Robyn and Michael and Lynda and Glen and Bob and . . . what's her name again?'

Liv stared blankly up at him. 'Rick, what are you doing here?'

'Watching the boys play cricket,' he said, like it was obvious.

'But it's not your weekend,' she reminded him.

'Come on, Liv, when have we ever been strict about that sort of thing?'

Well, never. When Rick was 'busy' for whatever reason, he was more than happy to palm the boys off onto Liv on his weekend. But to willingly come to watch them play sport when it wasn't his turn . . . that was a first, and it was troubling.

'Seriously, Rick, I want to know what you're doing here,' Liv said.

'Just enjoying some family time,' he replied.

Now she was really beginning to feel queasy. 'This has to stop,' she said plainly.

'You're going to stop me from seeing my kids?'

'Don't be dramatic,' said Liv. 'I'm entitled to some notice when you're going to show up at times outside the usual. That's only polite.'

'Fair enough. But speaking of polite, we should go join the others.'

Liv sighed. So that was that. He was staying, and she just had to put up with it. And not only that, she was expected to join 'the others'. This could blow her cover forever, but what choice did she have? If she held her ground, she'd look like a weirdo; besides, Rick wouldn't leave her alone until she gave in – that was his MO, wear her down until she lost the will to refuse.

So for the next few hours Liv had to stand around making strained conversation, trying desperately to keep up her carefully cultivated shy persona. Rick made it almost impossible. He didn't get it, of course, so he was constantly trying to buck her up, throwing an arm around her shoulders and telling her to cheer up. All she could do was grit her teeth, occasionally stealing a wistful look across at her shade shelter. Liv had a feeling it was never going to be the same again. And that just wasn't cricket.

When the game was finished, Rick suddenly made himself very helpful packing up her shade shelter and carrying all the gear back to her car, despite Liv insisting she and the boys could handle it. He closed the boot with a satisfied slap. 'So, who wants to come in my car?' he asked the boys.

No! That meant he would have to come back to their place. Before Liv could protest, Lachie called, 'Shotgun!'

'But there's no need, Rick,' said Liv, trying to sound firm but polite. 'We can all fit in my car. It's how we got here, after all.' *And who invited you anyway?*

But Rick was oblivious. 'First one home . . .' he cried, grinning at Lachie as they took off together across the carpark.

'Don't you dare speed with him in the car!' she called after them, for what it was worth. She stood there fuming, and then noticed Dylan staring at her. She swallowed down the lump of rage rising in her throat and fixed a smile on her face. 'Well, we better get going, too.'

Rick had done this to her all her life, with complete strangers, with their friends, in front of the boys – he took over and Liv was forced to go along with it or else look like the bad guy. It didn't matter what she said, he just waved it away as though he was swatting a fly. She always seemed to lose her power around him, and it made her so angry, as much at herself for allowing him to do it to her, again and again.

As they drove out of the carpark, Dylan turned to look at her. 'Are you okay, Mum?'

She glanced at him. She obviously didn't want the boys seeing her angry at their father. God, it was hard sometimes, keeping up appearances. 'I'm fine,' she said lightly.

'Are you mad that Dad came today?'

'No, not really . . .' Liv wondered which was worse, criticising Rick or lying through her teeth. 'I just wasn't expecting it, that's all. But it's fine, I know you want to spend as much time as you can with your dad . . .'

Dylan shrugged. 'Must bug you, but. If you divorce I guess that means you don't really want to be together, but you have to spend some time together because of us. That has to suck.'

He had always had an old head on his young shoulders.

'Anyway, I reckon it'd be weird if Dad was around all the time.'

'Really?'

'This is all I've ever known, Mum,' he said. 'We were too little to remember when he lived with us.'

'That's true.' She pulled up at a red light and looked at him. 'Do you ever wish things were different, though? That we were a normal family?'

'What's a normal family?' said Dylan. 'Half the kids I know, their parents are divorced, some more than once. They've got half-brothers, or stepsisters, or stepmothers, or just some dude who's dating their mum staying over all the time. Compared to all that we're like some lame family from way back in the seventies. Even *The Brady Bunch* was more out there than us.'

Liv had to laugh at that.

'I reckon the family you're in is the best, whatever it is,' said Dylan.

'I'm glad you think so. When I was a kid I always wished I could be from some other family.' Liv sighed. 'Any other family.'

He turned his head sharply at that. 'Didja?'

Whoops. That was inappropriate. The boys loved their nan, and she loved them, unconditionally. Funny how good parenting could skip a generation.

'Yeah . . . but I was just rebellious for the sake of it,' said Liv, covering herself. 'You boys haven't been through that stage.'

'Give us time,' Dylan said with a glint in his eye. 'Give us time.'

Such an old head.

When they turned into the driveway at home, Rick and Lachie were sitting on the front step of the house.

'He didn't have his keys with him,' Rick explained as Liv and Dylan got out of the car. 'And he didn't realise that till we got all the way here. Nong,' he added, giving Lachie's head a playful shove. 'Come on, boys, let's unpack the car for your mother.'

Liv steeled herself as she walked past them into the house. She was not going to extend any kind of invitation to Rick, not that he seemed to think he needed one. But maybe if she just ignored him and carried on as usual, he might get the hint. She went straight to her bedroom, closed the door and got ready to take a shower. The other thing Liv liked so much about cricket was that the boys were usually worn out after a full day standing out in the sun, and they crashed early, leaving her to enjoy a glass of wine and a chick flick in peace. But she had a feeling that wasn't going to happen tonight. She stood under the stream of water, trying to quell the simmering rage, but it was persistent. And it was accompanied by a growing sense of dread. What in the blue blazes was Rick up to?

Liv took her time in the shower, and dressed in her comfiest, daggiest clothes, finally emerging from her room to wander down the hall. Rick and Dylan were sprawled across the sofa, watching Lachie play a video game.

'Ah, there you are,' said Rick. 'We were thinking you must have got washed down the drain hole.'

Liv ignored that. Dylan's hair was damp, and he'd changed his clothes, so he must have had his shower. 'Lachie, you need to get out of your cricket gear and have a shower, mate.'

'Yeah, as soon as I finish this level,' he said, not taking his eyes off the screen.

Famous last words. God, she was sick of hearing that mantra. 'Okay, but the plug's coming out in five minutes no matter what level you're on.'

'Righto, Ma,' he said anxiously, 'don't have a cow.'

Liv walked over to the fridge. She was going to pour herself a glass of wine, just as if Rick wasn't there. And while it went against every polite instinct in her body, she wasn't going to offer him one.

'So I was telling the boys about this great curry place that delivers in the area,' Rick said, coming to lean on the other side of the breakfast bench.

Liv didn't respond. She didn't want to encourage him.

'I thought we could order in.'

'I've already got chicken thawing for dinner. Thanks anyway.'

'Oh, give yourself a night off,' said Rick. 'Besides, you probably won't have enough for me as well.'

'That's right,' Liv said pointedly.

'So it's agreed then! I'll call the curry place.'

What just happened?

*

Despite Rick's best efforts, the boys flagged early as usual after a day of cricket – Dylan first, then Lachie not long after. Liv was glad; she'd been working herself up to it all evening, and had decided she was definitely going to speak to Rick about his behaviour. She wasn't going to let him keep blindsiding her. If he wanted to play like that, then Liv had to be prepared to go ahead and look like the bad guy, but she would take him down with her.

As Lachie sauntered off up the hallway to bed, Liv was wiping down the benches and loading the last stray glasses into the dishwasher.

'Would you like a drink?' Rick asked as he came into the kitchen.

Nice of him to offer her a glass of her own wine. 'No thanks.'

'Okay, well, do you mind if I help myself?' he said, opening the fridge.

Liv turned to face him, leaning back against the bench. 'Yes, I do actually.'

'Huh?'

'I do mind if you help yourself.'

His face dropped, and he closed the fridge door again. 'What's the matter, Livvie?' he said, in his most patronising tone. 'You haven't been yourself today.'

'That's right,' she said, folding her arms. 'Because you barged in and hijacked my entire day.'

'I think I salvaged it, actually,' he said. 'I can't believe that in all this time you haven't made friends with those people and you needed me to break the ice.'

'I didn't need you to break the ice,' said Liv. 'I've chosen to keep to myself.'

'Well, that's not healthy, Liv.'

'It's very healthy, Rick,' she retorted. 'It's peaceful and relaxing. I can watch the boys and have some time on my own. And I don't have to explain myself to you, especially when you shouldn't have been there in the first place.'

'And that's another thing,' said Rick. 'Why are you trying to stop me from spending time with the boys?'

Liv groaned. 'I'm not, but we have a schedule, Rick, and the only time you've ever strayed from it in the past is when you've wanted to get out of seeing them, not to see them more often.'

'So I'm making up for lost time.'

'Not on my time you're not.'

He looked nonplussed.

'I mean it, Rick, I want to be very clear about this,' said Liv. 'From now on you have to call me if you want to visit them when they're with me.'

'Well, that might not be necessary.'

She frowned. 'Why's that?'

He glanced over his shoulder up the hall. 'There's something I need to talk to you about. Can we go and sit down so we don't wake the boys?'

Liv knew the twins would have crashed as soon as their heads hit the pillow, but she was wary as to what this was about, and she didn't want to risk them overhearing. 'Okay,' she said, 'but make it snappy. I'm tired and I want to go to bed.'

Rick followed her out to the family room; although he headed for the sofa, Liv took a seat at the table. She wanted to keep things businesslike. He traipsed over, pulled out a chair and dropped into it, doing a fairly good impression of a petulant child.

'So, what is it?' said Liv. 'What's going on?'

He took a breath. 'You see, the thing is, I might have to stay here for a while.'

Her jaw dropped. 'I beg your pardon?'

'Carly and I are breaking up.'

Liv realised that the news had absolutely no effect on her. There was only one thing she wanted to know. 'What's that got to do with you staying here?'

'Well, I didn't think you'd want the father of your children to be homeless . . .'

She rolled her eyes. 'No, I want you to do what any responsible adult would do, and find yourself somewhere to live.'

'But this is my house too.'

'No it isn't. Don't you remember the property settlement, Rick? When I bought you out?'

'Yeah, but they gave you eighty percent of the house. It was hardly fair, Liv.'

She gritted her teeth. She had got eighty percent because she was the primary caregiver for the kids, and she didn't take a share of Rick's super, which was far more substantial than hers. Liv's lawyer had been adamant that the court would give her the house, free and clear, given the age of the boys and the value of the super, but Rick had made such a fuss about not having any capital, asking how he was supposed to buy a place of his own . . . And then Liv's mother had weighed in, said it was a disgrace, 'taking a man's house away from him'. Never mind that they'd bought it together, and that Liv had contributed as much financially as Rick until the twins were born. She didn't even care about the house itself; she would have happily sold up and gone somewhere else, made a fresh start. But by the time they were finalising the settlement, the boys had started school, and she didn't want to uproot them. Rick had grudgingly agreed to that at least – he didn't want them to have to leave the house either. So against her lawyer's advice, Liv had worked out an amount she could afford to add to the mortgage to buy out his share, and the end result was an eighty–twenty split.

'Rick,' she said now, 'you know the settlement was actually in your favour. You got your super *and* twenty percent of the house.'

'Yeah, but after the GFC, my super took a hit, so –'

'Are we really going to do this now?' Liv said, stopping him. 'It's history, it's the law even, this house is mine. Deal with it. Or don't, I don't really care.'

'Okay, okay.' Rick held up his hands in defeat. 'I know, technically the house is yours. But theoretically . . .'

She sighed. 'Okay, then in theory, you could stay, but in reality, you can't.'

'Look, I just can't afford a hotel right now,' he said. 'Or the bond for a place.'

Liv didn't believe that for a second.

'Carly's making things very . . . difficult. You see –'

Now Liv held up her hands, blocking him. 'I don't care, Rick. I'm not interested.'

'That's a bit harsh.'

'The only reason you're still in my life at all is because of the boys,' she said. 'I'm not your BFF. I don't need to know what's happening in your relationship, unless it impacts on them.'

'You don't think this will? You're happy for them to stay with me in some seedy hotel?'

God, he was such a drama queen. Rick wouldn't stay in a 'seedy hotel' if his life depended on it. 'You are responsible for the boys' welfare when they're with you. I trust you to do the best for them.'

He looked a bit rattled. 'We're getting bogged down in details here – there's a much bigger picture to consider.'

'Oh, what's that?'

He sat back in his chair, meeting her eyes directly. 'I've been doing a lot of thinking, Liv. You know that I've been with a . . . a number of women since we split.'

'And before.'

He ignored that. 'The thing is, you can't say I haven't tried to make a new life. But it hasn't worked. Because – and this is what I've come to realise, Liv – you and me are the only thing that works.'

'Oh, for fuck's sake.'

'Settle down and hear me out,' Rick said, leaning forward. 'I know I did the wrong thing by you back then. I won't make excuses, but it was a really difficult time for me. I don't know if you were ever aware just how hard it was for me. All of a sudden you were a mother of two, and it didn't give you much time to be a wife, to be honest.'

This was Rick not making excuses.

'I'm not suggesting I chose the right way to cope with what was happening . . . Some men take up golf, and they don't lose everything. But on the positive side, I have actually learnt from my mistakes. I know now, without a shadow of a doubt, that you're the best woman, the only woman for me.'

Liv wanted to laugh. 'Well, it's never too late to take up golf, Rick.' She couldn't listen to this anymore, she went to get up.

'Just wait,' he said, taking hold of her arm. 'Try and tell me it isn't the same for you.'

'It's not the same for me,' she said flatly.

'Then why, in all these years, have you never found anyone, Liv? If you really believed there was someone else for you, why haven't you put yourself out there? Don't you think you should be asking yourself why that is?'

Liv was so astounded by his logic, she thought her head might actually explode. So not only do you get treated like a loser if you haven't managed to snare another bloke, it must mean that you're still holding a torch for the last one. If you dared to protest that you were in fact happy on your own, then of course that was protesting too much, methinks. The only way to shut everyone up was to partner up. No wonder Jennifer Aniston got married.

Suddenly Liv saw the perfect solution, written in code on that little slip of paper in her drawer.

'Liv, you're not saying anything,' Rick prompted her after a while.

She stirred, looking straight at him. 'You're making some pretty huge assumptions about my personal life, Rick. When in actual fact you have no idea what I do, or who I might be doing it with.'

He started to blink rapidly. 'You're not seeing anyone,' he sneered.

'How do you know that?'

'Well . . .' He was floundering. 'The boys would have told me.'

'The boys don't know,' she said calmly. Neither did the man in question, for that matter, but she could soon fix that. Besides, she wasn't actually saying anything specific. She wasn't lying, she was just planting a seed, and allowing Rick to fertilise it . . . No, wait, she didn't like that analogy at all. What she was doing was just allowing Rick to fill in the blanks with his own imagination.

'You see,' Liv went on, 'I decided a while ago that it was best not to over-share with the boys. They're at a delicate age, developmentally, and the way they think about their mother . . . well, I'm sure I don't have to remind you how Oedipus turned out. I have every second or third weekend to myself, I have my own life, Rick. I've moved on, and I've never looked back. I'm sorry that all your alternatives haven't worked out, but I've been having a great time. And I wouldn't go back for anything.'

Sunday

Liv was still reeling when she woke up the next morning. Rick had left soon after her revelation, obviously unsettled and out of ammunition. For the meantime. Now she had to cover her tracks. She waited until the boys were occupied after breakfast and it was a respectable hour on a Sunday morning to ring someone – she figured ten was acceptable. Then she grabbed her mobile and ducked into her bedroom, closing the door behind her. She went to her desk and took out the slip of paper. She perched on the end of the bed as she smoothed it out and thought about what she was about to do. Was she really going to call this guy just to prove something to Rick? No, she couldn't, that would be wrong. She had to do it because she wanted to do it for herself.

Well, she had salvaged it from the wastepaper bin the other day.

But that was only in reaction to her mother winding her up.

Liv bit on her lip as she stared at his name, for so long that it started to look weird. Funny how that happened, the letters no longer seemed to spell anything, and it looked like gibberish. So now she was just procrastinating. All right, what were the facts? He seemed like a nice person – he was nice looking, neat and well groomed. Of course, that was usually said about serial killers and mass murderers after the fact.

Why are you doing that, Liv? No need to go there.

Back on track. He was certainly easy enough to talk to, and he was a reader – both points in his favour. The fact that his daughter had lived with him was probably also in his favour, but as Liv had no idea of the circumstances, she couldn't necessarily put that in the pros column just yet. Though the chance to hear that story was in itself a good reason to go out with him.

In the cons column . . . well, she didn't know what he did for a living – not that that had to be a negative. Perhaps she needed a column with a question mark as well. She didn't know about his previous relationship, or relationships, plural. She didn't know if he was just divorced, if he was on the rebound, or if he was a compulsive flirt, handing out his number willy-nilly to any woman he sat next to on a plane or a bus or whatever, batting his eyelids and telling them all the same sweet tale about making promises to himself . . . Now that she thought about it, it was beginning to sound like a very well-rehearsed line.

Liv stopped for a second and heard her own voice reverberating inside her head. What the hell was wrong with her? Seriously? Madeleine would remind her it was only coffee. And if Mad was in the same position, Liv would be telling her to go for it. In fact, that's exactly what she had done. Cripes, Liv had encouraged Madeleine to go to the other side of the world for Henry.

And now they were getting married. Liv didn't want to get married – she hadn't wanted to get married in the first place.

Oh, for heaven's sake, *what was wrong with her*? She was just being a wimp. Without further ado, she entered the number into her phone and tapped *Call*. She was startled when it was answered almost immediately.

'David Lessing.'

'Oh, hello, David. I hope this is a convenient time.'

'Look, if you're selling something –'

'No, no,' Liv said quickly. 'I don't know if you'll remember, but I sat near you on a plane last week –'

'Liv!' he said. 'Named after the actress.'

She smiled. 'That's right.' She supposed he couldn't be handing his number out to every woman he sat next to, or he could never have come up with her name like that, unless he was some kind of voice-recognition freak.

'You called,' he said.

'I did. I am . . . calling.'

'Well, I'm glad. What made you change your mind?'

'I hadn't exactly made up my mind,' said Liv. 'So I didn't change it, as such. I just got to thinking about what you said about, you know, putting yourself out there, and how people are always asking you, and saying you should, and they act like that's the norm, that it's weird if you're not, so there must be something wrong with you, or that it means something that it doesn't at all, you know? They judge you on your inaction, when it might not even be inaction but an actual active choice . . . not to act. You know what I'm saying?'

'Not really,' he said in a bemused tone. 'But would you like to have coffee sometime?'

Liv breathed out. 'Yes, I would. I'd like that very much.'

Pittwater

'I really don't mind going the whole way,' Madeleine said as she backed the car out of the garage.

'That's what she said.' Aiden looked at her sideways.

'Stop it.'

He was taking a late flight to Brisbane, where he would be met by a delegation of aid workers who were going to escort him – via two more flights and several hundred kilometres in a four-wheel drive – to an Aboriginal settlement in Far North Queensland. But Aiden had refused the offer of a lift to the airport in Sydney.

'Just get me back to the edge of civilisation,' he was saying now. 'I can find my way to the airport from there.'

Madeleine grinned. 'It's not quite as bad as all that.'

He shook his head. 'It was like déjà vu when Henry brought me to your house the first day.'

'What do you mean?'

'Well, it's so much like his place in the Hamptons.'

'Really?' Madeleine said uncertainly. 'He took me there when I visited New York. I don't think the houses are anything alike.'

'Not architecturally,' Aiden said. 'That's true. And the terrain is different in the Hamptons, it's a lot flatter mainly. But the distance, and the isolation, they're just the same.'

Madeleine didn't know the place well enough to comment, but the observation didn't sit comfortably with her. The three of them had had a wonderful weekend of swimming, and barbecues, and a fabulous lunch at a restaurant in Palm Beach that Madeleine had been wanting to try. They'd even played board games on Saturday night, which was hilarious. She hadn't had so much fun at home since they'd moved up here. They never had visitors, and on the weekends it was too far to go back to the city, especially when Madeleine had to make the trip every day during the week. So they'd go for walks, or to the beach, now that it was getting warmer. They did have the odd meal at a restaurant or café, and once they'd gone to the local cinema. But it was a quiet life, to say the least.

'How do you feel about living all the way up here?' Aiden asked after a while.

'It's okay. And Henry needs a quiet place to work.'

'Fair enough,' he said. 'I just can't help wondering what's in it for you.'

Madeleine hesitated. She didn't want to answer that right now, because she didn't have an answer. 'Well, just take a look out there,' she said, nodding her head towards the expanse of ocean on their left. 'I could think of worse places to live.'

They drove on, as she breathlessly rattled off the attractions of the peninsula at every turn, thereby preventing Aiden from repeating his original question. She just didn't want to talk about it with him: she still had the vague feeling that it would somehow be a betrayal of Henry.

When they drove into Dee Why, Aiden spotted a taxi rank, complete with waiting taxi. 'There you go,' he said. 'You can drop me here.'

'But I haven't taken you very far at all,' Madeleine protested.

'You have to drive all the way tomorrow,' he said. 'This is far enough for me, Maddie.'

He must have been really bored with her monologue, she decided. She knew she was. Madeleine hopped out of the car and came around to the passenger side as Aiden dragged his bag out of the back seat. 'So don't forget,' she said, 'lunch at my sister's next Saturday, if you make it back in time. And if you want to.'

'What? Of course I want to,' said Aiden. 'I'm looking forward to meeting your family.'

'Henry doesn't know why we're putting you through it, when you'll meet them soon enough anyway.'

'Henry should get that giant stick out of his ass,' Aiden said with a wink. 'I'm sure I'll be back. In fact, I'm hoping to get back no later than Friday.'

'Well, you've got my mobile number – I can pick you up if it's in the afternoon, and you can drive home with me.'

'Sounds like a plan.' He leaned in to give her a kiss on the cheek and half a hug, as he had only one arm free. It was better than no hug at all.

'Have a good week,' she called, as he walked up to the taxi and opened the back door.

'Sydney airport, thanks,' she heard him say.

Madeleine went back to the car and headed for home, without much enthusiasm. It was going to be quiet without Aiden. And when she walked into the house, she realised just how quiet. The place felt empty, yet it was no more empty than usual. It was just more noticeable now.

She crossed the living room to take the stairs down to Henry's office. He was working, which was why she'd offered to take Aiden, and why he'd stayed behind.

'Hi,' she said as she came in through the doorway.

Henry was in his usual position, hunched over his drawing board. He swivelled a half-turn on the stool as Madeleine walked over to him. 'How did it go?' he asked. 'Did Aiden get away okay?'

She nodded, propping her elbow on his shoulder. 'He got a taxi at Dee Why. How's it going here?'

'All right.' He sighed heavily. 'But I've got a fair bit to catch up on, I lost a lot of time with Aiden here.'

He had laid out a sequence of drawings across the top of the board and was now working on the story. Sheets of writing paper were spread out over the remaining available space, each covered with clusters of words, crossed out, reinstated, scribbled over. Henry didn't write on a computer, not because he was a Luddite – though there was some truth in that – but because there wasn't a great deal of text involved, and he needed to visualise the words with the pictures. He sweated so much over every element, right from the first draft, when there were so many more stages and opportunities to tweak further. But that's what made him so good. It always amused Madeleine when she heard people suggest that writing children's books must be easy – they had no idea.

Henry shifted a little to block her view; he was always self-conscious about a work in progress, even with Madeleine. Writers. Typical.

'Do you think you'll be long?' she asked.

He looked apologetic. 'I wanted to keep at it, at least until I nail this draft.'

Which meant he would be 'at it' half the night.

'I guess I'll go and do some reading then,' she said.

'Okay, don't wait up.'

So he definitely intended to be at it half the night.

'If that's the case, you better give me a kiss goodnight now, then,' said Madeleine, circling her arms around his neck. He didn't resist, but his lips did: they were unyielding, remaining firm under pressure. She remembered that they hadn't had sex since the morning after Aiden arrived, and it obviously wasn't going to happen tonight either. She drew back to look at him. 'Well, goodnight,' she said.

'Goodnight, Madeleine.'

Back upstairs she wandered around, feeling that odd restlessness again. They'd had an early dinner with Aiden, and Henry had cleaned up after they'd left, so there was nothing for her to do. She really should take the opportunity to read; that was what she normally did when Henry was occupied downstairs. Which was often.

She went to her room to fetch her e-reader and then walked back out and onto the balcony. It was cooler outside, but pleasantly so. The only sound breaking the deafening silence was the deafening chorus of crickets. Madeleine started to read. It was a debut novel by an actress slash model turned budding author. They wouldn't have any trouble getting publicity for her, but Liv had asked Madeleine to give some thought as to which publicist would be a good fit, someone who wouldn't be too starstruck. Ren was an obvious choice, but then she might not be starstruck enough. Natalie was probably panting for it, but they suspected she'd enjoy the celebrity scene a little too much, and forget that it wasn't all about her. Madeleine had been surprised to discover that the book wasn't too bad, and the last time she'd picked it up she had been quite absorbed. But after clicking through a few pages tonight, she realised that she couldn't recall a word she'd just read. She sighed, closing the cover of her reader. Her restlessness was rapidly escalating towards agitation. If this kept up, she was going to have trouble getting off to sleep tonight, especially without Henry, or sex.

Then she remembered that there was an opened bottle of wine in the fridge. They'd had wine with meals while Aiden was here – it was only polite, he was on holiday, after all. But Madeleine had been very careful not to overindulge again. Ever conscious of Henry's watchful gaze, she'd only had one glass at a sitting, not even allowing Aiden to top it up. But she could really do with a glass right now; she knew it would smooth out the jagged edges. She tapped her fingers on the cover of her reader. There was nothing wrong with having one glass. She was an adult. And if she wasn't getting sex tonight, then surely she was entitled to a measly glass of wine.

Madeleine got up and walked back inside and into the kitchen. She made some noise filling the kettle and switched it on. Then she went to the fridge. The bottle was in a shelf in the door. She carefully lifted it out to inspect it, relieved to see that there was more than a glass left. So she could have one and Henry wouldn't notice, unless he'd measured it, and she doubted he'd go that far.

Madeleine quietly removed a glass from the cupboard – just a water glass, there was no need to use a wine glass. Her hand trembled a little as she carefully poured half of the remaining wine into the glass. She held it to her lips and breathed it in before taking a mouthful, letting it pool on her tongue, and then swallowing it down. She swallowed again and again, feeling the warming sensation as it travelled through her chest, and then the slight tingling buzz in her brain. And then the glass was empty. She quickly returned the cap to the bottle, and the bottle to the fridge, exactly where it had been. She rinsed out the glass, wiping it dry with a tea towel before replacing it in the cupboard. The kettle boiled and then clicked off. She didn't want a cup of tea anyway. She switched off the lights, and walked up the hall to their bedroom. In the bathroom, she brushed her teeth vigorously, then used a little mouthwash, rinsing her mouth out repeatedly. She changed into her pyjamas and climbed into bed, pulling the pillow over her head to muffle the sound of the deafening bloody crickets.

Monday

Madeleine sat down at her desk and switched on her computer. She'd been feeling a vague sense of unease, or ennui or something, all the way into work this morning. Even walking into the office hadn't given her the usual reliable buzz. As her screen came to life she noticed the date. The wedding was drawing inexorably closer, and she still had so much to do. Which only served to heighten her complete lack of motivation.

She had to snap out of it. Emails filed into her inbox, one by one. There was nothing from Emily Tanner yet, but that was okay, Madeleine knew she wouldn't rush her response. There was, however, a brisk reply from Lydia Carlyle. Madeleine had sent a copy of *Jane Eyre* by courier to her the same day as her dummy spit, the day Aiden had arrived. Plenty of time for Lydia to have read the cover blurb, and hopefully the foreword, written by a devout Brontë scholar. Her email contained one line:

> You can inform the event manager that I approve her press release.

There was nothing further, just her florid automated email signature with bonus soft-focus headshot. Madeleine glared at the photo. *Why yes, Lydia, my pleasure. No, don't thank me. Oh, wait . . .*

'Boo!'

Madeleine looked up to see Liv smiling down at her.

'What's up with you, Debbie Downer?' she asked.

Madeleine dropped her chin in her hand. 'I don't like Mondays.'

'Well, before you take a shotgun up to the roof, cheer up. I'm going to take you to lunch.'

'What, now?'

'No, silly!' Liv said. 'At lunchtime. Are you free?'

'Free as I'll ever be,' said Madeleine. Which wasn't very free at all. She really had to snap out of it.

'Okay, I'll call for you at twelve thirty, one o'clock,' said Liv. 'Toodles!'

Madeleine forced herself to get down to work. She didn't have the energy to instigate anything today, so cold calls were out, and she wasn't going to start ringing up her contacts to pitch for radio spots or print interviews – that required too much enthusiasm. The most she could manage was confirmations; she could do those largely by email, so she didn't have to be all chirpy on the phone.

At twenty to one, her phone beeped with a text message. It was from Liv. *Meet you out at the elevators in five. Be discreet.*

Madeleine wondered what all the subterfuge was about. When she got around to the elevator bay, Liv was holding one open, beckoning her to hurry up. They stepped inside and the doors closed behind them.

'What's going on?' Madeleine asked.

'Nothing, I just didn't want any hangers-on today.'

She knew what Liv meant: if you left the office at the same time as anyone else, you invariably ended up lunching with them. 'So I'm assuming it's Poppy's today?'

'You assumed right.'

Liv and Madeleine had discovered Poppy's a couple of blocks from the office, around a corner and tucked into the back of a pub. The food was fine, but the real attraction was that nobody else from work had found it. There were a couple of lunch spots handy to the office that their coworkers frequented. They were all very nice if you wanted company at lunch, but not when you needed some privacy. So they had kept Poppy's to themselves, using it whenever they needed to discuss sensitive work issues. And also gossip. Madeleine was really not up to talking about work today, she didn't think she could wrap her head around it. They ordered at the counter and took the buzzer that would alert them when their meals were ready. Madeleine wasn't very hungry, so she'd only ordered a small salad, and wasn't even sure she'd get through that.

They sat in a corner booth and she turned to Liv. 'I have to tell you I'm not much in the mood for shop talk.'

'That's not why I brought you here,' said Liv.

'Sounds ominous.'

'Rick was hanging around again this weekend,' Liv began. 'He gatecrashed the boys' cricket game.'

'Oh no,' said Madeleine. 'Your alone time.'

'And that's not the worst of it,' said Liv. 'He came back to the house afterwards, and stayed for dinner, uninvited. Then, after the boys went to bed, he announced that he and Carly are splitting up, and so he might have to stay with us for a bit.'

'I beg your pardon?!'

'Which is exactly what I said.' Liv shook her head. 'The man has the hide of an elephant.'

'So what happened?'

'I put him in his place for now,' Liv said. 'But he's not going to give up that easily.'

'Surely he doesn't think he can just freeload at your house?'

'Apparently he does. And that's not all,' said Liv. 'He thinks it's high time we got back together.'

Madeleine's eyes grew wide. 'No!'

'And wait till you hear his rationalisation,' Liv went on. 'He's tried on a whole lot of women for size, and none of them have fitted, whereas I haven't tried on anyone else, so, like Cinderella's slipper, he's the only true fit for me.'

Madeleine screwed up her face. 'Did he actually use that line?'

'No, that was mine,' Liv said airily. 'But it was his sentiment. He thinks that because I'm not whoring around like him, I must still be in love with him.'

'Wow, he's really got tickets, hasn't he?' said Madeleine. 'So what did you say to him? Did you use the Jennifer Aniston line?'

'Well, I can't now that she's gone and got herself married,' said Liv. 'But anyway, I preferred to let him believe that I'm seeing someone.'

Madeleine hadn't expected that. 'So you lied?' she asked.

'I didn't have to.'

'What does that mean?'

The buzzer went off on the table between them. 'Food's ready,' said Liv. 'I'll go.'

'And then you'll tell me what's going on.'

Madeleine watched Liv make her way to the counter. She had such an air of confidence about her, but Madeleine was well aware how much of a beating that had taken over the years. She wondered how Liv had felt leading up to her own wedding day – though considering where her marriage had ended up, perhaps it was best Madeleine didn't know.

Liv returned to the table and passed Madeleine her salad, then sat down to her grilled salmon.

'So, continue,' Madeleine prompted her. 'You told Rick you're seeing someone, but you weren't lying . . . ?'

'I said that I "let him believe".'

'Oh, okay, so you're just doing semantic gymnastics, not lying.'

'Don't be smart,' said Liv. 'And before you judge, there's something else I have to tell you, but you're not to get excited, okay? Keep it in perspective.'

'Okay,' Madeleine said warily.

'Yesterday I called the guy from the plane.'

'What?'

'The guy I talked to on the plane.' Liv watched Madeleine's face, waiting for the penny to drop. 'Last week, remember I told you?'

'But you also said that you threw out his number.'

'I fished it out again.'

'Fished it out of where?'

'That's not important,' said Liv. 'I called him, we're having coffee next weekend.'

Madeleine frowned. 'Are you doing this just to keep Rick off your back?'

'No, I'm doing it to keep everyone off my back,' Liv said. 'I'm putting myself out there. Are you happy now?'

'Well, I don't know,' Madeleine said, pushing her salad around with her fork. 'Doesn't seem very fair to the poor guy . . .'

'He'll be fine,' Liv assured her. 'You're the one always telling me it's only coffee, not a marriage proposal.'

'But at least you should be honest with him.'

'It's only coffee,' Liv repeated, mildly exasperated.

Madeleine just shrugged her shoulders in response.

'Boy,' Liv was shaking her head, 'I thought you'd be excited. In fact, I thought I was going to have to hold you back from turning yours into a double wedding.'

'Hardly,' Madeleine sniggered.

Liv looked at her. 'Is something up?'

'No, nothing's up. Nothing's ever up. Everything's the same. Day in, day out.'

'How very nihilistic of you,' said Liv. 'Am I sensing a little trouble in paradise?'

'Nope, because that would mean something had happened, and nothing ever happens.'

'All right.' Liv stopped cutting into her salmon. 'Spit it out, Mad. What's going on?'

'Nothing, that's what I'm trying to say.' Madeleine sighed. 'Since Aiden came to stay –'

'Uh-oh.'

Madeleine blinked. 'What do you mean by that?'

'What?'

'That "uh-oh"?'

'I was just wondering what Aiden has to do with it,' said Liv.

'What are you implying?'

'Why do think I'm implying something?'

'Because nothing's happened with Aiden.'

'I wasn't implying *that*.' Liv was clearly shocked. 'Why would you even go there?'

'I didn't,' Madeleine said, flustered. 'I thought you . . . Oh, jeez, this is confusing.'

'Then stop speaking in riddles, precious,' said Liv. 'You sound like Gollum in *The Hobbit*.'

Madeleine took a breath. 'All right. I mentioned Aiden because we've had so much fun with him staying with us. He and Henry have all these in-jokes, they clown around. Henry's not like that with me. Maybe I don't bring out the best in him.'

Liv snorted. 'What are you talking about? He adores you.'

'That's not what I said. I'm just not sure we bring out the best in each other.'

'Are you kidding me?' said Liv. 'You're a different person since you've been with Henry.'

'Yes, a quieter, more sedate, more boring person.'

'You're not boring.'

'Maybe I mean bored.'

Liv put down her knife and fork. 'Is this as serious as you're making it sound?'

'No . . . I don't know,' said Madeleine. 'I love that Henry's so solid –'

'He's your rock, that's what you always say.'

'I know, but that also makes him impervious, inflexible, resistant to change.'

'But you just said yourself that he livened up around Aiden. He's obviously not completely inflexible. You're yoyoing all over the place, Mad, like you're looking for problems.' Liv clicked her fingers. 'That's it!'

'That's what?'

'That's exactly what you're doing.'

Madeleine wasn't following.

'You're looking for problems,' said Liv. 'A few weeks out from the wedding, this is classic cold feet behaviour.'

'I don't know . . . You think?'

'I do. You're blowing even the slightest thing out of proportion, looking at everything through a long-range lens, asking yourself, "Is this what it's going to be like forever? Can I do this for the rest of my life?" You should be more worried about the things you can't see coming.'

Madeleine looked askance at her.

'Sorry, that's not helpful,' Liv dismissed. 'Look, I don't know what to tell you, except there is no doubt in my mind that you and Henry are going to live happily ever after. I'd bet my house on it.'

'Is that the way you felt right before your wedding?'

'God no,' said Liv. 'I've told you before, I didn't even want to get married.'

Madeleine sighed, resting her chin on her hand.

'Look, there's no comparison, Mad, it's apples and oranges, and you know it. Like you always say, Henry's solid, he's one of the good ones, he's not going to let you down. Rick . . . he's not even in the same ballpark.'

'Speaking of whom, what are you going to do about him?'

'I don't know,' said Liv. 'I guess I'm just going to have to keep him at bay until he finds the next girl silly enough to take up with him.'

'You should look for some girls whose names start with D,' Madeleine suggested. 'Introduce them.'

Liv smiled. 'I've got my own problems right now. My mother's coming to dinner tonight, and I have no idea what I'm going to cook.'

'I wouldn't stress,' said Madeleine. 'From what you've said, nothing will be good enough anyway, so it doesn't matter what you serve her.'

<h1 style="text-align:center">5.30 pm</h1>

Liv only wished it worked like that. She was wandering along, scanning the shelves of meat at the supermarket, waiting for something to jump out and grab her. Actually, after she got over the initial shock, she'd be quite happy if one of these plastic-wrapped packs leapt into her trolley of its own accord – better than having to make the decision herself. She would never again complain about cooking if her fridge was neatly stocked with the ingredients for each night's dinner. Better still, have all the ingredients chopped, measured and ready in those little glass dishes the TV chefs use . . . Even better still, have the 'Here's one I prepared earlier' option appear magically . . .

'Excuse me!'

Liv looked up into a very unhappy face, glaring at her. Liv was blocking the free-range chicken section, and obviously ruining this woman's life in the process.

'Sorry!' she chirped, moving on.

Deciding what to have for dinner with her parents coming was a nightmare. She could feed the boys almost anything, as long as it was served by the shovel, but her parents weren't so easy to please; in fact, her mother was almost impossible to please. She insisted they weren't fussy eaters, but this very insistence on *un*fussy food made them fussier than anyone else Liv knew. The safest option tonight would be a baked dinner, one might think, but only if Liv cooked it exactly the same way as her mother would. Sprigs of fresh rosemary were 'fancy' and regarded with suspicion, a slight on dried packet rosemary. A leg of lamb, while traditional, was extravagant these days. And one doesn't roast vegetables such as carrots and brussels sprouts! For goodness sakes, they were meant to be boiled to death on the stovetop.

But if Liv were to serve her parents the kind of food she and the boys normally ate – a stir-fry, for example – that would freak them out, especially her father. Even spag bol was a little too exotic, though at least it was mostly mince; if she didn't go too heavy on the tomato sauce, and left out the garlic, it might be acceptable, albeit too bland for everyone else. Then Liv spotted a tray of lamb shanks. Bingo! She could serve them with mashed potatoes and green beans to make a good old-fashioned meal. Her mother would never guess how expensive they were these days, or how 'fancy'.

*

'Well, it's a long time since I've had a lamb shank, love,' said her father, sitting back and giving his stomach a pat. 'That was beaut.'

'Yeah, Ma, it was totes amazeballs,' said Lachie.

'Can we have that again?' Dylan asked.

'I'll second that,' said her father. 'What do you think, Joy? Olive, you'll give your mother the recipe, won't you?'

Liv cringed inside, while her mother remained tight-lipped. She had been unusually quiet throughout dinner, because, Liv suspected, the lamb shanks had been such a success. She hadn't been able to find anything to criticise . . . oh, except the portion size.

'This is way too much for me,' she'd declared when Liv set the plate down in front of her.

'Don't worry, Mum, I'm sure Lachie will be happy to finish off anything you can't manage.'

'You might have to fight me for it, Lachie,' his pop chuckled.

'Well, let's see how I go first,' said Joy. 'Olive seems to be able to manage a very large portion, so I might be all right.'

Liv sometimes looked wistfully at mothers and daughters out and about together, shopping, at the movies, apparently enjoying each other's company. They didn't have to be best friends –

Madeleine and her mother didn't do an awful lot together, and poor old Margs was a bit dithery, but she was the sweetest woman on earth, and she clearly loved her daughters. Liv envied that; she didn't know why she and her mother had never had that kind of relationship. Maybe it was her fault? But she'd certainly never known anyone so ill-suited to their given name.

Before Liv could start to clear up, they were interrupted by a knock on the door.

Joy looked concerned. 'Who could that be, so late?'

It was seven o'clock. 'I'll go find out,' said Liv, getting to her feet.

'You answer the door at this time of night?' said her mother. 'That's not a very safe practice, Olive.'

'But I know you've all got my back.'

At least that got a laugh out of Lachie and Dylan.

As she walked up the hall, Liv was a little intrigued as to who would be visiting right on dinnertime. But when she opened the door, intrigue quickly gave way to irritation.

'Hi, Livvie,' Rick said expansively as he went in for the swoop-and-kiss manoeuvre again.

Liv managed to sidestep it this time. 'What are you doing here?' she demanded.

'Just visiting.'

'I asked you to call first, Rick.'

'But I was already out this way, and I needed to talk to you about something.'

Liv crossed her arms. 'It's not a good time.'

'Why, is your boyfriend here?' he sniggered. Dick.

'No, my parents are.'

His face lit up and he called down the hall, 'Joy, Ken!'

'Is that you, Rick?'

'Yes, Joy,' he cried, pushing past Liv. She gritted her teeth as she closed the door and walked down the hall to join the family reunion. Her parents had both sprung to their feet, delighted to greet the prodigal son-in-law. It got her goat how they made such a song and dance around him. Never mind that he was the arsehole who had cheated on their daughter, and effectively their grandsons – he was a man, and a man had to be shown respect, even fawned over.

'Have you eaten, Rick?' Joy was asking.

'Your wife cooked some ripper lamb shanks for us tonight,' Ken added.

'There's none left,' Liv said flatly. 'You guys ate the lot.'

'*So* awesome, Dad,' said Lachie.

'I'm sure we could put together a plate of something,' Joy said, beginning to scuttle her way around the table to the kitchen.

Liv stopped her. 'Rick can't stay, Mum.'

'Well –'

'No, no, it's fine, Rick, you mustn't feel obliged,' Liv said over the top of him. 'You see, Carly's expecting him. It'd be terribly rude to keep her waiting. You remember Carly, Mum and Dad? Now that I think of it, you've never met her, have you? She and Rick live together.'

Ah, *that* was the uncomfortable silence she was going for.

'Say goodnight to your father, boys, you'll see him on the weekend. And I'll walk you out, Rick.'

They said their farewells and Rick followed her back down the hall to the front door, probably pouting, but she had her back to him so she couldn't care less. She opened the door. 'We'll talk outside,' she said, waiting for him to pass. Then she stepped out and pulled the door to behind her. She wasn't going to have her mother trying to listen in.

'That was a bit mean,' Rick said, shoving his hands in his pockets.

'You ambush me like that, and I'll do what I have to do.'

'Ambush you . . .' he scoffed, as though she'd just made a joke.

'Rick, you really have to stop this,' Liv said firmly. 'You're showing a complete disregard for my wishes, and absolutely no respect for me. If you think this is going to get you anywhere, you're seriously deluded. I don't respond to bullying.'

He stared at her. 'I would never bully you.'

'Um, correction, you frequently have, and you're doing it right now.'

He looked a little shocked. That was the thing about Rick, he believed his own press that he was a great guy, universally adored by all.

'Now, what was it you wanted to talk to me about?' Liv kept her tone businesslike. 'I have to get back inside.'

'It's about this weekend, actually,' he said.

His weekend with the boys. 'What about it?'

'You know how I've got to find a place, seeing as you're not letting me stay here . . .'

Liv was unmoved. 'That's right.'

'Well, all the inspections are on Saturdays, so . . .'

'So?'

'I don't see how I can have the boys.'

'I do,' said Liv. 'Take them with you. They'll probably enjoy it.' For a while.

'But they've got cricket.'

Liv shrugged. 'They'll just have to miss it then, I guess.'

'I don't think that's sending the right message, letting down their teammates . . .'

'Whatever you think. It's up to you, they're your responsibility on the day.'

'What I think is that you should have them. I've done the same for you often enough when you go on tour.'

'Rick, you know very well that I've always made the time up to you in advance. I don't owe you.'

'Fine, then I'll owe *you*, and I'll make it up to you after,' he said, his tone smarmy.

Liv gave him a look of feigned regret. 'Gosh, Rick, I'd help if I could, but I can't this weekend, I've got plans.'

'With your boyfriend?' God, his fourteen-year-old sons sounded more mature.

'Not that it's any of your business, but yes, as a matter of fact.' She enjoyed watching the smarm dissolve into uncertainty. 'I have to go now. I'll get Lachie to call you about cricket, you can work it out with him.'

With that she turned and walked back into the house, closing the door behind her.

Friday afternoon

'Madeleine Pepper,' she said automatically, picking up her phone without looking at it. She was staring at the computer screen in a daze. Genevieve had sent her a link to the place where they were booked in for a cake tasting. Madeleine didn't even know that was a thing, but apparently it was, and so Genevieve had taken over, and found some hip designer bakery that she wished had been around when *she* got married.

'Hello, Madeleine Pepper, it's Aiden Carmichael.'

'Aiden!' she said, holding out her phone to look at the screen as if she'd see him there. She put it back to her ear. 'Where are you?'

She and Henry hadn't heard from him all week – not that they'd expected to, he would have been well out of mobile range most of the time. Then yesterday he'd sent Madeleine a text: *Starting the long trek back, will make it to Sydney tomorrow, all going well. Call you then. xa*

'I'm heading into the city,' he was saying now.

'What do you mean?'

'I grabbed a taxi at the airport, I thought it was easier to come to you.'

'You shouldn't have,' she admonished him. 'If you'd told me when your flight was due in I would have been happy to pick you up from the airport.'

'It's fine, I'm on my way. What's the address of your building?'

Madeleine gave it to him, and Aiden relayed it to the taxi driver.

'I'm just finishing up here,' she said. 'I'll meet you on the street, we can get down to the basement garage from there.'

'Listen, my sweet, I've travelled several thousand miles in the last twenty-four hours, and I would like to pause to rest at a watering hole before we begin the final leg to Mordor, if it's all the same to you.'

She smiled. 'Of course.'

'I'll call you when I get there.'

Madeleine hung up the phone and closed the cake webpage, before shutting down her computer. She felt excited for the first time all week. She had managed to lift herself a little out of the rut she'd been in on Monday, but Henry had been chained to his desk, so it had remained quiet on the home front, and there had still been no sex. Madeleine knew things would brighten up again with Aiden around.

Twenty minutes later she was beginning to wonder where he'd got to, when her phone rang. This time she checked the screen as she picked up her bag and started out of the office. 'Hi, was the traffic bad?' she asked.

'Not overly,' said Aiden. 'But I'm already at the helm.'

'What? Are we sailing home?'

'Ha. No, it's a bar. I asked the taxi driver where was the closest place with a view, and he dropped me here.'

'I know it. I'll see you there soon.'

When Madeleine walked into the Helm, she saw Aiden waving to her from a table right over by the wall, looking out across Darling Harbour. He jumped off his stool as she approached, and scooped her up in one of his signature hugs. 'Hey, Maddie,' he said. 'It's so good to see your face.'

'Yours too.'

'Let me get you a drink,' he said.

But she waved him off. He still had more than half a glass of beer, and she should avoid drinking with the long drive ahead of her. 'I've just finished a coffee,' she said. 'I'm right for now.'

'If you say so.' He took her hand to help her up onto the stool beside him. 'When the taxi driver said "harbour" I thought I'd be able to see your bridge and your opera house.'

'Not from Darling Harbour,' said Madeleine. 'Would you prefer to go down to the real thing? Though it's a bit of a hike from here.'

'No thanks, I don't want to move. Besides, this will do very nicely.'

'So how was your trip?' Madeleine asked.

'Exhausting,' he said. 'I've never travelled so far and stayed in the same state before.'

'You should try Western Australia.'

'I think I've had enough outback for now.'

Madeleine gave him a sympathetic smile. 'So do you think you're going to be able to do something for the communities you visited?'

'They put together some good proposals,' he said. 'I'll certainly be recommending that we fund what we can. We have the money, but I don't know if it's going to help all that much.'

'Why do you say that?'

Aiden took a swig of his beer. 'Your government has really screwed around with those poor people. I thought we did badly with our Native Americans, but I think you guys might have outdone us.'

'Wow, that's depressing.'

'Sorry, I shouldn't come out here like a loudmouth Yank criticising your government. I'm not taking sides – left and right, they've both been as bad as one another.'

'No, I agree,' said Madeleine. 'But it's not just the government, it's all of us. Out of sight, out of mind. Whenever I think about the plight of Aboriginal people, I just feel guilty. The issues seem so overwhelming.'

'They are,' said Aiden. 'That's what I meant before. We can throw all the money we like at the problems, but it's such a mess I don't know what could possibly make it right, except going back in time to undo everything that's been done to them since the white man came.'

Madeleine leant her chin in her hand, thinking. 'Have you heard of *The Chant of Jimmie Blacksmith*?'

'No, what is it?'

'It's a novel, but it's based on real incidents. We had to read it in school. It's by Thomas Keneally.'

'I have heard of him.'

'So Jimmie Blacksmith was a half-caste, and he was taken in by a minister and his wife. There was this line, where the minister was encouraging Jimmie to marry a white girl, because their children would be only a quarter Aboriginal, and then their children would be hardly black at all – it was something like that, but I'm sure I'm remembering that phrase right, "hardly black at all". It's always stayed with me, the sheer arrogance of it, that actually breeding out an entire race was a good thing. And then around the same time, I was at an old aunty's place, and Evonne Goolagong was mentioned on the news, she'd won some kind of special achievement award. She was a hugely successful Aboriginal tennis player back in the seventies.'

'Yep, heard of her,' said Aiden. 'My parents were big tennis fans, and that's not a name you easily forget.'

'Well, anyway,' Madeleine continued, 'she married a white guy, and my aunty was saying how good it was that her children were only half black, because their children would only be a quarter black, and that was *hardly black at all*. She actually said the same words. I couldn't believe what I was hearing. It's like nothing ever changes.'

Aiden shook his head. 'I know, seems that way sometimes.'

'It's not like I have any right to point the finger,' she said. 'I don't do enough, I don't do anything. Sometimes I look at my job and I'm embarrassed, it's just so frivolous in the big scheme of things.'

'Don't talk like that. Supporting and promoting the arts isn't frivolous.'

Madeleine looked at him doubtfully. 'It's not exactly saving the world, like what you do.'

'I wish you'd stop saying things like that,' he said, a little tightly. 'I'm not saving anyone, I'm not a hero. I don't even do anything particularly virtuous. I get invited to these places, shown around, I tick a few boxes on a report, and the obscenely wealthy company I work for drops some money that it won't even miss. I get paid well, and I get to go home afterwards, not like the people on the ground doing the actual work. Anyone could do what I do.'

Madeleine would have argued with him, but he didn't sound like he was being falsely modest, if anything he sounded irritated. 'Okay, but I still think what I do is a little frivolous,' she said. 'My father wanted me to be a teacher, like him. Now there's a noble profession.'

'Stop being so hard on yourself,' said Aiden. 'You wanna talk frivolous, the man you're going to marry writes children's books.'

Madeleine raised an eyebrow. 'You of all people should know how amazing Henry's books are . . . And besides, books are incredibly important for children.'

'Yeah, I guess . . . but don't we have enough already?'

She was starting to feel quite indignant. 'There can never be enough children's books!'

Aiden drained his beer and put the empty glass down on the table. 'Well said.'

'What?'

His face broke into a wide grin. 'Had you going then, didn't I?'

Madeleine elbowed him. 'Aiden Carmichael, in these parts, you're what we call a stirrer.'

'I had to lift the mood, it was all getting too depressing and serious.'

A young woman in a tight singlet top and even tighter shorts leaned across the table to pick up Aiden's empty glass, flashing him a smile, along with some generous cleavage. He seemed to appreciate it. Madeleine shook her head as the girl walked away.

'What?' he said, playing innocent. 'Just enjoying the local attractions. Are you ready for a drink yet?'

She pulled a face. 'I shouldn't.'

'Why not?'

'I have to drive.'

'What kind of drink-driving laws do you have in this country? Surely you can have one?'

'Yeah, but . . .' Madeleine hesitated.

'But what?' said Aiden. 'Come on, don't make me drink alone.'

'Okay,' she surrendered, 'I'll have one. But only one.'

'One, I promise.'

Aiden went to line up at the bar, and Madeleine leaned her elbows on the table, propping her chin in her hands and gazing at the sky, splashed with vivid streaks of orange and purple as the sun sank low beyond the western suburbs. She wondered why

Aiden was so down on himself and the job he did, and recalled his frustration the other night as well. She supposed the job must take its toll after a while, but it didn't seem right that he was downplaying his role like that. Maybe he wasn't irreplaceable, but that didn't mean what he did wasn't valuable and important. Madeleine was so lost in thought that she didn't realise Aiden had returned to the table until he placed a glass down in front of her. An empty one. She looked around as he lifted a bottle of champagne out of an ice bucket.

'Aiden! What did I say?'

'I know, I only got one bottle.'

'Oh, come on,' said Madeleine. 'You knew what I meant. I have to drive!'

'One bottle between us is only a couple of glasses each,' he said.

'More like three and a half.'

'You really are a pedant.'

'Well, it doesn't matter, I'm still only having one *glass*,' Madeleine stressed. 'You'll just have to drink the rest.'

'Okay with me,' he said, pouring the champagne. 'All the communities we visited up there were dry, and I don't think I've ever needed a drink more.' He returned the bottle to the bucket and lifted his glass in a toast. 'What shall we drink to?'

'Not getting drunk.'

'You can't drink to that. Come on, something positive.'

She thought about it. 'Okay. To making the world a better place.'

'So now you've gone from the sublime to the ridiculous.'

'All right, what do you suggest then?'

He paused for a moment. 'How about we drink to friendship?'

Madeleine smiled. 'To friendship.'

They clinked glasses and drank. It was good stuff, cold and crisp and delicious; it tingled on her tongue and flowed down her throat like liquid silk. Madeleine took another mouthful, and another, and then she realised that her glass was already half empty. She had to slow down. She set it back on the table, sliding it a little away from her.

'Do you have any more big trips planned while you're here?' she asked Aiden.

He shook his head. 'I've got some meetings in Sydney, and I might have to go down to Canberra, but that's not very far, I understand?'

'No, half an hour by plane,' she said. 'You can use the apartment as much as you like. But I hope you'll still join us in Mordor too – you bring a bit of life to the place.'

He smiled. 'That nickname seems to have stuck.'

'We better keep it between you and me though,' said Madeleine. 'Henry might be offended, he loves that place.'

Aiden took a swig of champagne and set the glass down on the table. 'You know what's been so surprising about seeing Henry again after all these years?'

Madeleine shook her head.

'Nothing,' he said. 'There *are* no surprises – except for you. But Henry hasn't changed one bit.'

She wasn't sure he meant that as a good thing. 'How do you mean?' she asked.

'He's still the same quiet, reserved guy,' said Aiden. 'Still happiest in his own company . . . and yours, obviously,' he added quickly.

'He's not that quiet around you. You should see him the rest of the time.'

Aiden raised an eyebrow. 'Still, you wouldn't exactly call him a party animal,' he said. 'You know, when Henry told me he was moving to Australia, I thought, wow, that's huge, I was really happy for him. We haven't had a lot to do with each other over recent years, but we always caught up when I went home to visit my folks. I used to worry about him, especially after he got that place up in the Hamptons. My uncle had all kinds of trouble getting him to meet his publicity obligations. I mean, if you're a literary writer, fine, you can be a little reclusive, but not when you're a children's author.'

Madeleine didn't say anything, she just picked up her glass and gulped, stopping short of draining it entirely. It was the word reclusive that rankled.

'But hey,' Aiden went on, 'suddenly he was up and heading over to the other side of the world, for a woman, no less. I knew you had to be something special, and in those five minutes at the airport, I was convinced of it.'

'You are an incorrigible flatterer,' said Madeleine. Not that she could say she minded, exactly.

'I'm only telling it like it is,' he said. 'When I met you, it was strange, I felt like I already knew you.'

'I felt the same way,' she said quietly.

Aiden smiled at her. 'Anyway, then we drove up to the house, and I couldn't believe how far it was. I thought about you, having to drive all the way from the city that evening, and every evening. It seemed to me that Henry had just re-created here what he had back home, except that now he had you for company. Which is great for him, but . . . I don't know.' He paused, looking at her, but she didn't say anything. 'Sorry, I'm making you uncomfortable again.'

She shook her head. 'I told you, Henry needs quiet to work.'

'But what about your work? I gather this apartment of yours is much more convenient. Why is Henry so against you keeping it?'

'He's not . . . but, you know, it's a bit extravagant for occasional use.'

Aiden grunted. 'He can afford it – don't forget, he kept an apartment in New York.'

That thought had crossed Madeleine's mind before too, but she didn't have the right to tell Henry how to spend his money.

'He keeps the reins pretty tight, doesn't he?' Aiden said carefully.

'No, no, he doesn't. He's not like that.' Though she wondered who she was trying to convince.

Aiden lifted the bottle out of the ice bucket but she covered her glass. 'Not for me.'

'Oh, why not?' He gave her a nudge.

'I have to drive, remember?'

He let out a heavy sigh, rubbing his eyes. 'To be honest, Maddie, I don't know if I'm up to that long drive back. Can't we just stay here in the city?'

'Of course,' she said. 'I can take you to the apartment if you like, and then Henry and I can pick you up tomorrow on our way to lunch.'

Aiden frowned, filling his own glass. 'Where does your sister live?'

'In Strathfield.'

'Which might as well be on Mars for all I know.'

'Sorry,' Madeleine said. 'It's not far, a few suburbs west of the city.'

'So it's not on the way to Mordor from here?'

'Oh no, it's in the other direction.'

'And your apartment's somewhere in between?'

She nodded. 'About ten, fifteen minutes from my sister's place.'

'Then why on earth would you drive all the way back, and then down again tomorrow? That isn't fair on you.'

'It's fine. I don't mind.'

'Seriously, Maddie, you have to help me understand,' said Aiden. 'Would Henry be angry if you stayed?'

'Of course not. He doesn't get angry . . .' Sulky, maybe.

'Then what's the problem? Is there only one bed in the apartment?'

'One bedroom, but there's a fold-out sofa as well.'

'Then we're all set,' he declared. 'Come on, you can have another drink with me and relax, instead of spending the whole night in the car.'

Madeleine could feel herself wavering. The champagne was good, the evening gorgeous, the company was all right too. If she made that long drive home, without Aiden, she'd be going back to the deafening silence, while Henry worked the night away in his study.

Aiden was watching her. 'I'm going to call Henry,' he said, taking out his phone.

'No, don't!' she pleaded.

'He's not going to argue with me,' he said, tapping his finger on the screen to bring up the number.

'It's not that.'

Aiden stopped to look at her. 'Then what is it?'

She hesitated. 'Just . . . don't say it's because we're drinking, okay?' Oh God, why did she say that? He was giving her such a strange look.

'Sure, no problem,' he said, in a tone one might use to placate a mental patient. 'Darrow!' he said, moments later. 'Yep, I'm finally back . . . Yeah, good. Listen, my flight was delayed, and your magnanimous fiancée waited all this time . . .'

Madeleine's eyes widened and her mouth dropped open at the barefaced lie. But Aiden just winked at her.

'I'm too shattered to go any further tonight, Dazza . . . Do you like that? I heard it up in Queensland, it's my new nickname for you . . . No? Well, we'll see. Anyway, why don't we just meet at Maddie's sister's tomorrow? We'll stay at the apartment . . . Yeah? . . . Sure, I'll put her on.'

Madeleine's throat felt tight as she took the phone from Aiden and held it to her ear. She didn't want to lie to Henry, they didn't lie to each other. 'Hi,' she said warily.

'Hi, are you okay?' he asked.

'Sure, of course. I can drive home if you want?'

Aiden gave her a stern look, shaking his head as he picked up her glass to refill it.

'Look, it's fine with me,' said Henry. 'To be honest, I'm working really well. If Aiden came back tonight I'd have to stop.'

'Oh, I see.' He wouldn't stop for her.

'I'm glad you two are getting along,' he was saying. 'This gives you a chance to get to know each other better.'

'Well, if you're sure it's all right.'

'Of course. Have a good time.'

'Thanks. And you eat something, won't you?' Henry sometimes got so absorbed when he was working that he forgot about everything else.

'I will, don't worry about me. I'll see you tomorrow.'

'Okay . . . 'night.' Madeleine hung up and handed the phone back to Aiden, and he slipped it into his pocket.

'So there we go, it wasn't a problem at all, you had nothing to worry about,' he said, raising his glass.

She picked up her full glass and took a decent slurp. She was annoyed now. So if she wanted to stay at the apartment for the sake of her work, it wasn't okay, but if Henry wanted her to stay away for the sake of his, then that was fine.

Aiden was watching her. 'Hey, I thought you'd be pleased – now you can relax.'

'You shouldn't have lied to him.'

'Well, you asked me not to mention the drinking . . .'

Madeleine could feel herself reddening.

'What's that about?' he asked.

'Nothing. It's sounding like a bigger deal than it is.'

'So if I'd said we were staying down here because you wanted to have a drink, that wouldn't have been a problem?'

'Of course not.'

'Then why did you ask me not to mention it?'

This was beginning to feel like an interrogation. She had to tell Aiden something, he'd just lied to his best friend for her. 'It's not like I'm an alcoholic or anything . . .'

He looked surprised by that. 'I didn't say you were, Maddie. I wasn't even thinking it.'

But now he was. Damn it.

'Does Henry think you're an alcoholic?' he asked.

'No, but you know how people who don't drink much can be . . .'

'Yeah, boring,' he joked.

But Madeleine just gave him a pained look.

'Hey, Maddie.' Aiden put a hand on her knee and gave it a rub. 'Lighten up. I understand. I'm sure Henry's just a bit sensitive because of his father.'

She frowned. 'What do you mean?'

'You know about his father, right?'

'I know they fell out of contact after his mother died,' she said. 'Which I did find pretty strange. Especially when they didn't seem to have any other family, except the grandmother he used to visit.'

Aiden was staring down at his glass, looking decidedly uncomfortable.

'What do you know, Aiden?' Madeleine asked.

'I'm not sure I should say . . .'

'Come on, you brought it up.'

He took a breath. 'You're at least aware Henry had a tough time of it growing up?'

'I don't know if you'd call it tough, exactly. Lonely, for sure.'

Aiden looked at her directly. 'Maddie, I think having two addicts for parents, a mother dying from what was basically a prolonged overdose, and then a father disappearing – I'd call that tough.'

She stared at him, shocked.

'You didn't know any of that?' said Aiden. 'What has Henry told you about his parents?'

'He never said anything about them being addicts,' Madeleine said. 'Addicted to what, exactly?'

'His father was a chronic alcoholic.'

'Oh.'

'And his mother was a chronic enabler, so his father was able to hold down a job, but they kept to themselves, pretty much. He didn't like people coming to the house, knowing their business. He was a mean son of a bitch, apparently.'

Madeleine was stunned. 'Was he violent?'

'I don't think he ever laid a hand on Henry, from what he said, anyway. So I suppose the guy had some boundaries. No, he stuck to emotional and mental abuse. His mother turned to pills eventually, to cope. That's what killed her.'

'Henry said it was kidney failure.'

'It was, from prolonged abuse of pharmaceuticals,' said Aiden. 'I think she was slowly killing herself, timing it for when Henry was independent and out of the house.'

Madeleine's heart was breaking for Henry, for his mother. 'So . . . what about his father?'

Aiden sighed. 'I can't believe he hasn't told you this,' he said. 'Henry went back home for his mom's funeral, naturally. His father gave him a cheque. It was for a few thousand dollars – not a fortune, but enough to tide him over for a while. Henry tried to keep in touch, calling the house, but there was never any answer. After a while the phone was disconnected, letters Henry sent were returned . . . They'd never been close, but he started to worry. He went back the next chance he could, and his father was gone. There was a whole other family living in the house, total strangers. And no sign of his father.'

Madeleine sipped her wine, trying to imagine what that would have been like – devastating, surely, especially on top of the death of his mother. Aiden went on: the new owners of the house were kind, Henry had told him, they even showed him the papers with his father's signature and invited him to take a last look around, but he didn't feel comfortable. He might have done if they weren't there, but he could hardly expect them to leave him alone in the house. So he handed over his keys and left. He made a few enquiries – with the realtor, and some other local businesses that his father may have had dealings with – but no one could tell him anything, and his father had left no forwarding address. Henry never heard from him again.

'I can't understand why he wouldn't have told me any of this.' Madeleine was shaking her head.

'I don't know, maybe he's embarrassed by it all,' said Aiden. 'Maybe it's just too hard for him to talk about. I mean, he was abandoned by his own father. I can't imagine how that must have affected him, deep down.'

Madeleine couldn't imagine it either. It was beyond imagining. She drained her glass. 'I think I need another drink,' she said finally.

Aiden lifted the bottle out of the ice bucket. 'I'm not sure I should have told you all that.'

'No, it's fine, I'm glad you did.' She paused. 'I do have a right to know, I'm about to marry him.'

'That doesn't mean it was my place to tell you.'

Madeleine met his gaze. 'You're the best man. If not you, and not Henry, then who?'

He looked pensive as he refilled her champagne glass. Madeleine reached over to cover his hand with hers. 'Don't worry, I won't tell him you told me.'

'That doesn't bother me,' said Aiden. 'I can answer to Henry myself. But you do probably need to clear the air with him before the wedding.' He splashed the last of the champagne into his glass. 'That's it for this bottle,' he said, upending it into the ice bucket.

'I'll get the next,' said Madeleine.

'Are you sure?'

'Yes, you don't have to buy all the drinks.'

'No, I meant are you sure you want to get another bottle?'

She groaned. 'Now you too?'

'Sorry.'

'I'm not driving, so I'm going to relax like you said. And besides, I think I need a drink after all that.'

'Fair enough,' said Aiden. 'Do you know if they serve food here?'

'I think so.'

'All right, well, let's at least have something to eat with the next bottle.'

'Deal.'

Aiden went to the bar to ask for a menu, and Madeleine looked out at the sky, dark now. The sun had set completely. She hadn't even noticed.

She couldn't understand why Henry had never told her any of that. It couldn't be healthy to suppress it so completely. Maybe he had worked through it in the past, but surely that meant he should have been able to talk about it freely with his fiancée. He had never lied outright, she supposed, but he'd certainly omitted all but the barest details. And Madeleine couldn't help but think that the omissions meant he hadn't dealt with it all. She thought about their future, shut up in Pittwater, away from everyone. What about when they had children? What sort of a father would Henry make with all this suppressed pain and rejection bottled up inside of him? It was all quite unnerving. He should be able to face the past and share it with the woman he was going to marry, for godsakes.

Madeleine was going to marry Henry in just a few short weeks, and suddenly she felt like she didn't know the first thing about him.

The morning after

'Maddie . . .'

Oh. My. God. Her head was literally splitting. Yes, literally. It would not surprise her at all if she opened her eyes right now to discover that her head was halved like a rockmelon, her eyes staring out at opposite sides of the room.

'*Owwwww*,' she squeaked.

'Maddie . . .'

Who was that? Henry never called her Maddie. Maybe this was a dream . . . but why was she in so much pain if it was only a dream?

'Maddie!' the voice repeated, a little more urgently now.

'Go away,' she groaned. 'You're not real.'

'Maddie, it's Aiden. And you really have to get up. Henry called, we have to be at your sister's in, like, an hour.'

She opened her eyes wide, and closed them again immediately. Too bright. 'What are you doing here, Aiden?' she said weakly, keeping her eyes shut fast.

'That's funny,' he said dryly. 'I'm going to help you sit up now.'

Madeleine felt his hands under her arms, and next thing he hoicked her up the bed and propped her against the bedhead. She gasped.

'Are you all right?' he asked.

'No.'

'Here, open your eyes and take a sip of water.'

'No water,' she murmured, turning her face away. 'Coffee.'

'No coffee until you've rehydrated a little.'

'I want coffee,' she whimpered, 'and Panadol.'

'What's Panadol?'

Oh . . . damn . . . what was it? 'Headache tablets,' she said finally.

'No, you're better off taking ibuprofen.'

'What's that?'

'It's a painkiller too, but it's also a vasoconstrictor.'

'A what?' She blinked, opening her eyes in a squint.

'An anti-inflammatory. The pain you're feeling is from the blood vessels in your head expanding. Ibuprofen will relieve that.'

'Then give me some . . . stat!' she cried.

'You can't take it on an empty stomach. Drink some water and I'll bring you your breakfast.'

'Can only manage Vegemite on toast,' Madeleine said wearily, listing sideways. It was too hard to stay vertical.

'Not that nasty black gunk you Australians eat?' he said, curling his lip. 'No, I've made you eggs.'

'The fatty fry-up doesn't work for my hangovers, I'm telling you.'

'It's not a fry-up,' said Aiden. 'Now sit up properly and hold on to the glass.'

She did so unwillingly, bringing the glass to her lips and taking a tiny sip that she could barely swallow. As it trickled down her throat and into her stomach, it created a wave of nausea. She felt like crap. She had forgotten that one of the advantages of living a more sober life was never having to wake up with a hangover. It was totally worth it. Madeleine might never drink again.

'I don't know why I feel so bad,' she said in a small voice.

'To be honest, I don't know why you do either,' said Aiden. 'We didn't drink all that much, a couple of bottles between us . . . I mean, I know that's not nothing. But we had food, and we didn't mix drinks. Then all of a sudden, it seemed to hit you hard, right at the end.'

'It must be because I hardly ever drink anymore.' She groaned. 'This is terrible, I don't even remember getting home.'

'That was no big deal, we caught a taxi.' Aiden stood up. 'Now, try to keep some more water down, and I'll get your breakfast.'

'I have to use the bathroom first,' said Madeleine, slipping her feet out the side of the bed. Her legs were bare – hold on, what was she wearing? She stopped, waiting for Aiden to leave the room.

But he was watching her. 'Are you okay? Are you going to be sick again?'

Her face dropped. 'Again?'

He didn't say anything – he didn't have to, the expression on his face answered the question for her.

'Can you give me a minute?' she said feebly.

'Sure.' He walked out of the room, closing the door behind him.

Madeleine pulled back the covers all the way. Okay, so she was wearing underwear – relieved to note – and the top she'd had on yesterday. A good top, bugger it, it was almost new. And now she'd slept in it, stretched it out of shape and probably vomited on it. She got up to inspect it in the bathroom mirror, stepping over her discarded skirt on the way. All right, at least no one – namely Aiden – had had to change her clothes or do anything untoward. No matter how drunk she was, Madeleine was sure she would have been capable of slipping off her skirt and falling into bed. She checked herself in the bathroom mirror. Ugh, grim. Very bad case of bed hair. She held out her top to inspect it in the light. There was a decent splodge of something down one side. Hopefully it was just champagne. That would leave a mark on this fabric, wouldn't it? She didn't want to think about what else it might be. Whatever, she'd have to give it a good soak, but she wondered if it would ever be the same again. She wondered the same about herself.

Madeleine was splashing water on her face when she heard a knock out on the bedroom door. 'Can I come in?' Aiden called.

'Just a sec!' She dashed back into the bedroom and grabbed a pair of tracksuit pants, pulling them on. Uh-oh, she'd moved too quickly, and now she was dizzy, and she could feel sweat breaking out across her forehead. She crawled gingerly back onto the bed and lay on her side, curled up in the foetal position. 'You can come in now.'

The door opened and Aiden walked in carrying a tray. 'Hey, are you feeling worse?' he asked, concerned.

'I'm sorry, I don't think I can eat, Aiden.'

'You have to,' he said firmly. 'I promise it'll make you feel better. And Henry called again –'

'Oh God.' Madeleine hauled herself upright. 'I should ring him.' She glanced at the bedside table. 'Have you seen my phone?'

'No. He said he'd been trying to call you all morning but it kept going straight to voicemail.'

Shit. 'It's probably flat. I hope I didn't lose it, I can't remember when I used it last . . . Have you seen my handbag? I did come home with it, didn't I? Please tell me I did.'

'No, I did – I grabbed it when we were leaving.'

While she was busy throwing up, probably. This just kept getting worse.

'I think it's out in the living room. I'll get it for you.' Aiden lowered the tray onto her lap. 'You stay put and eat something, or else you're not going to be in any fit state to go to your sister's. And then I'll be in trouble.'

'Thank you.' Madeleine stared at the food. The smell was almost making her sick. There was a neat mound of scrambled eggs, and two triangles of dry toast. And some clear pinkish liquid in a glass. She took a cautious sip; it was okay, kind of semi-sweet. Aiden came back into the room with her handbag.

'Did you find my phone?'

'I didn't look.'

'Why not?'

'I was brought up not to look in ladies' purses,' said Aiden. 'There's scary stuff in there.'

'What, like tampons? They don't bite, you know. Give it here.'

He handed her the bag, and Madeleine rooted through it until she found her phone. 'As I suspected, it's flat.'

'Do you have a charger here?'

She nodded. 'It should be plugged in under the bedside table.'

Aiden got down on his hands and knees and found the lead, passing it to Madeleine. She plugged in the phone. 'I should call Henry.'

But Aiden stopped her. 'I've spoken to him twice already. And now he's on his way, so –'

'Oh God, he's already left? We have to get going.'

'Settle down. He has a much longer trip, remember? We have time, and you have to eat something.'

'I really don't think I can, Aiden,' she said again.

He sat down on the bed, facing her. 'You can't take the ibuprofen unless you have something in your stomach.'

She sighed. 'Why does it have to be eggs?'

Aiden picked up the fork and scooped up some scrambled egg. 'Because eggs have an enzyme called cysteine that mops up the toxic chemicals produced when alcohol breaks down in the liver,' he said, holding the fork in front of her. 'Open.'

Madeleine did so and Aiden popped it into her mouth. She moved the egg around on her tongue a little. She supposed it was all right. She swallowed gingerly.

'Those toxins are what's causing that poisoned feeling,' Aiden went on. 'And eggs are loaded with cysteine.' Madeleine accepted another mouthful. 'The dry toast is whole wheat,' he continued his infomercial, 'and carbohydrates help restore your blood sugar, which is why doctors recommend dry toast or crackers for morning sickness. They fill the stomach without aggravating the nausea.'

'And what's in the drink?' Madeleine asked, taking a bite of toast.

'It's an electrolyte replacement, a real one, from the pharmacy, not one of those useless sports drinks.'

She blinked. 'Did you go out this morning and buy all this?'

'It's all right,' he said dismissively. 'Just eat a couple more mouthfuls and then I'll give you the drugs. And later when we get to your sister's, you should have a beer.'

Madeleine grimaced.

'There is something to the hair-of-the-dog theory,' said Aiden. 'But you should only have one, and drink it slowly.'

'How do you know all this?'

'Years of hard-won experience,' he said with a rueful smile.

To her surprise and relief, Madeleine was gradually starting to feel a little better. 'How are we going for time?' she asked.

'We're okay, keep eating.' He leaned across her outstretched legs, planting his hand on the mattress beside her. 'Maddie, I can't help feeling responsible for this.'

She looked at him. 'Nonsense. I'm a big girl, Aiden. You weren't to know it was going to hit me so hard.'

'That's not what I meant.'

'Then what?'

'I feel responsible because I told you all that stuff about Henry, and his father . . .'

It all came rushing back to her now. Madeleine dropped the toast on the tray, her appetite gone again. Fragments of the night before started to filter through into her consciousness. There were tears, a lot of tears . . .

'I'm sorry, Aiden. I was a weepy drunk, wasn't I?'

He smiled indulgently at her. 'You were okay,' he said, giving her leg a pat. 'You had a lot to process last night, you just had to get it out of your system.'

Why did he have to use that particular turn of phrase? She had to know . . . 'Where did I throw up?' she asked in a weak voice, praying it wasn't in the cab, or worse, his lap.

'Straight into the toilet bowl,' he assured her. 'Don't worry about it.'

She sighed. 'I hope I at least did you the courtesy of taking myself to bed after that, and leaving you in peace.'

'Oh, sure,' he said. 'I had to fight you off for a bit, but eventually I convinced you that no means no.'

Madeleine gave a nervous laugh. 'When you say you had to fight me off . . .'

'You were trying to get me to sleep with you, that's all.'

Madeleine was horrified. 'That's *all*? I came onto you? Oh God! How embarrassing. What must you think of me?' She gasped. 'What's Henry going to think?'

'Steady on,' Aiden said. 'It wasn't like that, you weren't coming onto me. You wanted me to sleep in the bed with you – like, *beside* you – because you felt bad that I had to sleep on the couch. And as for what Henry might think, he's not going to hear anything from me, so don't worry about it.'

'You think I should lie to him?'

'No, I think you should tell him nothing, because there's nothing to tell. I slept on the couch, that's the truth . . . Nothing to tell, Maddie.'

'I'm so sorry,' she said in a small voice.

'Nothing to be sorry about either, you were actually very sweet,' he said, giving her another reassuring pat on the leg. 'Now, you need to take a shower, and be quick about it.' He lifted the tray off her lap and stood up.

'What about my drugs?' she pleaded.

'All right, all right, you don't have to beg.'

*

Once she was showered, dressed and medicated, Madeleine felt like a new person, although still not quite back to her old self. The food had helped, and the drugs were working – her head wasn't throbbing any more – but she still felt debilitatingly fragile. She didn't know if debilitatingly was a word, but that was how she felt. The thought of negotiating the Saturday morning traffic on Parramatta Road was more than a little daunting.

And then it dawned on her.

'Aiden, how did we get here last night?' she asked as she joined him out in the living room.

'By taxi, I told you. Why?'

'That means my car's still at work!'

'Oh yeah.'

'Shit! Shitshitshit!'

'Calm down,' said Aiden. 'We'll just get a taxi to your building and pick it up.'

But she was shaking her head. 'We don't have enough time.'

'Well, what do you want to do?'

'I could call Henry,' she said, 'get him to pick us up on the way.'

'Nah, that's not going to work. He rang again while you were in the shower, he's already there.'

'What?' Madeleine said, alarmed. 'He's at my sister's?'

'I assume that's where he meant.'

'Oh no. Did he sound cross?'

'He didn't sound too happy when I said we hadn't left yet.'

'Shit.'

'It's not the end of the world, Maddie.'

'You don't understand,' she said. 'He doesn't get on all that well with my family.'

'Well, it's about time he did, he's about to marry into it.'

'I don't think that's how Henry sees it,' she muttered. Madeleine knew he only tolerated her family at best. He was all right with her mum, it was Genevieve who really pressed his buttons. And who could blame him. Genevieve had elevated pressing people's buttons to an art form, while Mark was just plain rude a lot of the time, constantly taking phone calls and ignoring his children, who all seemed to behave worse around their father, no doubt in a vain attempt to get his attention. At least he wouldn't be there today.

'Then we'll just get a taxi from here,' Aiden said. 'You said it's not far.'

'I suppose you're right.' She picked up her handbag and checked that she had her keys. 'It's just that the more urgently I need a taxi, the longer it always takes me to find one.'

'And tell me,' said Aiden, holding the door open for her, 'how long have you been experiencing these paranoid delusions?'

Madeleine pulled a face at him as she walked past him out the door. Her pessimism wasn't entirely unwarranted – it did end up taking more than ten minutes before a taxi finally pulled up for them. When they joined Parramatta Road, Madeleine's anxiety levels rose as she saw the traffic snarl ahead of them. It would be like this until they passed the used-caryard stretch, and there was no guarantee the traffic would move any faster beyond that either.

Genevieve and Mark had moved to Strathfield after Declan was born. They wanted their sons to attend a good private boys school from prep, and there was one such establishment just up the road. Jonathan Pepper would be spinning in his grave: he was a firm advocate of public schooling, having taught in the system his whole career. But that wasn't a subject Madeleine was ever going to broach with her sister. 'Mark's never home,' Genevieve had said at the time. 'Boys need a firm hand, discipline, structure. They're only going to get that at a private school.'

Madeleine knew that Genevieve was just trying to do the best with the disappointing hand she believed life had dealt her. Things hadn't turned out quite the way she'd planned. Instead of re-creating her family with a loving husband and two daughters of her own, she had a largely absent husband and three sons. One after the other. She'd tried again for a girl after Declan, and Madeleine had been quietly horrified when Genevieve had mused out loud about terminating the pregnancy when the ultrasound confirmed another boy. 'Don't look at me like that,' she'd snapped at Madeleine. 'I'm not going to actually do it, but you can't blame me for thinking about it.'

Madeleine had a soft spot for Declan out of the three boys; as the second child of the same gender herself, she'd experienced the vaguest of niggles from time to time that maybe her parents had hoped for a boy. They had never made her feel anything but loved and wanted, but she sometimes wondered if there had been even a split second of disappointment when she was born. Poor Declan didn't have to imagine it – Genevieve's favourite war cry when the boys were running amok was 'I wanted girls, you know!'

'So prepare me,' said Aiden. 'Who am I meeting today exactly?'

Madeleine roused herself. 'Right, well, first there's my mum, Margaret. She's very sweet, but a little . . .'

'What?'

Madeleine was about to say 'ditzy', but that felt mean. There was no need to telegraph her mother's shortcomings. And besides, her ditziness was endearing as much as anything, despite what Genevieve had to say about it.

'She's very sweet.' Madeleine left it at that. 'And my sister's Genevieve, who's married to Mark, but he won't be there.'

'Oh, why not?'

'He has to travel for work quite a lot. All the time, in fact. She's pretty much bringing up those boys on her own.'

'Those boys?'

'My three nephews,' said Madeleine. 'Gabriel is eight, Declan's five, and Archie is about twenty months.'

'She's got her hands full,' said Aiden. 'What does she do?'

'Hm?'

'Genevieve – what does she do for a job?'

Madeleine looked at him. 'Well, like you said, she's got her hands full already.'

'So she's a stay-at-home mom? I didn't know there were any left.'

'They're not extinct yet.'

Genevieve was caught in a trap of her own making. With three kids, and Mark away so much, it would be a nightmare for her to work outside the home. But once upon a time, she'd been crazy ambitious. She had qualified as a high school teacher, although everyone joked that she would be running the entire Department of Education before long. But then after their dad died she was in such a hurry to start a family that she didn't wait to be appointed to a permanent position before she fell pregnant with Gabriel. Madeleine assumed she had probably dropped off the eligibility list altogether by now. At home with a baby, and planning another one, Genevieve had pushed Mark to seize every opportunity and apply for promotions, even though they both knew this would mean he would be around less, especially when he became manager of Asia Pacific operations. His predecessor had actually based himself in Singapore, but Genevieve wouldn't even consider relocating, so it was hardly surprising that Mark was never home; he was barely ever in the country. Madeleine sometimes wondered if that's the way Genevieve wanted it. Though she carped and complained about being a virtual sole parent, when Mark was home she carped and complained even louder. They weren't an easy couple to be around, and Madeleine couldn't really blame Henry for his reluctance to spend time with them.

She just wished he had known her family while her dad was still alive. They were all so different then. He brought out the best in them, he brought out the best in everyone who had anything to do with him. Genevieve had become so brittle over the years, but she hadn't always been that way. Maybe she'd been a little bossy – that came with being the eldest child – but she was also caring and fiercely protective of her little sister. Madeleine didn't know how to define their relationship now. Sometimes Genevieve seemed disdainful of her, at other times she seemed envious. A lot of the time it was both at once, which was confusing, frankly.

The rumba started playing loudly from her handbag, and Aiden shot her an amused look. She fumbled inside her bag for her phone, quickly pressing answer to stop the interminable ringtone before she'd even checked who it was, though she expected it would be Henry.

'Where are you?' Genevieve demanded as soon as Madeleine put the phone to her ear.

'We're almost there,' she said, wincing at the volume of her sister's voice. 'The traffic's been crazy.'

Genevieve responded with a dubious-sounding grunt. 'Well, your fiancé managed to make it on time, and he had to come three, no, *four* times further.'

'Is Henry all right?' Madeleine asked.

'What do you mean? Of course he's all right. He's not a child.'

She would have liked to speak to him, but trying to gauge his mood over the phone with Genevieve around was unlikely to achieve anything but make Madeleine more uneasy. She couldn't imagine how they were filling in the time, what they were talking about. She hoped Henry wasn't going to be too annoyed with her by the time they got there.

'Okay, tell him we'll see him soon.' Madeleine hung up and looked at Aiden. 'We're in trouble.'

'I won't be in trouble,' said Aiden. 'I'm the guest.'

That was true. Aiden's presence was likely to change the dynamic considerably today, and that could only be a good thing.

Strathfield

They eventually pulled up at the house about half an hour late. As Aiden stepped out of the taxi he gave a low whistle. 'Nice place,' he said.

To say the least. A grand Federation pile, meticulously restored, set in an exquisite garden in one of the best streets in Strathfield, it was indeed a very 'nice' place. If she couldn't have daughters and a doting husband, then Genevieve went for the next best thing – conspicuous wealth and the envy of others.

Pressing the doorbell summoned what sounded like a charge for the door; it wasn't so much the patter of tiny feet as the thunder of heavy footsteps on the polished floorboards of the hall, the two older boys squabbling, the baby crying, and finally Genevieve's voice booming over the top of it all, 'Stop right there!'

There was a pause while muffled voices carried out tense negotiations on the other side of the door. At last it opened and Genevieve stood looking harassed, flanked by Gabe and Declan. She had one hand firmly on Gabe's shoulder – perhaps more correctly the scruff of his neck – as she held the door back with the other. Declan had tucked himself under her arm, his face half-buried. 'Everything has to be a competition!' she said, pink-faced. 'Even who gets to open the door.'

'Sounds pretty normal to me,' said Aiden.

It was cool and dark inside the hall, so Genevieve wouldn't have been able to make out their faces clearly when she first opened the door and her eyes hadn't yet adjusted to the bright spring sunshine outside. Now she turned her head towards the deep voice, and blinked rapidly. Madeleine observed the transformation. Genevieve quickly released Gabe, coyly smoothing her hair back from her face, the colour deepening in her cheeks.

'You must be Aiden,' she said, sounding like a teenage girl. For the record, Genevieve had never sounded like a teenage girl, even when she was one.

'But you can't be Genevieve,' Aiden was saying, taking a step towards her. 'I was told she's the older sister.'

Oh brother. Genevieve would never swallow a line like that.

But it looked like she was, along with the hook and the sinker. In fact, she was giggling. Her sister was giggling!

'Oh, stop,' she said. 'There's only a couple of years between us, it barely counts at our age.'

Madeleine was about to say, 'Speak for yourself,' but Genevieve hadn't seemed to register she was even there.

'It's so nice to meet you, Aiden,' she purred, extending her hand. 'Welcome to my home.'

Aiden took her hand. 'Aren't we family now?' he chided, drawing her into a hug. It didn't quite qualify as one of his signature hugs; Madeleine supposed he had to be careful not to squash Declan, who was still clinging to his mother like a barnacle to a boat.

'Hi, Gen,' Madeleine said finally, to announce herself. 'Hello, Gabe.'

'Gabriel, kiss your aunty,' said Genevieve, her voice undulating weirdly. Madeleine suspected it had started out as an order, but remembering Aiden was right there she'd quickly modified her tone to something sweeter.

Gabe kind of slouched towards her; Madeleine did the hugging and the kissing, he was just the receptor.

'And Deccy, how are you, mate?' she said. He ducked around behind his mother and Gabe, probably to avoid Aiden, and then clung on to Madeleine as if to dear life. She ruffled his hair.

'Now say hello to Uncle Aiden,' Genevieve said in a voice now resembling a fairy godmother in an old Disney animation.

'They don't have to call me uncle,' he said. 'Unless that's a respect thing you'd prefer,' he added quickly.

'Oh no, whatever *you'd* prefer, Aiden.'

'It's your home, your rules . . .'

Madeleine was going to need a bucket soon. She stepped forward and planted a kiss on her sister's cheek. 'I'm going to find Henry.'

Scooping Declan up into her arms, she carried him on her hip down the long hallway and out into the massive family room at the back. The house had been sympathetically renovated by the previous owners. They hadn't gone with the postmodern trend of sticking a big box – however artfully – up against the old structure, but instead had simply opened up what was there, reproducing the same features and details, and echoing the elegant proportions of the existing rooms. It really was a lovely old house, and Genevieve had done an amazing job decorating it so that it was comfortable for adults without being too precious for the kids.

Henry was over in the kitchen when she entered. He was standing at the island bench, occupied with some kind of food preparation, Madeleine assumed. He looked up but didn't say anything, just gave her a nod. Yikes. He wasn't happy. And making up was going to be nigh impossible today with everyone around. So she just said, 'Hi.'

'Hello, Maddie, darling. You made it.' Her mother went to get up off the sofa, but Archie was blocking her, busy piling toys onto her lap.

'Don't get up, Mum,' Madeleine said, as she deposited Declan back onto his feet. He immediately scrambled up onto the sofa and snuggled into his nan. Madeleine bent to kiss her on the cheek and then crouched down to Archie's height. 'Hello, gorgeous boy!' she said, giving him a gentle poke in the tummy. 'Look at you, getting bigger all the time!'

He turned a very snotty, tear-streaked face towards her, showing the remnants of the crying bout they'd heard through the door, but he seemed contented enough now. He gave Madeleine a big cheesy grin and leaned towards her as though to kiss her.

'Hold on, you don't want to smear that face all over Aunty Maddie,' said Margaret, wiping his cheeks and nose with the magical appearing tissue mothers always seemed to have at the ready.

'Arn Maddie!' he exclaimed, throwing his arms around her neck.

Madeleine hugged him tight; at least the youngest males of the family were pleased to see her. Archie was a sunny-natured little charmer – how could Genevieve have wanted anyone but him? She looked over his shoulder at her mother. 'How are you, Mum?'

'Oh, not too bad. My back's playing up again. Why, hello there.'

Madeleine turned. The star had entered the room, and even her mother was bedazzled.

'Mum, this is Aiden Carmichael,' she said. 'He's going to be Henry's best man at the wedding.'

Aiden walked over to join them. 'Please don't get up,' he said to Margaret, then, 'May I?', indicating the sofa next to her.

'Of course, please, take a seat.' Was her mother blushing? Not her too.

Aiden sat down, taking her hand in his. 'Mrs Pepper, it's such a pleasure to meet you.'

'You can't be calling me Mrs Pepper, you'll make me feel old. I'm Margaret.'

'And who is this little man?' he said, as Archie toddled over and grasped onto his knees. As natural as you please, Aiden scooped him up onto his lap. And Archie didn't protest a jot.

The Aiden factor clearly worked across all demographics. They would all be occupied for a while, basking in the warm glow of their mutual admiration session, so Madeleine pulled herself up and meandered over to the kitchen to face Henry.

'What are you doing?' she asked, leaning over the bench to see for herself. He was peeling prawns. Her sister had given him the worst job. 'Do you want some help?'

He shook his head. 'No point in us both stinking of prawns. I just want to keep going until I finish and I can wash my hands.'

'Genevieve's been keeping you busy, then?' said Madeleine, walking around the bench to join him on the other side.

'I had to do something.'

She sighed. 'I'm sorry we were late.'

He nodded, intent on pulling the head off a prawn. Madeleine came right up beside him. 'Don't I even get a kiss hello?' she said in a low voice. There was a burst of feminine laughter from across the room. 'No one's paying any attention to us.'

He gave her a glance that was somewhere between awkward and irritated, she suspected. Quite possibly Henry didn't even know what he was feeling, so she had to build the bridge.

'I missed you.' She reached up on tiptoes and pressed her lips against his cheek, holding them there until he gave her something. He finally paused, resting his hands on the edge of the bowl and leaning into her. Madeleine put her head on his shoulder and drew her arms through the crook of his elbow.

'Did you have a good time last night?' he asked eventually.

'It was nothing special,' she said. 'You didn't miss anything.'

He turned his head to look at her properly. Madeleine saw his eyes had softened as he opened his mouth to speak, 'I was just –'

'So, Darrow, what's cooking over there?' Aiden called loudly from the sofa.

Madeleine felt Henry stiffen immediately, and she released his arm, stepping back. 'I'm just the unskilled labourer,' he said. 'Genevieve's the chef.'

'All right,' Aiden said, turning to her. 'How can I help?'

'No way, you're the guest of honour,' she insisted.

'You have to let me do something. What if I pour the drinks?'

'Drinks!' Genevieve exclaimed, holding her hands to her face. 'I'm so sorry, Mark usually takes care of the drinks.'

Though Mark usually wasn't here.

'Then that'll be my job today,' Aiden said, getting to his feet. 'Now, I know Madeleine's having a beer, what are you two ladies drinking?'

'You're having a beer?' Henry frowned, glancing at her.

Before she could speak, Aiden answered for her. 'A little hair of the dog, old man. Your betrothed had a big night last night.'

Madeleine drew her breath in sharply, turning her face away from Henry and glaring at Aiden. What the hell?

'It was all my fault,' he said quickly. 'I'm afraid I led her astray.'

Was that supposed to make it better? Now everyone was looking uneasy.

Aiden took a breath. 'What I'm saying is, we only had a few drinks,' he said. 'Poor thing's obviously not used to it, so she was feeling a little worse for wear this morning. I suggested that a beer might help. So what's everyone else having?' he finished, clapping his hands together.

*

Lunch was a convivial affair. Genevieve always put on a good spread – she had the hostess thing down pat, and she never did anything by halves. So even for a Saturday lunch with the family she had arranged an extravagant centrepiece of fruits and flowers, and each linen napkin was tied with a twist of the same flowers, like a corsage. The food itself was fit for a restaurant. It was, as Genevieve put it, 'only' salads and cold meat, but she was also a fabulous cook, so the 'salads' weren't your standard tomato and lettuce variety, and the 'cold meats' hadn't come from the deli at Woolies that morning, but had been marinated and roasted in her own kitchen the day before, then carved and presented on platters as though they were going to be photographed for a magazine shoot. Her attention to detail was frankly exhausting.

Madeleine was glad to see that her sister had mellowed nicely after a while, with the help of a couple of glasses of wine and the fact that little Archie had obliged by going down for his nap without a fuss, just before they sat down to eat. After the older boys were fed, they happily retired to the far end of the house to watch a movie. Madeleine herself hadn't indulged in more than that one beer. It might have helped a little, but the thought of wine turned her stomach.

'So you grew up on Long Island, Aiden?' Genevieve was saying. 'In the movies it always seems like such a glamorous place.'

Aiden smiled. 'Everything seems more glamorous in the movies, but really it's just regular suburbs. When you get up to the Hamptons, that's where things get fancy. Henry has a place up that way.'

But no one was much interested in Henry – he was old news, which was just the way he liked it. He'd remained stilted during lunch, and hadn't so much as touched her – not that he was ever very demonstrative, particularly in front of her family. If Henry's arm brushed up against hers and he let it linger, it was almost the same as someone else making out in public. She wished he would just relax. No wonder Genevieve thought he was a stick in the mud.

She certainly wouldn't be thinking that about Aiden. He continued to hold the floor throughout the meal while Genevieve conducted an in-depth, *60 Minutes*–style celebrity interview. They learnt that Aiden had an older brother (Owen) and a younger sister (Abigail). That his father (Sheldon) was an investment banker, but his mother (Cindy) was a former schoolteacher, so that kept her husband honest. Cue laughter. Aiden skirted around it, but Madeleine knew he came from money, Henry had told her that much. After Henry's mother died, he was invited to the Carmichaels' house for Thanksgiving, and he said he'd never seen anything like it. It was an estate, not a house. Aiden did not live in 'just the regular suburbs'.

They also learnt that on graduation, Aiden didn't follow his brother into the family business, but according to him no one was really too bothered. 'Lucky for me, my brother was your garden-variety eldest child, he got all the ambition and sense of responsibility,' he told them. 'And my sister – well, what can I say, she was the baby and the only girl.'

He'd demonstrated some aptitude with computers and technology, so his father took advantage of connections and secured him an internship with one of the big tech companies in Silicon Valley. It was during the boom years, so Aiden stayed on, but he eventually grew bored with the work. He was more of a people person, an observation Genevieve and Margaret enthusiastically seconded, despite only knowing him for about five minutes.

'I just hated being cooped up in an office all day,' said Aiden. 'Then a chance came up to represent the company as part of a delegation to Africa. They were investigating ways to bring the wonders of the internet to the poorest communities. It changed my life. I realised there were bigger issues to work on than the next new operating system. Fortunately for me, my employer was keen to be part of the brave new world of venture philanthropy.'

'You're kidding – is that what they're calling it?' Genevieve asked.

Aiden nodded. 'I've also heard "philanthrocapitalism" bandied about.' He grinned.

'That's not a word,' Madeleine scoffed.

'But it is a PR opportunity,' said Aiden. 'This was all before the crash. A lot of these corporations were swimming in money, and people were starting to feel uneasy about it. To be fair, even some of the head honchos were. Bill Gates – or maybe I should say his wife – was setting a pretty impressive precedent. So no corporate entity wanted to be seen as a greedy holdout. As fast as I could put together proposals, projects were greenlighted, and before long it became a full-time job.'

'I think it's a little more than a full-time job,' said Madeleine, drawing on her Google research. 'You head up their entire global benevolent fund.'

Aiden shook his head. 'Ha, there's a CFO behind a desk somewhere at headquarters making all the important decisions and moving the money around,' he said. 'I just do the legwork, on the ground, and get a fancy title.'

'I'm sure you're being modest,' said Genevieve.

'I assure you I'm not.'

'So what do you love most about what you do?' said Margaret, who had seemed mesmerised throughout.

Aiden hesitated only a moment. 'I guess it's being in the position to make a difference. I mean, doesn't everyone want that?'

Madeleine was intrigued. He was giving no hint of the disillusionment or frustration he'd expressed more than once to her. She thought that maybe he was so used to keeping up a confident mask for the sake of the cause that he could rarely let his guard down the way he had with her. After all, if the people out there 'on the ground', as he put it, stopped believing in what they were doing, how could they ever keep the world at large interested and reaching into its collective pocket? It was spin, but if you were going to be a spin doctor, it might as well be for a worthy cause.

'You know what I don't get?' Genevieve said, looking at Aiden.

'What's that?'

'How a man like you is still single. You must have had women throwing themselves at you all your life.'

'Not so much,' he said with a modest shrug.

'I don't believe it.'

'Well, maybe I just haven't met the right girl.'

Genevieve lifted an eyebrow. 'What, never?'

Aiden paused for a beat. 'There was one girl,' he said with a sly look in Henry and Madeleine's direction. No, was he really going to make up a story like he did the first night? After telling her it was just a line to get sympathy, and even get him laid?

'Go on.' Genevieve propped her chin in her hand and leant towards him, intent.

Aiden drew a deep breath. 'I met her at college . . .'

Henry shifted uncomfortably in his seat. He must have heard Aiden's stories countless times. This was clearly a variation on the theme.

'She was sweet, and very smart,' Aiden went on. 'I really thought she might be the one.'

'So what happened?' Genevieve asked.

'We were in our senior year, both looking at our options after graduation,' he said. 'Everything we wanted to do was going to take us in different directions. We had the talk, you know, the one about sustaining a long-distance relationship, and we decided that we could make it work – we could talk on the phone, spend the holidays together . . . So she went east and I headed west. She was the one who drifted first.'

'She was obviously a fool,' Genevieve declared.

Henry stood up abruptly, his chair scraping loudly on the polished floor. 'Would anyone like coffee?' he said, turning towards the kitchen.

'I'll help,' Madeleine said, jumping up and following him. He was already at the sink, filling the reservoir for the coffee machine, his back to her. She had an impulse to press herself into his back and wrap her arms tightly around him, to breathe him in. She felt so disconnected from him lately. They really needed to have sex tonight, whether Aiden was in the house or not. She wasn't going to let Henry put her off again.

She suddenly had a flashback to what Aiden had told her this morning, that she had invited him – or rather, tried to pressure him – to share her bed. He'd assured her it was completely innocent, but Madeleine had to wonder if she'd been craving Henry then too, and that in her state any warm body would have done. She really shouldn't drink so much.

'What?' Henry stood holding the full reservoir, looking expectantly at her.

'I'm sorry?' she said blankly.

'You were just standing there staring at me.'

She smiled. 'I guess I can't help myself.'

He looked faintly embarrassed. 'Well, you're in the way.'

'Oh.' She realised she was leaning against the bench, blocking the coffee maker. 'Sorry.' She moved away to fetch cups while Henry set up the machine. 'Is everything all right?' she asked carefully, lining up the cups along the bench.

Henry glanced at her. 'Why wouldn't it be?'

'Just asking,' she said. 'I haven't seen you. It's weird being away from you overnight, and then not being able to catch up properly.'

'Whose fault is that?'

That stung. 'It's no one's fault, Henry,' she said. 'You were okay with it last night.' When he wanted to work.

The boys suddenly burst into the room, full-flight and mid-altercation. Declan was wailing at some injustice inflicted by Gabe, but in his heightened distress he couldn't make himself understood. Meanwhile, Gabe proceeded to defend his actions, presenting his case like a seasoned lawyer. Poor Dec was always at the mercy of his older, more articulate brother. It was another reason Madeleine had a soft spot for him: she could remember Genevieve lording it over her in exactly the same way. The curse of the second-born.

'Keep your voices down!' Genevieve hissed. 'If you wake Archie, so help me . . .'

'Okay, boys,' Aiden said, standing up, 'outside.'

Inexplicably, they stopped dead, staring up at him. Declan released a tremulous sigh, his eyes glued to Aiden, as he watched him walk across to the French doors that led out to the garden.

'Come on, then,' Aiden said, beckoning to them. He opened the doors and both boys trailed him outside without a peep.

'It's like he's the Pied Piper or something,' Genevieve said breathlessly.

Madeleine carried two cups to the table. 'Who's having coffee?'

'Not for me,' said Genevieve, picking up her wine glass and craning her head to see what they were doing outside. 'Do you think I should go out there with them?'

'Definitely not,' said Madeleine. 'He works with kids overseas. You can trust him.'

'Of course I trust him,' Genevieve said. 'The man's a saint.'

There was a sudden loud noise from the kitchen. Madeleine looked across to see Henry banging the filter basket against the sink to empty it.

'Coffee, Mum?' she said.

'Thank you, Maddie,' said Margaret, taking one of the cups. 'I'll just have this, and then I'll be on my way. I don't like driving at night.'

'Mum,' Genevieve sighed, 'it won't be dark for another couple of hours.'

'Dusk is worse,' Margaret said, stirring her coffee. 'Late in the afternoon the light is terrible. The sun is so low driving up Park Road I can barely see three foot in front of me.'

'That doesn't sound very safe,' said Madeleine, concerned.

'No, it doesn't.' Genevieve's tone was less sympathetic than her sister's. 'What age do they start mandatory retesting for driver's licences?'

Margaret tsked. 'It's not my driving,' she protested. 'I can't help where the sun sets.'

'You should be able to drive in all conditions, Mum,' said Genevieve.

'And I can,' Margaret said.

'When do they start retesting?' Genevieve repeated. 'Just out of interest.'

'Genevieve!' Madeleine frowned at her.

'I believe it's not until you reach your eighties,' Henry said, joining them at the table with his coffee. 'So you've got nearly twenty years, right, Margaret?'

'Thank you, Henry.'

'And it sounds to me like you're making sensible decisions anyway.'

Madeleine caught Genevieve rolling her eyes, but Margaret was nodding. 'Well, basically, I like to get home while it's still light.'

'That's a sensible decision right there,' said Henry. 'We have a long drive, Madeleine, we should think about leaving soon as well.'

'Sure.'

Madeleine and Henry were clearing the table a few minutes later when Aiden opened the French doors and the boys trooped back in, all smiles, their faces flushed.

Genevieve was coming down the hall, carrying Archie on her hip. 'Well, you all look pleased with yourselves,' she remarked.

'We had a rumble,' said Declan, giggling.

'Rumble in the jungle!' Gabe cried, raising his fist.

'I hope you said thank you to Uncle Aiden.'

'Thank you, Uncle Aiden!' they chorused.

Aiden was wiping his feet on the mat outside the door. 'My pleasure, boys. It was fun.'

'You better go get ready for your baths, then,' said Genevieve.

They scampered off together without protest, Gabe even flinging a big-brotherly arm around Declan as they went. Genevieve watched them with a look of mild astonishment. 'What kind of spell did you put on them? And can I have it bottled, please?'

Aiden grinned, coming into the room. 'They just had to blow off some steam. Boys need a little roughhousing sometimes. As long as there's adult supervision, it's good for them.'

'Mm, an adult, like a father?' Genevieve said tightly. 'You see, this is what I keep telling Mark. They're boys, they need a male role model around, they need to do boy things. I'm not being sexist, but –'

'I don't think it's sexist,' said Aiden. He was washing his hands at the kitchen sink. 'There are differences between the genders, and we're all the better for it – I say *vive la différence*. It's only sexist when you make out one sex is superior to the other.'

Genevieve nodded thoughtfully. 'That's a very good point,' she said. 'Oh, can I get you anything?' she asked. 'You missed out on coffee.'

'I'll just have a drink of water, thanks,' he said, filling a glass from the tap.

'And I'll say my goodbyes now,' said Margaret as she picked up her handbag and jacket.

'We were going to get moving too, Aiden,' said Henry. 'Oh, that's right, we have two cars, don't we?'

Aiden and Madeleine exchanged a glance.

'What?' said Henry.

'I'll see you out, Margaret,' Aiden said, stepping forward and holding out his arm for her. Coward, Madeleine thought, leaving her to face Henry alone. Genevieve followed the pair up the hall, calling to the boys to come and say goodbye to Nanna. Madeleine turned away to find her handbag, still scrambling to come up with an excuse to explain why they didn't have two cars here at all. There was no way around it, she finally decided, she would have to confess that she had drunk too much last night to drive. Well, she rationalised, it didn't take that much to be over the limit, better safe than sorry.

She picked up her handbag from where she'd left it by the sofa and turned around to face Henry again. 'Actually, I don't have my car here,' she said.

'You don't?'

'I couldn't drive –'

'Are you telling me you were so drunk that you were still over the limit this morning?'

'Oh no . . .' Madeleine was about to blab that the car was at the office garage, when she remembered that she'd supposedly picked Aiden up from the airport . . . Why would her car still be parked at work? Bugger. 'Of course I wasn't over the limit, Henry, but I felt a little green. It really hit me hard, I can't hold my liquor anymore,' she added with a nervous laugh. Henry remained stony-faced. 'Anyway, Aiden just took over, had me out the door and was hailing a taxi before I knew what was what.'

'Yes,' Henry muttered, 'he can be like that.'

Genevieve and Aiden came back down the hall, arm in arm, sharing some private joke and having a great old laugh. Genevieve was positively enamoured of the man. 'So, would you like a coffee now?' she asked him. 'Or one for the road?'

'We have to go,' Henry said bluntly. 'We have to call by the apartment to pick up Madeleine's car.'

Madeleine exchanged another glance with Aiden. 'Oh no, it doesn't matter, Henry,' she said. 'There's no need to drive two cars home. I'm not going to need it tomorrow.'

'But you'll need it for work on Monday.'

'I'll take the bus.'

'You hate taking the bus.'

'No I don't.'

'You do, you're always complaining.'

'I don't complain,' she returned. 'I don't *love* it, but I do it when I have to. Like I did the other day, so we'd only have one car to drive to the airport, remember?'

'Whatever,' he almost snapped. 'Can we just go?'

'My, my, tempers are getting frayed,' Genevieve remarked.

Madeleine felt her stomach clench. That would just piss Henry off more – the last thing he needed was Genevieve judging him.

'Never mind,' Genevieve went on, 'I'm sure it's just a little dose of pre-wedding jitters. Which reminds me, Mad . . .' She walked over to open the pantry door. 'Can I check that you've marked the cake tasting in your calendar?'

'I'm sure I did.'

'Is it going to kill you to check? You've bailed on me before, don't forget, because I certainly haven't.' Genevieve ran her finger down the calendar hanging inside the pantry door. 'It's the twenty-sixth, that's Monday week, at ten, gives me plenty of time to get the boys to school and drop Archie off at the sitter's.'

Madeleine was frowning at her phone. There was nothing recorded on that day in her calendar.

'You didn't write it down, did you.' Genevieve sighed like a disappointed parent. 'Hopeless.'

'I did write it down, I know I did – I must have done it at work,' said Madeleine, scrolling through the dates. 'I've got my dress fitting next week, that's here.'

'Who's going to be with you for that?' asked Genevieve.

Madeleine shrugged. 'The dressmaker.'

'You really should take someone with you. It's the final fitting, isn't it?'

That sounded so ominous, like the final countdown, the last supper, the end of the world as we know it . . .

'What day is it, Mad?' Genevieve persisted.

'Wednesday, in my lunch hour.'

Genevieve was shaking her head. 'There's no way I can call in any more favours for babysitting right now.'

'Honestly, it's fine, Gen.' Madeleine was quite touched by her interest. Or perhaps she was just trying to impress Aiden. 'Thanks, but my dressmaker's really great, I'm not worried.'

'Maybe you can take your friend from work . . . Olivia?'

'Liv? I don't know, I could ask –'

Henry cleared his throat, loudly.

'We should go,' said Madeleine, taking the hint.

'Well, good luck with the fitting.' Genevieve took her by the arm as they started up the hall. 'The main thing you have to check is that you can actually move freely, and above all that you can sit down without strangulating a hernia or something.'

'Right.'

'And that includes going to the toilet without having to take the whole dress off.'

'Okay, you've made your point.'

They paused at the front door. 'And I hope you haven't gone all puritanical on us, that you've got some cleavage showing.'

'*Gen!*'

'What?' Genevieve said undeterred. 'Jeez, Mad, if you're not going to look sexy on your wedding day, what's the point? Everyone knows what you're going to get up to that night. The reception is basically foreplay, in public, with dancing and a cake.'

Madeleine had seen Henry look mortified before, but that little spiel took it to a whole new level. 'I'm speechless,' she said on his behalf, 'and we're going.' She kissed her sister on the cheek and stepped outside ahead of Henry and Aiden.

'So I suppose I'll see you at the wedding, partner,' Genevieve said to Aiden.

'If not before. We can have a wedding-party party.'

'But we're the only two in the wedding party, apart from the bride and groom.'

'Then it'll be a very exclusive party.'

Madeleine could hear Genevieve's girlish giggle from here. She still couldn't get over her sister giggling.

'Oh, Mad?' Genevieve called after them. 'Did you take my advice about your bridal underwear?'

'For godsakes, Genevieve,' Madeleine hissed, turning around to glare at her.

'I just wanted to know if you bought the duplicate –'

'I'm not going to discuss my underwear with you! Goodbye.' Madeleine shut the gate behind her with a clang.

*

The traffic heading back towards the city was lighter at this time of day. They drove in total silence. Total. Awkward. Silence.

'It was great to meet your family, Maddie,' Aiden said from the back seat, finally lifting the embargo. 'They're lovely people.'

'Thanks.'

'Genevieve's a character.'

Henry grunted. Madeleine glanced across at him. 'Are you all right?' she asked.

'I'm just tired.'

'You shouldn't work so late.'

'I have a deadline,' he said curtly. 'What difference did it make to you, anyway?'

Ouch. They lapsed into silence again, it was better that way.

'You know what, guys?' Aiden said after a while. 'I just realised, I left all my stuff at your apartment, Maddie.'

Madeleine turned around. 'What stuff?'

'My bags from the trip. I left some of my clothes back at the house, but there's my shave kit, and –'

'We have anything like that you might need,' said Henry.

'I was about to add,' said Aiden, 'that, most importantly, I left my laptop and all the paperwork from the trip. I'll need it all before my meetings next week.'

'Madeleine could bring it home for you on Monday, couldn't she?' said Henry. 'It's just if we go via the apartment now, we'll have to go all the way across town.'

'Henry,' Madeleine chided.

'Look, why don't you just drop me off somewhere,' said Aiden. 'I can catch a taxi to the apartment, easy.'

'But then how will you get up to our place?' said Madeleine.

'Well, I'm thinking, if you don't mind, that I might stay at the apartment.'

Great, they'd scared him off.

'I have to be in the city next week,' he said, 'and I have to review the submissions before that, so I'll need everything before Monday night. I'll take the opportunity to catch up with some people, it'll be fine.'

'You know people in Sydney?' said Madeleine.

'Some of the aid workers I met in Vietnam last year were Australian. They're usually in high rotation, so there's sure to be someone home on leave.'

'Do you know how to find them?'

'We keep in touch,' he said. 'Facebook mostly, you know. So, Henry, just drop me wherever's convenient. As long as you give me the address of the apartment, I'll find my way.'

'No,' Madeleine said firmly, looking at Henry, 'of course we'll drive you to the apartment.'

Henry glanced at her, frowning. Then he shrugged. 'At least you can pick up your car.'

Damn and bother, there was no way out of this. She was just going to have to hoof it into the city to get her car from work, and that was the last thing she felt like doing right now. Blasted tangled web.

When they arrived at the apartment building, Henry pulled over to the kerb but kept the motor running.

'See you later, Darrow,' Aiden said as he jumped out of the car. He walked off briskly towards the entrance, keeping his back to them, being discreet. Or perhaps getting out of the firing line.

'I won't be far behind you,' Madeleine said to Henry. He just nodded, staring ahead through the windscreen. She leaned over and kissed him on the cheek, then stepped out of the car. He drove off the moment she closed the door behind her.

'So I guess you have to go and get your car now?' Aiden asked when she joined him at the entrance to the foyer.

She nodded. 'What a hassle.'

'Do you want me to come with you?'

'No, it's all right, but thanks. I'll let you into the apartment. There's some spare keys inside you can keep on you, that way you can come and go as you please.'

She swiped them into the building, and then again into the elevator, and when the doors slid closed, Aiden turned to her. 'So what was up with Henry?'

'He's pissed off, obviously.'

'About you staying out last night?'

'I don't know,' she said. 'He didn't seem to mind yesterday. I don't think it helped that you blabbed about me having a drink, or rather, how did you put it – "a big night"?'

'Sorry,' he winced, smacking his hand to his forehead. 'It just came out. I wasn't thinking. I forgot you wanted to keep it a secret.'

Madeleine cringed. She really wished he wouldn't put it like that. But then, that's what she'd led him to think. 'It's only because Henry's too sensitive about it. And now I know why.'

The doors slid open and they stepped out and started up the hall.

'Are you going to tell him that I told you?' asked Aiden.

'I don't know . . .'

'It's okay with me,' he assured her.

Madeleine looked at him. 'I really don't know. I'll just have to see if the moment presents itself.'

'Then I'm glad I'll be out of your way.'

They came to the door of the apartment and Madeleine smiled at him as she pushed the key into the lock. 'That's why you made up that story to get out of coming back with us, isn't it?'

'I really did leave my stuff here,' he said. 'But it also seemed like you guys needed some time alone.'

'You're probably right.'

She opened the door and he followed her inside. Madeleine found the spare keys and security card for the building, and handed them to Aiden. 'I don't think there are any tricks to the place you should know about,' she said, glancing around.

'Everything seemed pretty straightforward this morning.'

'Oh, and please use the bed, you don't have to sleep on the sofa.'

'Are you sure?'

'Of course,' she said. 'Though you might want to change the sheets, I was a bit manky last night. Linen's on the top shelf of the wardrobe.'

Aiden nodded.

'And the shower door sticks a little . . .' Madeleine saw the bemused look on his face. 'And now I'm just stalling. I'm sure you'll figure it out.'

'I'm sure I will.'

She took a deep breath. 'I'd best begin my journey, 'tis many miles to Mordor.'

'I think we may have taken that nickname too far,' said Aiden. 'Henry's not exactly a dark lord waiting up there for you.'

'I know. He's a pussycat most of the time, if a slightly repressed one.' She sighed. 'I just wish I hadn't lied to him.'

'I wouldn't make too big a deal of it, they were pretty inconsequential lies.'

'Not so inconsequential: I have to go out of my way now to pick up the car, remember.'

'So you only hurt yourself,' he said. 'I never get why lying is made out to be the greatest sin of all, especially in relationships. Most lies are about sparing somebody's feelings, or not making matters worse.'

'I've never thought about it like that.'

'The truth and nothing but the truth is for catching out criminals. The rest of us are just trying not to hurt anyone.' He paused. 'Now give me a hug and get out of here.'

She stepped into his open arms. He wasn't so exuberant this time, but rather warm and reassuring. It was quite remarkable how close they'd become in such a short time.

Aiden drew back to look at her. 'Go home and clear the air with Henry. Everything will be fine, trust me. Like Genevieve said, this is probably just pre-wedding jitters.'

She hoped they were both right.

Pittwaters

What with hailing a taxi and the detour to work, it was another half hour before Madeleine was on her way across the bridge. The drive home on her own was long and boring, as usual. She was tired, but she certainly wasn't in any danger of nodding off. She was too on edge; her mind was racing, still trying to process all this new information about Henry. She probably should tell him what she knew, even though it would be confronting for him. But she was going to be his wife, she should have known all this already, and he should have been the one to tell her. It was very odd that he'd kept it from her, even a little upsetting. One thing Madeleine knew for sure, Henry had to get her drinking into perspective. It was beginning to become very clear that it was his issue, not hers.

Finally she pulled into the garage, changed into her Crocs and negotiated the stairs in the rapidly fading light. When she let herself in through the front door, the house was eerily quiet. Henry's car was in the garage, so she knew he'd made it home. She called his name as she wandered through the main living area, then checked their bedroom and bathroom. There was only one other place he could be.

She walked over to the stairs that led to the lower level and his study, and saw the glow of a light from under the door. 'Henry?' she called loudly.

'Down here,' came the muffled reply.

Madeleine started down the stairs. If the first thing he did was come down here to work, she was going to be very pissed off. When she opened the door of the study he was leaning over his drawing board, his back to her.

'You're working?' She said it like it was an accusation, because it was.

'Just until you got home,' he said, dropping his pencil and swivelling around on his stool.

'I said I'd be right behind you.'

He glanced at his watch. 'Well, you couldn't have been *right* behind me.'

She ignored that. 'How can you just switch off and go back to work? I'm not going to put up with you being stuck down here for another night. If you would have downed tools for Aiden, you can do it for me.'

'I *am* doing this for you – for us.'

'What, for this honeymoon I keep hearing about? It better be bloody worth it.'

He looked upset by that, but so? She was upset too, and she had a right to say it.

'We have to talk, Henry,' she said in a firm voice.

'I realise.'

She folded her arms. 'Why were you in such a bad mood today?'

'I wasn't –'

'Were you angry that I stayed out last night?'

'I wasn't angry.'

'Well, you sure did a good impression of being angry.'

'I wasn't angry, I was worried.'

'What?' Madeleine frowned. 'Why would you be worried?'

'When I spoke to you last night it was fine, it really was fine.' He stood up and crossed to the window. 'But then this morning your phone wasn't picking up, and then you were late. I was worried. Okay?'

It was unusual for her not to keep her phone charged, so she supposed she could understand that being somewhat unsettling. 'But you spoke to Aiden.'

'Yeah, several times, and you were never "available". I didn't know what was going on.'

'I think I was asleep first, then in the shower. This is crazy, Henry, there was no need to be worried.'

'I can't help it,' he said. 'I worry about you, okay? I always worry about you when you stay in town. I wanted to hear your voice so I knew you were all right. That's all.'

Madeleine was torn between feeling touched that he cared and suspicious that he didn't trust her. The latter was winning. 'I think the truth is that you don't trust me,' she said. 'What could you be worried about? I was with Aiden, I was perfectly safe.'

'I know you were safe. That's not what I meant.'

'Then what do you mean? Nothing happened.'

He turned his head sharply to look at her. 'Why would you even say that, Madeleine?'

She felt a pang of guilt. Aiden had been perfectly well behaved, but she couldn't necessarily say the same for herself. It still bothered her that she had drunkenly tried to force him to share her bed; the mental image that conjured up made her cringe – she imagined herself all slobbery and grasping. Ugh. Aiden had said she was sweet, but she found that hard to believe. And even if her motivation was completely innocent, it would have been a compromising situation, to say the least. Just as well Aiden had the good sense to steer clear.

'Exactly,' said Madeleine. 'I shouldn't have to say it.'

'No, you shouldn't.'

'So it's the drinking, isn't it?'

Henry didn't respond, he just stared out the window again.

'That's what this is about, that's why you don't want me to keep the flat – you don't trust me out of your sight,' she accused him. 'Well, you need to get over it, Henry. I didn't ask you to be my keeper.'

He turned to look directly at her. 'Didn't you?'

Madeleine's stomach lurched. 'You're going to go there? So much for forgiveness, eh?'

'I forgave you, you know I did.'

'Certainly doesn't sound like it.'

'Fine.' Now he was angry. 'Newsflash, Madeleine, I don't want to be your keeper either.' He walked right past her out of the room.

'Where are you going?'

He didn't answer so Madeleine hurried out the door to catch up to him. When she came up the stairs he was in the kitchen, taking a bottle of wine out of the rack above the fridge. He slammed it down on the bench, grabbed a glass from the cupboard and filled it. 'Go ahead,' he said, sliding it towards her. 'Drink it, if that's what you want. I don't care.'

'I don't want it,' she cried.

'Fine, I'll have it then.' He picked up the glass. 'I need a drink right now.'

'But I don't. I don't need it, Henry, I'm not an alcoholic. I'm not like your father.'

He put the glass down again, staring at her. 'What did you say?'

Her heart was in her mouth now. 'I know your father was an alcoholic.'

His expression was grim. 'Aiden told you?'

She nodded.

'He had no right.'

'Don't blame him,' she said. 'He thought I must have known – I am going to be your wife, after all.'

Henry flattened his palms on the bench and hunched over, staring down at the floor. Madeleine suddenly didn't feel angry any more. She took a step towards him. 'Henry . . . it's okay.'

'I wasn't keeping it from you,' he said, his voice quiet. 'It's just . . . it's the past, I don't like to talk about it.'

She came closer, placing her hand gently on his back. He breathed out heavily. 'I suppose you have questions?'

Madeleine could hear the hurt and frustration in his voice. She didn't want to make him talk about something that was clearly painful for him, but she knew she wasn't going to be able to let it go either. 'I don't even know what questions to ask, Henry,' she said. 'I get why you might not want to talk about it, but to suppress it so completely . . .'

'Madeleine, do you understand how long ago all this was?' he said, straightening up and turning to face her. 'I was in college, I was a kid. Don't assume I "suppressed" it and that I haven't dealt with it because I don't talk about it now. I know it's taken you a while to come to terms with your father's death, for very different reasons, but if you were still having issues in another ten years' time, I would think there was something up with that.'

'But I can talk about my dad, I don't pretend he never existed.'

'I've never pretended my father didn't exist,' said Henry. 'There's just nothing much to say, we barely even had a relationship. And I know there's a whole bunch of psychoanalysis you could do on a boy growing up without a strong male influence, but it's hardly unheard of. Besides, I've had some pretty great role models, not least Gene.'

'What about your mother?'

His expression darkened. 'What did Aiden tell you about my mother?'

'Nothing, that's why I'm asking.' God, the lies were just getting easier and easier. But maybe Aiden was right about lying, she was only trying to avoid making matters worse. And mentioning his mother had obviously upset him.

'My mother was a saint,' said Henry. 'She just married the wrong man. At least an early death was a release for her – it was the only way she was going to get away from him.'

That suggested Aiden's theory that she slowly killed herself might not be too far from the truth. But Madeleine suspected that trying to get any more from Henry would be like pulling teeth, and probably just as painful. She knew he wasn't telling her everything, though – he hadn't mentioned half of what Aiden had told her. But in a way it didn't matter. This wasn't about forcing Henry to own up to his past, or to share more than he was comfortable with, this was about what was happening between them now. And it all seemed to come down to one thing, that Henry didn't cope with her being away from him. That might be all well and good, it could even be considered romantic, but it didn't feel like that. It felt controlling, or like he didn't trust her. He didn't want her to keep the flat, he didn't want her to have the option. Of course, if they weren't stuck up here, it wouldn't even be an issue. Aiden was right: Henry had everything the way he wanted it, but what was in it for her?

'Tea?'

Madeleine looked up. Henry was holding the kettle.

'Sure, thanks.'

He filled the kettle and plugged it in. She watched him in a daze as he took cups out of the cupboard, teabags from the canister, milk out of the fridge . . . They had to clear the air, like Aiden said.

'Henry?'

'Hm.'

'I think we still have to talk about last night.'

He turned around. 'What do you mean?' he said, leaning back against the bench, his forehead creased in a frown.

'Last night, this morning, whatever – this issue you have with the flat.'

'I didn't know it was an issue anymore. I thought we'd agreed that you were going to give it up after the wedding.'

'What if I don't want to do that?'

He seemed a little taken aback. 'Well, I can't force you.'

'No, instead you can just go all passive aggressive, make snide remarks, and sulk when I do stay there. Why can't you just be honest?'

Madeleine bit her lip as soon as the words came out. That might have been a bit harsh. The kettle was boiling behind him, Madeleine could see the steam rising. It clicked off, and Henry turned around to make the tea.

'I thought I was being honest,' he said evenly. 'I thought I'd made it very clear I didn't want to keep the apartment any longer. I want us to live together all the time, like any normal married couple.'

'And what am I supposed to do when I have to be at the airport at six in the morning?' said Madeleine. 'Or at a function until late at night?'

'I thought you wouldn't be doing any more of that after we're married.'

'Where did you get that idea?' she cried, her agitation growing. 'Do you know how precarious things are at work? You expect me to tell them, "Sorry, I have to leave promptly at five every day, my husband wants his dinner on the table"?'

'Now you're just being ridiculous, Madeleine. I'm the one who puts dinner on the table,' he said, placing her cup of tea in front of her.

'And clearly you resent it.'

'No, I don't, I just thought things would change after we're married.'

'Why would my job change?'

He paused. 'I didn't think you'd keep working that much longer.'

Madeleine was stunned. 'Why would you think that?'

'Well . . .' He hesitated. 'Aren't we going to start a family?'

'What? You've been thinking all this time I'm going to start popping babies out as soon as we say "I do"? We haven't even talked about babies.'

Now Henry looked stunned. 'You don't want to have children?'

'I didn't say that. I said *we haven't talked about it*,' she repeated, sounding out each word. 'But you've decided it's going to happen straight after the wedding.'

'I didn't say straight after.'

'Then when?'

'I don't know, I guess I presumed . . .'

Madeleine was shaking her head. 'You ASSumed, and you know what they say about that.'

'All right, I'm sorry,' he said, raising his voice. 'I was wrong to ASSume that we were going to have children, and I'm suspicious because I worry about you, and I'm weird because I want to live together in the same house!' He took a breath. 'What's really the matter here, Madeleine? You seem very intent on picking a fight and finding fault with everything about me.'

She was trembling . . . from anger, indignation, frustration. She stared down at the tea in her cup. She didn't even want it anymore. She didn't know what she wanted, or why it had come to this. Henry had a closet full of skeletons, and who knew how many unrealistic expectations. And when it came to the crunch, Madeleine realised she'd never really been honest with Henry, or herself, about living up here, about what their life together was going to look like. And now she had to wonder if they just wanted very different things.

She picked up her cup. 'I'm going to bed,' she said, tipping the tea down the sink.

Henry gave a loud sigh. 'So this is how we're going to do things now? Go to bed angry?'

'I don't know. How did we do things before? When do we fight? When do we properly have things out and say what we mean? For godsakes, when do we even spend time with other people? We're always stuck up here on our own. And now you're saying you want me to give up work and hang around here, barefoot and pregnant? Well, I can't live like that, Henry, not for the rest of my life.'

He looked like she'd just slapped him.

'I'm going to bed now,' she went on. 'I don't want to talk about this anymore. I'm tired, and confused, and if I stay up I'm going to keep saying things to hurt you, which isn't going to get us anywhere. So yes, I'm going to bed angry – that's the better option right now.'

She turned away, because she really couldn't bear the expression on his face, and walked out of the kitchen, down the hall and into their room. He didn't follow her.

Sunday

Liv drove through the winding streets of Como on the way to her coffee-only date with David Lessing. When they were organising where to meet he'd asked her where she lived, and when she told him Oatley, he seemed surprised.

'Do you know it?' she said. 'People have usually never heard of it, unless they come from the south of Sydney.'

'I know it well.' Before she could ask him where he lived, he added, 'What about the café at Como? It's a nice place, and it's close for you.'

'Sure.'

Liv could have driven five minutes down to the footbridge and then walked across the Georges River, that was by far the fastest route, but she had decided to drive all the way to the café, which meant going the very long way around via Tom Uglys Bridge and through the Shire. If she was being completely honest, she just felt more comfortable having her car close by in case she needed to make a quick getaway. Not that she was worried; it was broad daylight, and the quick-getaway option was more in case she wanted, well, to get away quickly – 'Thanks, that was nice. Bye!' – and jump straight into her car, instead of having to walk back to the bridge, giving him ample opportunity to follow her to arrange another date.

But she was being an idiot. She was an adult, she could hold her own and leave when she was good and ready. She had actually been surprisingly calm about the whole thing, considering she hadn't had a 'date' in what felt like a hundred years. It helped that they'd already met in person and been able to hold down a conversation. But really, the brutal truth was that Liv had nothing invested in it. She wasn't expecting, or even particularly wanting, this to go any further. It was like going for an interview for a job you didn't desperately need – it took all the pressure off.

Still, it didn't hurt to have a getaway vehicle handy.

It was a beautiful sunny day. Liv parked in the shade and stepped out of the car. The café was right on the banks of Georges River, with seating outside. She wondered if she would recognise David. Ever since the phone call she'd been trying to remember what he looked like; she could see the salt and pepper hair, but his features were indistinct in her mind. She hoped he had a better visual memory than she did.

As she approached the café, Liv thought she spotted him sitting at one of the outdoor tables. Well, she spotted the hair. But goodness knows how many men with salt and pepper hair frequented this café, there could be any number. He was in profile, not looking in her direction, so she slowed down to check him out as she drew quietly, stealthily closer. She should recognise his profile – they'd been sitting side by side the whole flight. He was wearing sunglasses, so she couldn't see his eyes, but she supposed that could be his jaw.

'Were you trying to sneak up on me?' he said, suddenly turning to look at her.

Liv jumped. 'You startled me.'

'Sorry.' David got to his feet and smiled down at her. She remembered the smile. Then he lifted his sunglasses, and, ah, there were the blue-grey eyes. She remembered that she'd liked his eyes. He had a nice face, a kind face. Quite a handsome face. All good so far.

'Hello, Liv,' he said, extending his hand. 'It's nice to see you again.'

'Hi, David,' she said, returning his smile and taking his hand. His skin was quite soft for a man's, not that she was making any kind of judgement. It probably just meant he didn't do manual work. So what did he do? They hadn't got around to that on the plane – they'd only discussed her job. At least that gave them something to talk about.

'Is this all right with you?' he said, releasing her hand and indicating the table.

'It's great,' she said, taking the seat opposite.

He raised his arm to alert the waiter, and then sat down again. 'I thought you'd be coming from that direction,' he said, nodding towards the bridge.

That explained why he was facing that way.

'Oh, I decided to drive,' said Liv. 'I have some errands to run on the way home.'

He slipped his sunglasses back into place, but not before she saw a flicker of something approaching wry amusement cross his eyes.

'So which direction did you come from?' she asked. 'I mean, I guess I'm asking where do you live?'

'Well . . .' He paused. 'Actually, I live in Hurstville Grove.'

Liv was surprised. 'God, we're almost neighbours.'

'Yes we are. I didn't want to say at first, I worried you might think I was a stalker or something.'

'Why would that make you a stalker? Unless you moved there after I told you I live in Oatley?'

He smiled. 'No, I've lived there for some time, I promise.'

She shrugged. 'Then it's just another small-world story.'

'It certainly is.'

The waiter arrived at their table and went to pass Liv a menu but she shook her head. 'Just coffee, thanks. A latte.'

'Sure you don't want something to eat?' David asked.

'No, coffee's fine.'

'For me too,' he said to the waiter. 'Long black, double shot, thanks.'

The waiter left them, and Liv looked at David. 'You take your caffeine strong and to the point?'

'Like my women.' Then he winced. 'That was a reflex. Please pretend you didn't hear it.'

Liv certainly wished she hadn't, especially the reflex part – did he use that line on all the women he met for coffee?

David was watching her. 'Seriously, it was a joke, Liv, a very bad one.' He took a breath. 'I'm a shift worker, strong coffee is how I get through the nights.'

She supposed she could give him a pass. 'So, what do you do?'

'I work in a hospital.'

That was vague. Was he a doctor, like his daughter? Made sense. But why put it like that? Was he too embarrassed to say he was a cleaner or an orderly or something? Not that there was anything wrong with either of those occupations, but for some reason David didn't look like a cleaner. As if she had any idea what a hospital cleaner looked like in civvies out in the light of day . . .

'So what exactly do you do in this hospital?' Liv asked.

'I'm a team leader,' was all he offered.

He really was being evasive. Liv decided she had to make it all right, show him she wasn't the kind of woman to judge a man on his occupation. At least, she hoped she wasn't the kind of woman to judge a man on his occupation.

'What kind of team do you lead?' she asked.

He clasped his hands on the table in front of him. 'A team of nurses.'

She wasn't expecting that. 'How do you get to lead a team of nurses?'

He breathed out. 'By being the most senior nurse on any given shift.'

Liv knew she must look surprised, but she couldn't help it. 'You're a nurse?'

'Guilty as charged.'

'Okay, so I'm just going to say it . . .'

'Go right ahead,' he said in a resigned tone.

'You know what's coming?'

'You've never met a male nurse before.'

'You know, I don't think I have,' said Liv. 'Not that I have a lot to do with hospitals, touch wood,' she added. 'My parents are still in good health, so the last time I was around hospitals was when the boys were little, and that's more than fourteen years ago.'

'There's a lot more of us around these days,' he assured her.

The waiter returned with their coffees and put them on the table. 'Can I get you anything else?' he asked.

David glanced at her and Liv shook her head. 'We're right for now, thanks,' he said.

'So, that's an interesting twist,' said Liv. 'Dad's a nurse, and daughter is inspired to become a doctor?'

'She was the one who inspired me, actually.'

'Oh really? How is that?'

'Well, her mother was very sick, for a long time, when Scarlett was a little girl,' he explained. 'She decided then that she was going to be a doctor, and she never wavered from it. Never so much as took a passing interest in anything else. She can be very single-minded.'

'Clearly,' said Liv. 'I can see how it would have made a big impression on a child. The doctors must have seemed like gods, being able to make her mother better.'

David's expression became serious. 'Unfortunately, they didn't make her better. She died when Scarlett was eight.'

'I'm so sorry.' Liv was trying to recall what he'd said about his relationship with his daughter's mother. She certainly would have remembered if he'd said she'd died. No, he'd said they didn't last, and later, that Scarlett had come to live with him. Liv could understand why he didn't want to talk about her death to a total stranger.

'I told you that we didn't last,' David said, as though he'd read her mind. 'Because we didn't. We broke up when Scarlett was a baby.' He leaned forward a little on the table. 'We were very young – Amanda found out she was pregnant just after we finished the HSC.'

'That is young.'

'I had got into medicine, but I didn't think I'd be able to handle the course with a baby coming, so I deferred.'

'What did you do instead?'

'Oh, I became a complete arsehole,' he said with a sheepish grin. 'Excuse my language, but that's the only way of putting it. I bummed around taking part-time jobs and losing them again, drinking, partying – you know, trying to squeeze as much of my youth into the time I had left before the baby arrived. But I got used to the lifestyle, and Amanda gave up on me, quite rightly. My mother did more to support her than I ever did. When it was my night to have Scarlett, I'd just leave her with Mum and go out as usual. I told you – complete arsehole. I really put my heart and soul into it.'

Liv smiled. 'You were very young, though.'

'So was Amanda, but that didn't stop her from taking the responsibility seriously. She was brilliant with Scarlett. Then after a couple of years she enrolled at TAFE to do childcare. She'd originally planned to be a schoolteacher, and she was intending to get to that. She never made it. She was diagnosed with ovarian cancer when Scarlett was four. It was brutal, but she fought it so hard. She wanted to see Scarlett start school, and then it was the end-of-year dance concert, and then it was her first game of soccer, sports carnivals, more concerts. Every one of Scarlett's milestones was another incentive for her to stay alive long enough to see it. She was beginning to believe she'd be there when Scarlett started high school, but the cancer had other ideas. It spread everywhere. She had so many operations, there was nothing left they could take out. She was only twenty-seven.'

Every response Liv could think of felt inadequate – that it was awful, horrible, sad, tragic . . . In the end she just said, 'I don't know what to say . . .'

'What can you say?' He shrugged. 'Scarlett lost the only decent parent she had, so I had to step up to the plate. I had to get my act together so I could give her a future, I owed Amanda that. I couldn't go back to medicine – the hours would've been impossible, even if I'd managed to get back in, and there was certainly no guarantee of that. It was my mum who suggested nursing. I laughed it off at first, but gradually it became the obvious choice – I'd be trained in half the time it would take to become a doctor, and I could be out earning an income.'

'Still, it couldn't have been easy with a young child,' said Liv. 'How did you manage the shift work?'

'My mother came to the rescue again.' He smiled. 'Scarlett slept at her place whenever I was on night shift. I have to admit, being male, and a single father, I did benefit from a little reverse discrimination. My supervisors used to take pity on me, give me more day shifts and weekends off so I could be with Scarlett. It got a lot easier once she was in her mid-teens and was more independent.'

'I'm noticing that with my boys now,' said Liv.

'Tell me about them,' said David. 'I've talked way too much about myself.'

'Not at all,' she said. 'You've got a pretty impressive story, you should write a book.'

He laughed. 'Spoken like someone who works in publishing. Really, enough about me. So your boys are becoming more independent?'

'Starting to, at least enough so that I can get out on the road again. My mother helps out too, and they do have a father.'

'How long have you been on your own?'

'Almost a decade,' she said.

'What went wrong? If you don't mind me asking.'

She didn't. He was as easy to talk to as when they were on the plane. 'My ex couldn't handle real life, and the twins were the straw that broke his back, poor camel. He was telling me only the other day that I never realised how hard it was for him when the boys came along.'

That seemed to amuse David. 'So he's still in your life?'

'In the boys' lives, and by extension mine. What can you do?' Liv said. 'Boys need their father.'

The waiter returned to take their empty cups. 'Would you like another?' he asked.

'Not for me,' David said.

Liv felt an unexpectedly keen sense of disappointment. She'd only intended to stay for one coffee too, but she was enjoying herself. David was not only harmless, he was also interesting and engaging, and she felt at ease in his company. This wasn't what she'd expected at all; she didn't know if that was because she'd had no expectations, or whether, as she suspected, David was actually a nice guy.

And right now, he and the waiter were patiently waiting for a response. 'Oh, nothing for me either,' said Liv.

'Listen, I'm on night shift tonight,' David explained. 'I'll be mainlining caffeine later, so I can't have any more now. But please, you go ahead.'

'Oh, it's okay.'

'Really, I've got nowhere I have to be,' he said. 'Unless you do?'

'No, not right away.'

'Then stay, have another coffee.'

'All right. A latte again,' she said to the waiter.

'And could we have some water for the table?' David added. 'Thanks.'

So they stayed and they talked, and then they talked some more. David asked endless questions about the boys, apparently still fascinated that they were twins. He told her that he'd finished Cameron's book, and loved it, and they talked about other books they'd read, and movies they liked. He even admitted that he'd rented out a Liv Ullmann film when he happened across one at the video store the other night. 'No offence, but it was weird.'

'No offence taken,' said Liv, who had never seen a Liv Ullmann film in her life. 'I told you, my mother just liked the name.'

'Your bag's tweeting,' David said.

'Huh?' Then she heard it too. It was her text message alert. 'Sorry,' she said, digging for her phone in her bag. 'I know it's rude, but I have to check, because of the boys.'

'Completely understand,' he assured her.

It was Lachie, of course, asking what was for dinner that night. Liv's heart lurched as she checked the time on the screen. It wasn't anywhere near dinnertime, but she realised they had been here for more than two hours. She hoped Rick hadn't dropped the boys off early.

'I have to reply to this.' She gave David an apologetic look, but he waved his hand for her to go ahead.

Liv quickly texted Lachie, asking where he was. He replied almost as quickly: *Still with Dad. Just thinkn bout dinner.* As usual.

'Is everything okay?' David asked as she slipped her phone back into her bag.

'Everything's fine,' she said. 'But I'm going to have to get a move on. It's later than I thought.' She took out her wallet.

'I'll get this,' he said.

'No way,' said Liv. 'I invited you, and I had two cups to your one.'

'It's only coffee,' he said.

'Exactly, so what's the big deal?' She left a couple of notes to cover it, tucking them under the sugar bowl. David stood up as she got to her feet. 'Are you parked in the carpark?' she asked.

'No, I walked across the bridge.'

Liv was suddenly wishing she had too. 'I had a really nice time,' she said.

'Me too,' he smiled.

She liked the way his eyes crinkled when he smiled, she liked that he smiled, often. She liked him. And she was staring at him. Time to go.

'Okay then, well, bye.' She turned to leave.

'Is that it?' David said.

Liv glanced over her shoulder. 'You've got my number. I called you last time. Tag, you're it.'

She walked back to her car feeling pretty pleased with herself, especially that exit. She felt like the sassy one in a TV series about independent career women and their zany dating adventures.

As she got into the car, her phone rang. She took it out and checked the screen. It was David. Her heart did an involuntary little jump. That better not become a habit. She held the phone to her ear. 'Did I leave something behind?' she asked.

'No. You said it was my turn to call.'

'Wow, you don't waste any time.'

'I can't at my age,' he said. 'Would you like to go out again, Liv?'

She hesitated, but only for a second. 'I guess . . .'

'How about next weekend?'

Keen. 'Sorry, I have the kids. Every second weekend.'

'And they're with you all week?'

'Yep.'

'Okay . . . how about lunch on a weekday?'

'You know I work in the city?'

'That's okay. I work shifts, remember, I get some weekdays free.' That was a bonus.

'Let me check my roster,' he said, 'and I'll get back to you.'

'All right.'

'Good. Talk to you soon, Liv.'

'Bye, David.'

Monday

'I shouldn't have been so easy.'

'What are you talking about?' said Madeleine. 'You had coffee. Or are you worried that two cups sends a message that you're some kind of loose woman?'

They were lining up at the café on the ground floor, and Liv had already spilled about her still surprising coffee-only date with David. It really was utterly surprising; she had never expected that it would be so easy, and comfortable, and basically just . . . nice.

So, of course, all night she'd had second thoughts, eventually deciding it was a bad idea to take it any further, and that she should nip it in the bud the first chance she got.

'What I'm saying is that I shouldn't have agreed to another date so readily,' she explained to Madeleine. 'I should have said that *I* need to check *my* schedule.'

'Why?'

'To give me time to think about it.'

'Why?'

'Because thinking about it is . . . a good thing.'

'Why?'

Liv rolled her eyes. 'You sound like Dylan when he was little – why, why, why?'

'Well, if you were giving him lame answers like that, then no wonder.'

'My answers are not lame,' Liv said indignantly. 'What's wrong with taking time to think? It might give you the chance to realise that maybe you don't want this to go any further. Whereas if you answer on the spot, you're under pressure to say yes. And then what do you do?'

'You go out again?' Madeleine suggested. 'With a nice guy, with whom you had a nice time? Just an idea.'

'You're being a smart-arse today.'

Madeleine just shrugged.

'Anyway, he hasn't got back to me, so it's all academic,' Liv said. 'This is why I've avoided the whole dating thing. Men are weird. He could barely let me leave his sight yesterday before calling me, and then he doesn't get back to me? What's that about?'

'Didn't you say he was on night shift last night?'

'Oh yeah.' Liv had forgotten about that.

Madeleine smiled at her. 'Look at you, getting all antsy, waiting for the call.'

'I am not,' Liv said. 'I'm getting antsy that there's a call to wait for in the first place.'

'You know you're not making any sense, right?' said Madeleine.

'Look, I only intended to meet him once, for coffee, to get the monkey off my back, so to speak. And now I'm waiting for a call that I'm not even sure I want.'

'Well, looks like he's not going to call, so you'll be off the hook. Won't that be a relief?'

Liv pulled a face. '*Such* a smart-arse today.'

'Sorry,' she grumbled. 'I had a crappy weekend.'

'Why, what happened?'

Their orders were called and they picked up their coffees at the end of the counter.

'Do you want to drink these down here?' said Madeleine. 'Have you got time?'

'Sure, my first meeting's not for an hour.'

Madeleine led the way to one of the bench tables over against the window. They sat down with their backs to the entrance so they probably wouldn't be noticed if anyone from the office came in.

'What's up?' said Liv.

Madeleine was staring down at her coffee. 'I'm not sure where to start . . . I'll try to give you a brief synopsis.'

'You sound like you're pitching a book.'

She didn't respond to that. 'Aiden got back on Friday afternoon, and, well, he and I had a few drinks. He ended up telling me all this stuff about Henry's family. You know how he never talks about them?'

'Uh-huh.' So Liv had to wonder why Aiden felt so free. And where was Henry while they were having their cosy little D&M?

'So, here's a revelation,' Madeleine went on. 'Turns out Henry's father was an alcoholic, a full-on, nasty alcoholic.'

'Oh.'

'Explains an awful lot about Henry.'

'Such as?'

'Well, why he's so sensitive about me drinking, for one thing.'

Liv didn't know what to say to that, and frankly it made her uncomfortable. While she'd never gone so far as to think of her as an alcoholic, she did know that Madeleine had abused alcohol for a while there. That had all changed when Henry came into her life, so Liv had decided Madeleine's behaviour must have been an aberration, not an addiction. However, Liv had once looked after the author of a book on co-dependency and had been fascinated to learn that people were often drawn to the same dysfunctional environment they'd grown up in, so children of alcoholics were drawn to alcoholics, and so on. If Henry's father was an alcoholic, and Henry had been drawn to Madeleine . . . But she didn't know enough about it, and she certainly didn't have any right to judge.

'Anyway, long story short,' Madeleine was saying, 'I confronted Henry about it on Saturday night.'

Poor Henry. 'How did he take that?'

'Not very well. He didn't really want to talk about it, he claimed it was all a long time ago. But it brought up all this other stuff . . . like, he's been assuming that I'm pretty much going to give up work as soon as we're married, and start having babies.'

'Are you serious?'

'That's what he said.'

'And this has never come up before?'

Madeleine shook her head. 'I was thinking about it afterwards, wondering how had we got this far without talking about kids. It's a pretty major oversight. I racked my brain, trying to remember conversations we've had. Certainly neither of us has ever had a strong position *against* having children. I did recall one time when Genevieve was complaining about Mark never being around, and we said how great it was that Henry worked from home because that would never be an issue for us.'

'So you do want kids?' said Liv.

'Oh sure, one day. We just haven't talked about when, or what it will mean for my career.'

'Okay then, you've got some stuff to sort out. Welcome to married life.'

'But I don't know, the thought of living up there, so far away from everything and everyone I know, and having kids . . .'

'Did you say that to Henry?'

'More or less, but he just looked hurt.'

'You can't leave it at that, Mad. You have to talk about it.'

'That's the thing,' said Madeleine. 'The next morning he just says to me, "Are we all good?" *Are we all good*?' she repeated incredulously.

'So what was your answer?'

'Well, he did say a little more than that,' Madeleine admitted. 'He said he knew we had some important things we have to talk about, and that we will, but he just needs to meet his deadline and then we can discuss it all with a clear head.'

'Maybe a little dispassionate,' said Liv, 'but that is quite sensible, when you think about it.'

Madeleine sighed. 'It just feels like it's all galloping ahead too fast to the wedding. I want to stop and take a moment to think about all this.'

'Mad, it's not like the wedding is some point of no return, that suddenly you're in lockdown and you can't talk about anything ever again, or negotiate your future. You're panicking at the last minute, but it's not the last minute.'

'I guess.'

'Marriage is a constant negotiation,' said Liv. 'You two are really going to have to learn how to fight properly.'

'That's the problem, we don't fight,' said Madeleine. 'We have these little flare-ups and then they die down again. But this was more than a little flare-up. I just hope Henry realises that.'

'That's why I say you have to learn how to fight,' Liv said. 'You have to see things through all the way to the bitter end, or else all you'll be left with is bitterness. In the right conditions, all those little smouldering flare-ups can easily turn into a great big bushfire that will destroy everything in its path.'

'That was some metaphor.'

'I know, right?' said Liv. 'I'm so wise today.'

Her phone tweeted to announce a message. She slipped it out of her pocket and read the screen, and her heart did that skippy-jumpy thing again. She really had to do something about that. 'It's from David,' she murmured.

'Ah, there! You see?' said Madeleine.

Liv clicked on the message to read it in its entirety. *Hi, still at work so will call later. Just wanted to let you know asap that I have Wednesday off, is that good for you?*

'What does it say?' asked Madeleine.

'He's free Wednesday.'

'Oh.'

Liv looked at her. 'What?'

'Nothing,' said Madeleine. 'I have my final dress fitting that day. I was going to ask you to come, but –'

'Fine, I'll tell David I can't –'

'No, you will not,' Madeleine said firmly, grabbing her hand to stop her. 'It was Gen's idea anyway. I don't need to have someone with me – Lucy's great, I'm completely comfortable with her. I don't even know why anyone has to be with me for the final fitting; it's too late if you tell me you hate it.'

'I'd love to see it though . . .'

'Well, bad luck, you're going to have to wait for the wedding like everybody else. Now tell David yes.'

Liv bit her lip. 'I don't know . . .'

'Take a piece of your own advice, seeing as you're so wise. You're backing away because of potential problems in a long-term relationship that doesn't even exist yet. Who's having cold feet now?'

Tuesday

Flying to Canberra tomorrow. Thanks for letting me stay at apartment, see you when I get back end of the week xa

'Who was that?' Henry asked absently.

They had finished dinner and were clearing up when Madeleine's phone buzzed.

'Aiden,' she said. 'Just to let us know he's off to Canberra, and to thank us for letting him use the apartment.'

'Hm.' Henry was so intent on scrubbing out a pot, he didn't even lift his head.

It wasn't the first message Aiden had sent since he'd left them. He'd texted Madeleine on Sunday to see how things had gone with Henry, if they were okay. In a series of texts she'd filled him in on what had transpired, while Aiden offered consolation and encouragement in response. She had begun to feel as though he understood her better than Henry.

She didn't hear from him all day yesterday, and so last night when Henry went down to his office to work after dinner, she sent him a message. *Very quiet here without you. Henry locked away in study. As usual. xm*

She had added a sad face, but then thought better of it and deleted it again. She didn't want to sound like a teenage girl. Aiden sent a whole run of texts in reply, one after another, a list of suggestions of ways to get Henry's attention, mostly involving the wearing of some very silly outfits, until finally he suggested wearing nothing at all . . . *If that doesn't do it, I'm afraid he's a lost cause.* Madeleine had blushed sitting there in the living room all on her own.

The next day Aiden texted: *Dozing off in meeting. So bored!*

Madeleine had texted back: *I'll see your boring meeting and raise you two hours' scheduling – tedious!*

To which he replied: *I'm calling your bluff. There's no emoticon for a poker face, so you'll just have to imagine it.*

And on it went. At one point Ren had walked past and asked her what was so funny.

'Nothing,' Madeleine said, placing her phone face down on the desk. But the truth was, Aiden's messages were becoming the highlight of her day.

Henry was now meticulously wiping the scrubbed pot with a tea towel. He was nothing if not thorough, this man.

'Henry?' said Madeleine. He looked up. 'I was thinking, now that the flat's free . . .' She watched the beginnings of a frown form on his face, but she pushed on, '. . . I might stay down in the city for a few days.'

'Oh?'

'I've got so much to do for the wedding, tomorrow's the final dress fitting . . .' She let her voice trail off as though she was about to recite a list.

'I thought you were doing that in your lunch hour?' said Henry.

'I am, but I'll have to take a long lunch, so I should work back to make it up.'

He slid open the pot drawer. 'So what else do you have to do?'

Madeleine felt herself bristle. She didn't appreciate the interrogation, especially because, truth be told, there wasn't all that much left to do before the wedding. But she couldn't get out of her head something Aiden had said in one of his texts: *You should take some time out for a few days, down at the apartment, while you still can. You know what they say, absence makes the heart grow fonder.* The phrase that had stayed with her was 'while you still can'.

'I have to go by the reception place to confirm the menu and some other details,' she told Henry. 'I'll probably do that after work one night. And Gen's been hounding me to go over to sort out a few things . . .' Seriously, could she sound any more vague?

'Anything I should know about?' asked Henry.

'What do you mean?'

'Well, it's my wedding too.'

'Huh,' she grunted, 'not that you'd know it.'

'What's that supposed to mean?'

'You're not exactly interested.'

'And yet I just asked.' He sighed, turning to her. 'What's the matter?'

'Nothing's the matter, this just feels like an inquisition, like you don't believe how much I have to do. You have no idea what's involved in organising a wedding.'

'I know I don't, which is why I asked, that's all,' he said, keeping up that calm, honey-smooth voice of his. It annoyed the life out of her sometimes. 'It worries me how much this is stressing you out.'

'What are you talking about? I haven't been stressed out.' She could hear her own shrill voice bouncing off the walls back at her.

'You just seem very tense lately, not quite yourself,' he said. 'And we're fighting all the time.'

'And that's my fault?'

'I didn't say that, I didn't mean that.' Henry sighed again, heavily this time. 'I'll just be glad when the whole damn thing is over.'

Madeleine blinked at him. 'I don't even know what to say to that. I didn't know you had a problem with the wedding.'

'I don't. I would marry you anywhere, anyhow. This is what you want, so it's fine with me.'

Fine? 'Why did you even ask me to marry you?'

'Oh, for godsakes, Madeleine.' He rubbed his forehead. 'It wasn't so that I could have a wedding, that's for sure. Is that why you said yes, just so you could wear a white dress and walk down the aisle? Because I hope to God there was more to it than that.'

She suddenly felt silly and self-indulgent for wanting a regular wedding. It wasn't even going to be over the top, in fact it was pretty modest by today's standards. This was why Henry didn't want to write his own vows, she decided – he didn't even want to be part of the whole thing in the first place.

'Hey . . .' He walked around to where she was standing on the other side of the bench and tucked his fingers under her chin to lift her face. Her eyes had teared up, she could feel them stinging. She tried to turn her head away, but he'd already seen.

'Madeleine.' He drew her into his arms and held her close, swaying gently as though he was rocking a baby. She couldn't stop the lump rising up in her chest, and finally she let out a forlorn sob. 'Don't cry,' he soothed. 'I didn't mean to make you cry. I'm sorry.'

She pulled back to wipe her eyes. 'This is all just a bit much to find out so close to the wedding. It's too late to change things now.'

'I don't want you to change a thing,' he said. 'I want you to have whatever you want, whatever makes you happy. Please don't let this put a cloud over it.'

Too late for that.

Henry lifted her face again. 'Go, have a few days, take all the time you need, but give yourself a break as well. Okay?'

She nodded.

'There's just one thing I'd like to do before you go.'

'What's that?'

He took a breath. 'I think we should have sex. We haven't since –'

'The day after Aiden arrived,' she blurted. 'I know!'

And suddenly he was kissing her with uncharacteristic urgency. Madeleine found it quite thrilling as his mouth ravaged hers, and their bodies gyrated eagerly against each other. But when she started to pull up the back of his shirt, Henry reached around and took hold of her hands, murmuring something about taking this to the bedroom. Madeleine's heart sank, and she traipsed after him as he led her by the hand, the flame already ebbing. He managed to fire her back up again, but as always it was the slow, steady build, and her orgasm was a little tame. She just wasn't as into it as at the start.

Afterwards she lay in his arms, her head nestled into the usual spot, feeling vaguely unsatisfied. It wasn't that the sex wasn't good – it was – and she didn't really want to change this about him, it was part of who he was. She certainly could never say anything about it; like any man, he'd be mortified. Their egos just couldn't take it, even someone like Henry who didn't have a great deal of ego. But God, sometimes she wished he'd just chase her around the house, or take her on the kitchen bench, or even throw her down on the bed with a little unbridled passion. In her dreams . . .

Wednesday

As Madeleine drove south to the city and freedom, she wasn't sure she felt so free. She felt confused and conflicted and, most of all, guilty, that she had so quickly become used to lying to a sweet man who wouldn't hurt her for the world. On top of that, when she'd gone to kiss him goodbye, he'd taken her in his arms and given her a big Hollywood kiss. It was unexpected, and lovely, and had left her feeling pleasantly lightheaded. Maybe she was underestimating him.

'I'll miss you,' he said.

'Henry . . .' She reached up to brush a lock of hair from his forehead. 'It's not unusual for a couple to have a little time apart before the wedding, you know.'

A flicker of hurt had passed across his eyes. 'Is that why you're doing this?'

'No,' she gently assured him. 'I've got a wedding to organise, remember?'

At least work was busy, helping to keep her mind occupied instead of spinning around off its orbit. In the morning, she and Liv met with Jane to discuss which authors to pitch for the main festivals next year. Publicists had an unabashed passion for festivals – their natural habitat. They were exciting and inspiring and buzz-creating – but there was always a tug-of-war between the publicists' enthusiasm, and the publishers' pragmatism.

It was getting close to lunch by the time Madeleine got back to her desk, and soon after, her mobile rang. It was Aiden.

'Hello,' she said brightly. 'How are you finding our nation's capital?'

'I'm still in Sydney,' he said. 'My flight was cancelled, some mechanical fault, they had to ground the plane.'

That always sent chills. 'I'm glad they discovered it,' said Madeleine. 'Doesn't it freak you out?'

'This is nothing, you should see some of the planes I've travelled in,' he said. 'Anyway, they can't get me on another flight until later this afternoon, so I've got a few hours to fill. I was wondering if you wanted to grab some lunch?'

'I can't, sorry,' she said, genuinely disappointed. 'I have to go to my dress fitting.'

He said nothing for a moment.

'Aiden, are you still there?'

'Yeah, I was just thinking . . . I could always tag along?'

'Why would you want to do that?'

'It might be fun, and I'm sure I can make myself useful.'

Madeleine smiled at that. 'Oh? How so?'

'I can check that you can sit down, like Gen was saying, and use the bathroom –'

'Enough.'

'And what else did she say? Oh, to make sure you've got plenty of cleavage showing.'

'Aiden!' she scolded.

'I promise to behave myself,' he said. 'What do you say?'

Madeleine pressed her lips together. She wasn't sure if it was the proper thing to do, and she was even less sure what Henry would make of it. 'I don't think you're supposed to see me in the dress,' she said finally.

'You're getting me confused with the groom,' he said. 'As the matron of honour's partner, doesn't it make sense that I go in her place?'

That was a good point; he was a bona fide member of the wedding party, there was no need to get all weird because he happened to be a man. Most wedding traditions had sprung from the eighteenth century and earlier, but they were now living in the twenty-first century, after all.

'All right, Aiden, if this is how you want to fill your time, you're welcome to join me.'

'Excellent!'

Madeleine offered to pick him up from the airport, but he said it would be quicker if he jumped in a taxi and met her there. So she gave him the address, and they agreed to meet in front of the salon.

She stopped by Liv's office on the way out. 'I'm taking a long lunch,' she reminded her. 'I forgot to mention it earlier.'

'That's right, it's your dress fitting today.' Liv sat back in her chair. 'Are you excited?'

'I suppose.'

'Whoa, calm down, Mad, you might blow a gasket.'

Madeleine rolled her eyes, unimpressed.

'Anyway, take all the time you need.'

'I'm staying at the flat for a few days, so I can work back if I have to.'

'Why are you staying at the flat?' Liv asked.

'I've got a lot of wedding stuff to do,' Madeleine said. 'It's easier if I'm close to town.'

'How does Henry feel about that?'

'Henry has to be a grown-up and handle it.'

Liv raised an eyebrow. 'Have you two come to some kind of understanding?'

'Not exactly . . .' Madeleine didn't want to get into it with Liv now, her thoughts were way too chaotic. Besides, she had to go if she wasn't going to be late for her appointment. 'You were right that I should stop treating the wedding as some kind of scary deadline. We've got plenty of time to sort things out.'

'The rest of your lives.'

'Indeed.'

'Well, I'm glad to hear you're putting things into perspective,' said Liv. 'You certainly look a lot brighter than you did earlier in the week.'

Probably not for the reason Liv was thinking. Madeleine wondered about asking her if she thought it was weird that Aiden was coming to the fitting, but decided not to, because she didn't really want to know.

'Oh, I just remembered, you've got your date with *Daaaave*,' she said.

'And you're never going to call him that again.'

Madeleine smiled. 'Have fun, catch ya.'

Trousseau

Aiden was waiting on the footpath when Madeleine turned her car into the street, and he gave her an enthusiastic wave. She found a park a little way past him, and he walked up to meet her.

'Hi, Maddie,' he said as she got out of the car.

'Hello to you.' She joined him at the kerb. 'Are you sure you're ready for this?'

He leaned in and planted a kiss on her cheek. 'I can't wait.'

The salon was in a street off the main drag in Newtown, and wasn't open to the general public. As Lucy was the owner, designer, seamstress and receptionist in one, all fittings were by appointment only. Madeleine pressed the intercom when they arrived at the door.

'Hi, it's Madeleine Pepper,' she said when Lucy answered.

'Come on in.'

There was a buzz, and the door released. Madeleine pushed it open, stepping inside as Lucy came down the hall into the reception area, a tape measure around her neck, her signature oversized red-rimmed glasses perched on the end of her nose.

Madeleine had clicked with Lucy from the start. After the engagement, she had spent a couple of Saturdays traipsing around the big bridal salons in the city, but nothing grabbed her. She knew what she didn't want – too much fuss or frou-frou – but she didn't really know what she did want. Lucy was the first person to be able to make sense of that. Madeleine had found her on the internet, and fallen in love with the dresses on her website – delicate, vintage-inspired, subtle not showy.

'Hey, Madeleine,' Lucy cooed. Then she stopped dead, her cheeks turning pink. She'd obviously just spotted Aiden coming in behind her. 'Well, I hope this isn't your future husband,' she said, regaining her composure. 'You know it's bad luck for him to see your dress . . . And, well, I don't know, it might bring bad karma to the whole place.'

'Don't be concerned,' Aiden assured her, flashing her one of his most charming smiles. 'I'm merely the best man.'

'Merely is definitely not the word that comes to mind . . .'

'Aiden Carmichael, Lucy Chu,' Madeleine said, introducing them. 'Aiden's standing in for the matron of honour, she couldn't make it today.'

Aiden took Lucy's outstretched hand. 'Nice to meet you.'

'Am I detecting an American accent?' she asked.

'You are,' said Aiden. 'Henry and I went to college together.'

Lucy looked at Madeleine. 'I didn't know your fiancé was American,' she said. 'Are you living here too, Aiden, or just visiting?'

'Just visiting, sadly.'

'That is sad. It's a tragedy, in fact.'

'So, I'm excited to see the dress,' Madeleine said pointedly, to drag Lucy away from whatever little fantasy scenario she had going on in her head.

Lucy roused herself, blinking at Madeleine as she pushed her glasses back up on her nose. 'And I'm excited to see you in it! I'm pretty thrilled at how it's turned out. Come along,' she said, turning back into the hall.

The salon was originally a single-storey terrace house. The front bedroom wall had been knocked out to form the reception area. The next bedroom off the hall was the changing and fitting room, and the former living room beyond it was the 'salon' proper, replete with chandelier, red velvet lounges, and gilt-edged mirrors positioned around the room at various angles. It was more like a waiting room in a bordello than a bridal salon, but that was one of the reasons Madeleine had loved the place the first time she visited. By then she was a little over all the virginal, hearts-and-flowers bridal confectionery. Perhaps Genevieve had a point about sexing things up a bit.

Aiden was shown into the salon, where an old record player was cranking out crackly music from the thirties. Lucy was all about setting the mood.

'There's champagne in the ice bucket over there,' she told him, 'and orange juice in the bar fridge, if you think it's too early to have it straight.'

'It's never too early.' He winked at her.

'Man after my own heart,' said Lucy. 'I wish,' she muttered under her breath to Madeleine. 'Make yourself comfortable, Aiden, while I go and transform your . . . gosh, what are you to him?' She frowned at Madeleine.

'A very dear friend,' Aiden said.

Lucy released a wistful sigh. 'We'll see you in a little while.'

As soon as she closed the door of the fitting room, she turned to Madeleine, eyes wide, making exaggerated pointing gestures towards the salon. 'He's hot!' she said, her whispered voice similarly exaggerated to match her gestures.

But Madeleine was distracted by the dress draped on the dummy in the corner of the room. It was just as she'd pictured it . . . no, it was better than she ever could have imagined, from the richly beaded bodice to the ivory silk that swirled down to the floor in gentle folds. Madeleine drew closer to look for the tiny monogrammed *M* and *H* entwined around each other at the centre of the bodice, and a lump rose in her throat.

'Lucy, it's so beautiful,' she said, her voice barely making it out of her throat. She wanted to wear this dress, she wanted Henry to see her in this dress . . . But then she remembered what he'd said yesterday, and her excitement evaporated. She was never going to be able to feel the same way about the wedding now. No matter how well it turned out, and how much he tried, she was going to feel a little silly, like an overgrown girl having a princess party.

'Madeleine?' Lucy was saying.

She stirred. 'Sorry, I was a million miles away.'

'Playing out the wedding in your head?' Lucy said. 'Brides always do that when they see their finished dress for the first time. Now let's get you into it.'

Madeleine stripped down to her underwear. She actually had followed Genevieve's advice and bought two bras, the one she was wearing now, and an identical twin, wrapped in tissue paper and tucked away in a drawer at the flat, to be worn for the first time on her wedding day. She had also bought a few pairs of those seamless long-line tummy-flattening pants. She didn't need to lose weight, but even so, she could never get rid of the curve of her belly. Henry said he didn't know why it bothered her, he thought it was sexy . . .

Lucy held the dress for Madeleine to step into, then carefully drew the gossamer-fine cap sleeves up her arms and positioned them on her shoulders. The sleeves formed a line that plunged down into a deep V-neck – Genevieve needn't have worried, she was showing enough cleavage. Lucy had started on the buttons at the back. Madeleine remembered that there were close to thirty tiny pearl buttons, and as Lucy patiently proceeded to do them up, the dress took shape around her, and tears crept into her eyes.

Lucy looked over Madeleine's shoulder at her reflection. 'Uh-uh, no tears on the dress!' she warned. She darted around in front of her and quickly blotted her cheeks with a tissue. 'Water marks silk, you know.'

'It's just so beautiful, Lucy,' said Madeleine. 'I'm actually quite overcome.'

'That's all well and good, but no tears!'

She knelt down to help Madeleine into her shoes. Lucy had helped her find the perfect pair, and then had them sent away to be covered in the same fabric as the dress. She'd left them here at the salon; Lucy said it was better that way, fittings were a complete waste of time without the shoes, and harassed brides-to-be were all too prone to forgetting them.

She helped Madeleine up onto the small dais, and walked around her, pinching in the fabric here, adjusting there, narrowing her eyes as she assessed the dress from every angle. 'You've lost more weight,' she tutted.

'I haven't been trying to,' said Madeleine.

'Well, I should hope not,' said Lucy. 'You certainly don't need to lose any more. But this happens to a lot of brides. It's all the stress. You have to try to make sure you keep eating healthy. Waif is not a good look for a bride – you want to look glowing, ripe for the picking, so to speak. Fecund, even.'

Madeleine raised an eyebrow. 'Did you just use the word "fecund"?'

'I did,' Lucy said. 'You know, when you think about it, it's entirely appropriate for a bride to look fecund, even if people don't marry to have babies any more.'

Try telling Henry that.

After Lucy had trimmed and tucked, and Madeleine had performed the full range of movements to her satisfaction, she finally walked out into the salon. Aiden looked genuinely stunned.

'Well done,' said Lucy, watching him. 'Excellent reaction.'

'It's not an act,' he said, holding a hand to his heart as he gazed with unabashed admiration at Madeleine. 'Maddie, once again, I have to say that Henry has to be the luckiest man alive.'

'You don't think it's too much?' she asked, checking herself in one of the mirrors.

'What?' He frowned. 'What are you talking about? It's very understated, very elegant.' He took her by the hand and held it up to lead her into a pirouette. 'I think congratulations are definitely in order, Lucy,' he said.

'Why, thank you, sir.'

'Now, the matron of honour said to remind Maddie to check that she can sit on a toilet without the help of a special ops team.'

'We've already checked,' Madeleine assured him.

'I'm extremely particular about that kind of thing,' said Lucy. 'My designs are always wearable, I don't believe the poor bride should be all trussed up like a turkey at Christmas. It's her day, she should be able to enjoy it in comfort.'

'It's true, it really is very comfortable,' said Madeleine, looking over her shoulder to check the view from behind in the mirror.

'Now, what are you going to do with your hair?' Aiden asked, and unexpectedly he brought his hands to the base of her neck, lacing his fingers through her hair to hold it up. Madeleine felt shivers right down her back, but not the kind that was like someone walking over her grave. Different to that.

'What do you think, Lucy?' he asked. 'Personally, I'd like to see her in a veil.'

'Aiden –'

'Me too,' said Lucy. 'I tried to talk you into that in the first place, Maddie.'

'I just don't want to look . . .'

'What?' they said in unison.

'Well . . . too bridey, I guess.'

Aiden released her hair, and Madeleine was able to breathe out again. 'You know,' he said, 'you're not exactly in disguise. People are going to realise you're the bride.'

'Very funny,' she said.

'Why don't we just try it?' Lucy suggested. 'I think I have the perfect one.'

'That doesn't mean I'm going to wear it,' Madeleine warned.

'But it doesn't hurt to try.' Lucy whisked out to her studio, and Aiden smiled down at Madeleine.

'Henry is going to be totally knocked out. You look gorgeous, really.'

She could feel tears pricking at the corners of her eyes again, and she swallowed hard to keep them at bay.

Aiden was watching her thoughtfully. 'Would you like a glass of champagne?' he asked.

'Sure, why not?' she said with a brave smile.

As he crossed to the ice bucket, Lucy came back into the room, a piece of silk organza draped over her outstretched arms. 'Okay, let's try this.'

She positioned the veil, catching it into place at the back of Madeleine's head. She supposed it did frame her face. It made her feel . . . regal or something. And self-conscious. She wondered what Henry would make of it.

Aiden turned around, holding a glass of champagne for her. 'Now there, you see – I'd marry you.'

'There's an offer you couldn't refuse,' said Lucy, only half joking.

A phone started ringing from the back of the building. 'Sorry, do you mind if I get that?' she asked.

'Of course not,' said Madeleine. 'Please, take your time.'

As Lucy skittered from the room, Aiden passed Madeleine the glass of champagne.

'Oh,' said Lucy, popping her head back in, 'and there's a layer you can wear over the face, if you want to try how that looks.' She disappeared again.

'I do,' Aiden declared.

'I don't know –'

'Just humour me,' he said, feeling behind her for the layer. 'I think there's something very . . .'

'What?' Madeleine prompted him.

He drew the veil over her head and let it fall softly over her face. 'I don't know. It's mysterious, even a little sexy,' he said, gazing straight into her eyes through the filmy fabric. 'And it's such a great moment when the groom lifts back the veil,' he said, as he did the same, 'like he's opening a present.'

'That's the whole problem,' said Madeleine. 'Isn't it a bit outdated? I mean, he's literally unveiling his newly acquired chattel.'

'No.' Aiden frowned. 'Don't be so cynical, it's all part of the ceremony.'

A ceremony Henry wasn't even all that keen to be taking part in. Madeleine took a gulp of her champagne as 'The Way You Look Tonight' started to play on the stereo.

'Now this is a beautiful song,' said Aiden. 'You know what else we should make sure you can do in that dress?'

'What?' she asked warily.

'Dance.' He slipped the glass out of her hand and popped it on a side table. Then he took her hand in his and scooped his other arm around her waist, pulling her close.

Madeleine brought her hand to rest on his shoulder as Aiden started to waltz her around the room. 'Hey, you're not bad,' she said.

'My mother made us take dancing lessons when we were young.'

'Really?'

He nodded. 'Me and my brother, before our high school prom. She said girls will always fall for a boy who can dance.'

Madeleine didn't think Aiden needed dancing ability to get girls to fall for him, but it was a nice bonus. And he was very light on his feet.

'How's Henry on the dance floor?' he asked.

'Are you kidding? He would never get up and dance in front of people.'

'He's going to have to at his wedding.'

'I wouldn't count on it.'

Aiden paused to look down at her. 'He has to do the bridal waltz with you on your wedding day.'

Damn tears again. Madeleine steeled herself.

'What's wrong, Maddie?' he said kindly.

She tried to shrug it off. 'I've just found out Henry's not that crazy about having a big wedding, he's only doing it for me.'

'Well, he wouldn't be the first man to feel that way,' said Aiden, starting to sway to the music again. 'The bride's the driving force behind most weddings, but the groom usually gets into the spirit of it on the day. You shouldn't worry, Henry'll come around.'

Madeleine sighed. 'I don't know. I hope so.'

The song built to its climax as Aiden swept her around the room, finally dipping her low to the closing strains.

'Bravo!' Lucy stood in the doorway, applauding enthusiastically. 'I hope your husband can dance like that, Maddie. Or else I'd be tempted to hire Aiden here as his stand-in.'

Thursday night

'Not hungry tonight, mate?' asked Liv, watching Dylan push the food around his plate.

'No, not much,' he said.

'Do you feel all right?'

'Just tired.'

'Maybe you should try to get an early night,' she said. 'You too, Lachie.'

'Just because we're twins doesn't mean I feel the same way,' he said.

'Yes, but you've both got your big sleepover party tomorrow night,' Liv reminded them. Like they needed reminding. Dylan in particular was very excited. His brother was the popular one, and since starting high school they didn't automatically both get invitations to things anymore. Liv had known this would happen one day: they had to establish their separate identities, all the literature on twins said so. But still, she felt for Dylan sometimes. Not that he ever complained; he was happy in his own company, and he didn't really fit in with a lot of Lachie's friends anyway. But they played cricket with Jared, and he'd invited the whole team to his birthday bash, and Dylan had clearly been thrilled to be included. He'd probably tired himself out from the anticipation.

'I tell you what,' said Liv, 'I'll clear up and stack the dishwasher –' usually the boys' evening chore – 'if you both head off now, get ready for school tomorrow and pack what you need for the sleepover.'

'But I finished my homework this afternoon,' Lachie whined. 'I wanted to go on the PlayStation.'

'Okay,' said Liv. 'So I'll leave the stacking to you?'

He groaned, and trudged off up the hall after his brother.

They were going straight to Jared's house from school, and they had a bye for cricket this week – part of the reason Jared's parents had chosen this Friday for the sleepover. So Liv would have the night free, and she didn't have to pick them up until ten on Saturday morning.

She hadn't mentioned this to David. Not that he'd asked – he thought she had the boys all weekend, and there was no need to correct that assumption. They had enjoyed another extremely pleasant date, with food this time. When he arrived to meet her in the city, he'd already booked them into a very nice harbourside restaurant. Liv would have been worried about his intentions – and his expectations – if it had been for dinner, but for lunch it was quite safe. But Liv wasn't sure how much longer she'd be 'safe', so to speak. It wasn't David, it was her – that wasn't a line, it was fact. She was having a great deal of trouble finding anything wrong with him, and that was just unnerving. Nobody's perfect, so there had to be something, surely. And the deeper it was hidden, the worse it probably was.

Madeleine had said she was obviously guarding her heart, and Liv asked if she had an app that generated sappy sayings. Mad had given a fake laugh and said she should bring David to the wedding as her plus one. Liv had given a genuine belly laugh and said she should have her head examined.

The truth was – and she was too embarrassed to admit this even to Madeleine – the place she was guarding was a little south of her heart. Liv knew she came across as all confidence and sass, but the very idea of sex paralysed her with fear. It had just been so long. When the boys were little she was so exhausted she hardly ever thought about it. Back then she was in no fit state; her heart was too battered and bruised, she needed time to heal, and who had the energy anyway? But lately there had been stirrings. She found it quite physically uncomfortable to watch movies with hot sex scenes, or any sex scenes, or just the suggestion that sex might happen sometime in the future. She'd even had to give up her addiction to the BBC series of *Pride and Prejudice*, which was her extra-strength comfort binge watch, right up there with chocolate, wine and bedsocks. But that kiss in the very last few seconds – the *only* kiss in the entire six hours! – was enough to set Liv off, imagining what Mr Darcy was going to get up to with Miss Elizabeth Bennet when they got back to Pemberley.

But sex in real life wasn't like sex on screen. It was clumsy and awkward, and sweaty and physical, and you had to be really comfortable with the other person before it all clicked into place. That had been Liv's experience anyway. She'd had her share of casual sex in her early twenties, pre-Rick, but it had never really done it for her. She knew that as a liberated woman she was supposed to love it, and be all in tune with her body and free with her sexual expression. Perhaps she wasn't as liberated as she thought, because she'd only enjoyed it when she knew the guy at least a little, when there was some chance of tenderness and regard.

So what was she worried about? She knew David at least a little now. They were grown-ups, verging on middle-aged, actually. They ought to know what they were doing. Who knows, it might turn out to be pretty good.

And once she'd opened the floodgates, then what? She had been doing fine without it, so why scratch the itch now, so to speak? Everyone knows that scratching an itch only makes it worse, and that you can't stop scratching once you start. Nuns managed to live without sex, and they were okay, weren't they? Liv had read somewhere that they were more likely to get cervical cancer . . . No, wait, that was the one they didn't get, because they didn't have sex. So there were health benefits to celibacy, clearly. Anyway, there was some kind of cancer that nuns did get at a higher rate, but that had more to do with not having children, and Liv had two. Though only one pregnancy, so she couldn't really count them as two, in terms of protective effects.

Liv was standing in the middle of the kitchen, holding a plate in each hand and trying to remember what had started her off thinking about nuns and babies. Sex! That was it. And right then her phone started ringing like some kind of alarm, snapping her out of it.

It was Rick – that really snapped her out of it. Like being doused with a bucket of cold water.

'I know the boys have a sleepover tomorrow night,' he began. 'So I was wondering if you'd come with me to look at an apartment I'm considering. I could ask the agent to take us.'

She wondered what planet Rick was living on, thinking a real estate agent was going to give him his own private viewing on a Friday afternoon, on a *rental*. It was a buyer's market, not a renter's, making him a beggar, not a chooser. He could get in line like everyone else.

Rather than explain all that to him, she just said no.

'You don't want to see where the boys will be spending part of their time?'

'I'll say it again, Rick: you're their parent, I trust you to look after them adequately when I'm not around.'

'You know, you've become really hard lately, Liv,' he said, his tone glum. 'You haven't even asked me about my break-up.'

'Because that would imply I was interested.'

'Jeez, Liv.'

Okay, maybe that was a bit harsh. 'Rick, we're not friends, we're co-parents.'

'But as co-parents, shouldn't we try to be friends?'

'Friend*ly*, there's a difference.'

'You've changed since the phantom boyfriend suddenly appeared.'

'If he's only a phantom, why would that have made me change?'

'All right then, give me a name.'

'That's none of your business.'

'So I was right, he doesn't exist.'

'It's David, okay?'

There was a silence down the line for a moment. 'That's so generic,' he muttered. 'You just pulled that out of a hat.'

Liv was flabbergasted. 'Yes, Rick, I have a hat handy at all times, filled with random names on slips of paper, just in case you ask.' She sighed. 'I have to go.'

'But Liv –'

'Goodnight, Rick.'

Amblin Press

'Who's up for Friday lunch?' Liv announced, walking out of her office.

She was met with a rousing chorus of whoops and hollers from everyone on the floor. Friday lunch was a bit of an institution, whenever they could swing it. If they came to a Friday that was completely free of events – no author lunches, no library talks, no festivals – they went to lunch as a department. It was always a very *long* lunch: no one came back to the office afterwards. There was no point really – Friday afternoon wasn't a good time to conduct business. You couldn't find a journalist to save your life, and authors didn't want to be bothered with publicity matters at the start of a weekend.

'You've all done a wonderful job on the great desexing campaign,' said Liv. 'I met with Jane only this morning, and she's thoroughly impressed. So let's celebrate our collective awesomeness. I can't even remember the last time we had a Friday lunch.'

'Too long,' Ren called out.

'So,' Liv clapped her hands together, 'what are you all waiting for? Grab your hats! Let's get outta here.'

Friday lunch was always held at Durango's. It was a happy, vibrant place, and sitting in the sunny internal courtyard surrounded by Mexican kitsch, you could forget you were in the middle of the CBD. But most importantly, they served tapas. No self-respecting single girl wanted to be seen in public tucking into a full plate of food, but salad was a bit insubstantial when one was imbibing. Rocket leaves didn't soak up alcohol as well as fatty little morsels of chorizo and battered squid, not to mention the delectable variety of bacon, cheese and potato pastry thingies. The other clear advantage of Durango's was that the bar was popular with the Friday afternoon office crowd. In truth, this was the main attraction for the single women, who comprised most of the department.

It was such a big part of the attraction of Friday lunch that Madeleine had been feeling for some time now that she didn't really fit in any more, so she usually didn't mind having the excuse that she had to drive home. She liked a bit of fun as much as the next person, she just believed there was fun to be had in other ways than keeping scores on a list of 'hotness indicators', or playing 'Root, Shoot or Marry' or any number of inane games that basically centred around perving on, and fantasising about, the male patrons who filed through the door. Madeleine knew that if a group of men sat around a table rating women in the same way they'd be derided as sexist pigs. But she also knew she could never point that out to her colleagues for fear of being branded a feminazi killjoy.

Perhaps they were right, it was only a bit of fun. But the best thing about working in publicity was also the worst thing – it was staffed entirely by women. Madeleine couldn't help but think that a few good men added to the mix would do something towards correcting the hormonal imbalance in the office, especially come Friday afternoon.

'A toast!' Liv declared when the first round of drinks arrived at the table. 'To working hard and working smart. Especially you, Madeleine. You did a fantastic job with those press releases. You effectively gave the girls a script to work from, and for that matter, the authors as well.'

Madeleine smiled graciously and raised her glass.

Liv peered at it. 'What are you drinking?'

'Mineral water,' she said.

'Are you going home tonight?'

'No, but I'm pacing myself. I'll have something when the food comes out.'

'That's very sensible of you,' Liv said, clearly approving.

Madeleine had been sorely tempted to order one of those Mexican beers with a wedge of lemon. But after her experience with Aiden last week she didn't want to risk getting sick later on, and she knew if she started drinking too early that was on the cards. She wanted to enjoy herself, prove once and for all that she could handle a few drinks without dire consequences – and definitely without a hangover.

Still, she should probably call Henry before she started drinking, in case he tried to call her later. They had talked on Wednesday night, and twice yesterday. He had hoped that she would be coming home tonight, until she told him she had essential wedding-related shopping to do on Saturday. Only she didn't. Madeleine felt mean about lying, but then she remembered what Aiden had said about sparing the other person's feelings. This might be her last chance to have a night out with the girls, and what Henry didn't know couldn't hurt him.

Her phone started to play the rumba – that might be him now. She fished it out of her handbag and checked the screen, and her heart jumped. It was Aiden.

She turned away from the table. 'Hi! Where are you?'

'I'm at the airport, I've just flown back from Canberra. I'm a little ahead of schedule . . . I guess you're not going home for a few hours yet?'

'Actually, I'm not going home at all. Henry's not expecting me until tomorrow.'

'Well, well,' he said. 'Do you want to grab a drink after work? When do you get off?'

'I'm off already,' she said. 'I'm out for a long lunch with the rest of my department. We won't be going back to work this afternoon.'

'Oh . . . okay then. Well, maybe I can meet you later?'

'No, come meet us now!' she said.

'Are you sure? I don't want to crash your party.'

'Don't worry about that, you're going to be a very welcome addition to the party. Though I should warn you, you'll be the only male.'

'Now you're talking.'

She gave Aiden the address of Durango's and he said he'd be right over, he just needed to take a detour by the apartment to drop off his bags. Madeleine hung up, turning around again to face the table. The girls were chattering excitedly, and Ren had called over a waiter to order another round. Madeleine couldn't help feeling a little chuffed that she was going to get to show off Aiden. She only hoped he would survive it.

One hour later

'Oh em gee!' Ren hissed. 'Get a load of what just walked in.'

Heads turned left and right, and no doubt the force of all those eyeballs drew Aiden's gaze towards them. He smiled broadly and held up his hand in a wave. A frisson of electricity literally travelled the length of the table. Yes, literally – Madeleine was quite sure she would get zapped if she were to touch anyone right now. Aiden was utterly delectable in jeans and a crisp white shirt with a casual dark jacket. It was like seeing him for the first time all over again, imagining how he looked to the girls. His features were positively chiselled, as though his face had been carved out of honey-coloured wood, and you could tell all the way across the room that his eyes were blue. Madeleine rose to her feet as he made his way over, those bluer-than-blue eyes trained solely on her. This was going to be fun.

'Maddie,' he exclaimed, throwing his arms around her with his customary exuberance. 'It's good to see you. I missed you.' He drew back to look at her. 'So, are you going to introduce me to your friends?'

When she turned back to the table it was like staring into a fish tank – all open mouths and goggling eyes. 'Everyone, this is Aiden Carmichael, he's going to be the best man at our wedding.'

Their expressions shifted from shock and awe, to dawning realisation, to barely contained excitement. This was the man they'd been waiting to meet. He was tall, handsome and available. Let the games begin.

Suddenly the table broke into a simultaneous cross-examination, like a pack of journalists at a press conference, or seagulls fighting over a chip. They were all talking at once, and Aiden didn't have a hope of keeping up with them.

'One at a time, girls,' Liv said loudly, getting their attention. 'You'll frighten the poor man away.' They all looked duly chastened. She turned to Aiden and held out her hand. 'Hi, Aiden, I'm Liv. Pleased to meet you finally. We've heard so much about you.'

'Liv,' he said, taking her hand. 'But aren't you the boss? You must have started working when you were twelve.'

Madeleine didn't think she'd ever seen Liv blush before. Aiden seemed to have this effect on everyone. 'Aiden,' she said with a sweep of her arm, 'this is Stacey, Lauren –'

'Call me Ren.'

'Sarah, Natalie, Katie and Amy.'

'I hope there's not going to be a test,' he joked, at which they all laughed, a little too loudly.

'Let me get you a drink,' said Liv. 'You need to catch up with this lot.'

'No, I should be buying the drinks.'

'No way,' said Natalie, jumping up from her seat. 'I'll get it.'

'Or I will!' Sarah offered, getting to her feet. 'I'm closer.'

'I said it first,' Natalie hissed. 'What will you have?' she asked Aiden, starting to walk backwards in the direction of the bar in case anyone tried to overtake her.

'A beer would be great. Thank you.'

He didn't buy another drink all afternoon. Publicists were accustomed to looking after people, and Aiden was the main attraction, the guest star. He took to the role with aplomb, holding the floor with stories of his work abroad.

'What's the worst thing you've ever seen?' Natalie asked.

'Tasteless much?' said Ren. 'Do you slow down to gawk at car accidents too?'

'Piss off.'

'Ladies,' Liv chimed in.

'It's okay,' said Aiden. 'I'd have to say it's always the children that get to me. We can do a lot for them, we have done a lot –

immunisation alone has probably saved somewhere in the vicinity of two to three million lives. But sometimes I wonder what we're saving them for.'

'What do you mean?' Sarah asked.

'Their lives are just so relentlessly grim. In the west we often talk about kids falling through the cracks, but in these places the cracks are great, wide chasms of the most bone-crushing poverty you could imagine. Millions of children live on the streets in India, and I do mean children, living alone, on the streets. Here, someone would report them, someone would pick them up, and yes, maybe they wouldn't have the best of lives, but they would have a chance. These kids have no chance, they live and work in the trash, next to open sewers. They're at a much higher risk of disease, but they're frightened of authority figures, so we can't get anywhere near them to give them medical attention, to give them anything.'

He paused, staring at the label on his bottle of beer. 'Even worse are the ones you don't see. There are Nepalese girls as young as nine being sold into brothels in India, children from Sudan and Yemen trafficked into the Gulf states to be camel jockeys, of all things, entertainment for the rich. It's very dangerous, you know, a lot of them are killed doing it, but it's okay, because they're disposable.' Aiden was shaking his head. 'Then I go back home, and I see my nieces and nephews complaining about being bored, or turning up their noses at food – and look, they're great kids, I love them, they don't know anything else. But . . . remember when your mom used to tell you to finish your dinner and think about the starving children in Africa? Well, now I do. I can't stop thinking about them.'

Suddenly Madeleine understood why Aiden was so overwhelmed, and why he felt so hopeless. She really wanted to give him a hug right now.

'Have you ever thought about writing a book?' Liv asked him.

He shook his head as all the women made noises in agreement. 'I wouldn't have the patience,' he said.

'Well, you tell a good story,' she said. 'I'm quite certain our nonfiction publisher would be interested. And she could always hook you up with a ghost writer, or even a co-writer.'

'I dunno,' he said with a self-deprecating grimace, 'I think I'd rather be out there doing it than writing about it.'

That unintended innuendo set off a schoolgirl titter around the table. They had all been in Aiden's thrall since he arrived, and although the early office crowd had started to file in, no one at the table seemed to have noticed. Natalie was leaning forward, directly across from him, her chin resting in her hands, gazing at him with blatant adoration and drooling so badly she was in danger of leaving a puddle. Honestly, they were all well on the way to tipsy town. Madeleine was glad she'd decided to take it slow; she was feeling quite smug and proud of herself. She could totally do this.

'So, I think it might be time to move this party on,' Aiden announced. 'Who's with me?'

'This place kicks on into the night,' said Sarah. 'There's no need for us to move anywhere.'

'You don't think so?' he said.

'You don't like it here?' Natalie was dismayed.

Aiden treated them to an adorably apologetic expression. 'Here's the thing. I've spent a lot of time in Mexico, and seeing as I'm in Sydney, I'd like to go someplace that looks like Sydney. Maybe down near the harbour? I haven't seen the Opera House up close yet.'

'Okay,' said Liv. 'The Opera Bar it is then, obviously.'

'Yes!' Ren agreed. 'Then we'll be close to The Rocks, we can probably find somewhere with live music later on.'

'I know a place . . .'

They started excitedly discussing the range of options for the night as Aiden shepherded them out onto the street. Madeleine suddenly realised that her phone was ringing, and she scrabbled in her bag for it. Just as she plucked it out and looked at the screen, it stopped ringing. It was Henry. Damn, Aiden's call earlier had distracted her, and she'd forgotten to ring him.

She touched Aiden's arm to get his attention. He turned and leaned in close to her. 'Henry just rang, I have to call him back, away from the noise.'

'Sure, we'll wait for you.'

She ducked around the corner of the building and tapped the screen to return the call.

'Hi, Madeleine,' Henry answered.

'Sorry, I just missed you. I couldn't hear the phone in the restaurant.'

'You've left work already?'

'Um, actually we left a while ago for lunch, but we're finished now.'

'Oh, do you want to ring me back when you get home?'

She swallowed. 'No, it's fine. I can talk. How's everything there?' she added quickly.

'Good, getting plenty of work done,' he said. 'I think I can finally see light at the end of the tunnel.'

'That's great, Henry, you've been working so hard.'

'Listen, you haven't heard from Aiden, have you?'

She froze. She didn't know what to say.

'Madeleine? Madeleine, are you there?'

'Yes, I'm here . . . you dropped out for a moment.'

'Can you hear me now?'

'Yeah. What were you saying?'

He repeated the question while she gathered her thoughts. She couldn't speak for Aiden, she didn't know what he wanted to tell Henry about his whereabouts.

'He hasn't been in touch with you?' she said, avoiding an actual lie.

'No, I haven't heard a word. He said in that text message the other night that he'd see us at the end of the week, didn't he?'

'I think so,' said Madeleine. 'But that could mean tomorrow. I wouldn't worry, he's a big boy.'

'Of course,' he said. 'Let me know if you hear from him.'

Bugger. 'I'll tell him to give you a call.' Talk about semantic gymnastics.

'Do you know what time you'll be coming home tomorrow?' he asked tentatively.

'Not sure,' she said vaguely. 'Depends how I get on . . .'

'Well, good luck with the shopping.'

Madeleine cringed.

'Maybe you can buzz me when you're on your way home?'

'Sure.'

'I'll let you go, I know you're out on the street.'

'Okay, have a good night.'

'You too. I love you, Madeleine.'

'Love you too.'

She hung up, feeling sick. What if Henry tried Aiden again? She had to speak to him immediately. She hurried around the corner, where only Aiden and Liv were left standing by the kerb. 'Where is everyone?' she asked.

'Stacey and Amy had somewhere else they had to be,' said Liv. 'They said to say goodbye.'

'And the others are already on their way down to the harbour,' said Aiden. 'We couldn't all fit in one taxi.'

'You should have seen the carry-on.' Liv rolled her eyes. 'They were all trying to angle a ride with Aiden.'

'Stop it,' he said. 'We ready to go?'

As Madeleine nodded, she grabbed Aiden by the arm, manoeuvring him between herself and Liv. 'Have you had a call from Henry?' she said close to his ear.

'What? No . . . I don't know.'

'Don't answer if he calls, okay? Not till I get a chance to talk to you.'

Liv had managed to hail a taxi, and it pulled up in front of them.

'Is everything okay?' Aiden said, under his breath.

'Yes, of course.'

He gave her hand a squeeze. 'Okay, don't worry.'

Opera Bar

The girls were waiting eagerly when their taxi pulled up at Circular Quay. It was a perfect spring evening – when Sydney got it right, the superlatives just didn't do it justice. As they walked along the concourse, Aiden got his first real view of the Opera House up close, and his face nearly split in two from grinning.

'This is more like it,' he sighed happily.

So he was positively delirious when they came to the bar, which was tucked into a sweeping curve on the water's edge, directly opposite the Harbour Bridge and in the shadow of the Opera House.

'Okay, we have to get some photos of this, with everyone,' he declared.

'I think we better find a table first,' said Madeleine. On such a gorgeous afternoon the place was humming. However, it was still relatively early, so they managed to grab one of the bench tables at the southern end, giving Aiden a panoramic view from the peaks of the Opera House sails to right across the harbour. He was clearly rapt. The girls scurried to gather up enough stools to seat them all while Aiden snapped away with the camera in his phone. Eventually he lined them all up along the stone wall edging the water, with the bridge behind them, and then he asked a waiter to take a shot so that he could be in the photo as well . . . and then he asked for one of just him and Madeleine.

'Now just with me,' Natalie blurted.

'Oh, come on, we're not going through everyone,' Liv said, rescuing Aiden from a potentially lengthy photo shoot. 'We'll be here all night, and I'm thirsty.'

'This round is definitely on me,' Aiden insisted. 'And I think it has to be champagne. Is that okay with everyone?'

It was, and Natalie scampered after him like a puppy to help.

'Why didn't you tell us how cute he is?' Ren demanded of Madeleine, as soon as Aiden was out of earshot.

'Because he's not.'

'What?'

'Cute.'

'Why?'

'He's not sixteen,' Liv answered for Madeleine. 'That man is way past cute.'

Sarah was nodding enthusiastically. 'And it's not just his looks, he's *so* utterly charming.'

'And funny,' said Katie.

'And fascinating,' added Sarah.

'And *hot*,' said Ren.

'And that voice!' said Sarah.

'You mean the accent?' Katie asked.

'Not just the accent, his voice comes from right down in his chest.'

'I wonder what his chest is like?' Ren mused. 'Have you seen him without a shirt on, Mad?'

'Okay, this is getting weird.'

'Well, you get to live with him,' said Katie. 'You can at least throw us a bone.'

'A boner, more like,' Ren snorted.

'That's disgusting,' Madeleine frowned.

'And physically impossible,' said Liv. 'You want her to throw you his erect penis?'

'I wouldn't throw it back.'

'That's enough,' Madeleine hissed. 'He'll be back any minute. Show a little respect. He's like a brother to Henry, which makes him like a brother-in-law to me.' Not that she thought of Aiden that way. He was nothing like her real brother-in-law, Mark. Ugh. Nothing to fantasise about there.

And nothing to fantasise about here, either! All this talk was messing with her head. She needed a drink. It was one thing to show Aiden off, but it was quite another to have them lusting after him like a piece of meat, for anyone's consumption.

'It's warm out here,' she remarked, fanning herself with her hand. 'Is anyone else warm?'

'I'll see if they have any jugs of water at the bar,' Sarah offered, heading off in that direction.

All three soon returned with two bottles in ice buckets, and a tray of champagne flutes. Sarah handed Madeleine a glass of water. 'Sorry, there weren't any jugs.'

Aiden lifted the first bottle out of the ice and began to fill the glasses. 'They said they had to pop the cork behind the bar. Some health and safety issue apparently, courtesy of the fun police.'

'That makes them the popping party poopers.' Natalie giggled.

'Cripes,' Liv muttered, grabbing two full glasses from the tray and passing one to Madeleine.

When the glasses had all been distributed, Aiden raised his. 'This really does call for a toast.'

'I think we should drink to the best man,' Natalie gushed, and everyone readily agreed, raising their glasses and saying his name at once.

'No, wait,' Aiden spoke over the top of them. 'Hold on a minute, I'm only here because of this beautiful woman,' he said, putting an arm around Madeleine. 'We should be drinking to Henry and Madeleine's health.'

'But Henry's not here,' said Ren.

'Good point,' said Aiden. 'To Madeleine.'

'And to Aiden.'

'To Madeleine and Aiden,' they all chorused. And Madeleine quickly downed a couple of mouthfuls of champagne to drown the guilt she was feeling. She mustn't forget to tell Aiden about Henry's call.

'So this could be your last night out for a while, I guess?' Liv said to her.

'Especially after you give up your apartment,' said Aiden. 'Along with your freedom.'

Madeleine gave him a nudge.

'But isn't your house, like, nearly on the Central Coast?' asked Sarah. 'What if you have to work late?'

'It's not on the Central Coast,' Madeleine scoffed.

'Yeah, it's actually quicker to get to the Central Coast,' Liv said, 'with the freeway.'

'Nonsense, that couldn't be right.' Could it? 'Anyway, I'm going to try to avoid working long hours after we're married.'

'Oh? You are?' said Liv, raising an eyebrow.

Yikes, she shouldn't have said that in front of the boss. She didn't even think it, so why was she saying it? It wasn't like Henry could hear her.

'Well . . . I can always stay at my mum's place if . . . *when* I work late,' she said finally.

'I've just had a brilliant idea,' said Aiden. 'Why don't we make this your bachelorette party?'

Natalie grinned. 'We don't call it that here.'

'What do you call it?'

'A hens' night.'

'Why? That's terrible,' Aiden said with a grimace.

'I know, isn't it?' said Liv. 'Men get a bucks' night.'

'We call it that too,' said Aiden, 'or a bachelor party. How did "hen" get partnered with "buck"?'

'Buggered if I know,' said Liv. 'I remember when it used to be called a does' night. I don't know when it changed to hens.'

'But it doesn't even make sense. Why "hen"? It's not a baby shower.' Aiden shook his head as though it was beyond his comprehension. 'Well, I'm sticking with bachelorette party,' he decided. 'What do you say, Maddie?'

'I wasn't going to have a hens' or a bachelorette night, or anything.'

'Why not?'

Madeleine sighed. 'I don't know . . . Gen is my matron of honour. She wouldn't have time to organise it, and she probably couldn't get a babysitter so she could come herself. It just hasn't come up, to be honest.'

'Well, it's coming up now,' said Aiden.

'We should have organised something, Mad,' said Liv. 'I feel bad.'

'It's fine, I'm really not fussed,' said Madeleine. 'Henry's not having a bucks' night.'

'Isn't that up to me?' said Aiden. 'I'm the best man.'

'He's not going to want one,' she said. 'Besides, you're probably the only person he could ask.'

'So I'll take him out for a drink,' said Aiden. 'But I'm your best man too, and if this is going to be your last big night out, then I'm calling it a bachelorette party. And that's all there is to it.'

'A man of action,' said Liv, raising her glass to him. 'I like it.'

Aiden clinked his glass against Liv's and took a swig of his champagne before putting it back down on the table. 'All right,' he said, clapping his hands together. 'It's too late to organise a male stripper. What else goes down at a bachelorette party?'

'Interesting choice of words,' Ren remarked.

Aiden gave her a sideways look, more of a leer really, Madeleine noted.

'I know, I know!' said Natalie. 'What about the game where you have to design a wedding dress out of toilet paper?'

'Borr*ring*,' said Ren.

'And I think management might take issue if we started wrapping ourselves in their toilet paper out here in full view,' said Madeleine.

'I have an idea!' Sarah jumped off her stool and bolted off. 'I'll just be a sec,' she called over her shoulder.

She came strolling back a few minutes later, her arms crossed in front of her and a conspiratorial grin on her face. At the table she pulled out a large scrunched wad of toilet paper she had tucked under her arm.

'I'm not going to wear a toilet paper wedding dress,' Madeleine said flatly.

'No,' said Sarah. 'Just a veil!'

'Yes!' Katie jumped off her stool to come around behind Madeleine. 'Who's got bobby pins?'

'No, wait,' Madeleine protested as they all started searching in their handbags. 'I don't want to go round with toilet paper on my head.' That made Aiden laugh. 'I'm not even wearing a veil at the wedding.'

'You're not?' said Aiden. 'But Lucy and I both thought the veil was perfect.'

'What?' said Liv, looking confused.

'I was lucky enough to accompany Maddie to her fitting the other day,' Aiden explained.

Madeleine could feel them all gaping at her, especially Liv. 'M-my sister couldn't make it,' she stammered, 'and it was my final fitting, so . . .'

'Well, aren't you a gorgeous best man going with her?' Natalie gushed.

'What's the dress like?' Sarah gasped, her eyes wide.

'My lips are sealed,' said Aiden. 'Except to say that she looks amazing. Especially with the veil,' he added.

'Enough about the veil,' said Madeleine. 'I didn't say I'd wear it.'

'Well brides always wear veils on their hens' night,' said Katie. 'Haven't you ever noticed them?'

'Yes, and they look tacky, and they're not even made of toilet paper!'

'Settle down.' Sarah patted her on the shoulder. 'Promise we won't make you look stupid.'

As far as toilet paper veils went, Madeleine supposed they could have done worse. Between them, Sarah and Katie fashioned a rosette for a headpiece, with a few lengths flowing down her back.

'Now that's a bride.' Aiden raised his glass when they were finished. 'To Madeleine.'

She could feel people staring. She took a sip from her glass, and then another, more of a gulp really. It was excellent champagne; she almost smacked her lips. She hated to think what Aiden must have paid for it.

'All right, so now we need a wedding-related game,' he said.

'I've got one!' said Ren. 'We did this at my friend's hens' night.'

Aiden winced. 'I wish you'd stop calling it that.'

'Anyway,' Ren went on, 'there was a game show like this on the telly, yonks ago. You ask the bride questions about the groom to see how well she knows him.'

'That's *The Newlywed Game*,' said Aiden. 'We had it in the States as well.'

'We would have got it from you.'

'How are we going to play it here?' Liv asked. 'With no groom?'

'We ask Madeleine questions about Henry,' Ren explained, 'and if she gets them right –'

'But wait, we don't really know Henry,' said Natalie, 'so how will we know if she's getting them right?'

'You could trust me?' Madeleine suggested.

They ignored that.

'Aiden could speak for Henry,' said Liv. 'You've known him the longest, right?'

'Sure,' he said. 'I can do that.'

'And if Mad gets the answer wrong, she has to drink a shot,' said Ren.

'Hold on a minute,' said Madeleine. 'You didn't say anything about making it a drinking game.'

'Why not? You're not driving,' Aiden said. 'And it's not much of a game if there are no stakes involved.'

Madeleine didn't know, shots might be taking things too far.

'Look,' said Aiden, 'this will be entirely based on you answering a series of questions about Henry, so how can you lose? You know everything about him, you live with him.'

That was the thing, Madeleine felt like she didn't know everything about Henry at all, but she could hardly say that out loud. Everyone was watching her, waiting, coaxing. She finally caved to the pressure.

'Okay,' she relented.

'That's the spirit,' said Aiden.

The girls started establishing the rules and the way the game would be played. They set Madeleine and Aiden up on stools on one side of the table, while the rest of them sat facing them like a panel. They would ask the questions in an orderly fashion, one at a time. Aiden had the last word on whether an answer was acceptable, and no further discussion would be entered into. They were about to begin when Aiden reminded them that they didn't have any shots to drink.

'You go with Aiden, Mad,' said Ren. 'We need to organise our questions.'

As soon as they were alone, Madeleine grabbed Aiden's arm. 'I haven't told you about Henry's call,' she said.

'Oh yeah, what was that about?'

'He asked if I'd heard from you,' she said. 'And I kind of avoided telling him.'

'Okay . . .'

'It was just that we'd already been talking for a few minutes, then he asked if I'd heard from you, and if I suddenly said you were with me . . . I don't know.' She gave up. She didn't really know how to explain herself.

'It's okay, I get it.' They joined the queue at the bar.

'You see, I didn't know what you wanted to tell him . . .' She hesitated. 'I didn't even say I was going out tonight.'

Aiden nodded. 'Well, he won't hear it from me.'

'I don't want to keep lying to him.'

'Don't worry, Maddie, I get it, and Henry probably wouldn't. So it'll be our little secret.'

She looked dismayed. 'Did you have to use that expression?'

'Hey, it's okay,' he said, slinging an arm over her shoulders. 'You just want to have a bit of fun tonight, and, as we've established, it might be your last chance. And what Henry doesn't know won't hurt him.'

Which was exactly what she'd thought too. The very same words, which was kind of unsettling.

As they moved further in the queue, Madeleine looked up at Aiden. 'About this game. You haven't spent time with Henry in years, there's probably a lot you don't know about him.'

'"Give me a child until he's seven and I will give you the man,"' he quoted.

'But you didn't know him when he was seven.'

'Seven, seventeen, not much difference,' said Aiden. 'And Henry was set in his ways even then. I don't think much has changed.'

He was right. As Aiden had pointed out before, Henry was living the same life here as he had in the States. He was set in his ways . . . even in the bedroom.

Aiden was watching her. 'What, don't you trust me?'

She stirred. 'No, no, it's not that.'

'Because I'm an honourable guy, you know.'

She smiled. 'I know you are.'

When they got to the bar, Aiden ordered a bottle of tequila.

'Seriously?' Madeleine grimaced.

'Would you prefer something else? You're welcome to choose your own poison.'

'Well, it's just a bit messy, isn't it? Don't you need lemon and salt?'

'If you're a *girl*,' he said sardonically.

She wouldn't point out the obvious.

'And a shot glass,' Aiden said to the barman when he placed the bottle on the bar.

'Only one?' Madeleine asked.

'You're the only one being put to the test,' he said.

Great.

*

'We're going to start with some easy questions, like they do on lie detector tests,' said Sarah, with an air of authority.

'They do that to establish a baseline for your blood pressure and heart rate,' said Madeleine.

'Whatever.' Sarah waved the remark away. 'I'll go first.' She cleared her throat importantly. 'What's Henry's favourite colour?'

Madeleine frowned.

'You're kidding? You don't know?'

'No, I just don't know that he has a favourite colour. I mean, he loves colour, he works with colour, he's an artist . . . But I couldn't tell you his favourite.'

'Wow, you're bombing out on the easiest question!' Natalie declared.

'Shot!' Ren called, grabbing the bottle.

'Hold on,' said Aiden. 'You're supposed to check with me first. And Maddie's right, I don't think Henry would have a favourite colour.'

Madeleine was relieved. He was being honourable.

'Okay, what's his favourite food?' asked Ren.

She was thinking . . . thinking . . . but nothing came. She'd drawn a total blank.

'She's got nothing,' Ren cried. 'Shot!'

'Really, he's just not fussy,' Madeleine tried to explain. 'He'll eat anything.' She paused. 'Oh, will this do? Anything except strawberries. He has an allergy.'

'She's right,' said Aiden. 'He tried one at a party at our place once, and his lips all swelled up till he looked like a duck, poor guy. Though it was pretty funny.'

'We're asking the wrong questions,' Ren grumbled.

'What about his favourite film?' said Katie.

'He's not really into movies.'

'Summer or winter?' Sarah tried.

'I don't think he has a preference.'

'Dog or cat?' asked Liv.

'Well, we don't have a pet, and he didn't have one growing up, so . . .'

'It's true,' said Aiden. 'Henry never had a pet.'

'He never had a pet?' said Ren. 'That's a bit weird, isn't it?'

Madeleine bristled. 'Not necessarily.' Though she had often thought it was sad that his parents hadn't bought their only child a dog, for some company if nothing else. Because of that, Henry didn't really have an affinity for animals now. It wasn't his fault.

'How about . . .' Katie paused. 'Chocolate or vanilla?'

'He's not keen on chocolate,' said Madeleine. 'So I'd have to say vanilla. But he doesn't eat ice cream anyway.'

'White or red?'

'He isn't much of a drinker, he'll have a glass of whatever's opened with dinner.'

'Oh, for crying out loud.' Ren finally broke. 'We need a more interesting groom!'

Madeleine felt defensive on poor Henry's behalf. 'He *is* interesting,' she said. 'He's just easygoing. Isn't that right, Aiden?'

'Absolutely,' he agreed, giving her hand a squeeze. 'But easygoing makes for a dull game, I'm afraid.'

'We need more drinks,' said Ren. The two champagne bottles were empty and upturned in their ice buckets.

'Oh, let me –'

'No way, Aiden,' said Ren, 'not this time. Our shout.' They took orders and Sarah and Ren went off to the bar.

'We need to bring this bachelorette party to life,' said Liv.

'We could try some hypotheticals,' Aiden suggested. 'They do that in these kinds of games, don't they?'

'What do you mean by hypotheticals?' Natalie asked.

'If Henry was faced with a moral or ethical dilemma,' Liv explained, 'how would he handle it?'

'So how do we test that?'

'It'll still be up to Aiden,' said Liv.

'You'll just have to take my word for it,' he said.

When the others returned from the bar, they went into a huddle to devise some scenarios, and then began to put them to Madeleine. If Henry was given too much change in a shop, and he realised, would he return it? Madeleine said that of course he would, and Aiden had to agree; they could both give examples of when Henry had done just that.

After a couple more scenarios treading similar ground – cheating on tax and petty theft generally – the situations became more complicated, and more morally ambiguous.

'What if you were sick,' Ren proposed. 'Like, really sick, you were going to die. And there was this medicine that could cure you, but you couldn't afford it. Would Henry steal it, or steal the money to pay for it, to save your life?'

'We have Medicare in this country,' said Madeleine. 'That could never happen.'

Ren groaned. 'Okay then, let's say you've gone to live in the US with Henry. It could happen there, right?' she asked Aiden.

'Yes, unfortunately.'

Madeleine was frowning. 'Still, it would have to be a ridiculous sum of money for Henry not to be able to afford it. I'm not saying he's ridiculously wealthy, but there would be a way that we could pay for it.'

'No, there wouldn't!' Ren was getting frustrated. 'We're talking hypothetically, remember?'

'Fine,' Madeleine said. 'So it's millions of dollars. How would Henry go about stealing that amount of money? How would anyone who wasn't a professional criminal?'

'He hires someone, okay?'

'But –'

'Do you understand what hypothetical means?' Ren said loudly.

'All right, all right,' said Madeleine. 'So I'm going to die if I don't get this medicine . . . and Henry has some way of stealing it . . . Okay, I think he would steal it, and then, once he knew I was all right, he would turn himself in.'

'Really, even if he'd got away with it?' Sarah asked.

'Yep.'

'I have to agree,' said Aiden. 'That's the kind of guy he is.'

Although there followed a collective groan, Madeleine didn't care. Henry wasn't uninteresting, he was just a very decent man.

'This isn't working,' Aiden said. 'We're never going to get you drunk at this rate.'

'I didn't think that was the object of the game,' said Madeleine.

'Of course it is,' he said with a grin. 'What if I quiz you on how much you know about Henry's past?'

'You told me Henry doesn't have a past,' she returned.

'Oh, he has a past all right.'

Madeleine raised an eyebrow. 'Are you still going to be honourable?'

'Depends on how you define honourable.'

'Aiden!'

'I promise to tell the truth, the whole truth, and nothing but the truth, so help me, God,' he declared with a hand on his heart, and the whole other side of the table visibly swooned, starstruck.

'All right,' said Madeleine, 'do your worst.'

Aiden thought for a moment. 'Okay, easy one first. Where did Henry grow up?'

'Oh, that's way too easy!' said Ren.

'I'm just working my way up,' he assured her.

'We've been working our way up all night!'

'Trust me,' he said. 'Maddie, what's your answer?'

'Columbus, Ohio.'

'Correct.'

'Whoopee,' Ren said glumly.

'Next question,' said Aiden, ignoring her. 'What was Henry's major at college?'

'Well, he did a Liberal Arts degree . . .'

'Yeah, but what was his major?'

She pressed her lips together, thinking. Damn. She should know this. They'd had conversations about the differences between the university system here and in the US, where undergraduate degrees were often more general, unless you were doing pre-law or pre-med. Henry had started off taking classes for pre-law but then realised he didn't like it. He had dabbled in literature, they'd talked about that . . .

'Tick, tick, tick,' said Aiden.

She looked up at him. 'I don't know,' she said in a small voice.

'What was that?'

Madeleine cleared her throat. 'I don't know.'

'Bam!' Ren cried, picking up the bottle of tequila to pour her a shot.

'So what was his major?' Madeleine asked Aiden, as Ren passed her the shot glass.

'Women's studies,' said Aiden.

There was a ripple of barely suppressed chuckles around the table, which Madeleine chose to ignore. 'Are you sure?'

Aiden nodded. 'After his sophomore year he realised he'd taken a class in just about everything. When he started to focus on getting published, he wanted to take the fastest route to graduation, which turned out to be via women's studies.'

'Why has he never told me that?'

'Why do you think?' Ren snorted. 'Now, shot!'

Madeleine took a deep breath, then drank the tequila. It took her two attempts. There was a slight burning sensation as it went down, before the warmth radiated out into her chest. Not too bad.

'All right,' said Aiden, clapping his hands together. 'Now we're getting somewhere.'

She was beginning to wonder if his motives really were honourable.

'What was the name of the first girl Henry kissed?'

That caught her by surprise. Henry wasn't what anyone would call a Lothario . . . But she was being silly. He was already in his thirties when they met, as *if* he hadn't kissed a girl. But whoever was first couldn't have been all that memorable – he'd never mentioned her, Madeleine was sure of that at least.

'Pour me another,' she said to Ren, surrendering. She got a round of applause for knocking it back in one go.

'Who did he take to his high school prom?' Aiden asked next.

'Was she also his first kiss?'

'Maybe . . . but how does that help? You didn't know who that was either.'

Madeleine picked up the glass Ren had already refilled. Her head was starting to feel a little woozy. She needed a moment. 'So what was her name?' she asked Aiden, stalling.

He shrugged. 'Becky, Betsy . . . something like that. I can't remember.'

'So you don't even know!'

'I just can't remember her name. I know his prom date was the first girl he kissed. Which is more than you knew.'

'Well, I think it's only fair that you take a shot.'

'Gladly,' said Aiden. 'After you.'

Madeleine sighed. Fine. She took a breath and sculled the shot. 'Refill, thanks, Ren.'

Aiden picked up the glass and threw it back before slamming it down on the table. 'Fill it up, bartender, she'll be needing another one before long,' he drawled.

'As long as you ask questions that you actually know the answer to,' Madeleine said.

'Fair enough.' Aiden met her eyes directly. 'Who was Henry's first love?'

Madeleine blanched. Had there been a first love? A real first love? 'I don't know.'

'Uh-huh! Shot!'

She tossed back the shot to get it out of the way. Besides, she was beginning to enjoy the tequila's anaesthetising effect.

'Next question –'

'No, wait,' said Madeleine. 'Aren't you going to tell me who his first love was?'

'Not if Henry hasn't told you himself.'

'You said you'd only ask questions that you knew the answer to.'

'I do know the answer, but I don't think it's my place if Henry hasn't told you.'

'It's just never come up,' she said. 'It's not like he wouldn't tell me.'

'Then ask him,' Aiden said simply. 'Moving on, who was the first girl who broke his heart?'

Henry had had his heart broken? So there *was* a real first love? Perhaps there'd been more than one. Perhaps there'd been many. Madeleine had no idea. He'd never confided in her.

'I don't know,' she muttered, picking up the shot glass and gulping it down. Then she grabbed her champagne flute and drank some of that too. It was flat by now, and a little warm, but she didn't care.

Aiden was watching her. 'Who was the first girl he moved countries for?' he said gently.

She looked wide-eyed at him. 'There was someone else?'

'No, no . . .' He brought his arm around her shoulder and gave her a squeeze. 'Silly.'

'Oh. Then that's me.'

She went to pick up the shot glass but Liv grabbed her wrist. 'Wait,' she said, 'you were right that time. You don't have to take a shot.'

'Maybe I just want to,' Madeleine retorted. She didn't like the look Liv was giving her.

'Take it easy, Mad.'

'Fine,' Madeleine said, putting the shot glass down again.

'How about we have an open round,' Aiden announced to the table.

'What do you mean?' asked Sarah.

'A free-for-all,' he said. 'Anyone can ask a question.'

'What sort of questions?' said Katie.

'Anything you like,' Madeleine said, draining her glass of warm, flat champagne. Hopefully Liv wouldn't have a problem with that.

'Let's make it general,' Aiden suggested. 'You know, funny questions about being a guy, whatever.'

'I know,' said Liv. 'What's Henry's most annoying habit? There has to be something, all men have at least one.'

'That's very sexist,' said Aiden. 'Not all men have annoying habits. I, for one, have no annoying habits at all.'

They actually all laughed at that. Big proper belly laughs. At least they had stopped being impossibly besotted with him.

'Okay, spill, missy,' Liv prompted Madeleine. 'Henry's most annoying habit.'

'I guess . . . well, he cracks his knuckles. I can't stand it.'

They all started talking at once. 'I hate that.' 'Eew!' 'Why do guys do that?' 'What is wrong with you?'

'Why are you asking me?' Aiden objected.

'You don't crack your knuckles?'

'You mean like this?' he said, clasping his hands together and stretching his arms out in front of him, before quickly inverting his hands and releasing the most spine-curdling crunching sound, setting them off all over again.

'You should have to take a shot for doing that,' said Katie, still cringing.

'Or be shot,' Liv added.

'No,' said Madeleine, grabbing the glass first. 'I need one after that.'

The game morphed into a version of truth or dare. Not that there were any dares, per se, just increasingly personal questions, and Madeleine hit back every one like she was an ace tennis player in front of one of those ball machines. She didn't so much as flinch.

'Does he put the seat down?'

'Never!'

'Boxers or briefs?'

'Boxers!' she declared. 'Baggy cotton ones. I hate them, but he refuses to wear anything else.'

'Does he snore?'

'On occasion, but then so do I sometimes, so I can't complain.'

'Favourite sexual position?'

Madeleine paused. 'What do you bloody well think? Missionary, of course!' She threw her head back so far laughing that she would have tipped backwards off the stool if Aiden hadn't grabbed her in time.

'Whoa!' he said, righting her and the stool. 'Careful . . .'

Madeleine leaned her head against his shoulder and clung to him as she waited for her brain to stop swishing around. She could smell Aiden through his shirt, and a flush crept up her chest and across her face. Someone had asked before if she'd seen him without a shirt on, and she had, at the beach. All three of them were together, so Madeleine couldn't exactly stare, but she had managed to steal the odd furtive glance. And no surprise, Aiden did look amazing without a shirt – he was broad-shouldered, with tight abs, and he had a *very* nice chest. Madeleine smoothed her hand across it now. This was her bachelorette party, her last night of freedom . . .

*

Liv was watching as Madeleine blatantly pawed at Aiden, and decided she had to put an end to this. 'I think it's time to call it a night,' she announced, slipping off her stool.

There was a loud protest from around the table.

'It's not that late,' Madeleine slurred. 'And besides, it's my bachelorette party.'

She could hardly get the word 'bachelorette' out. Liv came around and leaned in close to Madeleine. 'Don't you think you should quit while you're ahead?'

Madeleine gave her a petulant glare. 'You're as bad as Henry.'

Okay, that was it. Liv reached behind Madeleine and tapped Aiden on the shoulder. He looked around. 'Can I speak with you for a minute?' she said in a low voice.

'Sure.' He disentangled himself from Madeleine and propped her up against the table, and then stepped away to face Liv.

'You have to take her home,' Liv said.

'Why? She's having fun.'

'She's had too much to drink and she's not handling it. What do you think Henry would want you to do?' she said pointedly.

Aiden frowned. 'But I can't just order her.'

'Well, I can,' said Liv. 'If you won't take her home, I will. Then you can go off with your little cheer squad over there.'

He rubbed his forehead with his hand. 'No, I got her into this, I'll take care of her. You're right, I'm the best man.'

'Then act like one.'

They turned back to the group, and Madeleine grabbed Aiden's arm. 'We've decided – next stop, karaoke!'

'I'm sorry, Maddie, I'm suddenly feeling shattered.'

'*Awww!*' The girls chorused in dismay.

'Are you all right?' Natalie asked Aiden. 'Can I get you anything?'

'Thanks,' he said. 'But I just need to go home. I've been in meetings for three days solid, I haven't got the energy for karaoke.'

Madeleine pouted. 'But it's my bachelorette party!'

He took her by the hands. 'And it's been a good one, but I'm with Liv, I think it's best to call it a night while we're all still standing.'

'Come on,' said Liv, 'we'll walk back to the taxi rank together.'

The others decided they were going to kick on anyway, so everyone gathered around to give Liv, Aiden and Madeleine the kind of farewell that drunk people do, as though they were seeing off loved ones on a journey abroad and didn't know when they would meet again. They finally extricated themselves and started off down the concourse. Madeleine was a little wobbly on her feet, but Aiden seemed to have a firm hold of her, and they made it to the Quay with her dignity intact.

There was a long line of taxis waiting. 'You guys go first,' said Liv.

'Are you sure?' Aiden said.

'Absolutely. Bye now, Mad, have a good night's sleep.'

Madeleine threw her arms around Liv with a dramatic flourish, and planted a sloppy kiss on her cheek. 'I love you. You're my best friend in the world,' she slurred. 'She's my best friend in the world,' she said to Aiden as he peeled her off Liv.

'I know,' he said. 'She's a very good friend.'

'The best.'

Liv waited while Aiden helped Madeleine into the taxi. He turned back to her. 'It was good meeting you, Liv.'

'Well, aren't you going to give me a hug? I don't bite, despite all the evidence to the contrary.'

He smiled, and bent down to hug her. 'Thanks for the voice of reason. I promise I'll take good care of her.'

'You better. See you at the wedding.'

He climbed into the taxi and closed the door behind him, giving her a wave through the window. Liv walked down to the next taxi and got in.

'Oatley, thanks,' she said. The driver should be pleased with that, it was a decent fare, though she was never sure – they didn't much like being stuck out in the suburbs on a Friday night. But he just said okay and pulled away from the kerb.

'You don't mind the music?' he asked, turning up the radio.

'Not at all,' said Liv. That meant she wouldn't have to make conversation. She didn't mind talking to cabbies, they were often quite interesting in their take on the world. But tonight she was tired, and it was a fairly long drive, too long to sustain a conversation with a stranger. So she settled into her seat, resting her head against the back. She'd done the right thing sending Aiden and Madeleine on their way, even though she'd felt like house mother doing it. She was worried about the amount of alcohol Mad had put away. She'd started off so well, pacing herself, but it was the shots that had been her undoing. Liv wasn't sure what to make of Aiden. He was charming, no doubt about that. And he seemed to genuinely care about Madeleine. But what was that about him going to her fitting? Mad hadn't mentioned that – not surprisingly. It was a little odd, and she wondered if Henry was okay with it, if he even knew about it. She must remember to call Madeleine in the morning to check on her.

Liv was also glad for her own sake that she'd called it a night. She had a nice buzz on, but at this point it would be so easy to take it further, and such a mistake. She was getting too old to deal with hangovers; years of early-morning soccer games had cured her of that.

But she had to admit it was fun to have a night out. At different times throughout the evening she'd found her thoughts turning to David, wondering how he would fit in with everybody – say, for example, she were to bring him to Madeleine's wedding. Not that that was going to happen. Liv didn't know why she was even entertaining the idea. But still she wondered, idly, what it would be like to be out with David socially. She supposed it would have to happen eventually, if they kept seeing each other. He was a nice man, an attractive man; she would be proud to have him as a date.

She took out her phone now and scrolled through her contacts to his name. It occurred to her that she could just ring him. Might be a bit strange – it was kind of late – but she could ring him if she wanted to. What do they call that? A booty call. She could give David a booty call . . . She grinned to herself in the back seat in the dark. Hilarious. And tempting. Lucky she'd stopped drinking when she had.

She must remember to call Madeleine in the morning.

Chippendale

'Maddie, we're here,' Aiden said gently.

'Where?'

'Home. At your apartment.'

Madeleine squinted, peering out the window. When did they get in a taxi? Last she remembered they were going to karaoke . . .

She must have dozed off. Aiden started to shift away from her; she could feel his hand on her arm, keeping her upright. Okay, she had to get her act together. She sat up straight, wiping a trail of drool away from the corner of her mouth. Gross, she hoped she didn't slobber all over Aiden. Her head felt a little clearer now. She fumbled for her handbag.

'Oh Aiden, I don't have my bag,' she said, alarmed.

'It's okay, I've got it,' he said. 'Come on, slide across the seat. Now give me your hand.'

'Wait, we have to pay the man,' she said urgently.

'It's all taken care of.'

She reached for his hand; he was already out of the taxi. She stepped out onto the footpath and he helped her up to standing. All good.

'Thank you,' she called to the driver as Aiden closed the door.

'Are you right?' he asked, linking his arm through hers and clasping her hand to support her.

'Yep.'

They walked slowly down to the entrance, where Aiden swiped them in, and then into the elevator. Madeleine leaned back against the wall, hanging on to the railing as they ascended. Not so good.

'Are you all right?' Aiden asked again.

'I feel a little dizzy.'

He drew in closer, bringing his arms around her and holding her head firmly against his chest. 'It's just the movement of the elevator,' he murmured into her hair. 'It'll be over in a minute.'

Madeleine leaned into him, feeling safe, and secure . . . There were other nice men in the world. Henry wasn't the only one.

'Thank you for looking after me,' she said. 'Sorry I'm such a bother.'

'You're not a bother,' he said, and kissed the top of her head.

He took her arm again when the doors opened, and they walked up the hall to the door of the flat. Aiden unlocked it, letting her through ahead of him.

Madeleine kicked off her shoes and sauntered across the living room.

'Do you want to go to bed?' said Aiden.

She swung around. 'Is that an invitation?'

'Don't tempt me.'

She supposed she should have been mildly outraged, but she knew he was only joking, so she just laughed. 'What time is it anyway?'

Aiden checked his watch. 'Not quite eleven.'

'Well that's not late at all,' she declared. 'I wonder if I've got anything to drink here,' she said, heading for the kitchen.

But as she opened the door of the fridge, Aiden was suddenly behind her, scooping his arm around her waist and drawing her out of the way as he closed the door again. 'I don't think that's a good idea,' he said.

'*Ohh*,' she whined, 'not you too!' She turned around to face him, looping her arms around his neck. 'I'm perfectly fine, you know.'

'Mm,' he grunted dubiously. 'Have a glass of water first, and then we'll see.'

Madeleine kept her arms around him as they shuffled over to the sink, only removing them when he handed her a glass. But even so, she didn't step back, and neither did Aiden.

She sipped the water. She did feel fine now, the sleep must have rejuvenated her. In fact, she felt better than fine. That was one thing she missed about drinking, she always felt so free and loose, and horny. Like the other night, and Henry had rejected her. Old stick in the mud.

'Can we see if there's anything to drink now?' she pleaded.

'Not until you finish your water,' he said.

'All right.' Madeleine brought the glass to her lips and tipped it back too far. She couldn't drink fast enough, and the water dribbled down her chin and onto her neck.

'Maddie,' Aiden scolded, taking the glass from her, 'you're making a mess.'

'Sorry.'

He wiped his thumb across her lips and her chin, gazing intently at her. Madeleine arched her head back, as his hand moved down her throat, coming to rest flat on her chest.

'I can feel your heart beating,' he murmured.

'That's a relief,' she said. 'I hope yours is beating too,' she said, lifting her head again to look at him, as she undid the top button of his shirt.

'What are you doing to me, Maddie?' he said in a low voice.

'Just checking on your heart,' she said simply, as she slipped her hand under his shirt, grazing the skin on his chest with her fingers.

He released a shuddery breath, bringing his hand up to cup her face and draw her closer. He pressed his cheek against hers, and breathed her name into her ear. Madeleine's chest was heaving now. They had to be careful, or something might happen. But this was okay. She could feel his lips on her cheek, nothing wrong with that, he'd kissed her on the cheek many times. He tightened his other arm around her, just like one of his signature hugs. Then his lips made their way to hers, brushing against them. That was still fine, it was nice, they were just playing. Now his lips were not so much brushing, as caressing . . . she supposed that might be another way of saying he was kissing her. So it seemed they were kissing, but it was okay, really, they were just friends . . . Madeleine could feel every nerve ending tingling all over her body. Her lips parted, and his tongue plunged into her mouth.

Hold on, that wasn't right, was it? They weren't supposed to kiss like *that*. But it was so . . . hot. She was losing it. She felt his hand on her breast, and then his lips left hers as he pushed aside her top and her bra, and bent to take her breast in his mouth, sucking and nipping. Madeleine could feel it all the way down to her groin. As if he could read her mind, he pushed his thigh between her legs and she pressed herself hard against him. She heard a loud moan . . . oh, that was her! Wait . . . she should stop this. But Aiden was lifting her up now. She glanced around. She was on the kitchen bench! This was a dream! It was what she'd always dreamt. It was okay to *dream* about having sex with Aiden. She lay back and closed her eyes, throwing her arms above her head, and knocking over something that clattered to the floor. Madeleine giggled. She could feel Aiden's tongue, sliding across her belly . . . it was excruciating and delicious . . . He was easing her zipper down, and his tongue was following . . . *Jesus!* He tugged at her jeans, pulling them all the way off, and then he took hold of her bare legs, bending them at the knees and pushing them wide open. Her pelvis rutted involuntarily, and then he was inside her. Madeleine gasped, opening her eyes. Aiden was standing at the end of the bench, thrusting into her, over and over, his eyes glazed, his expression contorted into that sex face guys always pulled.

Shit, this was really happening. *Fuck!* She couldn't have sex with Aiden, that was wrong, it was definitely wrong. Damn, why did she have to drink so much? Why couldn't she just control herself? She'd asked for this, she'd begged for it, now she was just going to have wait it out. Surely it couldn't take much longer. She steeled herself as Aiden grasped hold of her breasts, kneading roughly, as he rammed harder into her, her body jerking against his. This wasn't like she'd imagined in her fantasies. The bench was hard, and cold, and uncomfortable. She wasn't feeling lust anymore, only disgust, with herself . . . She just wanted it to be over.

Aiden suddenly let out a loud grunt, grabbing onto her shoulders to push himself in further, and that was it. He was done, thank God. He rested his head on her stomach, catching his breath. She was going to be sick.

'I'm going to be sick,' Madeleine cried out loud.

Aiden jolted upright, grabbing her by the hands to haul her up. 'Are you okay?'

'No, I'm going to be sick,' she repeated, cupping her hand across her mouth.

He lifted her off the bench and onto her feet, and she staggered half-naked to the bathroom. She dropped onto her knees, holding onto the toilet bowl, and threw up, again and again, her whole body shaking violently. Saliva streamed from her mouth along with the tears pouring from her eyes, even her nose was dripping; she was a mess. She slumped beside the toilet, finally spent, and reached up to yank a towel off the rail. She buried her face in it, sobbing. What had she done? And what was she going to do? She couldn't even get up. Her head was swimming as she rested it against the towel, leaning on the rim of the toilet. She would just stay here for now.

Morning

Suddenly a loud, shrill, urgent noise crashed into Liv's dream. Her eyes sprang open. Was that her alarm? What day was it? No, it was her phone. She fumbled for it on the bedside table, blinking furiously to clear the blurry film of sleep from her eyes. She squinted at the screen. Fuck, it was Lachie. What time was it?

'Lachie,' she croaked. 'What's up, did I sleep in?'

'Mum,' his voice was trembling, 'you have to come, Dylan's sick.'

She bolted upright, instantly awake. The boys were at the sleepover. She glanced at her clock: it was 6 am.

'Tell me what's happening,' she said in a steady voice as she leapt off the bed and strode over to her wardrobe.

'He's been throwing up heaps,' Lachie said, and she could hear the tears in his voice.

'For how long?' She grabbed a T-shirt off a hanger and tossed it on the bed.

'It started a few hours ago. They thought it was all right at first.'

'Who's they, Lachie? Who thought it was all right?' Her voice was completely calm, not accusing.

'Jared's mum and dad. They tried to get him back to sleep, but he's got a really bad pain in his stomach, it won't stop.'

'Is Jared's mum or dad there?'

'Yeah.'

'Put one of them on, okay?'

Liv switched the phone to speaker and grabbed a pair of jeans off the shelf as a woman's voice came on the line. 'Hello, Liv, it's Allison.'

'I'm here.' Liv put the phone down on the bed. 'Can you hear me?'

'Yes.'

'What's going on?' Liv stepped into her jeans while Allison spoke.

'Poor Dylan's in a bad way, I'm afraid. At first we thought he'd just eaten too much, but now he's doubled over, and I think he has a fever.'

'Okay, I'm on my way,' Liv said, before pulling her nightie up over her head.

'I wasn't sure if we should call an ambulance.'

Liv caught her breath. 'Do you think it's that bad?'

'I don't know, it's just that nothing we do seems to help. He's getting distressed, poor kid.'

Liv knew Dylan would only be more distressed with sirens wailing and ambulance officers prodding at him, especially if she wasn't there with him. She picked up the phone. 'Allison, I'm coming right now. I'll be out the door in sixty seconds, and you're only ten minutes from here, so we can make a decision when I get there. I'm sorry you're having to go through this.'

'Don't even say that,' Allison assured her. 'I think Lachie wants to talk to you again.'

'Could you tell Lachie that I'll call him from the hands-free in the car in, like, three minutes? Tell him not to worry.'

'Of course, see you soon.'

Liv hung up and threw the phone on the bed. She pulled on the T-shirt as she walked into the bathroom to the vanity. She splashed water on her face, breathing deeply. Something always came over Liv in a crisis, she became incredibly calm and focused, almost unshakable. It wasn't that she was not affected, she was, but it usually hit her a day or two later, when the danger had passed, and then she collapsed in a heap, sobbing uncontrollably. But in the moment it was incredibly efficient, and not a bad quirk for a parent to have.

Liv was in the car and on her way in under three minutes when she called Lachie as promised. She'd never heard fear like that in his voice, and it was unsettling, given the psychic connection that many people – Liv included – believed existed between twins. She didn't know if Lachie was just feeling his brother's pain or if he was foreshadowing something worse.

Okay, that kind of thinking is really not helpful, Liv.

'I'm not far away, Lach,' she said clearly down the phone. 'Everything's going to be all right. Okay? You have to be brave for your brother. Are you with him?'

'Yep, I haven't left him the whole time.'

She felt a lump in her throat. That was the only thing that could set her off right now. She swallowed. 'Well, God knows what strange powers there are between you two. You stay with Dylan and I know he's going to be all right.'

'How far away are you?'

'I could count it in blocks,' she told him. 'I'm just coming up to that intersection with the lights, near the servo, you know the one?'

'Yeah.'

'Damn, it just went red.' She started to slow down, looking around. 'There's not a soul on the road, I'm going to go through.'

'No, Mum, what if something happens?'

She didn't want to frighten him. 'It's okay, Lach, I'm coming up to it now, slowly, I can see in every direction, either side . . . and I'm through!'

He actually laughed. 'Mum, you're such a badass.'

She was where her boys were concerned.

Less than a minute later she pulled up outside the house, and Allison was coming out to meet her; Lachie must have alerted her after she'd hung up the phone. Allison took her straight inside and down the hallway.

'The place is quiet for a sleepover,' said Liv.

'They're all out the back in the family room, Doug's watching them. We brought Dylan in here, kept everyone right away.'

'Thank you.'

Allison pushed open a door and Liv walked in. It was the master bedroom, she assumed. Dylan lay curled up like a pretzel in the middle of the large bed, Lachie hunched over him, stroking his head like he would a puppy. Lachie looked up, and she saw the relief wash over his face. 'Dyl, it's okay,' he said. 'Mum's here.'

'Hey, matey,' she said gently as Lachie shifted out of the way. She climbed up next to Dylan, and he winced as the mattress moved under her weight. His face was twisted in pain and he was pale as a ghost, his damp hair plastered to his skull. Liv touched his forehead; he was burning up. 'Does it hurt anywhere else but your stomach?' she asked him.

'No, and yes . . . my skin, all over,' he breathed.

'Okay, we're going to get you to the hospital,' she said, her voice calm and soothing. 'That's where they keep the good drugs, they'll stop the pain in no time.'

'Should I call an ambulance?' Allison asked from the doorway.

Liv turned around. 'You know, what are we, ten minutes from St George? There's no traffic on the roads, I think it'll be quicker if I just take him straight there. Lachie will stay with him in the back seat, won't you?'

'Yep.'

'But I think we'll need Doug to help us get him into the car?' Liv said.

'Of course.'

Allison left, and Liv turned back to Dylan. 'Doug's going to carry you out to the car, okay?' she said, and he winced and grunted in response. 'It might hurt for a bit, but it'll be better than walking. Quicker we can get you into the car, quicker we get you there, and the quicker you get rid of this pain, okay?'

He nodded, reaching out to grasp her hand.

Thank God Doug was a big man – he scooped Dylan up as though he was a baby. Getting him into the car proved more of a challenge. Doug told him to stay scrunched up in a tight ball, and he kind of launched him into the back seat. And then they were on their way, Lachie cradling his brother's head on his lap, his face pinched with fear.

When they arrived at the hospital, Liv drove straight into the emergency entrance.

'Hey, Ma,' said Lachie, 'it says emergency vehicles only.'

'We are an emergency vehicle,' she said, pulling up right in front of the doors to casualty.

'Told you she was a badass, Dyl.'

'You wait here,' said Liv. 'I'm going to go and grab the first person I see in a uniform.'

Chippendale

Madeleine gradually drifted into consciousness, taking in the sounds around her. She was at the apartment . . . and someone was breathing right next to her . . .

She jumped up onto her knees in one movement, shimmying away from Aiden, bringing the sheet with her. 'Shit, *shit*!'

He was lying on his stomach, his face turned towards her, and he started to blink, peering out at her. 'Maddie . . .'

'Aiden, what have we done?' she said tearfully. 'This is bad, this is really bad. *Oh my God*!'

'Maddie, calm down,' he said, reaching over to plant his hand on her knee. 'It's okay –'

'*Are you fucking kidding me?*' she cried, backing away from him to the edge of the bed. 'Do you realise what we've done? This is so bad, Henry will never forgive me for this.' She dropped on her knees to the floor, the sheet twisted awkwardly around her as she rocked back and forth.

Aiden pulled himself over to the side of the bed, still on his stomach. His face was level with hers, but she couldn't look at him. 'Maddie, listen to me.'

She didn't respond, she just kept rocking.

'We were drunk, it just happened, it's not the end of the world.'

'How can you say that?' she said, her voice hoarse.

'Because it's true. It was just sex. You had a bit too much to drink and you let loose. It was your bachelorette party, it happens.'

She raised her head slowly to look at him. 'Why didn't you stop it?'

'What?'

'If you knew I was so drunk, you should have stopped it,' said Madeleine. 'Were you as drunk as me? You couldn't have been, you got me home, I don't even remember getting home. You must have been all right.' Her voice was becoming shrill. 'Why would you do that, Aiden, when you knew I was so drunk?'

'Hold on just a minute,' he said, drawing himself up onto his elbows. 'What you're implying . . . I mean, you were all over me, you knew what you were doing, and you didn't once try to stop me.' He paused, shaking his head. 'For fuck's sake, Maddie, I didn't rape you.'

She winced, hearing the words. 'I know, I'm sorry. I shouldn't have said . . . It was as much my fault.' She clutched her hands to her face. 'I kept seeing it last night, in my sleep, but I kept telling myself that it was only a dream,' she said, a lump welling in her throat, choking her. 'Because we didn't do *that*, we couldn't –' She began to sob. 'What am I going to do?'

'Grow up, Maddie,' he said harshly.

That stung. Aiden had never spoken to her like that before.

'This was just waiting to happen,' he went on. 'And if you ask me, Henry had it coming.'

'*What?*' Now she was shocked. 'How can you say that? I don't even . . .' She got up and staggered into the bathroom, slamming and locking the door behind her. What did he mean, Henry had it coming? And why was he being so nasty? Why wasn't he feeling as bad about this, too?

Henry . . . that was it, she'd done it, she'd ruined everything. She couldn't expect forgiveness, not again. He would never understand – how could he? She didn't understand it herself. How could she get so drunk to let that happen? She racked her brain, trying to recall how it started, but it was hazy. They were standing in the kitchen . . . she *was* all over Aiden, like he said. But Madeleine remembered suddenly realising she wanted it to stop – when he was fucking her on the benchtop. It was a bit late then. She could blame the drink, but she had definitely been aware of what she was doing. She just hadn't cared, she hadn't even thought about the consequences. Henry hadn't come into her head. Then through the night, when it all played out again in her dreams, she'd convinced herself the whole thing had only happened in her subconscious: Henry kept walking in and finding them together, and she'd jump, momentarily alert, reassured it was only a dream.

But it wasn't a dream. She had betrayed Henry in the worst possible way, and he would never forgive her for this.

Madeleine emerged from the bathroom sometime later, wrapped in a towel. She had stood under the shower for ages, sobbing, until her skin was puckered and she had no tears left to cry. She felt calmer now, but in a hollow, desolate kind of way. Aiden had made the bed, and she could smell coffee.

He appeared in the doorway, fully dressed. 'I made coffee,' he said.

She nodded. 'Can you give me a minute?'

'Sure.' He stepped out again, closing the door.

She dressed slowly, methodically. Her body ached all over. Well, she'd fulfilled her fantasy to be taken fast and hard, so much for that. She thought of Henry's tender lovemaking; how could she ever have imagined that wasn't enough? She examined her face in the mirror. Her eyes were swollen and red, her lips too. She checked her neck, but there were no damning hickeys. Thank God for that at least.

Aiden knocked after a while.

'Yes?'

He opened the door holding a cup of coffee.

'No, I'll have it out there,' she said.

He nodded, and backed out again. Madeleine followed a minute or so later. She wanted to take this right out of the bedroom – that was until she caught sight of the kitchen bench. She had to stop herself from audibly gasping as she turned away and headed for the sofa. No, not there either; she preferred to keep some distance between her and Aiden. She finally dropped into the armchair her mum had let her take from the house. It had been her dad's favourite. What would he think of her now, she wondered dully.

Aiden walked over and handed her the cup of coffee. She took it without looking at him, and he sat down on the sofa. 'How are you feeling?' he asked.

'Numb, and in pain, all over. I don't know how that can be, but that's how it is.'

He sighed heavily, rubbing his eyes. 'I don't know what to say, Maddie. I don't know what you want me to say. But what happened, happened. And I can't say I'm sorry it did.'

'What?'

'I wouldn't undo it for anything.'

'And I would give anything to undo it,' she retorted.

'Don't tell me you didn't see this coming.'

'*What*? I don't know what you're talking about.'

'For Chrissakes, Maddie, this has been brewing since the day we met. How can you pretend you didn't know what was happening between us?'

'I didn't know *that* was going to happen,' she protested, but Aiden just kept on over the top of her.

'You've been miserable since I got here, and I don't know for how long before that.'

She was shaking her head. 'That isn't true. I love Henry.'

'Well, that was a little hard to tell last night.'

'Enough!' She slammed her cup down on the coffee table and stood up. 'That's unfair. Just because we . . .' She couldn't say it, so she rushed on, '. . . it doesn't mean I don't love Henry. You have no right to say that.'

'Okay, fine,' he conceded. 'You still have feelings for Henry. But is that enough?'

Madeleine started to pace, her head was hurting. 'My feelings for Henry are more than enough, but I don't know if his feelings for me will be enough to overcome this.'

'Then he doesn't deserve you.'

'Don't make it his fault.'

'You don't think it is?' said Aiden.

'Of course not,' she declared, turning to glare at him. 'How can me getting drunk and sleeping with his best man be Henry's fault?'

'Because he hasn't been paying attention,' said Aiden, raising his voice. 'He's had everything his own way, and you've been left lonely and unhappy. I could see it from the start, but Henry hasn't even noticed. And this is what it's led to. You don't sleep with someone else when everything's fine.'

Madeleine was bewildered. 'My God, Aiden, you have to at least admit that what we did was wrong. Don't you feel any loyalty towards Henry at all?'

'Look, it's not as though I planned it. But like I said, Henry had it coming.'

'What could you possibly mean by that?' she asked, lowering herself to perch on the edge of the armchair.

'Don't you see?' Aiden sat forward. 'Henry just floats through life, and everyone rushes to help him. Even I did, at the beginning. He has this way about him . . . My parents couldn't do enough for him,' he said, clenching his jaw. 'Even my sister was infatuated with him, until I put her straight.'

Madeleine couldn't believe what she was hearing.

'I remember you said, first day I was here, that you played easy to get. Typical. Henry doesn't actually have to do anything, people are just drawn to him. And someone like you lands in his lap, and he doesn't even put in any effort after the fact.'

Madeleine was almost too stunned to speak. But she had to say something. She certainly had to defend Henry.

'You have no idea what Henry's done for me,' she said. 'You don't know anything about us, you don't know what I've already put him through.'

'What are you talking about?'

She sighed heavily, slumping back into the armchair. 'This is not the first time . . . I've cheated on Henry.'

'What?'

A lump was rising in her throat as the details surfaced again in her mind, details she'd pushed down so far, she had allowed herself to believe that it didn't happen, or that it was so small, and so long ago, that it didn't matter.

But it wasn't so small, and it wasn't all that long ago.

'The first time Henry and I were together was in New York,' she began. 'I fell in love with him, but neither of us said the words – it seemed too soon, too unreal. But after a couple of months he came out here, and we were so happy, but still we didn't say it. He told me later that he didn't feel it was right to bind me to him when we lived in different countries, until he worked out what he was going to do, what was possible.' She paused. 'He went away again, and I felt lost. In those months since I'd first met him, I'd calmed down, got my life back together. Remember how I told you I was going off the rails?'

Aiden nodded.

'But after he left that time I started drinking again, heavily. I couldn't bear not knowing what was going to happen. We kept in constant contact, like before, but there was no certainty I was ever going to see him again. And then I went away on tour with an author. He was a big drinker, so we kept staying up late, long after his events, getting smashed. The third night, we slept together. It was never going to lead to anything – he was married, I wasn't even attracted to him. It was a stupid, drunken mistake. But I still felt so strongly that I'd betrayed Henry . . . just like I do now.'

'Did you tell him?'

'I did,' said Madeleine. 'When I got back from that tour, Henry said he was coming out again, in a week or two, and as soon as he got here, he told me he loved me, that he wanted to be with me, that he was going to find a way. So I had to tell him.'

Aiden looked disinterested. 'What did he say?'

'He was hurt, obviously, but he also understood. He said he hadn't given me a firm commitment before then, so he didn't have any right to expect fidelity. Then he said we should put it behind us . . . He forgave me.'

'So why don't you think he'll forgive you now?'

'Because now he has every right to expect fidelity!' She raised her voice again. 'Aiden, it's . . . fuck, it's two weeks *today* until I'm supposed to marry him!'

They sat for a while, in silence, except for the distant hum of traffic from the street below. Two weeks, and she'd ruined it all, ruined everything, and she was about to ruin Henry's life . . .

'I have to work out what I'm going to do,' she continued after a while, 'how I'm going to break this to Henry. That's the worst part.' The painful lump had lodged in her throat again. 'If there was only some way I could avoid hurting him.'

Aiden sighed. 'Easy. Don't tell him.'

She looked at him. 'What?'

'He won't hear it from me, it can be our little secret.'

She cringed. 'I'm not going to lie to him.'

'You don't have to. It's not like he's going to ask you if you slept with me.'

Madeleine dropped her head in her hands. 'For godsakes, Aiden, you and your bending of the truth.' She looked up again. 'You know, that theory of yours, it's bullshit. People don't lie to protect the other person, they lie to protect themselves.'

'Then protect yourself.'

She stared at him. 'I can't. I couldn't live with that, and Henry has a right to know the truth.'

Aiden was shaking his head. 'Well, I think you're making a mistake.'

'No, I've already made the mistake. Now I just have to deal with it.' She sat up straight again. 'You're going to have to leave, Aiden.'

'What?'

'Surely you realise it's not appropriate for you to stay here any longer?'

He considered her for a moment. 'Fine,' he said. 'I'll go to a hotel.'

'There's no reason for you to stay in the country. There's not going to be a wedding,' she said. 'Even if there was, you could hardly be the best man.'

'You don't think I know that?'

'Then why not just go home?'

He grunted. 'I'll go when I know you're all right.'

'You don't owe me anything,' she said plainly. 'You owe Henry . . . I don't know, an apology, something, but you don't owe me.'

'Still, I'm staying for the meantime,' he said, getting to his feet. He walked off into the bedroom, and she could hear him moving around, zipping up bags. Madeleine felt drained. She wanted to curl up in a ball and disappear into oblivion, and then to wake up and for the whole thing to be over. But it wasn't over, not by a long shot.

Aiden came back into the room, carrying his bags. Madeleine stood up and walked over to the door. She turned around to face him, her hand on the doorknob.

'There's one thing I want to ask you to do.'

'What is it?'

She took a deep breath. 'I can't stand the thought of any more lies, but if Henry calls you –'

'You want me to lie for you,' he said flatly. 'Suddenly not such a bad theory, eh?'

Madeleine groaned inwardly. 'I am going to tell him the truth, I just need time, and I don't want him to hear or suspect anything until I have the chance to talk to him. Please, Aiden, it's the least you can do for me.'

'Fine, I'll tell him I'm staying with people I met in Canberra, or that I'm going on a trip or something. I won't let him know I've seen you, if it means that much to you.'

'It does.' Madeleine opened the door and held it while he walked out. Then she closed it again, leaning back against it. Henry was expecting her home tonight, but she wasn't ready to face him yet. She didn't know when she was ever going to be ready. She would have to come up with some excuse to delay it; she was getting so good at lying, but she told herself it wouldn't be for much longer. The truth would out, and that would put an end to everything.

She trudged wearily across the room, noticing her handbag on the dining table. She went to it and took out her phone. It was dead, and she had a sick feeling, wondering if Henry had been trying to call. She walked through to the bedroom and dropped onto her hands and knees to find the lead to the charger, then plugged it into the phone. After a moment it came to life. There were no missed calls from Henry, no messages; that was some relief. But he'd expected her to be out shopping, she remembered. She had some time, a little respite. She climbed up onto the bed, and eventually sleep overcame her.

*

She was stark naked, spread-eagled across the benchtop of the kitchen at the house. She lay there, listless and passive, as Aiden pumped her to the steady beat of the rumba, his eyes glazed, a manic grin on his face. Then suddenly Henry was leaning over her. *It's your phone, Madeleine, answer your phone.*

She sat bolt upright, her heart nearly thumping out of her chest. Her phone was ringing. She twisted around, fumbling for it on the bedside table.

'Hello,' she croaked.

'Madeleine,' Henry said. 'Are you okay?'

'Oh . . .' She was panting, trying to catch her breath. 'Henry, sorry, I was asleep.'

'Are you all right?'

She cleared her throat. 'Yes, the phone, it just startled me.'

'I'm sorry,' he said. 'I was getting a little worried.'

'What time is it?'

'Six thirty. You were going to call when you were on your way, so I thought –'

'Henry, I'm so sorry, I was exhausted . . . I lay down on the bed, and I must have fallen asleep.'

'Seems that way.'

He didn't sound cross; his voice was warm, and kind. Oh, Henry. 'I'm so sorry,' she said again, almost choking up.

'It's okay.'

'No, it's not, I promised –'

'Sweetheart, it's okay, really. Don't worry about it. You rest up.'

She took a breath. 'Are you sure?'

'Absolutely. I don't want you driving when you're so tired,' he said. 'Why don't you call me in the morning when you wake up, whenever that is, okay?'

She sniffed. 'Okay.'

'Go back to sleep,' he said gently.

'All right . . . Henry?'

'Yes?'

'I love you, I love you so much.'

'I love you too, Madeleine. Sleep now.'

St George Hospital

Liv shifted in the chair, trying to get comfortable. Not that she was in any danger of achieving that – her back was aching, and she had the beginnings of a crick in her neck. She realised there was someone moving around in the darkened room, and she sat up straight.

A nurse was standing at the end of Dylan's bed, reading his chart by the light of a small torch. She glanced at Liv. 'I'm sorry, did I wake you?'

Liv could detect a slight accent, maybe Indian? 'It's fine,' she said, stretching out properly. 'I can't really sleep in a chair.'

'Well, you were doing a very good impression of it just now.' She smiled.

'I think I only dropped off a little while ago. What's the time?'

'It's eleven forty-three,' the nurse said, looking at her watch. They were very precise, these medical folk.

'I'm sorry, I haven't met you yet, have I?' said Liv.

'No, I just came on night duty,' she said. 'My name is Padma. I'll be watching over Dylan tonight. Everything is looking very good. You were lucky you brought him in when you did.'

Liv had heard that several times today. She could hardly believe it was the same day. After she'd burst in through the emergency doors, she had grabbed the first person in uniform, as was her plan – the plan of a crazy person without much of a plan. Fortunately, Liv managed to keep the crazy sufficiently locked down, and after she'd explained the situation the woman hurried outside with her to the car. She'd crawled right into the back seat, checking his 'vitals' – Liv was fast catching on to all the lingo – and asking Dylan questions that he could only answer with grunts and moans. Then she backed out again and turned to face Liv.

'I'm going inside to get help, and we'll be back out with a gurney. Stay here, I'll only be a minute.'

'What do you think it is?' Liv called after her.

The woman turned back at the door. 'I shouldn't say until we've run some tests, but if I had to guess at this stage, I'd say appendicitis. It's good you brought him in. I'll be right back.'

Appendicitis had crossed Liv's mind, but her medical knowledge was derived solely from *Grey's Anatomy* – the TV show, not the textbook – so all she had to go on was severe abdominal pain accompanied by a fever, which, when she thought about it, would turn out to be something much more dramatic if it turned up on *Grey's Anatomy*. In Dylan's case, Liv hoped she was wildly overreacting and that it was nothing more than a tummy bug.

Moments later a gurney burst through the doors, wheeled out by two men, with the woman Liv had originally accosted following behind. They were all wearing the same blue scrubs, and Liv didn't know if they were nurses, doctors, orderlies or gardeners, though she supposed gardeners didn't wear scrubs. The men extricated Dylan from the car and had him strapped onto the gurney in a matter of minutes. As they started to wheel him in, the woman looked over her shoulder. 'You have to move your car.'

'But can't I come with you?'

'Just park it over there, see?' She pointed to a couple of marked spaces on the other side of the drive. 'They're for emergencies, for fifteen minutes only, but at least you can come in and see where we are.'

'But how will I find you?'

The woman glanced at Lachie, standing anxiously beside Liv. 'This is your son too?'

'Yes, Lachie – Lachlan. He's Dylan's twin.'

'Okay, come with us, Lachlan.' She looked back at Liv and smiled reassuringly. 'We'll be right up the far end of the corridor, he can stand outside so you'll see him. Oh, does Dylan have any allergies you're aware of?'

'No, nothing.'

Liv jumped into the car and manoeuvred it into one of the spaces, then ran back into the hospital and up the corridor. When she got to him, Lachie was standing outside a door, craning to see inside.

'What's happening?' she asked.

'I don't know.'

She looked into the room. There was a flurry of activity going on around Dylan, but it was orderly and calm, not all shouty and frenetic like on *Grey's Anatomy*. Liv decided that was probably a good sign. The two men and the woman had been joined by another man, and between them they were inserting tubes and hanging drips and checking monitors and talking to her son like he was a person. It was oddly touching.

'Here's Mum,' the woman said to Dylan. She waved Liv in, and Lachie followed.

'Not the boy,' said the man they hadn't seen before.

'It's his twin brother,' the woman told him.

He looked up, and then nodded. 'But keep back, please, both of you.'

'Come in, just stand at the end there,' said the woman.

'What's going on?' Liv asked.

'We've started intravenous antibiotics immediately, as a precaution,' the woman explained. 'And we've given him something for the pain – it's working already, see? He's much calmer now.'

'Hi, Mum,' Dylan managed to say in a weak voice.

'We have to get some details,' said one of the men who had pushed the gurney, materialising beside her with a clipboard. He started to run through a series of standard questions, name, age, allergies . . .

'When did the patient last take any food or liquids?'

'I wasn't with him last night,' Liv said. 'He was at a sleepover.' She turned to Lachie. He was chewing on his lip, his brow all furrowed like he was worried he'd get the answer wrong. 'It's okay, mate, just whatever you can remember.'

'Anything in the last six hours?' the man prompted him.

'Nah, I don't reckon. Jared's parents packed up the food around midnight, when we started playing the Xbox,' Lachie said. 'Dylan started chucking up a couple of hours after that, and Jared's mum just gave him ice to suck.'

'Very good,' said the man, jotting it down. He continued through the list: previous surgeries, pre-existing conditions, any medication he was on. 'And your name?' he asked finally.

'Liv, Liv Walsh.'

'You're the child's legal guardian?'

'Yes, I'm his mother. They have their father's surname.' Cripes, she had to call Rick as soon as she got the chance. 'Can you tell me what's happening?' she asked.

'Ms Walsh,' said the man at Dylan's side. 'I'm Dr Harding. Your son has suspected appendicitis. As Dr Ennis told you, we've started an IV of antibiotics to arrest the infection while we perform a CT scan and a CBC to confirm the diagnosis. The pain has localised in the right lower quadrant, and the abdominal wall is sensitive to palpation. Also, there is rebound tenderness in the lower abdomen but no rigidity, so we believe on initial examination that he is not exhibiting any signs of peritonitis. You were right to bring him straight in.'

'So you're going to have to take his appendix out?'

'That's the most likely prognosis. Although antibiotics have proved effective in treating uncomplicated appendicitis, the statistics of recurrence are not encouraging, especially as recurrence brings a higher risk of peritonitis, whereas a laparoscopic appendectomy under general anaesthetic, prior to rupture, carries the smallest risk and is therefore still the preferred course of treatment.'

A simple yes would have done. But she was soon to learn that nothing that could be said in a few words was said in less than a dozen multisyllabic, incomprehensible ones – or else they spoke in acronyms; there seemed to be nothing in between. Not that Liv was complaining. The staff had been nothing short of spectacular, even the humourless Dr Harding.

The rest of the day was spent in various periods of waiting. Waiting for the results of Dylan's tests, then waiting for him to be prepped for surgery, then waiting while he was in surgery, then waiting for him to come out of recovery. Liv wondered why waiting was so exhausting: it wasn't as if you were doing anything but *waiting*, yet she was sure she would have felt less tired had she run a marathon.

Rick arrived just after Dylan had been wheeled into surgery. He was a little frustrated that he hadn't got to see him, but Liv assured him it wouldn't have made any difference. 'He's been pretty well out of it since they gave him the pain relief when we first got here,' she told him. 'Poor kid, I think it was from exhaustion as much as anything. Lachie said he hadn't slept a wink last night.'

'Well, you still think they could have held on until his father got here,' Rick said, miffed.

Liv would have liked to remind Rick that this wasn't about him, it was about Dylan, and that his son needed to have the surgery as soon as the doctors were ready to perform it. But what was the point? Rick had never coped all that well with the boys being sick, not that he didn't care, he just seemed irritated by the inconvenience of having to care.

Throughout it all, Liv had remained in her hyper-calm state. There was a bubbling undercurrent of anxiety, sure, but it stayed well down, out of the way. She had to keep calm for Lachie, who was finding the whole thing pretty overwhelming, not surprisingly. He was restless and fidgety, asking questions nonstop, wanting to know where Dylan was at any given moment, and what they were doing to him. He particularly wanted to know everything about the surgery, and Dr Ennis had been extremely forthcoming, even resorting to sketching a diagram of the laparoscopy, with a blow-by-blow description of the procedure. Liv wasn't at all sure if this was helpful or necessary, but Lachie seemed to lap it up, so what did she know?

'Hey, Ma,' he said afterwards, 'you know, I could give Dyl my appendix.'

'What?'

'You hear about it all the time, people donating kidneys and stuff. And we'd be a perfect match, wouldn't we? Because we're identical.'

Liv's heart swelled. 'Sweetheart, it's okay, he can live without it, just like you'd have to if you gave yours to him. We have two kidneys, so people are able to give one and still keep one for themselves, and most other kinds of transplants come from people who've died. Anyway, they don't do appendix transplants, but it's very sweet of you to offer.'

'So if this happens to me, I'll be okay too?'

She nodded. 'But it's not going to happen to you.'

'We're twins, Mum, it's probably going to happen to me.'

Poor kid. Liv wondered about everything that must be running through his head right now as he tried to process all of this. No wonder he had so many questions.

'I'm almost certain appendicitis isn't genetic or hereditary,' Liv said. 'But that's something else you can ask one of the doctors next time they come around.'

Liv had decided not to inform her parents until Dylan was out of surgery, and even then she knew she'd have a fight keeping her mother away, if only for today. There was nothing Joy didn't like more than a little drama, and that was the last thing Dylan, or any of them, needed right now.

It was four in the afternoon before Dylan was finally settled into the post-operative ward, thankfully in a room to himself. Liv had been told she would only be able to stay with him if he was in a private room, so she was insistent that they find him one. She knew Dylan was old enough to stay on his own, but she just didn't want to leave him tonight. He was still groggy, coming in and out, and if he suddenly found himself wide awake in the middle of the night, she wanted to be here. In truth, she was getting a little anxious to actually see him wide awake, so she wanted to stay for her own reassurance as much as anything.

'Come on, mate,' Rick said to Lachie, 'we should make tracks. Dylan needs his rest.'

In other words, Rick had had enough. Not that she could blame him – it was pretty boring just hanging around. She was amazed Lachie had lasted this long without a game console or his phone, which he'd had to turn off in the hospital. But he hadn't complained.

'I'm not going anywhere,' Lachie announced. 'If Mum's staying, so can I.'

'I don't know if that's allowed, mate,' Liv said carefully.

'I don't care.'

'Listen, son,' said Rick. 'It's not up to us, there are rules –'

'I said I don't care, I'm not going. I'll hide when they come round, Ma, I'll go in the bathroom and get in the shower stall, they won't know.' Lachie was furiously blinking back tears, his jaw set grimly, his hands clenched into fists by his side.

Liv gave his arm a squeeze. 'I'll go and talk to someone, see what I can do.'

She walked out to the nurses' station, where a young nurse gave a rather automated-sounding response that it wasn't hospital policy to let siblings stay. But when Liv pushed a bit, pointing out that the boys were twins, she suddenly became animated, and quite eager to help. 'I'm not senior enough to make that decision, but I'll find you someone who is.'

Liv didn't have to wait long before another nurse arrived to discuss the issue. She was older than the first nurse, but not ancient, and not at all scary like the matrons Liv remembered from a long time ago. Liv realised she must be the team leader, like David. She was quite sympathetic, and with a few provisos – that the boy couldn't leave the room and wander the corridors, and that if there was any undue noise or disruption he would have to leave immediately – she agreed to let him stay.

'Thank you so much,' said Liv. 'He'll be so relieved.'

'Twins, what are you going to do?' said the nurse.

'I'll go give him the news.' Liv turned up the hall when she had a thought. 'Excuse me?' she said, coming back to the desk. 'I have a friend who works here, I believe he's the same rank as you.'

'We're not in the military,' she said with a smile. 'What's his name?'

'David Lessing?'

'Oh yes, I know David.'

'You don't happen to know if he's on tonight?'

'Sorry, it's a big hospital, I haven't seen him. And you understand we're not able to give out information about staff rosters to just anyone –'

'No, of course, I wouldn't expect you to,' said Liv. 'I'll give him a call myself tomorrow. Not a problem.'

As she started down the hall again, the nurse called after her, 'David never works down here anyway, he's usually up on cardio.'

'Thanks.'

*

'They've told you where the tea and coffee-making facilities are?' Padma asked Liv now. She had completed Dylan's obs, which he had pretty much slept through.

'Yes, thank you, everyone has been very helpful.'

'So sweet,' Padma remarked, gazing down at Lachie, who was crashed out on a camp bed alongside Dylan's hospital bed. 'He is sleeping very soundly.'

'Hm,' said Liv, getting up to stand next to her. 'When he insisted on staying I was worried he was going to get bored, but he was asleep as soon as his head hit the pillow. I realised he hadn't slept last night, worrying about his brother.'

'Twins are special,' said Padma. 'They are a blessing. And you have boys – in India you would be much admired. And your husband, too, for his virility.'

Liv decided not to tell the lovely nurse Padma just where her husband's virility had got them. 'Excuse me, Padma,' she said. 'The boys seem very settled. Do you think it would be all right if I went for a bit of a walk to stretch my legs?'

'Outside the hospital?'

'No, no, just around the corridors. I wouldn't bother anyone.'

'Of course, this is fine. I will not be far, your sons are safe.'

With a last glance back at the boys, Liv followed Padma out of the room. She walked down towards the elevator bay, where the corridors led off in various directions, and looked around. What if she got lost in the maze and couldn't find her way back? She mentally recorded the floor and number of the ward, and headed off towards a T-intersection where she could see a directory board suspended from the ceiling. As she approached, her eyes almost immediately landed on 'Cardiology', and her heart missed a beat. She wondered if she should . . . The chances of David actually being there were pretty remote – it would be something like less than one in twenty, considering there were three shifts in a day, and seven days in a week. But wouldn't the number of nurses on staff also affect that figure? And also how many shifts David had in a week? That was as far as Liv could go with statistical probability, she wasn't a numbers person. She was a people person, and a nosy person, and curiosity was getting the better of her. It would be interesting to see where David worked; if nothing else, it gave her a direction to head in.

However, after a while Liv began to think that Cardiology was about as real as the Land of Oz, as she went up stairs and down corridors and finally across a glassed-in bridge into another building. The hospital was eerily silent at this time of night, at least over this way, far from the emergency entrance. She hadn't passed a single soul to ask if she was heading in the right direction, and she was beginning to think she had strayed too far from the boys, that she should head back, when she came around a corner and saw a sign on the wall that read CARDIOLOGY WARDS E–K. She was here, finally. Liv walked tentatively down the hushed corridor. She could see the light coming from the nurses' station at the far end. Some of the doors she passed were closed, others open to show a light glowing above the bed, the outline of figures sleeping under the covers. As the nurses' station came into view she could see there was no one there, and decided she'd gone far enough. She felt like an interloper. She turned around, just as David came out of the nearest doorway, looking down at a clipboard. She drew her breath in sharply, and he raised his head. There was a look of stunned confusion in his eyes as he stared at her.

'Liv, what are you doing here?'

'Oh, I'm not here . . . I mean, I'm here . . . over there . . . it's Dylan.'

'Is everything all right?'

'He had surgery, appendicitis . . .'

And it had to happen now. The flood rose up in her chest, forcing a loud sob out of her throat. She clasped her hands over her mouth, as if that was going to be able to stop the tsunami. It was just like a tsunami, in fact. Liv had read that after the initial undersea earthquake, the water retreats, all is still and calm for some time, until the wave hits. That was exactly what was happening to her. Her shoulders shook as tears sprang from her eyes, and she felt David's arms close around her. She collapsed against his chest, heaving, unable to speak or do anything except allow herself to be led she didn't know where, while David kept his arms firmly around her, shushing her gently. He brought her into a brightly lit room, closing the door behind him.

'Here, sit down.' He eased her carefully into a chair. 'I'll get you some water.'

Liv had always wondered why people were offered a glass of water at times like this. Somebody died: here, have a glass of water. You've had a bit of a shock: here, have a glass of water. Was sudden dehydration a side effect of trauma?

She wiped her eyes with her hands as she tried to get her breathing back to normal. God, she must look a sight. David returned and crouched in front of her, handing her a glass of water.

'I'm so sorry about this,' she said in a ragged voice.

'Don't worry. Just drink a little.'

She did as he said, taking a few sips. Then he took the glass from her and put it down nearby. He reached for a chair, dragged it closer and sat facing her, taking hold of her wrist. 'Feeling better now?' he asked, staring down at his watch.

Liv realised he was taking her pulse, and that made her smile. 'Am I gunna make it, Doc?'

He looked up suddenly, caught out. Then he gave her a sheepish smile. 'Sorry, hazard of the profession. I can't help myself.' He released her wrist. 'Your pulse is still racing though, I should mention.'

'And I should apologise for that dazzling performance just then.'

'Stop it,' he said. 'When was the surgery?'

'This morning. I've been fine all day.'

'You had what's called a delayed reaction to shock.'

'Yeah, I know, it's my party trick,' said Liv. 'Usually it takes about a day to hit. I thought I'd have till tomorrow at least, so I could have had my breakdown in the privacy of my own home.'

'If only we could plan these things,' David said. 'Happens all the time in here: people are either hysterical when it's all happening, which is the worst, or it's some time after, out of the blue, when you tell them something random, like their husband needs pyjamas . . . Oh, not that I was implying you were hysterical,' he added quickly.

'But let's call a spade a spade.'

He gave her a warm smile. 'Well, sit here as long as you need.'

'No, I'm good,' she said, taking a deep, slightly tremulous breath. 'I have to get back, I didn't mean to leave them this long.'

'Them?'

'Yeah, Lachie's here too, he wouldn't leave his brother . . .' Her voice caught on the words, and she felt tears pricking her eyes. Great, so now she was going to constantly ooze emotion?

David reached over and covered her hand. 'How about I walk you back?'

'Oh no, that's okay, you're working.'

'It's fine, let me just tell someone. You sit here,' he said, getting to his feet. 'Take a minute. I'll be right back.' He passed her a box of tissues and slipped out the door again.

Liv looked around. It was some kind of break room, she assumed: there were the ubiquitous green vinyl hospital chairs, and a small fridge at the end of a sink unit, covered in stray cups; newspapers and magazines were strewn across the coffee table.

She was doing her best to clean her face with a tissue but no mirror when David came back in.

'Are you ready?' He reached out a hand to help her up, and then held the door open for her to go ahead of him. She felt his hand on her elbow as they started back down the corridor. When they had left the ward, David turned to her. 'So, how are you feeling now?'

'I'm fine, really. I don't want to take you from your work.'

'I told them I'm on a break. Come on, it's this way.'

Considering her state of mind, it was probably just as well he was with her; she didn't know if she would have found her way back on her own.

'Can I ask you something?' he said as they walked across the glassed-in bridge.

'Sure.'

'What brought you up this way?'

Liv looked sideways at him. 'Okay, I did ask after you, and the nurse mentioned you tended to work in cardio, and I was going for a walk to stretch my legs, and I just thought I'd wander up this way

. . . but I'm not a stalker or anything.' She took a breath. 'Please don't think I'm weird.'

'Are you kidding?' he said. 'I'm flattered. I've never had a stalker before.'

'David . . .'

'It was a joke.'

'I really didn't expect to bump into you,' said Liv. 'I mean, what are the chances?'

'Better than being seated next to each other on a plane,' he said with a grin.

When they got back to Dylan's room, David paused in the doorway. 'Do you mind?'

'No, of course not, come in.'

He crossed over to the end of the bed, picked up the chart, and then came around beside Dylan. He took out his own small torch, and propped the chart on the rail of the bed as he flicked through the pages. Liv found herself a little mesmerised. There was something about him in those blue scrubs, and his air of quiet authority, laced with a heavy dose of compassion, that was just so damned appealing. Seriously, men in uniform . . . *any* uniform. Put a woman in scrubs and she looked like a sack of potatoes, they were so unflattering. But not on a man.

David looked up and caught her watching him. 'I did it again, didn't I?' he said in a hushed voice. 'Playing nurse. Can't help myself, sorry.'

'No, please,' said Liv, coming around to join him beside the bed. 'Actually, can you tell me that everything's okay? I'd be reassured to hear it in plain English.'

'Everything looks great. His notes are all routine, you have nothing to worry about.' He gazed down at Dylan, bringing one hand to his forehead and gently smoothing his hair back. Liv found it quite moving.

'They're handsome boys,' he said.

He turned around and Liv was right in front of him. They both stood frozen for a moment, very close, breathing hard. Then David cleared his throat, and Liv stirred, moving out of his way.

'Now, have you been trying to sleep in that chair?' he said briskly.

'Yeah, it's fine. I gave Lachie the camp bed. I don't expect I'm going to sleep much anyway.'

'There'll be another mattress around,' he said, walking over to the door. 'You might not sleep but you should at least get horizontal, or else you'll pay for it tomorrow.'

He returned shortly with a mattress and bedding. 'I'll make it up for you,' he said, dropping the mattress onto the floor.

'No way, I'm not going to let you make my bed!'

'Are you sure? You should see my hospital corners.'

Liv smiled. 'Thank you, but you've done enough already – more than enough. And I'm starting to get worried about the heart patients you've abandoned back there.'

'Ah, they'll keep, I promise.'

They were standing facing each other again. Liv was quite overcome – it was the kindness . . . his compassion . . . the way he looked in those scrubs. It seemed there actually were a few good men left . . . but what were the chances of being seated next to one of them on a plane?

Impulsively, she reached up on tiptoes to kiss him on the cheek, and he leaned into her. She lingered for a moment, resting her cheek against his. When she drew away, there was a look in his eyes that was almost grateful, certainly pleased.

'I might come by and check on you tomorrow, if that's okay?' he said, his voice husky.

'That'd be great. I'll look forward to it.'

The next morning

Madeleine woke early, probably because pretty much all she'd done yesterday was sleep. Whenever she was conscious for a while, everything would come hurtling back into her head with a ferocity that made it ache. She couldn't bear thinking about it, she couldn't bear existing in the reality she had created for herself, so she would roll over again and go back to sleep.

But when she woke today her head felt much clearer, it was the pain in her heart that was threatening to engulf her. It occurred to Madeleine that part of what she'd been feeling yesterday must have been a hangover, so thankfully that was over with. But that was the least of it. She lay in bed for another hour, trying to imagine how she was going to tell Henry. She knew there was no getting around it: she couldn't make it more palatable, or less damning; she had to face the consequences of her actions, actions that were unforgivable. She wasn't even going to ask for forgiveness – she had no right.

Madeleine knew she was going to lose him, and it was breaking her heart. But what made it worse was that she was going to break Henry's heart. She was the one who'd done the wrong thing, but he was going to have to suffer for it. If there was any way she could take that away from him, she would; if she thought that leaving, disappearing from his life would save him the hurt, she would do it in a heartbeat. But there was no way out, and maybe that was her punishment, being forced to inflict pain on the person she loved more than anyone in the world, someone who'd done nothing to deserve it. It was cruel and unusual punishment, to say the least.

Her phone pinged to announce a text. It was still early, and Henry had said he'd leave it up to her to get in touch, so she wasn't expecting to hear from him. She held her phone up to check, and her stomach lurched. It was from Aiden. To think that only a week ago she'd looked forward to his messages. She was tempted just to delete it, but she had a feeling she wasn't entirely finished with Aiden.

Madeleine opened the message. *Just checking in, want to know you're ok. Are you home? xa*

She supposed she had to keep him in the loop for now, at least until she'd talked to Henry. *Not home yet*, she replied. *Still at the flat.*

Do you want me to come over? he asked.

NO.

Madeleine knew what she had to do, but as she held the phone in her hand, contemplating calling Henry, she also knew she needed more time before she could face him. Maybe she was only delaying the inevitable, but she still wasn't ready.

She took a breath. When she tapped on his name to make the call, his picture came up on the screen. It was a photo she'd taken of him at his house in the Hamptons. Just a snapshot in an unguarded moment, but she loved that photo, she loved the expression on his face . . . she loved him, so very much.

'Madeleine, hi.' She heard his voice, and quickly put the phone to her ear. He'd answered after only a ring or two; he must have had the phone right alongside him, which wasn't like Henry.

'Hi,' she said.

'Did you sleep well?' he asked.

'I did, thank you, I slept and slept.'

'Well, you must have needed it.'

'Mm.'

'So . . . what are your plans?' he asked.

She'd concocted a response in her head earlier, should she need it. She didn't know if it was going to sound reasonable, but it was all she had right now.

'Well, I was thinking, if it's okay with you, that I might get some things done around here. You see,' she went on quickly, 'the place really needs a good clean-out if I want to give notice before the wedding, which, you know, I might as well, we're going to be away for weeks.'

As soon as it all came tumbling out of her mouth she wanted to be sick. She was using the excuse of a wedding that wasn't even going to happen anymore, along with a teaser about getting rid of the flat – which likely wasn't going to happen now either – and thrown in a mention of a honeymoon that they were never going to have, all so that Henry wouldn't get annoyed with her for staying away another night before she fronted up to tell him she'd slept with his best man. It was a wonder she wasn't struck down by lightning on the spot.

'That's fine, Madeleine, whatever you need to do,' was all Henry said.

Why was he being so reasonable? She took a breath. 'The thing is, if I really want to get somewhere, I should stick at it, and stay tonight as well, then go straight to work tomorrow from here. But this will be it, okay? I promise, Henry, it's the last time.' At least that was the truth.

'It's really okay, Madeleine,' he said. 'Just try not to overdo it.'

'I won't,' she said weakly.

'So I'll see you tomorrow evening?'

'You will.'

'Maybe you could give me a buzz when you're on your way?'

'Of course.'

'I'll see you then,' he said. 'Love you.'

'I love you too.'

What was going on? There was no disappointment, no disapproval, no sulking. She'd been away since last Wednesday, and he was being nothing but supportive and sweet. Madeleine was starting to wonder if she'd been making it all up in her head. What was the matter with her? Why had she been so ready to see fault in everything he did?

It was too late now. She had a deadline. She had to face Henry tomorrow night, no matter what. She couldn't put it off any longer.

She thought about Aiden, what the hell was his issue? The things he'd said about Henry – it was almost as if he didn't know him at all. How could he suggest that Henry had 'floated through life', after what he'd told her about his childhood? He was supposed to be Henry's best friend, his *best man*. What was going through *his* mind when he was fucking her on the kitchen bench? He must have known that he was ruining everything, or helping Madeleine to ruin it for herself. She would take full responsibility for her own actions. Aiden hadn't forced or coerced her to do anything she didn't want to do – at the time – but it still left her with a very bad feeling about him and his motives. She may need to keep him in the loop, but she intended to steer well clear of him in person.

She fired off one more text message to him. *Staying at flat tonight, work tomorrow, then home to talk to Henry. Please come and leave keys after I've gone. UNDER NO CIRCUMSTANCES BEFORE THAT.*

A moment later he responded, *No need to shout.*

Sunday afternoon

The change in Dylan by the morning was nothing short of miraculous. Not that the staff seemed to think so; it was all very routine to them. Of course he'd be hungry, and of course he could start to eat – only clear fluids at first, but all going well, he could have solid food by tonight. One thing he couldn't do was jump around and risk bursting his stitches. So when Lachie's relief translated into playfully roughing up his brother – probably because he really just wanted to hug him – Liv had to pull him into line immediately. She explained that it was very important for Dylan to avoid any stress or strain to his stomach muscles, and that included fighting off his overexcited twin.

But it was so good to see Dylan smiling, his eyes bright and his cheeks pink again. Lachie was intent on grilling him for all the gory details, even though he probably knew more about it than Dylan did.

'Was it scary in the operating room?' he asked, his eyes growing wide. 'Were you lying under one of those humungous lights, with all the doctors staring down at you, their faces masked, as one of them holds up a scalpel, and it gleams in the light, and he's just waiting for you to count down from a hundred, so he can plunge it into your guts?'

'Lachlan James Foley!'

But Dylan was grinning, holding his stomach. 'Don't make me laugh!' he pleaded. He caught his breath again. 'Anyway, I don't remember much, it's all pretty fuzzy. The whole night is, but especially after I got the drugs. Hey, Mum, you were right about them being the good ones.'

He would have to remember that. 'Yes, but the good drugs are only available in hospitals, administered by doctors,' said Liv. 'All other drugs are bad.'

'Yeah, right.' Lachie snorted.

Rick came in after breakfast, giving Liv and Lachie the opportunity to go home for a while. Liv had never been so happy to have a shower and change her clothes. She put together a few things for Dylan, though the staff had told her he would in all likelihood be able to go home tomorrow, or Tuesday morning at the latest, so he didn't need much. Lachie packed up the console and some games, and Liv tossed in a couple of books that were sitting on Dylan's bedside table, getting an eye-roll from Lachie for her trouble.

When they got back to the hospital, Rick left again. He would return later to stay with Dylan throughout the evening, but not overnight. Dylan had been quite definite about that – he wasn't a baby, he pointed out. Liv was beginning to think he regarded the whole thing as an adventure, a rite of passage even, that made him worldlier than your average fourteen year old. Which was okay with Liv, as long as he was getting better.

The boys were absorbed with their gaming device when their nanna and pop arrived, and were reluctant to turn it off.

'Leave them to play,' said Joy. 'I'm just glad to be here and see my darling boy looking so well.'

'What about me, Nan?' said Lachie.

'Oh, you always look well, scruff,' she said, tousling his hair.

Before calling her parents yesterday, it had taken Liv ages to come up with an opening line that would simultaneously convey both the necessary information, and complete reassurance. She ended up starting with, 'So I just want to let you know that everyone's all right –'

'What's happened, is it one of the boys?' Joy interrupted frantically before Liv could get any further.

Honestly, her mother's antennae were fine-tuned for calamity. Liv remembered vividly when she was growing up, Joy glued to the news, keeping track of the rising death toll of the latest disaster. Each day when Liv got home from school, Joy would give her an update: 'It's up to sixty-eight dead in those terrible bushfires. I just know there's going to be more.'

'What did I tell you? Seventy-five now. And we haven't heard the last of it, mark my words.'

A week later: 'Well, they're still at seventy-five. The way they were carrying on you'd think there was going to be hundreds.' She'd almost sounded disappointed.

'When I think of what could have happened to you,' she was saying to Dylan now, shaking her head. 'You know, if your appendix bursts, you die. That's it, all over, red rover.'

'Mum . . .'

'I guess you were lucky your mother was even contactable, under the circumstances. I mean, she could have been anywhere, and then what?'

Rick poked his head into the room. 'Special delivery!'

He pushed the door all the way open and walked in carrying two huge McDonald's bags and a tray of drinks.

'Awesome!' cried Lachie.

'Rick,' said Liv, who so enjoyed taking on the role of Nancy No-Fun, 'Dylan can't have solid food until tonight, didn't you hear the doctor?'

His face dropped. 'Oh, really?' He said it as though it had been Liv's decision.

Dylan was trying not to show his disappointment, but he'd only just been saying to Liv that his hunger pangs were starting to get stronger, and that juice and broth weren't doing it for him.

Joy had sprung from her seat when Rick first came in. 'Well, what a generous and thoughtful thing to do, even so,' she exclaimed, helping to relieve him of his load.

No, once again, not thoughtful at all.

'Well, you can have a soft drink, yeah?' Rick said hopefully.

'Thanks, Dad.'

'Maybe a few chips wouldn't hurt?'

'I don't think so, Rick,' said Nancy No-Fun. 'He's not allowed solids until teatime.'

'I tell you what, mate,' said Rick. 'The minute they give you the all-clear, I'll duck out and get you a fresh McChicken meal, or whatever you want.'

'Awesome.'

Bugger him. Liv was pretty sure Dylan wasn't supposed to eat like that for at least another few days, though she didn't want to have to be the one to say it. But she knew it would have to come down to her. After all, she couldn't count on the staff to police it; they might not notice Rick come in with the McDonald's, or they might assume he'd brought it in for himself, not to feed to his son who'd just had abdominal surgery.

'I'm so glad we're getting to see you, Rick,' said Joy. 'Olive said you weren't coming back till later.'

'You know, Joy, I was driving along, thinking my whole family's back in that hospital room, including my favourite in-laws . . .'

Liv rolled her eyes.

'And I said to myself, where would I rather be? Going home to catch a few hours of the cricket? I don't think so. So you know what I did?'

Joy was hanging on his every word.

'I turned my car around that minute and headed straight back here.'

'See how much your dad loves you boys?' said Joy.

'Sorry, this looks like a bad time.'

Everyone turned. David was standing in the doorway, a tentative expression on his face. Liv thought he was probably right – it wasn't the best time, not for their sakes, but for poor David's. Talk about a baptism of fire.

But before she could warn him off, Joy piped up, 'Of course not, doctor, come in.'

'Oh, I'm not –'

'He's not Dylan's doctor, Mum,' Liv jumped in. She had to keep control of this, somehow. 'This is a friend of mine, David Lessing. This is my mum and dad, Joy and Ken Walsh.'

'How do you do?' David shook Ken's hand. Her dad seemed oblivious, but Joy was clearly starting to piece it together, largely because Rick was doing a very good impression of a stunned mullet.

'This is the boys' dad, Rick Foley,' Liv charged on valiantly.

'I thought only family were allowed to visit?' Joy muttered, not quite under her breath.

Liv continued over the top of her, 'And here are the boys –'

'Dylan and Lachlan,' David said, identifying them correctly, and giving them each one of those fist bumps that the young people do. The boys seemed duly impressed.

'How did you know which one of us was which?' Lachie asked, wide-eyed.

'Well, your mum told me you have a freckle on the right side of your nose . . .'

Lachie frowned, touching his nose doubtfully.

'And that Dylan just had his appendix out,' David added. 'Bit of a dead giveaway.'

'D'oh,' Dylan said, and Lachie elbowed him.

'Gently, please, Lach,' Liv warned.

'How are you feeling, Dylan?' David asked him.

'Good, but hungry,' he grimaced.

'I'm not surprised. Bit rough having to put up with the smell of hot chips when you haven't eaten.'

'Reckon.'

'But to be honest, you probably should wait a few days before you have anything greasy like that.'

Dylan's face dropped. 'Dad was going to get me Macca's tonight.'

David winced. 'You wouldn't want to let the nurses catch you with it.'

Bless him.

'Can I tell you something, Dylan?' David went on. 'You probably couldn't manage it, even if you think you could. A couple of bites in and you'd most likely feel sick – and take it from me, you don't want to get an upset stomach when you've got stitches. You'll enjoy it more in a few days, maybe give it a week.'

A further blessing upon his house.

'But what can I eat till then?'

'Let me see,' David said, reaching for the chart.

'Apparently they're letting just anyone read people's private records,' Joy sniffed.

David didn't seem to notice. 'What have they given you so far?' he asked Dylan, scanning the chart.

'Soup.' Dylan pretended to gag. 'And juice and soft drink.'

'Any problems keeping it down?'

'Nuh.'

'Well, you'll probably get some scrambled eggs later, bread, yoghurt or rice pudding, something like that. The best I can do for you now is jelly, how does that sound?'

'Cool,' said Lachie. 'Can I have some too?'

'No, you got Macca's,' said David. 'Your brother's getting the jelly.' He high-fived Dylan. 'I'll be right back.' He caught Liv's eye on the way out and gave her a wink.

'Nice sorta bloke,' Ken remarked.

But Joy turned up her nose. 'Treated the place like he owned it, if you ask me.'

No one did, Liv felt like saying.

'So that was David,' Rick finally spoke. By the look on his face, he was still reeling.

'Yes.' Liv jumped in to stop him from saying something inappropriate in front of the boys. 'He's a nurse, works up in Cardiology.'

'And how did you come to meet a man nurse from Cardiology?' Joy wanted to know.

'I didn't meet him at the hospital,' Liv said. 'He's a friend.'

'What kind of a *friend*?'

'A good one.' Liv decided to head David off at the pass – she couldn't let him come back into this. 'Excuse me,' she said briskly, and walked out of the room.

She was pacing the corridor outside when David walked up, carrying three tubs of jelly in different colours.

'Hi,' she said, smiling nervously.

'Hello . . .' He looked bemused.

'I'm just going to come straight out and say it,' Liv began. 'I think it's probably better if you don't go back in there.'

He nodded thoughtfully. 'Sorry, I didn't mean to make you uncomfortable.'

'You didn't,' she assured him. 'It's the rest of them. Not the boys, and not my dad. He said you seemed like a nice bloke.'

'But not a hit with your mother, or your ex,' David said with a wry smile. 'So they know . . . ?'

'Not really, but my mother has an eagle eye and a suspicious mind,' said Liv. 'And she thinks Rick is still my lawful husband . . . so, you know . . .'

'You *are* divorced?' David said, checking.

'Absolutely. It's just, she's religious, and a little crazy.'

'I see. Well, give these to Dylan,' he said, handing her the tubs of jelly. 'Tell him not to eat them all at once.'

'Thank you, that was really kind of you.'

'It was nothing.' He let out a sigh. 'I guess I'll see you?'

'Yeah . . . though I don't know when, things are going to be difficult for a while. Dylan will be off school, I don't know what I'm going to do about work . . .'

'Is there anything I can do to help?'

'God, no – I mean, no, thank you,' said Liv. 'I wasn't fishing, I was just saying I don't know when I'm going to have the chance . . . to see you again.'

The disappointment was evident in his eyes. 'Then I'll leave it up to you,' he said. 'Bye, Liv.' He turned and walked away up the corridor.

Bugger it, she thought as she headed back to Dylan's room.

Monday morning

The rumba started to play in Madeleine's head, insistent, ludicrous. She rolled over and it stopped. She must have been dreaming. Then it started up again. Her eyes sprang open.

She grabbed her phone off the bedside table and squinted at the screen. It was Liv. What day was it? She peered down at the numbers and letters on the display, trying to focus. It was Monday, and it was nine thirty.

Shit, shit, *shit*.

'Hi, it's me, I'm sorry,' Madeleine said all at once as she answered.

'Where are you?' said Liv.

'I'm . . . it's okay, I'm in the city, I can be there in . . . half an hour, tops.'

'Well, all kinds of shit is going down here, so you better hurry.'

Madeleine hung up the phone and tossed it onto the bed, rubbing her eyes. She didn't know why she hadn't set her alarm, but there was no time to dwell on that, she had to get her act into gear. She stumbled out of bed and threw herself under the shower just long enough to rinse off and wake up. She yanked a dress off its hanger – it was clean, it would do, and she wouldn't waste valuable minutes finding a top to match a bottom. Back in the bathroom, she checked her face in the mirror. God, what a disaster. Puffy red eyes, blotchy skin, and her hair could do with a wash, but there was no time. She quickly brushed mineral powder over her face in the hope it would cover some of the blotchiness, and dragged a mascara wand across her lashes; lips she could do in the taxi on the way. She grabbed a hairclip and her handbag, and ran for the door, twisting her hair up and catching it at the back with the clip.

As she burst through the foyer doors a minute later, a cold gust of wind almost picked her up and carried her away. What the hell? She looked up at the sky. It was grey and threatening, and she could feel fine rain spitting on her face. Her dress was thin cotton georgette, sleeveless, her shoes strappy slip-ons. She was going to freeze. She rooted around in her handbag in the vague hope she had one of her little cardigans, even a scarf buried away down deep. No luck. Madeleine hesitated for a second longer. There wasn't time to go back, there was nothing she could do. Bloody Sydney spring, it had no right to call itself that. Oh sure, it was halfway between summer and winter – but all that meant was that it was golden warm one day, shivering cold the next.

Twenty minutes after Liv's call, Madeleine was racing up the street, breathless, cursing herself; she really shouldn't have promised half an hour 'tops'. But then, contrary to her usual experience, she managed to grab a taxi almost as soon as she got to the main drag, so she was going to be pretty close to her ETA, after all. As she settled into the back seat, brushing the spots of rain from her bare arms, she suddenly remembered that her car was in the garage of the apartment block. Crap! Though on second thoughts, it was probably better she wasn't driving – she wouldn't have to park the car when she got to work, she could be dropped right at the door. And this gave her time to collect her thoughts, check her messages, breathe . . .

There were two, no, three messages from Liv, sent before she'd finally given up and called her. Madeleine didn't know why she hadn't heard the beeps; she must have been really out to it. The messages warned her that she was about to walk into a shitstorm, without giving any hint as to what it might be. What the hell was going on in there? She really didn't need this today. She scrolled further down the screen. There was nothing from Henry, not that she was expecting anything. Fortunately, there was nothing from Aiden either. It seemed he'd taken her at her word, and she wouldn't expect any more trouble from him.

Madeleine breathed out heavily, leaning her forehead against the car window as the streets sped by. It was raining properly now; droplets spotted the glass and dribbled down, blurring her view. But she wasn't really looking, she had too much else crowding her mind.

She hadn't been able to get to sleep last night, maybe because she had slept too much the day before, but also because her brain wouldn't switch off. She couldn't stop trying to analyse her behaviour, and Henry's, and Aiden's, going over the sequence of events since he'd arrived in the country, and trying to understand what had contributed to the clusterfuck that had resulted. From the start, Aiden's presence had seemed to cast Henry in a bad light, but now that had completely flipped. It was like looking at one of those pictures that played tricks on the eye.

Eventually Madeleine had given up on sleep and turned on her laptop, and soon she found herself googling 'effects of alcohol on inhibition', 'excessive consumption of alcohol', 'alcohol abuse', 'problem drinking' and, finally, 'alcoholism'. She did it to reassure herself as much as anything. Years ago, she used to be able to drink without any repercussions beyond a mild hangover, so she didn't see how she could actually be an alcoholic, or surely she would have always had a problem drinking? Not only that, she'd barely even drunk for the last year or so, ever since Henry had moved out here to live. And she hadn't suffered any withdrawal symptoms, she hadn't needed to go to rehab or support meetings, she'd just stopped. One drink occasionally didn't send her spiralling out of control, so the refrain that 'one's too many and a hundred's not enough' certainly didn't apply.

Her initial findings did reassure her. Alcoholism was a very serious condition, not a term to be bandied about lightly. It was classified as a disease: people lost their families, their jobs, they couldn't get through the day without a drink. None of that applied to Madeleine – well, except that she was going to lose Henry, but maybe alcohol wasn't the culprit.

The sites were littered with links to numerous questionnaires used by health professionals to diagnose the disease. She wasn't afraid to answer the questions, quite confident the results would prove once and for all that she didn't have a drinking problem.

Have you ever been treated by a physician for your alcohol consumption?

No.

Do you drink to boost your self-confidence?

No.

Does your drinking cause you to have difficulty sleeping?

No – it was the opposite, she usually slept better.

Do you ever feel like a drink the next morning?

Oh my God, you're kidding, aren't you?

Madeleine obviously wasn't an alcoholic. But then . . .

Has drinking ever affected your work?

Has drinking affected your home life, your relationships?

Have you ever had a loss of memory after drinking?

Have you ever done something after drinking that you would never have done sober?

Holy shit.

Madeleine tried to rationalise it. Okay, she might have a slight problem; certainly she didn't seem to be able to handle drinking *too much*. It might even be said that that actually made her the opposite of an alcoholic.

Then she came across the term 'functional alcoholic'. And a whole lot more literature debunking the myth that alcoholism was a one-size-fits-all condition, and the notion that you were an alcoholic from the first time you took a drink, leading Madeleine all the way to the uncomfortable truth that you could *develop* alcoholism at any stage of your life.

But what had probably left her most unsettled of all were the articles about alcoholics in relationships. Not the violence and other extreme behaviours, though they were certainly discussed at length. More typical and insidious was the alcoholic's need to deflect attention from their own actions by finding fault, picking fights and casting blame. This helped reassure them that the problem was not theirs, also giving them an excellent excuse to drink – spawning the notion that you could be 'driven to drink'. The only way an alcoholic could deal with their deep shame and guilt was to make it about the other person. Madeleine realised she had turned Henry into her scapegoat.

The taxi pulled up outside her office building and Madeleine roused herself into action. When she stepped out onto the kerb and into the cavernous wind tunnel of the CBD, it was even colder than before. But it was only a quick dash to the door and she was inside the air-conditioned foyer – still a little too cool for what she was wearing. She only hoped she'd left a cardigan behind at her desk sometime.

When she walked into the publicity area it was surprisingly quiet – there was no sign of the shitstorm that Liv had alluded to. She couldn't even see Liv. A couple of the girls were working quietly at their desks, while Amy was on the phone, speaking in hushed tones. Madeleine dumped her bag on her desk and yawned. She felt a little lightheaded, and realised she couldn't remember the last time she'd eaten.

'Hey,' Stacey said, appearing around the wall. 'Liv will be pleased to see you.'

'Where is she?'

'Not sure. She might be in a meeting, but she won't be far.'

'I thought things were supposed to be crazy in here?' said Madeleine, as she started to hunt around her desk for any items of clothing that might be lurking.

'That was an hour ago, it's settled down a lot since then,' said Stacey. 'Are you looking for something?'

'Yeah,' Madeleine said vaguely. 'You wouldn't have a spare cardigan, would you?'

'Sorry, no,' Stacey said. 'I thought you seemed a bit underdressed.'

'Tell me about it. I was in such a rush, I didn't even look out the window before I left the building.'

Stacey nodded. 'Let me go and check in editorial, there's sure to be a cardigan floating around there somewhere.' She turned to walk away. 'Oh, and have you had coffee yet?'

Madeleine gave her a pitiful look.

'Or anything to eat?'

She shook her head.

'I'll take care of it,' said Stacey, charging off.

'Thank you,' Madeleine called after her, and dropped down into her chair. She felt exhausted already, and she had a headache.

Not a real headache, just a caffeine vacuum, which left her head feeling hollow. She yawned again as she pulled her chair up to her computer to log in.

'Hey, Mad, I didn't see you come in.' It was Ren, popping her head around the nib wall.

Madeleine swivelled her chair to face her. 'Oh, hey, Ren.'

'Have you recovered from Friday night yet?'

She was never going to recover from Friday night. 'Sort of.' She attempted a weak smile.

'Have you seen Aiden?'

Don't blush, don't blush! 'Of course.' She really didn't want to get into an Aiden gabfest, but she had a feeling it was going to be hard to avoid. 'He's staying with us, so, you know.'

'He's amAHZing.' Ren gushed, propping herself against the wall. 'Did he say he had a good time? We didn't overwhelm him, did we?'

Madeleine shook her head. 'No, I'm sure he really enjoyed himself.'

'We put heaps of pictures up on Facebook. Have you seen them?'

'Oh? Um, no, I haven't.' Madeleine felt queasy. What kind of pictures? It wasn't as though Henry was likely to see them, he wasn't on Facebook, but she didn't like to think that there were potentially compromising photos of her and Aiden on display to the world, indeed, any photos of her and Aiden, compromising or otherwise. She would have to log on later and untag herself. For now she needed to change the subject. 'Where is everybody, anyway?' she asked.

'I know Sarah and Katie are off at events, but Nat is totally missing in action.'

'What do you mean?'

'She didn't show up for work, and no one's been able to reach her on her mobile or at home. Liv's pretty pissed off.'

That had to be at least part of the cause of the crisis this morning. Before she could think much about it, Madeleine spotted Stacey coming back into the office, carrying a coffee and a paper bag, and some kind of knitted garment over her arm.

'Oh, thank God.' Madeleine swooped, relieving Stacey of her booty. 'Thank you so much,' she said, and took a sip of the coffee. She opened the bag and tucked straight into the muffin, suddenly aware of how famished she was.

Stacey held up the cardigan. 'Sorry, this was all I could find. And I'm not surprised nobody's claimed it before now.'

'Lucky for me, then,' said Madeleine, pulling it on. It was a big, chunky long-line cardigan in the drabbest of browns, with a heavy rollover collar. 'As long as it keeps me warm, I couldn't care less about making a fashion statement.'

Stacey's expression as she took in Madeleine's appearance was somewhere between a smile and a grimace. 'That's just as well then.'

The brown didn't go with the blue tones of her floral sundress, and she was sure she must look bizarre, especially with bare legs and sandalled feet. But she was warm now, and the coffee was good, the muffin filling. She was starting to feel human again. As long as she tried not to think about the train wreck that was her life, she might just get through the day.

'I wonder where Liv's got to?' she said after she'd demolished most of the muffin.

'I'm right here,' Liv said, marching briskly into the open office. 'What the hell are you wearing, Mad?'

'I had a wardrobe miscalculation. Stace found this for me so I wouldn't freeze to death.'

'Rightio,' said Liv. 'Anyway, you want to come to my office?'

'Sure.' Madeleine got up, wiping crumbs from her mouth. 'Thanks again, Stace, I owe you.' She grabbed her coffee and followed Liv into her office.

'Shut the door, would you?' said Liv, sitting down at her desk.

Madeleine did so, then took a seat opposite Liv. 'What's going on?'

'Before we get into all that, I just want to let you know . . . Dylan had his appendix out on the weekend.'

'What?' Had Madeleine been so caught up in her own problems that she'd forgotten Dylan was having an operation? 'I didn't know that was happening.'

'No, none of us did. It was an emergency.'

'Cripes, Liv. What happened?'

'Remember the boys were at a sleepover? I got a call at six on Saturday morning.'

'Oh no.'

'Oh yeah. He'd been throwing up, severe pains in the stomach, fever . . . Anyway, long story short, I picked him up and took him straight to casualty, he was diagnosed with appendicitis, and they had it whipped out within a few hours.'

Madeleine was shaking her head, stunned. 'How is he?'

'He's fine – bounced back the next day, he was eating last night, and he'll be home tomorrow.'

'What on earth are you doing here then?'

'It's all right. Mum was going to see him today, and I will leave early, but I have to get things sorted out here first.'

'Why didn't you call me?' said Madeleine.

'Well, I did, this morning.'

'No, I mean when it happened?'

'Thanks, Mad,' Liv smiled, 'but really, what could you have done?'

There was more truth to that than Liv could have realised. Madeleine would have been absolutely useless if Liv had called her for help this weekend.

'After the initial shock, it was really okay,' Liv said. 'The staff were amazing. I don't get why people complain about public hospitals.'

'How did Lachie cope with it all?'

'He was just gorgeous, so protective. You know, he offered to give Dylan his appendix.'

'Bless.'

'I know, break a mother's heart,' Liv sighed. 'So, onto what's happening around here. Natalie has thrown the cat among the pigeons, and then decided to run off and leave us all to clean up the mess.'

'Ren said she hasn't shown up this morning.'

'And she's not answering her phone,' Liv said grimly.

'What did she do? What's the cat, the mess?'

Liv sat back in her chair, interlocking her fingers. 'Well, on Friday, just before we went to lunch, the stupid girl decided to fire off emails to two of her authors who have erotic books coming out next week, telling them there had been a change of plan and she was going to have to cancel some of their publicity. And that was it. Then she left the office for the day.'

'You're kidding.'

'Wish I was,' said Liv. 'I just can't understand it, she must have literally sent them off moments before we all walked out of the office.'

'Which authors are we talking about?'

'Cal Olson and Jennifer Finch.'

'Well, Jen'll be fine,' said Madeleine. 'She's experienced, and she's sensible. But this is Cal's debut, she wouldn't have known what to make of it.'

'Exactly,' said Liv. 'They both replied to Natalie's emails – Jennifer left it at that for the weekend. But Cal was understandably confused and probably a little thrown, so when she didn't get an answer, she tried to call Natalie to find out what was going on. But of course Nat was too busy mooning after your best man to bother answering her phone. That's all I can assume, because this morning the shit really hit the fan. Natalie hasn't turned up, and she's still not answering her phone, so I had to field calls from both of them. Jennifer was okay once I explained a little – I promised to call her later to have a longer chat about it.'

'And Cal?'

'Here's where it gets interesting,' Liv drawled. 'You see, Natalie forgot to inform the journalist who was scheduled to interview Cal over the phone this morning.'

'Oh God,' Madeleine groaned. 'Which journalist?'

'Anne Reynolds.'

Unfortunately, Ms Reynolds fell into the camp of journalists who would make a story out of anything.

'So of course, not knowing any different, Anne phoned Cal at the scheduled time, and from what I can understand, confusion reigned, with Cal playing straight into her hands, and Anne managing to prise the details of the email out of her, pretty much verbatim.'

'Bugger.'

'Next thing, I get a call from Anne, wanting some kind of scoop about the death of erotica, and the implications for the ailing publishing industry.'

Madeleine winced. 'What did you say?'

'I fudged some of the facts, and I think I've put her off for now.' Liv said. 'But she's determined to run a story on this, and she's going to, whether I cooperate or not. So naturally, if I don't cooperate, that will make up part of the story: "Head of publicity at Amblin Press refuses to go on the record, will not even acknowledge the existence of an email", et cetera, et cetera.'

'What are you going to do?'

'I have until tomorrow to pull something together,' said Liv. 'I'll have to let Jane know what's going on, though I would like to have my department under control before that.'

'But isn't this all on Natalie's head?' said Madeleine. 'Have there been any other slip-ups like that?'

'No, and I want to keep it that way,' said Liv. 'What I'd like you to do today is sit with any of the girls who are handling the relevant authors, and go over their strategies with them, just to make doubly sure. Try not to get into what Nat's done. I've already alerted them that a journalist is sniffing around, and that they should have strictly no comment.'

'Okay, I'll get onto it.' Madeleine was glad to have something to focus on.

'How are you doing?' said Liv, watching her. 'No offence, but you look a little beat.'

She nodded. 'My sleep is all over the place.'

'You were at the flat last night?'

'I was there the whole weekend,' she said.

'With Aiden?' Liv frowned.

'No, he left on Saturday.'

She couldn't get into it with Liv now, she'd find out soon enough, everyone was going to find out soon enough – but Madeleine was dreading telling Liv in particular. After what she'd been through with Rick, Madeleine couldn't expect any sympathy or understanding from her. Not that she deserved either.

There was a single knock on the door and Stacey popped her head in. 'Sorry to interrupt,' she said, holding up Madeleine's phone. 'This has rung out about three times. It was sitting on your desk. I didn't answer it, but "Genevieve" came up on the screen every time.'

Madeleine groaned: that was all she needed. 'Thanks,' she said, taking the phone from Stacey. 'I better call her back.'

She went to get up but Liv stopped her. 'Stay here. Unless it's private?'

'No, it won't be anything important.'

Stacey ducked back out as Madeleine tapped the screen to return Genevieve's call.

'Where are you?' Genevieve demanded before Madeleine could even get hello out.

'I'm at work.'

'Well, why aren't you here?'

'Where's here?' Madeleine asked blankly.

'At the Cake Walk, for your tasting!'

This could not be happening. 'Genevieve, I'm really sorry. Something's come up at work –'

'Don't you give me that,' she said. 'This is your cake tasting, for *your* wedding! What could be so important that you forgot?'

If only she knew. 'I'm really, really sorry, but I just don't think I can get away.'

'Are you serious?' Genevieve growled. 'Are you fucking kidding me? Yes, Mum, I said the F-word! Deal with it.'

Oh crap, her mother was there too.

'I've taken the kids to school, dropped Archie off at the babysitter's, picked up Mum, and driven here to Glebe, taken half an hour to find a park in these shitty little back lanes, and you're going to tell me you can't get away to come to your own wedding cake tasting?'

'Genevieve, I'm really sorry, you don't understand –'

'I understand all right. You are so *unbelievably* self-centred . . .'

Madeleine was distracted from Genevieve's rant by Liv waving madly at her from across the desk. 'Just a minute – can you hold on just one minute, please, Gen?'

She groaned loudly in response, and Madeleine muted the phone.

'What's going on?' Liv asked her.

'I'm supposed to be at my cake tasting, of all things.' Madeleine sighed wearily.

'Then go.'

'Oh no, it's fine.'

'Madeleine, go.'

'But you want me to meet with the staff . . .'

'Listen to me,' said Liv, leaning forward. 'How long's it going to take, an hour? You've got the rest of the day to talk to the staff, but I assume you can't put this off any longer – your wedding's less than two weeks away.'

Madeleine was dumbfounded. This was not only absurd, it was a complete waste of time. But how the hell was she going to get out of it? She was trapped between an angry sister on one end of the phone and an understanding boss on the other. She didn't have a choice.

'All right, thanks.' She took the phone off mute. 'Genevieve, I've talked to my boss. She said it's fine, I can come.'

'I should think you can bloody come!'

'I'll be there as fast as I can.'

'Make it faster,' Genevieve snapped, hanging up.

Liv was removing her jacket. 'Ditch that horrible grizzly bear coat. You can wear this,' she said, passing the jacket across the desk.

'Are you sure?'

'You can't go out in public looking like that,' Liv said. 'This doesn't really go either, but at least it's an improvement.'

The Cake Walk

A few minutes later, Madeleine was rushing through the foyer again, this time on her way out of the building. It must have rained heavily in the past hour, the pavement was wet and the awnings were dripping, but fortunately it had stopped for the moment. She stepped off the kerb to hail a taxi and landed ankle deep in a puddle. If there was a God, he was really messing with her today – not that she didn't deserve it.

When she managed to get a taxi she realised she didn't know the exact address, so she just told the driver to head towards Glebe while she looked it up on her phone. She wouldn't have remembered that much if Genevieve hadn't mentioned Glebe earlier. Cake tasting wasn't really up there on Madeleine's list of priorities, even before today, and she had kept postponing the appointment, much to her sister's chagrin. At least Madeleine had given plenty of notice on the other occasions, so she did understand the chagrin today. But she wasn't going to be able to explain to Gen why, this time, perhaps it was forgiveable.

When she found the address she relayed it to the driver, and then rested her head back against the seat. The irony of trotting off to choose between highly overpriced, overwrought cakes for a wedding that wasn't even going ahead was not lost on her. Perhaps she should consider it penance. And if she did enough penance, she wondered, could Henry be spared?

The taxi pulled up outside the Cake Walk, and Madeleine paid the fare and stepped out, watching where she placed her feet this time. But she was still squelching as she walked into the bakery. The sickly smell of sugar hit her immediately. And the decor was pretty sugary as well, all lolly pink. A long glass counter stretched before her, displaying rows of what could only be called cake sculptures. Most of them looked like they couldn't possibly be edible. There were cakes that resembled cars, and trains, and various animals, even insects – a vivid red ladybird and a pretty mauve butterfly. There was a cake made to look like a handbag, and another that looked like a fancy wrapped gift. Weirder still were a selection of cakes made to look like other food: a bar of chocolate, a hamburger, even a giant cupcake – a novelty cake of a cake.

The wedding cakes were set apart in their own glass cabinet at the glamour end of the showroom. There were no cartoonish creations here – it was all pomp and grandeur, cakes that were taking themselves a little too seriously. Gazing into the glass case, Madeleine remembered how little she had cared about this, and yet now she'd give anything to be choosing a cake for real, a cake that she and Henry would stand behind while photos were taken, clasping their hands together around the handle of the knife, making a wish . . .

A young woman in a pink smock appeared from a doorway behind the counter. 'Can I help you?'

Madeleine snapped out of her daydream. 'Yes, hello . . . I'm here for a cake tasting. I'm meeting my mother and sister, I believe they're already here.'

The woman smiled. 'Of course, I'll show you through.' She led Madeleine through the door behind the counter into a small well-lit room where Genevieve and Margaret were sitting at a white-clothed table.

'Finally,' Genevieve declared.

'Hello, darling,' Margaret said brightly. She looked relieved and Madeleine felt bad. She must have had to just sit there while Genevieve stewed and foamed at the mouth. Madeleine stooped to give her a kiss.

'My God, Madeleine, what kind of get-up is that?' said Genevieve, looking her up and down.

The tailored black jacket was an odd match for the blue sundress, as Liv had warned. Liv was also taller than Madeleine, so it was about a size too big. Madeleine pushed up the sleeves as she came around to give her sister a kiss.

Genevieve offered her cheek. 'Are you wearing one of Henry's suit coats?'

Did Genevieve think Henry was a woman's size twelve? 'I had to borrow it from my boss, I was a bit underdressed for the weather.'

'And your shoes are all wet,' Genevieve frowned. 'What did you do, walk here?'

'I stepped into a puddle getting into the taxi.'

'Oh no, darling,' said her mother. 'Are you all right? You look a bit tired.'

Madeleine took a seat at the table. It was already dotted with delicate little plates displaying delicate little samples of cake. 'I'm all right, Mum, it's just been a difficult morning at work.'

'So what was the big drama that kept you from getting here on time?' Genevieve asked.

'Just work stuff,' Madeleine said offhandedly. 'It's not very interesting.'

'Interesting enough to make you more than half an hour late,' said Genevieve. 'Anyway, we had to get started without you, we couldn't hold them up forever.'

There was a plate in Madeleine's place, and several cake forks laid out for their use. The cake samples were all labelled with elaborate place cards, including lists of ingredients.

'Mum and I have been trying some, taking notes,' said Genevieve. 'We like the almond cake layered with mocha ganache, and also the citrus with strawberry coulis, don't we, Mum?'

Margaret nodded obligingly.

'Henry's allergic to strawberries,' said Madeleine.

Genevieve narrowed her eyes. 'How allergic?'

'Allergic enough.' Madeleine stared at her sister in horror.

'Will Henry get to try the cakes?' Margaret asked.

That caused an involuntary spasm in Madeleine's heart. 'He's happy to leave it up to me,' she said. 'Actually, Henry likes the traditional fruitcake. So do I, to be honest.'

'Me too,' said Margaret.

But Genevieve was rolling her eyes. 'You can*not* serve dreary, old fruitcake in this day and age. People expect something more upmarket.'

Madeleine felt like saying that people who were getting a free meal really had no right to be 'expecting' anything. She knew her friends weren't like that. But what did it matter? This was all make-believe anyway; she felt like an actor in a surrealist play. She stuck her fork into the sample labelled RED VELVET and scooped up a portion.

A man in chef's garb suddenly appeared through the doorway. 'Ah, the bride has arrived,' he said, sweeping over towards her. 'Madeleine, I presume? Allow me to introduce myself. I'm Trevor, your pastry chef.'

At any other time, Madeleine might have been amused by the incongruity of a pastry chef being called Trevor. It was something she would have relayed to Henry over dinner tonight, and they would have had a chuckle.

She rested her loaded fork on the plate, and shook the hand Trevor extended. 'I'm so sorry I was late.'

'Not at all.' He waved her apology aside. 'We understand, brides are very busy people. Now, can I offer you a cup of tea? We prefer not to serve coffee for the cake tasting, it can overpower the flavours. But you do need something to cleanse the palate between tastes.'

'Black tea will be fine,' she said.

'Perfect!' he said. 'English Breakfast, or something else? We have a full range, herbal as well.'

'English Breakfast will be lovely, thank you.'

He gave a slight, oddly deferential bow and swept back out of the room.

Madeleine picked up her fork again and took a mouthful of the cake. It didn't taste like she expected. She wasn't sure what she'd expected a ruby-red cake to taste like, but if she closed her eyes, it might as well have been a rather mild chocolate cake.

'What do you think?' said Genevieve.

'It's okay . . .' Madeleine swallowed it down. 'Maybe a little bland?'

'I thought so too.' Margaret nodded.

'You didn't say that earlier,' said Genevieve.

She looked nonplussed.

'I think it must get quite difficult to differentiate after you've tasted a few,' Madeleine said, with a reassuring glance at her mother.

'Then you have to focus,' Genevieve said firmly, like the schoolteacher she should have been. 'The thing is, red velvet is a statement cake – just look at it. If you have it with some white chocolate ganache, I think you'll find that will liven it up.'

Madeleine's tea was served, and she set about sampling the samples, even though she felt sick in the stomach. She was finding it hard to differentiate, or to focus, as Genevieve conducted a running commentary, waxing lyrical about the various properties of your basic muds, and exploring the pros and cons of butter cream versus fondant icing versus ganache. It was all so unimportant in the scheme of things. Madeleine couldn't help thinking that if she hadn't wanted this wedding in the first place, everything would still be okay. They could have had a simple ceremony at the registry office, no need for a wedding party, no need for a best man, and therefore no need for Aiden to come out here. And none of this would have happened.

'Honestly, Madeleine, you could show a little more enthusiasm,' Genevieve said, breaking into her reverie. 'I think I care more about this than you do.'

She couldn't argue with that.

'She's just tired,' said Margaret. 'Aren't you, dear?'

'I am, Mum. I had a . . . a big weekend.'

'What did you do?' Genevieve asked, as if she wanted proof.

Had drunken sex with the best man.

'Actually, the girls from work threw me an impromptu bachelorette party on Friday night.'

'Don't you mean a hens' party?' said Genevieve. 'Bachelorette is a little American.'

'Whatever.'

'Nice of them to invite me,' she added.

'What?'

'Well, I am the matron of honour, after all.'

'Doesn't that mean you should've been the one organising it?' Madeleine snapped.

'And how do you expect me to do that, with three kids and an absentee husband?'

'So how would you have managed to come out to the city on a Friday night?' Madeleine threw back at her.

'If I'd had some notice, I would have made the effort,' Genevieve said airily. 'I hardly ever get a night out.'

'Well, I'm sorry that I didn't think to tell my work friends when they turned Friday afternoon drinks into a "hens' night" that they should have been running it by my sister first!' Madeleine's voice was raised and her eyes were glassy with tears. Her mother and Genevieve were staring at her. 'Sorry,' she said.

But instead of the retort she was expecting, Genevieve put her hand over her sister's. 'Hey, Mad, what's the matter?'

'She's just tired,' Margaret said again, rubbing her other arm.

'I don't think this is just tiredness,' said Genevieve, actually looking concerned.

Madeleine suddenly had a flashback of the big sister who used to look out for her. Who used to lie on her stomach on the bed opposite hers, in the room they shared as girls, chattering away till all hours – until their dad had to come in and have a stern word with them. Of course, being the eldest, and with far more interesting stories to tell, Genevieve did most of the talking. But Madeleine always knew she could tell her anything . . . That was a long time ago.

She cleared her throat. 'I'm . . . I'm afraid everything's not going to work out.'

Genevieve released a loud sigh of relief. 'You're just having cold feet, Mad.'

Madeleine was getting heartily sick of that expression.

'It's completely normal, so close to the wedding,' Genevieve went on. 'You shouldn't let it get to you. If ever there was a couple who had nothing to worry about . . .'

Madeleine wouldn't have expected that sentiment from Gen, and she was touched. 'Did you have cold feet before your wedding?' she asked.

'Not really,' said Genevieve. 'But I've got them now,' she added with a jaundiced laugh.

'I had cold feet,' said Margaret.

They both looked at her. 'You did?' said Madeleine. 'With Dad?'

'Oh yes, terribly cold feet,' she said. 'But your father was so good to me. Honestly, my feet were like blocks of ice sometimes in the winter, and he always let me curl them around his in bed, until they warmed up.' She had a faraway look in her eyes, and a dreamy smile on her face. 'Does Henry let you warm your feet up against his, Maddie?' she asked.

Tears crept into Madeleine's eyes. 'Yes, Mum, he does.'

'Then he's going to make a wonderful husband.'

Amblin Press

When Madeleine got back to the office it was even quieter than before. She couldn't see a soul on the entire floor, until Liv got her attention, waving from her office.

Madeleine walked over to the door. 'Where is everyone?' she asked.

'Gone to lunch,' said Liv, munching on a salad from a takeaway container on the desk in front of her.

Of course. Madeleine had totally lost track of the time; it had been a very strange day.

'Come in,' said Liv. 'Pull up a pew.'

Madeleine did so. 'Have you heard from Nat?'

Liv shook her head. 'Don't mention her while I'm eating, it'll give me indigestion.' She scooped up some leafy greens onto her fork, and they all dropped off again before she could get it to her mouth. 'Jeez, they make it hard for you to eat healthy. So how was the cake tasting?'

'All right, I guess.'

'Try to contain your excitement there, Mad.'

She shrugged. 'This was Genevieve's little project, I was just along for the ride.'

'Well, what did you choose in the end?'

'Umm . . . I think it was a tier of red velvet with white chocolate ganache, and a tier of coconut glazed with passionfruit and layered with white chocolate . . . No, hold on, the red velvet must have the dark chocolate ganache – I know they both didn't have white, and you wouldn't put dark chocolate with coconut, or would you?' Madeleine suppressed a yawn. 'I don't know, I just went along with whatever Gen said.'

'You shouldn't let her push you around.'

'It doesn't bother me, not about this anyway.'

'At least you didn't go with cupcakes.' Liv was shaking her head. 'More like schmuck cakes. They've been done to death. I quite like the traditional fruitcake, to be honest.'

'So do I,' said Madeleine. 'And so does Henry.' And the melancholy descended again with the mention of his name.

'Then why don't you have fruitcake?'

'Because Genevieve said it's daggy.' And because it didn't matter. She was going to have to call and cancel the order tomorrow anyway. It was all just a big charade.

'Phooey,' said Liv. 'I kind of miss getting that finger of fruitcake in the little bag – you know, the one you put under your pillow to make a wish. You couldn't put passionfruit glazed coconut cake with chocolate ganache under your pillow – can you imagine the mess it'd make?'

As Liv prattled on, Madeleine could feel the tears pricking at the corners of her eyes. It was all too hard, she couldn't keep this up – talking about this phantom wedding was breaking her heart. The floodgates suddenly flew open and a loud sob burst from her mouth.

'What's the matter?' Liv jumped up to close the door, and pulled a chair over close to her. 'Oh, poor Mad,' she said, giving her shoulder a gentle rub. 'It's all getting a bit much, eh? You know, weddings are one of the most stressful life events you can go through. How crazy is that? If everyone didn't bother with all the palaver and took themselves off to a registry office, they'd all be a lot happier.'

That just made Madeleine cry harder.

'Oh, I'm sorry,' said Liv, 'that was insensitive. Your wedding's going to be beautiful, I'm just being an old hard heart. You and Henry – you're the real thing, if anyone has a right to celebrate, it's you two.'

Wailing like a baby now.

'Oh for godsakes, what is it?' Liv pleaded with her. 'You have to tell me.'

Madeleine looked up at her, wiping her eyes with her hands, until Liv passed her a tissue. Liv was one of her closest confidantes, if not her *closest* confidante, after Henry. Maybe she would understand . . .

No, what was she thinking? Liv wouldn't understand. She had been the victim of cheating, why would she have any sympathy for Madeleine? Why would anyone? But maybe that was exactly why Madeleine needed to confess to her, even if she wasn't going to get absolution – maybe *because* she wasn't going to get absolution.

She sniffed, taking a deep breath to compose herself. 'This is in the vault, okay?'

Liv raised her eyebrows. 'The vault is hereby sealed. Out with it.'

God, this was so hard. Madeleine swallowed. 'Aiden and I . . . we . . .'

She watched Liv's face – the initial confusion, then the flutter of realisation passing across her eyes and landing with a thud. 'Maddie!' she gasped, barely audible. 'You didn't.'

Madeleine just looked at her helplessly, tears filling her eyes again. 'I'm such a bad person.'

But this time Liv didn't rub her shoulder or try to reassure her. She sat back in her chair, pensive.

'I'm sorry,' said Madeleine. 'I shouldn't dump this on you.'

'It's just hard for me, you know, because of Rick.'

'I know, I'm sorry.'

They lapsed into silence. Madeleine wondered what was going through Liv's mind, how disgusted she was with her right now.

'I'm just trying to understand,' Liv said after a while. 'Why would you do something like that? Why would you jeopardise your relationship?'

'I don't know.'

'Henry's a good man, he loves you, he *adores* you.'

'I know.'

'Then why?'

Madeleine didn't have an answer.

'Are you in love with Aiden?'

'God no, it was an accident.'

'You accidentally slept with him?'

'No, I mean . . . it was a mistake.'

Liv blinked. 'Fucking big one – excuse the French.'

'You don't have to convince me. I know how bad this is.'

'I gather Henry doesn't know?'

Madeleine shook her head. 'I haven't been back home yet.'

'When did this happen?'

'Friday night, when we got back to the apartment.'

Liv dropped her head into her hands. 'I knew I should have made you come home with me.'

'Why, did you suspect this was on the cards?'

'Of course not, or I definitely would have made you come home with me, even if I'd had to drag you.' Liv bit on the side of her thumb, thinking. 'You know, I wasn't sure about Aiden. I know he's gorgeous and charming and all, but there was something that bothered me. He seemed a little *too* charming, and a little *too* familiar.' She looked at Madeleine as if remembering something. 'Why did he go with you to your dress fitting?'

'That was nothing, he just had some time to kill before a flight.'

'It was a bit weird.'

'Nothing happened there. He was totally all, "Henry's the luckiest man alive." The whole time he's been so pleasant, and charming, like you said. So different to Henry.'

'But not in a good way, as it turns out.'

'No, not in a good way at all,' said Madeleine. Liv didn't know the half of it. 'But look, I can't make him the villain of the piece.'

'Well, I wouldn't exactly call him the hero. He slept with his best friend's fiancée.'

'And I slept with my fiancé's best friend.'

Liv shook her head. 'Why, Mad?'

'I don't know,' she said. 'Everything was getting to me – living way up there, Henry working all the time. Having Aiden around just brought it into sharp relief.'

'But why wouldn't you talk to Henry?' said Liv. 'Tell *him* all that, instead of sleeping with his best man. It's just so . . .'

'Tacky. And deplorable. And unforgivable.' Madeleine took a breath. 'I'm not making excuses, Liv, but . . . I think I might have a drinking problem.'

'Oh, you definitely have a drinking problem.'

Madeleine blinked. 'You've noticed?'

'Yeah,' she said like it was the most obvious thing in the world. 'You know you almost lost your job over it?'

'What – when?'

'A couple of years ago, during that "going off the rails" period you always refer to.'

'You were going to fire me?'

'Jane was getting close – she wanted to give you a warning, but I said I'd take care of it. That's why you only got one author at the festival that year. And that was Henry. And then everything changed.'

Madeleine pressed her lips together, trying to stem more tears.

'God, poor Henry,' Liv murmured.

'I know.' Madeleine's face crumpled. 'I can't stand that I'm going to hurt him. It's so unfair, he didn't do anything to deserve this . . .' Her voice trailed off, finally dissolving into tears. She felt Liv's hand on her back again, and then her arm drawing around her as she shifted closer.

'When are you going to tell him?' Liv asked. 'You *are* going to tell him?'

'Of course. I couldn't keep this from him, I could never live with myself. And I have to do it tonight. I've been putting it off, staying at the apartment.'

'With Aiden?'

'No! I sent him packing on Saturday morning.'

'He didn't go back up to Pittwater, did he?'

Madeleine shook her head. 'He's keeping a low profile. I told him not to come anywhere near me, and he said he was going to tell Henry he was taking a trip for a few days. Give me a chance to talk to him first.'

Liv was thoughtful. 'Tell me, did Aiden have any defence for his part in all of this, any justification?' she asked. 'I mean, I'd like to know what was going on in his head while he was screwing his best mate's fiancée. Sorry for being crass.'

'It's all right, it is crass.' Madeleine considered how to answer Liv's question. 'Aiden has some strange attitudes, some of the things he said . . . it's almost as if he's jealous of Henry. He said it had been "brewing" between us since the day he arrived. Reckoned he could see how unhappy I was and that Henry had it coming.'

'Bastard.' Liv looked disgusted. 'You know, he was playing you like a cheap guitar. He was the one who suggested the drinking game –'

'I don't know, I think it might have been Ren.'

'Well, he seconded it, and he bought the tequila,' said Liv. 'You know I had to pull him aside and tell him to take you home, when you were all talking about kicking on? Bloody hell, I should have kept my mouth shut. You would have been better off getting blind drunk – then maybe you would have just passed out instead of sleeping with him.'

Madeleine sighed deeply. 'There's a great pair of alternatives. Be a drunk or a slut . . . seems I managed to be both at once.'

Liv looked at her. 'How do you think Henry's going to take it?'

'How do you think?' Madeleine said. 'He's never going to be able to forgive me for this, and I don't blame him.'

'I don't know, Henry seems like the type who would forgive almost anything.'

'But I'm not even going to ask for his forgiveness. I don't deserve it, just like Rick didn't deserve yours.'

'It's not quite the same, Mad. Rick was a serial adulterer, and there's no coming back from that. But this is not who you are, I know that, and I'm sure Henry will too. This is a one-off, terrible mistake that you're never going to repeat.'

Now was not the time to tell Liv that it wasn't, in fact, a one-off.

'Is that how you thought about Rick after the first time?' Madeleine asked.

'I did, at least I hoped,' said Liv. 'It was after the second time that it got harder . . .'

Madeleine's heart sank. She had to face the consequences. Her father had always been big on that, accepting the consequences of your actions. It was the way he'd brought her up. She wondered what he would think of her right now. It was the first time she'd ever been relieved he wasn't here, so he couldn't see the mess she'd made of her life.

'Henry will come around,' Liv was saying. 'He has to, the wedding's less than a fortnight –'

'There's not going to be any wedding,' Madeleine said flatly.

'Really? You'd seriously call the whole thing off?'

'Of course. I can't make him go through with it just because I've bought a dress and we've paid deposits. That's the least of our worries.' Madeleine stared down at the floor. 'Henry didn't even want all the hoo-ha anyway, it's certainly not going to bother him to cancel.'

'Oh, Mad . . .'

'It's all right, I'm not going to fall apart.' She felt it was important to stress that to Liv. 'And I *am* going to get this drinking issue sorted.'

'How do you plan to do that?'

'I don't know,' said Madeleine. 'I'm not sure I'm ready for a group thing, but I'd like to talk to someone, like a drug and alcohol counsellor, who can help me figure things out. Maybe I am an alcoholic, I honestly don't know. All I know is that I was happy with Henry, and as soon as I started drinking, to excess anyway, I decided that he was the problem, not the drinking.'

'You should tell him all that,' Liv said. 'It's a pretty big deal, isn't it, admitting that you have a problem?'

'Doesn't mean he wants to take it on.' And besides, it was the same excuse she'd used the first time. How many chances was he expected to give her? Who could live like that? Madeleine knew this was going to destroy all trust they had between them. And without trust, what hope did they have?

They heard noises out in the office. People were starting to drift back in after lunch.

'Why don't you go home?' said Liv. 'You're not going to be good for anything until you deal with this.'

But Madeleine shook her head. 'No, I need to prove to you that at least I can do my job, that you can count on me. I'm going to lose Henry, I can't lose this as well.'

'You're not going to lose your job. I know from experience that you're capable of pulling yourself together, that you went to the brink and came back from it. You should tell Henry about that. He didn't really know you then, he's only seen you at your best.'

Not exactly. 'Anyway,' Madeleine really wanted to change the subject, 'you should be the one going home, Liv. You have a child recovering from surgery and I've been sitting here, dumping my problems on you.'

'Nonsense,' said Liv. 'In any case, I've still got to talk to Jane, and she couldn't see me until after lunch. I'll go after that.'

'Let me give you back your jacket,' said Madeleine, getting up and slipping it off her shoulders.

'Are you sure?' Liv said, standing up.

'Yeah, the rain looks like it's clearing. Besides, I'm not going to need it, I'll be going straight to the car from the office.'

Madeleine handed her the jacket, and as Liv took it, she suddenly wrapped her arms around her, holding her tight. 'You're not a bad person, Mad.'

'I'm going to cry if you keep this up.'

'Okay,' said Liv, drawing back to look at her. 'I hope it goes all right, or as well as can be expected, anyway.'

Madeleine managed a weak smile. 'Give Dylan a high five from me,' she said, before walking out into the main office.

4 pm

Madeleine decided to call it a day. She'd made it through the afternoon, meeting with the girls and focusing on work issues rather than her own. It gave her mind a break, and at least she felt she'd achieved something, apart from making a bogus order for a wedding cake.

Liv had left more than an hour ago, while Natalie still hadn't shown her face, and was unlikely to now. Madeleine collected up her things and got all the way down to the underground carpark before remembering that her car wasn't here, it was at the apartment. Nuts. When was she going to get it right today? She caught the lift back up to street level and then got a taxi to her building. There was no need to go up to the apartment, so she swiped her card and went straight down to the garage, relieved to finally get into her car. Then she remembered she hadn't messaged Henry yet. She took out her phone and typed, *Leaving city now.*

As she drove out of the carpark, she heard the beep of her phone. She checked it at the next lights. *Look forward to seeing you soon.* Madeleine doubted he was going to feel that way later.

While usually the trip seemed to take forever, today it felt as though she was turning into their street all too soon, and she'd even taken the long way home, along the coast instead of the Wakehurst Parkway, her sense of dread growing with every kilometre.

Madeleine pulled into the garage and cut the engine. As she climbed out of the car she could feel a chill rising off the water.

The sky was clear now, but the absence of cloud cover meant that as the sun started its descent, so did the temperature. She shivered as she slipped on her Crocs and made her way down the stairs to the front door. She paused with her hand on the doorknob for a moment, taking a deep breath, preparing herself. As though she could ever be prepared for this.

When she pushed open the door and stepped inside, the house felt warm and welcoming. There was even soft music playing in the background: Henry was clearly doing a bit of scene setting. Her heart felt heavy as she closed the door behind her, dropping her bag and keys on the table in the entranceway.

'Madeleine?' Henry called. He walked across the living area to meet her, wiping his hands on a tea towel before flicking it over his shoulder. Madeleine stopped short as he approached, unsure of what to do. It felt wrong to kiss him hello as though everything was normal. But what was she supposed to do? Block him? Not respond? That'd only be worse. She just had to go with the flow for now. She could hardly blurt, 'I slept with Aiden' right from the get-go, just for the sake of full disclosure.

She wouldn't have had a chance anyway, because Henry walked right over to her and caught her up in his arms, holding her tight. Madeleine felt like a fraud, but she relished it all the same. It might be the last time . . .

He drew back, cupping her face in his hands and planting a firm kiss on her lips. 'I missed you,' he said, taking hold of her arms. 'You're cold,' he added, giving them a gentle rub.

'I didn't dress very appropriately today,' Madeleine said. 'Actually, I was thinking of taking a quick shower, changing into something warmer?'

'Of course,' he said, releasing her. 'I was just starting dinner. It's still early.' He smiled down at her. 'It's good to have you home, Madeleine.'

She mustered up a smile in return, and then hurried across the living room towards their bedroom, while Henry returned to the kitchen. 'I won't be long,' she said, as she disappeared up the hall.

'Not a problem, take your time.'

Madeleine was relieved to get out of the flimsy dress and into the shower. She realised she hadn't felt really warm, through to her bones, all day. After standing under the blissfully hot stream of water for five minutes, she finally dragged herself out, drying herself as she drifted back into the bedroom. She pulled on her most comfortable jeans and a worn but cosy long-sleeved T-shirt. She probably looked daggy, but she was craving comfort right now. She slipped on some bedsocks and then walked back into the bathroom to hang up her towel, catching a glimpse of herself in the mirror. Her hair was bedraggled, and there were smudges of mascara under her eyes. Although it hardly mattered, she really should make at least a bit of an effort, Henry had been so pleased to see her. She cleaned her face and pulled a brush through her hair, staring at her reflection. How was she going to get through this? She wandered back into the bedroom, gazing at Henry's side of the bed, an ache rising painfully in her throat. She reached to pick up his pillow and sat down, hugging it to herself, breathing in the smell of him, missing him already. But she was only tormenting herself. She put the pillow back in place and smoothed out the cover.

When Madeleine returned to the living room, Henry was standing at the stove, stirring a large pot with a wooden spoon. 'Feel better?' he asked.

'Much better, thanks.'

'I poured you a glass of wine,' he said, picking it up and holding it out to her.

Ugh. Madeleine took it from him, but she had no intention of drinking; the very thought of it made her sick. But now Henry was raising his own glass to her.

'What shall we drink to?' he said.

'I don't know,' she said weakly. 'What do you suggest?'

'We could drink to the future?'

Hell. This was so hard. She held her glass up to his, trying to control the trembling in her hand. 'To the future.' She took a tiny sip, barely letting the wine touch her tongue. It made her feel nauseous. If this repulsion kept up, it was certainly not going to be difficult to give it up for good.

'What are you cooking?' she asked him. 'It smells amazing.'

'I made chilli.'

And just getting harder. Madeleine had never tasted American-style chilli before Henry made it for her, and now she couldn't get enough. He knew how much she loved it; he was trying so hard. And she was a monster.

'Thank you,' she said sincerely, sliding onto a stool. 'It's my favourite.'

'I know,' he said, turning back to stir the pot.

Madeleine watched him, thinking. She realised that this might be her last opportunity to find out all those things she couldn't answer about him the other night, and she suddenly wanted to know everything, before the ship went down.

'Hey Henry, what's your favourite food?'

'You know me, I'll eat anything.'

'Except strawberries,' she said.

He glanced across at her with a faint smile, like he was flattered she'd remembered. 'That's right.'

'So what happens if you eat them? You never told me.'

'Well, when I was little they just gave me hives, apparently. My mom eventually worked it out, so she stopped feeding me strawberries. Then there was this time, it was at Aiden's, actually, I'd forgotten all about it, and I bit into one. While it was still in my mouth my tongue started to swell up, and then my lips, and then I couldn't breathe.'

'Oh my God,' said Madeleine, 'that must have been awful!'

'Hm, but luckily someone had an EpiPen –'

'Are you serious? Someone just happened to have an EpiPen?'

'Yeah. It was a party, and their friends were all doctors and lawyers. One of the doctors stuck me with the EpiPen, and I was okay in a few minutes.'

'What if he hadn't been there?'

'I don't know,' said Henry, seemingly unperturbed. 'I suppose someone would have known CPR, called an ambulance.'

'You're terribly blasé about it.' As Aiden had been, cruel even. 'You might have died. Doesn't that worry you now?'

'No, because I know not to eat strawberries.'

She couldn't help smiling at that. 'Are you allergic to anything else?'

He shook his head. 'The Carmichaels insisted I get checked out by some allergy specialist after that, a friend of theirs. Strawberries are it. It's a rare allergy, but at least it's single-minded.'

Madeleine couldn't get over the way Aiden had joked about it. What was wrong with him? Henry's life had been threatened, you don't joke about something like that.

'What a horrible thing to go through,' she murmured.

'It was a long time ago.'

She rested her chin in her hand, gazing at him across the kitchen, thinking of her next question. 'Can I ask you something?'

'Sure.'

'What's your favourite colour?'

He looked intrigued. 'Why do you ask that?'

'Because I never have.'

He leaned back against the bench. 'I've never thought about it. I work with colour all the time, so I can't really play favourites.' But he seemed to be giving it some consideration. 'I guess if I had to choose one, it would be the colour of your eyes. I've tried to reproduce it, you know, but I've never been able to.'

He turned around to stir the pot again and Madeleine melted. He was doing that thing he did, saying the most incredibly romantic line imaginable like it was a simple statement of fact. She loved him. She really loved him. She wished she could go back in time . . . But it was fanciful and pointless to think that way. Still, she wanted to hold on to this moment for as long as she could. She knew she should just stop stalling and tell Henry the truth . . . but surely the cosmos could afford her just a little more time?

'Can I ask you something else?' she said.

'You have a lot of questions tonight.'

'Sorry.'

'No, I don't mind,' Henry said, turning around to face her again. 'You can ask me anything, Madeleine.'

'Okay.' She took a breath. 'Who was your first love?'

He blinked. 'Where did that come from?'

'Just something Aiden said one time. That there was a girl who broke your heart.'

'He told you that?' Henry didn't seem cross, more curious.

'He wouldn't tell me who, he wouldn't tell me anything about her – he said he didn't feel right if you'd never told me.'

'I didn't *not* tell you,' said Henry. 'It just hasn't come up, I suppose. It was a very long time ago. I haven't thought about it – her – for ages.'

'But she was your first love.'

'Not really. First crush is probably more accurate.'

'At college?' Madeleine prompted.

He nodded, staring into space as though it was slowly coming back to him. 'You remember when Aiden was talking about all the girls he used to pick up for me?'

'Uh-huh.'

'I know he thought he was doing me a favour, but Aiden and I were very different back then – we still are. I love him like a brother, I guess, because from what I hear, brothers, siblings, get on each other's nerves most of the time,' he said with a wry smile. 'Anyway, these girls really weren't my type. They were the kinds of girls who got drunk at parties and hooked up. I'm not judging, it just wasn't for me. Having said that, at that age a guy wants to get laid, it's pretty much all he thinks about, so I went along with it for a while. But it got tired pretty quick; I had to keep making excuses.' He paused. 'There was a reason my head was always bent over a sketchpad whenever he came looking for me. But that wasn't enough to put him off.'

'So what did you do?'

'Well, after his uncle took me on, things changed. Aiden was more understanding about my work, that it was something I had to spend time on. And I had to get my act together about college. I had no direction – I had to settle on a major once and for all and start working towards graduation.'

Madeleine's head shot up. 'Women's studies. You majored in women's studies.'

He glanced at her, mildly bemused. 'Yes, I did,' he said. 'And that's where I met Gillian.'

'That was her name, your first love?'

'Why do you keep using that expression?'

'I don't know, wasn't she?'

'Like I said, first crush is closer to the truth.'

'You don't have to water it down for me, Henry.'

He gave half a laugh. 'I realise that, Madeleine. It was a very long time ago. I wouldn't think you'd be bothered by a teenage crush.'

She propped her chin in her hand again. 'So tell me about her.'

'She was just a girl I met in class. We clicked right away; there weren't too many guys in that course, so I guess I didn't have much competition. But she and I had a lot in common, and we started hanging out together all the time. We became inseparable, you could say.'

'And?'

'Well, it went on like that for almost a year, and I still couldn't bring myself to make a move. I started to think I'd missed my chance, that if I did something it would only ruin the friendship. Our last summer break was coming up, and Gillian had decided to volunteer for Habitat for Humanity down in the south. I was working with Gene to get a couple of my manuscripts ready to submit to publishers, but I also had to support myself in the meantime, so Gene gave me a part-time job doing admin in his office. I stayed up at Long Island for most of that summer, in the Carmichaels' guest house.' He turned back to stir the pot.

'Henry,' Madeleine said, slightly exasperated. 'You haven't said what happened with Gillian.'

He glanced over his shoulder. 'Oh, because nothing did,' he said simply.

She frowned. 'I'm not following.'

He turned around again. 'A few weeks into summer break, Aiden decided to go volunteering with Habitat as well. When we all came back to college for senior year, they were together.'

'No.' Madeleine's eyes grew wide and her mouth dropped open. 'Did he know how you felt about her?'

'Of course,' said Henry. 'He'd tried to encourage me to do something about it, but I'd told him how I was afraid it would ruin our friendship. I suppose in the end he thought she was fair game.'

Madeleine was perplexed. Why would Aiden do that? This wasn't sitting comfortably with her at all. And then something clicked in her head. 'Oh my God. That story he told at lunch at Genevieve's – that was Gillian, wasn't it?'

Henry nodded. 'I admit I do get a little pissed when he talks about it, because it wasn't all nice and amicable the way he made out, and she wasn't the one who "drifted" first. There was no drifting – Aiden dumped Gillian right before graduation, said there wasn't any point continuing, that a long-distance relationship wasn't going to work . . .' He gave a rueful sigh. 'She was heartbroken, she felt like a fool. We were still good friends, so she cried on my shoulder. She also told me she'd been hoping we would get together senior year.' He paused, thoughtful. 'But that when Aiden came onto her, he told her I wasn't interested in her as more than a friend.'

'He *what?*'

'Oh, I don't know if it was true – I think she was angry with him and wanted to turn me against him as well. Mind you, it probably worked, I don't think we were ever as close after that.'

'So I don't get it. If you haven't seen him in years, and you weren't that close in the end, why did you ask Aiden to be your best man?' Madeleine wanted to know.

'You might recall I didn't exactly ask, he nominated himself.'

She didn't recall that at all. But it's not as though she'd listened in on the phone call.

'As soon as I told him I was getting married, he said, I'm coming over, you need a best man. Typical Aiden.' Henry leaned on the bench opposite her. 'Here's the thing you have to understand about Aiden. He really is a spoilt rich kid, and worse, a spoilt rich *middle* child. His older brother was smart and ambitious, and clearly his parents' favourite. And the girl was also doted upon, as you can imagine. So Aiden still spends his life trying to get their attention and approval. I think he succeeded for a while when he first got some good press for the work he's doing, but like all things, it eventually settled down. He's bored with it now, I can tell – he kept complaining that he wasn't achieving anything, but I think he's had enough. Which is okay, anyone would get burnout in a job like that. But you have to wonder what he's going to do next. For someone who's got so much going for him, he has one enormous chip on his shoulder. You probably couldn't tell, because he hides it so well, but I've seen it in action. He can be jealous and competitive, and he always needs to be the centre of attention. Anyway, enough with the psychoanalytical shtick,' he said suddenly. 'Your eyes were glazing over just then.'

'No, not at all.' Madeleine might have been in a daze, but not because she wasn't interested in what he was saying. She'd seen that enormous chip on Aiden's shoulder, all right, he certainly wasn't hiding it anymore. And jealous didn't even begin to describe his behaviour. She wished she'd known all this before he came to stay, she may just have tread more warily around him.

'Speaking of Aiden,' Henry interrupted her thoughts, 'I suppose you've heard from him by now?'

Her mouth went dry. 'Sorry, what?'

'You've heard from Aiden, I gather? You know what he's up to?'

'Um . . . No, not really.' Damn.

Henry was giving her a puzzled look. 'Oh, well, okay . . . He sent me a text to say he's going away up the coast for a few days, with some people he met in Canberra. He probably means down the coast, closer to Canberra, I imagine. Anyway, that's what he's doing for the rest of the week. Aiden never seems to have any trouble hooking up.'

Madeleine wished he hadn't used that particular expression. She watched Henry now, tasting the chilli, adding seasoning. They were having such a lovely night, and she was going to ruin it. She was going to ruin everything. It was so good to talk to Henry like this; he'd never shared that much about his past before, but he was being so open tonight. She wondered what had brought that on. And she was staggered by everything he'd said about Aiden. She didn't know if it was going to make what she had to tell him better, or worse; more fathomable, or perhaps just inevitable.

But she did know she had to stop putting it off. 'Henry?'

'Hm?'

'We have to talk,' she said, her heart in her mouth.

He turned to look at her. 'Yeah, we do.' He replaced the lid on the pot. 'Let's go sit, this can simmer for a while.'

Madeleine picked up her glass and headed towards the sofa.

'No, let's sit here,' said Henry, 'at the table.'

She noticed then that he'd set the table already, and he'd put out a bowl of olives, some sourdough and a dish of oil. More of the things she loved. What was he doing? Why was he being so nice? How the hell was she going to be able to go through with this?

They sat opposite each other, and Henry set his glass down in front of him, leaning forward and clasping his hands on the table. 'Do you mind if I start?' he said.

'What?' She wasn't expecting that.

'I know we have a lot to talk about,' he said. 'But there's something I want to say upfront, before anything.'

She knew she should just be firm and insist he let her speak first, because nothing he had to say was going to matter once he heard what she had to tell him. But she was too much of a coward. Every minute she put it off was only making it harder, but every minute was like gold to her.

'Sure, go ahead,' she said finally.

'I want to sell the house,' he said.

'What?'

'I want to sell the house. I've already spoken to a realtor – sorry, real estate agent. That's what you call them here, right?'

She was struggling to understand. 'Henry, does that mean . . . Do you want to go back to the States?'

'Oh, God no, Madeleine,' he said, reaching across the table to take her hand. 'Not at all. That's not what this is about. I want to stay here, with you. Just not in this house.'

'I don't get it,' said Madeleine. 'You love this place.'

'But you don't.'

'That's not true. It's a lovely house.'

'Madeleine, I'm sure you like the house well enough,' he said. 'But wouldn't you like it a lot more if it was, say, within half an hour of the city?'

He was doing this for her. He would have always done it for her, if only she'd asked.

'Of course you would,' he answered for her. 'So let's look for somewhere closer.'

'But . . . what about your work? You need peace and quiet.'

'Are you going to tell me there's nowhere between here and the city quiet enough for me to work?'

'I guess not,' she murmured.

'I went for a long drive yesterday,' said Henry. 'There are so many beautiful places I didn't even know existed. I'm thinking – but it's just a suggestion – that we should leave the peninsula altogether. The traffic's always going to be a problem with the Spit Bridge. Do you know Greenwich?' he asked suddenly.

'I know of it, not sure if I've ever driven through it.'

'Because you wouldn't, unless you lived there,' he said, becoming animated. 'It's a beautiful place, quiet streets, lots of trees, some views to the harbour. And I checked on Google maps, it's less than twenty minutes for you to work. But then there's also the whole other side of the bridge. We can look around closer to your mother, if you like, and Genevieve. I don't mind, I don't have an attachment to anywhere in particular. I just want to find somewhere we can both be happy.'

Madeleine nodded vaguely.

'And I hope you don't mind that I contacted the local agent before I spoke to you. It's just that I'm really quite resolved about this.'

'It's not up to me,' she said. 'It's your house.'

'Our house,' he corrected her.

'Henry –'

'We're not going to have that debate again, are we?' he said.

She felt queasy. 'No, all right . . . I just don't understand what brought all this on.'

'Don't you?' He took a deep breath. 'Madeleine, it's pretty obvious to me that things haven't been right between us lately.'

'And you think it's all about the house.'

He shook his head. 'Ever since I came here, you've done everything to accommodate me, you've agreed to whatever I wanted.'

Oh God. Don't give me credit. 'Well, it only seemed fair,' Madeleine pointed out. 'You moved from the other side of the world.'

'Because that was the only option,' he said. 'Your family's here, I would never expect you to move away from them.'

She hadn't realised her family had figured so much in his decision.

'After the other night, when we argued, I got to thinking about it, imagining us living up here with a baby. And I'm not saying that's a given,' he added quickly.

'Henry, I didn't mean –'

'It's all right,' he spoke over her. 'I understand you would have misgivings, trying to imagine having a baby living in this house. This isn't a place to bring up children. I mean, the area's great, but this house . . . You can't even wear your shoes to get down the stairs, how are you supposed to carry a baby and all the stuff that goes with it? How am I, for that matter?'

Madeleine suddenly had a mental picture of Henry carrying a baby – their baby – down the stairs. And it broke her heart.

'But it's not just that,' he went on. 'None of this has ever been fair on you, Madeleine – like driving more than an hour every day to work and then back again. It wasn't a sacrifice for me to move to Australia, because I was coming to be with you. But you've made all the sacrifices ever since, and I can't . . . I'm not going to ask you to make any more.'

She could feel tears pricking her eyes. 'Henry, I don't know what to say.'

'Say you'll come looking for a new place with me, somewhere we can both be happy.'

As much as she wished she could, Madeleine couldn't agree to that – it'd be meaningless, she'd feel like a bigger fraud than she already was. But she had to say something. Henry was waiting for an answer, his expression hopeful, and so full of love. So she said, 'All right, but now you have to let me talk.'

'I will,' he said. 'I'm just not quite finished yet.' He glanced across to the kitchen. 'I think dinner might be ready. Are you hungry?'

'No . . . thanks.' Madeleine knew she couldn't eat.

'Okay, I'd better turn it right down.' He went over to the stove, returning a moment later with the bottle to top up their glasses. 'Oh, you've hardly touched yours,' he said.

'I don't really feel like drinking tonight.'

'Do you want me to get you some water?'

'I'm fine.' On second thoughts: 'I'll get it.'

'No, you sit, I'm already up.'

He brought a jug of water and a glass back to the table, filling it for her, and then sat down, topping up his wine.

'I have to tell you some things I should have told you before,' he began. 'I should have told you a long time ago . . .' He sighed, dragging his hands through his hair.

'Henry, what is it?' she said in a small voice.

'I'm not sure where to start.'

'Just go ahead,' she said. This was exhausting, but she might as well let him get whatever it was off his chest. He was entitled to that much.

He nodded. 'Okay. Well, before I met you, before I came out to Australia . . . I was seeing a therapist.'

'Oh.' That wasn't what she'd expected.

'I'm not crazy or anything, Madeleine.'

'You have to be crazy to see a therapist, Henry.'

'Just troubled?' he suggested.

'I don't know, you tell me.'

'Well, that's the thing, there's a lot you don't know about me . . . When you asked me about my father the other day, I know I brushed you off, and that wasn't fair. We're going to be married, you've got a right to know.'

No, they weren't going to be married, and therefore she didn't really have a right, but she wanted to hear this from him. Not secondhand through Aiden. So she sat quietly listening while Henry recounted a lot of what Aiden had told her. He didn't say much more about his father, just that he was an alcoholic and that he'd made Henry's mother's life a misery. But the way Henry went on to talk about her was a revelation. He never once referred to her as an addict, as Aiden had. Instead he talked about how much he loved her, how good and kind and patient she was.

'Too patient, the way she put up with my father,' said Henry. 'I used to wish I was old enough to take her away from it all, and when I was a little older I said as much to her. But I was still only a teenager, and she used to shush me, tell me it was nothing for me to concern myself about. She said, "Your father's doing the best he can, he works hard, and he provides a roof over our heads, and food on our table." She explained that he'd had a hard life, that his father had died young, and he'd had to go out to work to help support the family when he was not much more than a boy himself.' Henry paused. 'I've always wondered if there was a cycle, if perhaps his father had died an alcoholic. I'll never know, there's no one left who could confirm it either way.'

Madeleine could tell him a thing or two about cycles, patterns of behaviour and alcohol. But not just yet. 'Can I ask you something?' she said.

'Of course.'

'I don't mean to pry –'

'Madeleine, you can't possibly pry, you're my family.'

She wished he hadn't said that. She took a breath. 'Okay, was there any . . . was your father ever . . . aggressive, or violent?'

He shook his head. 'I can't say for sure what he put my mother through before I was born, but I didn't see any evidence of it. Sure, he could be aggressive, surly, but there was never any physical violence. As for our relationship, we barely spoke, he had very little to do with me. I was fine with that. The best times were when he stayed out drinking and didn't come home until late, after I'd gone to bed. Those nights we'd watch television, me and my mom, have dinner on a tray in the living room, as a treat. We always watched sitcoms – I loved more than anything seeing my mother laugh. They're my happiest memories.'

He became wistful for a moment before continuing. 'But when I was a senior at high school, I was aware that something wasn't quite right with her. Sometimes when I came down into the kitchen in the morning she would hurry to close the lid on a canister, then tuck it high up in a cabinet, out of sight. I suspected she might be hiding money from my father, which I could understand, but one day curiosity got the better of me. She was out grocery shopping, so I decided to look in the canister for myself. It was filled with bottles of pills – amphetamines and sleeping tablets mainly. I asked her about them, but she just brushed it off, said they were for her nerves, that a doctor had prescribed them, so it was nothing for me to worry about. But after that I started to notice her hands were often shaky. I didn't know if they always had been, or if I was just becoming hyper-vigilant. When I asked her about it, she just said, "See, that's why I have to take those pills, it's my nerves."

'Anyway, then I was accepted into college, halfway across the country. I was thrilled to be getting away from my father, but loath to be leaving my mother. But she was so happy for me, so proud, I went for her sake as much as anything.' He stared down at the table, a deep frown creasing his forehead. It was a moment before he could speak. 'My father didn't even call to tell me she'd been taken to hospital. It took weeks for her to die, apparently, and I would have had time to see her, to say goodbye. More than anything, I'll never be able to forgive him for that.' He took a breath. 'My grandmother came down for the funeral. It was the first time she'd ever visited, though she wouldn't come to the house. She told me she'd never wanted her daughter to marry "that man", that he'd finally destroyed her. I was inclined to agree.'

'What happened to your father after that?' Madeleine asked carefully. She felt a little underhanded, like some kind of investigative reporter asking leading questions to get him to incriminate himself.

'I told you we lost contact,' said Henry, 'but it was a little more deliberate than that. He sold the house and moved away without telling me. He didn't leave a forwarding address, he just disappeared.'

Hearing Henry say it brought tears to her eyes. 'I'm so sorry.' He clearly didn't want to recount the shock of going to the house, and Madeleine certainly wasn't going to push it. But there was one thing she'd wondered about ever since Aiden had told her the story. 'Can I ask you something?'

'Madeleine, you can ask me anything,' Henry said with an indulgent smile. 'You just don't have to keep asking me that.'

'Okay, well, I guess I was wondering, if your father just disappeared like that, wouldn't you . . . I mean, I know you had no relationship . . .' What was she saying? This wasn't going to come out right. 'I don't know what I was thinking, it doesn't matter.'

'Madeleine, what is it? Just say it.'

She looked awkwardly at him.

'Go on,' he urged.

'I wondered why you wouldn't call the police, the way he just went missing like that. Anything could have happened.'

'I did go to the police,' said Henry. 'I was actually worried that he'd gone and done away with himself. The police thought that idea was valid under the circumstances, and so they started with a simple records search. According to his driver's licence, he was living in a small town in Minnesota. They weren't permitted to give me his address; they told me they shouldn't have mentioned that much. But they had police up there visit his house to make sure he was all right, and to get his permission to pass on his contact details to me.' Henry took a breath. 'He was there, he was fine, but he wouldn't give his permission. He said he wanted his privacy. So that was that.' He sat back, apparently spent.

Madeleine tried to imagine what that would feel like, but she had absolutely no frame of reference. She could relate to the grief of losing a father, but she had always felt loved and important and special. She was amazed that Henry had managed to become the man he was; she supposed his mother had had a large part to do with that. No wonder he was such a gentle soul.

'Why didn't you tell me any of this before?' she asked after a while.

He shrugged. 'I think I was ashamed, to be honest. You have such a loving family, your father was your hero. I didn't know what you'd make of me if I told you about my family.'

'Henry . . .' She reached her hand across the table and he took hold of it. She probably shouldn't have done that, but she couldn't help herself. 'You have nothing to be ashamed of.'

'Thanks for saying that.' He squeezed her hand. 'But it wasn't the only reason. I just didn't want to be that person anymore. I had a chance to start over – my history could be just a short blurb, like the one on the sleeve of my books.' He paused. 'But now I know you can't escape who you are.'

He didn't have to tell her that. 'Is that why you went to therapy?'

'Eventually,' he said. 'I had a few good years, productive years, when my books first took off. Gene was very good to me – he was my mentor, and probably the closest thing I ever had to a father.'

Madeleine's stomach lurched. She knew Gene was no longer Henry's agent, but she'd thought that was because he'd retired. 'Gene, he's all right isn't he?'

'Sorry, I shouldn't have spoken in the past tense,' said Henry. 'He's alive, and mostly well. He had some minor health issues, which is why he retired and moved to Florida. I would have asked him to the wedding, but I know he wouldn't be up to the trip, and I didn't want him to attempt it.'

That was a relief. Madeleine couldn't bear to think of any more sadness in Henry's life. And she was about to rain still more down on him. But she had to let him finish.

'Sorry, I interrupted you,' she said. 'You were saying your books were doing well?'

He nodded. 'With the first substantial money I made, I bought the house up in the Hamptons, long before I bought the apartment in New York. I loved it, I loved being on my own to work. I didn't think that was strange; writers, artists, our work is solitary, that's the nature of it. But after a while, Gene started to voice some concern. I kept pulling out of appearances, making excuses, cancelling on him. It was really unprofessional, and just plain wrong, considering everything he'd done for me. Finally, he sat me down and gave me some ultimatums. One of them was that I had to talk to a therapist.'

'How did you feel about that?'

'I was belligerent about it,' said Henry, 'but I owed Gene that much. So I made a promise to stick it out for three months. Roland, that's my therapist, he got through to me in less time than that. He made me realise that I was in danger of turning into my father. That scared the hell out of me. I wanted to do something about it, I wanted to change before it was too late. And I didn't want to do it with drugs – after what happened to my mother, the idea freaked me out. But Roland didn't believe I needed medication anyway, he was certain I'd respond to cognitive behavioural therapy.'

'Change in thinking leads to change in behaviour,' she murmured, recalling a snippet from the back of some book.

'You know about CBT?' Henry asked.

'I've read a little.'

He nodded. 'So, we developed a kind of contract. The main thing was that I wasn't allowed to say no to invitations. If I was tempted to say no, I had to come to him and talk it through. That's why I agreed to the trip to Australia.'

Madeleine's eyes widened, but all she could say was, 'Oh.'

'Best thing I ever did.'

She couldn't *not* respond to that. 'I think so too.' But he wasn't going to think so anymore.

'I wasn't sure at first – you were so frustrated with me at the beginning. I should have been saying yes to everything you suggested, but there was only so much I could handle. I didn't want to go to big parties, or "network".'

'I remember,' said Madeleine.

'But then you came to pick me up that day,' he said, smiling at the thought of it, 'all ready to take me out hiking. And I think that's when I started to fall in love with you.'

'Me too,' she blurted; she couldn't help herself.

He looked at her. 'Really?'

She nodded. She wanted to let him know how much he meant to her. Maybe he would remember after she dropped her bombshell. 'There was something about you that day . . . I've told you before, you reminded me of my father in a lot of ways. You seemed so calm and self-contained. You didn't need to talk all the time.'

'I was probably just terrified of saying the wrong thing.'

Madeleine smiled then. 'Well, it worked. I didn't want to let you go.' The words almost stuck in her throat. She still didn't want to let him go.

'I felt there was something between us,' said Henry, 'but I didn't know what I could do about it. And then I got home and your email was waiting for me. That's where my therapy came in: I never said no to you again.'

'But you did more than that,' Madeleine reminded him. 'You asked me to New York.'

'I did, with the help of Roland. I thought he was the crazy one when he suggested it. I kept talking about how I wanted to find a way to see you again, so he said to me, "What if you met a beautiful woman here, in New York, what would you do?" I told him I supposed I'd ask for her number. "Well, you already have her number," he said. "What then?" I said I'd ask her out on a date. He said, "So, what's stopping you?" I reminded him that there was the small issue of you living on the other side of the world. And he said, "Are you going to let a little thing like that stop you?"' Henry smiled. 'He took me through every conceivable outcome – what if you said no; what if you came, but you thought we were just friends . . . He showed me that nothing was as bad as not risking it in the first place. Turns out he was right.'

'Yes,' she said faintly.

'So here's to Dr Roland,' said Henry, raising his glass. 'Perhaps we should name our first-born after him?'

She looked at him, horrified, but not for the reason he was thinking.

'Hey, I was only kidding,' he reassured her.

'I know.'

'The thing is,' Henry resumed, becoming serious. 'Ever since then you've made everything easy for me, Madeleine. And because I had you, I really didn't need anything or anyone else. So I started slipping back into old ways. The house was the first mistake, and the biggest. And then I started to get irritated by your family. That was really unfair – it wasn't them, it was me. I found myself dreaming about the day you'd give up work, have a baby, and we could just exist up here, together. We wouldn't need anyone else, we wouldn't have to go anywhere. So I started to get grumpy about the apartment. I could feel it coming on, but I convinced myself it was reasonable.' He paused. 'I suppose Aiden being here brought it all to a head.'

He didn't know the half of it.

'That fight we had the other night,' said Henry. 'Have we ever fought like that before?'

Madeleine shook her head.

'And then when you said you wanted to have a few days away . . . I was a little terrified. I thought I was going to lose you, that you'd had enough. I knew I had to do something about it. So after you left, I called Roland in the States.'

'Oh.'

'I knew what I had to do, I just needed to talk it through with someone. So while you were away, we had a session over Skype, in the middle of the night. I was the one who suggested selling the house, he just validated my decision.'

Madeleine sat, barely breathing, racked with guilt. Henry had worked so hard to make everything right, while she had got drunk and slept with his best man.

He was watching her. 'I don't want you to worry, Madeleine, it's not like I'm going to have to keep my therapist on speed-dial.'

'It's okay. After my father died we saw a counsellor a couple of times, all of us. Then I just wanted to get on with my life. But I think I could have used more . . . Therapy, that is. Instead I used alcohol to numb the pain. When I met you, I started to get my life together . . .' And then it all fell apart again.

'I know, you told me all that, you've always told me everything,' said Henry. 'And I should have told you everything. Now I have. There shouldn't be any secrets between us, Madeleine. I want to have everything out in the open from now on.'

Oh shit. This was it. She had to tell him, she had to tell him right now. She'd put it off long enough. Her heart was hammering painfully against her ribs. 'Henry, I have to tell you something.'

'I know, you keep saying that, and I realise I've hogged all the time. But please, if you don't mind indulging me for one last thing, and then you can have the floor. I promise. There's just something I want to show you.'

'Okay,' she said, wondering what on earth this was going to be.

He got up and went over to the kitchen, where he opened a drawer in the island bench. When he came back, he was holding a wad of brochures. He moved the bowls and bread aside, and spread the brochures out on the table in front of her. 'I wanted to show you where we're going on our honeymoon,' he said. 'Why I've been working so hard . . .'

This really wasn't a good idea right now. 'I thought you wanted to keep it a surprise?' she said, trying to think of some way to stop him.

'I've had second thoughts,' he said. 'Let me show you . . .' He opened the first brochure and slid it closer to her, pointing out pictures as he gave a running commentary: from the luxury elevated tent at Uluru, to the breathtaking 5-star treehouse in an eco-lodge up in the Daintree, and finally, a few nights on a yacht sailing the Barrier Reef. Henry had booked the most romantic accommodation possible, in some of the most beautiful locations in Australia. He had outdone himself, totally surpassing her mean-spirited expectations.

When she looked up, her eyes glassy, he was watching her intently. 'I want you to know, this didn't happen since I talked to Roland,' he said. 'I've been planning it all along, it's already booked. I had wanted to surprise you, but I realised it wasn't any good if you were only feeling apprehensive. I wanted you to be excited leading up to the wedding. You see, it doesn't work to keep things from each other, no matter how good the intentions might be.'

She couldn't speak. It felt like her throat had seized on her.

'Madeleine, what do you think?' he prompted after a while. 'Say something.'

Her face crumpled. 'I can't take this anymore, Henry.' She burst into tears, sobbing convulsively.

He was suddenly at her side, crouched beside her chair, gathering her into his arms. 'Madeleine, what's the matter? Don't cry . . . What is it? Is it something I said?'

'No . . . and yes.' She pulled back from him, her face streaked with tears. 'You just have to stop. You have to listen to me.'

'Okay, okay. It's going to be all right,' he said gently, brushing her hair from her face. 'Just don't cry.'

'I can't help it.'

He stood up, reached for a napkin on the table and pressed it into her hands. Then he dragged a chair over to sit at her side, facing her. 'Go ahead, say what you have to say.'

She wiped her eyes with the napkin. 'This is just . . . it's hard,' she said, her voice barely more than a squeak.

'You don't think what I just told you was hard?' he said. 'It's okay, you can tell me anything. That's how it's going to be from now on.' He took her hands in his. 'Go on, it's going to be all right.'

Madeleine lifted her face to look into his eyes. 'But it's not, Henry. After what I have to tell you, nothing's going to be all right, and I'm sorry. I'm saying that up front, because you're not going to listen later, but I want you to know how desperately sorry I am, and that I would do anything if I could change this. If I could undo what I've done.'

'What are you talking about?' Henry was starting to look uncertain, and his hands went slack around hers.

Madeleine felt sick, but she had to get the words out. 'The thing is . . . I have seen Aiden . . .'

He dropped her hands. 'And?' he said, his voice low.

'Oh Henry, I'm so sorry.'

She heard the sharp intake of breath. 'Say it, Madeleine.'

'I can't.'

He stood up so abruptly that the chair toppled over. '*Say it!*' He was almost shouting.

'Henry, don't.' The picture he must be forming in his head, she didn't want to fill in the details.

'*Fuck.*' He turned away, dragging a hand through his hair as he strode across the room. 'When did it happen?'

She swallowed. 'Friday.'

He swung around again, glaring at her. 'Friday? Before or after we spoke?'

'After.'

'Was he with you then?'

Oh fuck. She couldn't lie to him anymore, and now every lie she'd ever told him was going to come out.

'*Madeleine!*' he barked to get her attention. 'Was he with you when I called?'

'Yes.'

'Jesus Christ! You were lying through your teeth, planning to spend the night with him?'

'No!' she cried. 'It wasn't planned. It just happened.'

'But you lied about him being there. You told me you hadn't seen him, hadn't spoken to him.'

It was no use trying to prove she avoided actually lying to him on the phone. That would just be insulting.

'I was out to lunch with the girls,' she said, her voice trembling, 'and he called to say he was back from Canberra early, so I invited him to join us.'

'And why wouldn't you tell me that if you weren't planning to sleep with him?'

'I wasn't,' she insisted. 'He wasn't around – near me – when you called. I didn't think I had a right to speak for him.'

'Oh for fuck's sake, Madeleine, that's just bullshit.'

Henry never spoke like that, she'd barely ever heard him swear.

'I know it sounds like that now,' she said, trying to keep her voice calm, 'but the only thing I was intentionally keeping from you was that we were all on our way out for drinks. I wasn't going home.'

'Why wouldn't you tell me that?'

'Because I knew you wouldn't approve. You don't like me drinking, or staying away. I just wanted to have some fun, a night out with the girls.'

'And Aiden,' he said grimly.

'Yes, okay, Aiden was coming too,' she said. 'I didn't think it was that big a deal.'

'You didn't think fucking Aiden was a big deal?'

'That's not what I said.'

He rubbed his forehead. 'How did it happen?'

'I got very drunk, and he took me back to the apartment.'

'And then what?'

She gave him a plaintive look. 'Henry, you don't want –'

'Who started it?' he demanded, looming over her now.

'I don't know, I don't remember.'

'How the fuck do you not remember?'

'I told you I was drunk.'

He sighed loudly, turning away from her. 'I can't believe this is happening again.'

'I know, I'm sorry. I don't expect you to forgive me a second time.'

He frowned, looking back at her. 'What?'

'You know, the other time, with the author on tour.'

'I'm not talking about that,' he dismissed. 'But this is the sort of shit I had to put up with from Aiden for years. When he used to drag me to those parties? Every time a girl came anywhere near me, he'd leap in and take over. He hated that his family liked me, he used to throw massive fits like a two year old. It was embarrassing. And then Gillian, he couldn't stand that she barely noticed him. That was his crowning achievement, stealing her from me. Until this.'

Madeleine was shaking her head. 'I wish I'd known all this.'

'Why?' he said harshly. 'Would that have stopped you from sleeping with him?'

'Henry, I didn't do it consciously, I was drunk.'

'Jesus, Madeleine! Do you think that excuses you?'

'No, I have no excuse, I know that.'

There was a long pause before Henry said, 'I need some air.' He walked to the doors to the balcony and threw them open. 'This is so fucked up, Madeleine.'

'I know.'

'Is that all you can say? If you knew so well, why did you fucking do it?'

'Because I was unhappy,' she cried, getting to her feet. 'I was lonely, I hated living up here, you were distant, always working . . .'

'So it's my fault?'

'No! It's my fault, it was wrong, it's the worst thing I've ever done in my life, and I don't expect you to understand or forgive me. I don't expect that, Henry. I have no right to expect that. You don't owe me anything.'

He turned slowly to face her. 'You want me to release you, so you can be with him?'

'*No!*' she cried, horrified he would even think that. 'I don't want that, Henry, I don't want to be with him. I told him to go, to leave the country. I don't want to ever see him again.'

Henry was breathing hard, glaring at her. She couldn't bear the look in his eyes. So much pain, so much disgust.

'I can't do this anymore,' he said finally. 'I can't look at you, I can't be around you.'

Her throat tightened so much she had to squeeze the words out. 'I understand. I'm so sorry.' She turned and ran away across the living room.

'Madeleine!' he shouted after her.

She grabbed her bag and keys from the hall table and flew out the front door and up the stairs, still in her socks. She jumped into the car, her trembling hands fumbling to get the key into the ignition. She dragged the gear into reverse and shot out of the garage. She had to get as far away as she could. Henry couldn't look at her. He didn't want her anywhere near him.

Chippendale

Madeleine turned into the garage and swiped her card, her hand still trembling. She didn't know how long it had taken her to get here; there wasn't much traffic at this time on a Monday night, but she'd had to pull over several times. She felt sick, and she was crying so much that at one point she couldn't see the road ahead. All she wanted was to crawl into bed and sleep. That single thought pushed her the rest of the way, and she didn't stop again until she drove into her space at the building and turned off the engine.

It was over. Henry said he couldn't look at her, and she'd seen in his eyes that he was never going to be able to look at her again.

She dragged herself out of the car. Her limbs felt so heavy, she could barely imagine getting herself over to the lift, let alone up to the apartment. But somehow she had to, and somehow she did. She stepped out at her floor and walked up the corridor, still in her bedsocks. She pushed her key into the lock and opened the door. Tears welled again, partly out of relief that she was finally here. She could go to sleep and blot everything out for now. She leaned heavily against the door to close it behind her.

'Maddie.'

Aiden appeared in the doorway to the bedroom, wearing only jeans, which he was hastily zipping up. She stared at him in a daze.

'What are you doing here?' he asked.

Madeleine blinked. 'What are *you* doing here?' she replied. 'I asked you to stay away.'

'But you said you were going home tonight.'

'Well, I'm back, so you have to leave.'

'What's happened, Maddie?' said Aiden, his voice dripping with concern. 'You talked to Henry?'

'I don't want to discuss it with you.'

'Are you all right?'

'No, of course I'm not all right,' she said, walking across the room. 'But I'm not going to talk about it with you. I just want to go to bed. You have to go,' she added, dumping her bag on the table. 'I'm going to use the bathroom, and when I get out I want you gone.'

Aiden didn't move, he just stood there in the doorway, like he was guarding it or something. 'You don't look very well, Maddie. Have you eaten?'

'I'm not hungry.'

'Maybe you should eat,' he said. 'Let me grab a shirt, and I'll take you somewhere.'

'No,' she sighed, exasperated, coming towards him. 'I don't want to eat. I just want to use the bathroom.'

He still didn't move from the doorway.

'Aiden, please get out of the way and let me through,' Madeleine said firmly. She thought she heard movement in the bedroom. 'What's going on?' She pushed him out of the way and walked in. 'For fuck's sake. Natalie?'

'Hi, Mad.'

Natalie was sitting up in *her* bed, *her* sheet draped loosely around her obviously naked body, with her just-fucked hair and a stupid just-fucked expression on her face. Madeleine wanted to slap her.

'This is awkward,' said Natalie.

'I can explain,' Aiden began.

Madeleine looked at him. 'I think this is fairly self-explanatory.'

'Maddie, I –'

'Shut up, Aiden,' she snapped, turning and heading out of the room.

'Wait, I'll go with you, we can talk about this,' he said, following her.

She spun around again to face him. 'What is there to talk about? You're a consenting adult, you can fuck whoever you want. Clearly you're not fussy. I just think it might have been prudent to find somewhere else to do it.'

'I live in a share house,' Natalie called from the bedroom.

Madeleine stormed back across the living room to the bedroom door. 'Did you get in touch with Liv yet?'

'No,' said Natalie, 'I haven't had a chance.'

'Well, you better call her, or better still, show up at work first thing tomorrow,' Madeleine snarled. 'Either way, I don't think you're going to have a job for much longer.' She turned away again, snatching up her bag and heading for the door.

'Wait, Maddie,' said Aiden, grabbing her arm.

She flung it off. 'Don't touch me, don't ever touch me again. I can't believe I ever thought you were a good guy. You're not, you're a manipulative, over-grown spoilt brat, and you're the one who needs to grow up, Aiden.'

He looked like she'd just spat in his face. Good.

'I've lost the best man I've ever known, because of you.' She stabbed his chest with her finger and he winced.

'Maddie, I'm sorry. Let me go with you now.'

'I don't want to go anywhere with you, and the greatest regret of my life will always be that I ever set eyes on you.'

With that she turned on her heel. Aiden didn't try to stop her as she marched determinedly across to the door, reefed it open and slammed it behind her. She almost ran down the corridor to the lift. When she got to the garage and into her car, she sat there, catching her breath. And that was when she realised she didn't know where to go. She couldn't gatecrash Liv's on a school night, what with the kids, especially one who was recovering from emergency surgery. Nor could she lob up to her sister's – she couldn't even imagine facing Genevieve and having to tell her everything . . . Madeleine didn't want to talk about it, she wanted to be left alone, and Genevieve would never be able to do that. She ached for Henry, but Henry said he couldn't be around her. A sob escaped from her throat. There was only one place where she would feel safe, and nurtured, and where she wouldn't have to explain herself. She started the engine and drove out of the garage.

Morning

Liv was in a mild panic. Her mother should have been here by now – she prided herself on her punctuality, so if she was late it was for a reason. And the reason no doubt was to punish her daughter for having the audacity to go to work when she had a child recovering from surgery.

When Liv had arrived at the hospital yesterday afternoon, they were all set to discharge Dylan.

'Are you sure he's okay to be going home already?' Liv said.

'Does your house have a lot of stairs?' Dr Ennis asked her.

'No, it's on one level.'

'Then it's the best place for him to be,' she assured Liv. 'He shouldn't be climbing stairs for a few days, or lifting anything, obviously. Apart from that, he's eating and his bowels have already moved, so there's nothing keeping him here. He's going to recover more quickly in his own home, but naturally he can't be left alone. That's not going to be a problem, is it?'

'Of course not.' But Liv's head was spinning. She had to go to work tomorrow, she really didn't have a choice. She'd talked to Jane and they'd come up with a plan of action to deal with the nosy journalist, and she had her own plan to deal with Natalie, if she ever showed her face in the office again.

So that meant she was going to have to bow and scrape to her mother, and ask her to come and stay with Dylan for most of the day. And for that her penance would be five disapproving grunts, ten loaded remarks and a whole shitload of judgement. Putting up with all that was surely proof enough that there was nothing Liv wouldn't do for her boys.

While Liv was packing up Dylan's things in the hospital room, Rick had called on the landline. 'Hi, is Dylan about?'

'He's just getting changed in the bathroom, they're discharging him.'

'Really? Already?'

'They gave him the all-clear, but someone's going to have to stay with him at home,' she said. 'I don't suppose you can take some time off work?'

'Nah, sorry, Livvie.'

And her mother would think that was perfectly reasonable.

'But I was planning to visit him tonight,' Rick went on, 'so's it okay if I call by the house?'

At least he was asking. 'It's okay, Rick, but you can't stay for dinner. You can't keep lobbing up uninvited and taking over. It really has to stop.'

'Okay, okay,' he said, 'I understand.'

She had a thought. 'In fact, you can actually make yourself useful tonight. I have to pick up some food, I can't drag Dylan around a supermarket, but he can't be left at home alone, and it's certainly not right to leave Lachie responsible for him.'

'No, of course,' said Rick. 'So, you go to the supermarket when I get there, I'll stay with him.'

His tone was unusually obliging and agreeable. Liv sensed a shift in attitude, but she wasn't to know quite how seismic a shift it was until he arrived at the house that evening.

'Okay, well, I'll get going now,' she said, picking up her handbag. 'They've eaten, I managed to throw together some chicken and pasta that wasn't too much on Dyl's tummy. And I'll bring home plenty of jelly and yoghurt and whatnot for dessert.'

'All right,' said Rick. He looked a little preoccupied. 'I'll walk you out.'

She frowned. 'No need.'

'I just want to have a quick word,' he said, lowering his voice.

Liv groaned inwardly. What now?

They stepped out onto the front porch and Rick pulled the door closed behind him.

'What's this about?' said Liv. 'I need to get to the shops.'

He nodded. 'I won't keep you. I just wanted to say . . .' But then there was a long pause while he seemed to be mulling something over.

'Rick?' she prompted. 'You know you haven't said anything yet?'

'Sorry.' He roused himself. 'I wanted to say . . . well, so, David is a real person?'

Liv sighed. So that's what this was about. 'I don't want to discuss David.'

'No, wait, Liv,' Rick said, holding up his hands. 'I'm not trying to have a go. He seems like a pretty decent sort of bloke.'

She was listening.

'It was a bit of a shock, that's all.' He folded his arms, leaning back against the door frame. 'The truth is, I always thought you and I would end up together.'

'What?' Now it was Liv's turn to be shocked.

'All this time you've been there, I thought you'd always be there, you were like this permanent fixture in my life. I still saw us growing old together.'

'So let me get this straight,' said Liv, but not unkindly. She was actually rather amused. 'You were going to work your way through the alphabet, dating, cohabitating, whatever, and then come back to me when you were old and grey, and probably needing a nurse, and you expected that I would be sitting out on the porch in my rocking chair, waiting for you?'

'Well, when you put it like that . . .' He flashed her one of his cheeky, boyish grins, and Liv couldn't help smiling back at him. 'Ahh, Livvie, I was a bloody idiot, wasn't I?' he said. 'I gave you nothing but trouble.'

'I don't know, there are two beautiful boys in there that you had something to do with.'

'Thanks for saying that.'

'Well, it's true.'

He straightened up. 'So anyway, I just wanted to clear the air, give you my blessing.'

'You know I don't need it, right?'

He looked sheepish.

'But I appreciate it all the same,' she added.

'I just wanted to wish you the best,' said Rick. 'You deserve to be happy, Liv.'

'I wish you'd tell my mother that.'

*

It was a quarter to nine when Liv finally heard the doorbell. She raced up the hall to let her mother in.

'Oh great, you're here.'

'Yes, of course I am, I just wanted to stop by the shops to pick up some things for Dylan. I've got jelly, yoghurt –'

'I already stocked up –' Liv stopped herself. 'That's very thoughtful, Mum, thanks.'

She walked her mother back down the hall, trying to move her along. 'I've laid out Dylan's medication along the bench here,' she said, as they came into the kitchen. 'And I've written down all the times, and the doses. Does that all make sense?'

'Honestly, Olive, I'm not an imbecile.'

'I know that, Mum. I just wanted to run you through it, because I have to get going.'

And there was the first disapproving grunt.

Liv ignored it and soldiered on. 'Lachie's already left for school, and Dylan was still asleep when I last checked.'

'Are you sure he's all right?'

'Yes, he's a teenage boy, they like to sleep in,' said Liv. 'Anyway, it's the first unbroken night he's had in . . . well, since before Friday. So I'm not surprised he's sleeping so long. It'll be good for him.'

'Hm.' And the second disapproving grunt. 'Well, seeing as the boys aren't around, I don't mind telling you that that little show you put on at the hospital the other day was a disgrace. You should be ashamed of yourself, Olive.'

Liv was stumped. 'What little show?'

'Parading your boyfriend around like that,' Joy scolded. 'How could you put Rick through that? The man has his pride, you know.'

'Hold on just a minute,' said Liv. 'There was no parade. David visited of his own volition, I didn't plan it. And if you want to know something, Rick has actually been very supportive. Only last night he came to tell me that he wished me well.'

'See what sort of a man he is? You never gave him a chance –'

'I gave him a dozen chances,' Liv stopped her. 'You don't even know the half of it, Mum.'

'But he's the best man for your sons, not this other . . . man, this nurse.'

'Of course Rick is the best man for the boys – he's their father,' said Liv. 'But that doesn't mean he's the best man for me.'

'And so this man is? This man nurse?'

'I don't know,' said Liv. 'I haven't had a chance to find out, but I'd like to. And Rick gave me his blessing, so why can't you?'

'You know how I feel, Olive,' she said. 'You're still married in the eyes of the church.'

'But it's not my church, I don't have to follow your rules.'

'And I don't have to like it.'

'Then what do we do?' said Liv, holding out her hands. 'Should we just give up?'

Joy stared at her.

'I can't do this anymore, Mum. We can't keep going on like this. I'm going to be looking after you in your dotage, you really have to be a little nicer to me.'

Now Joy looked affronted. 'Is that a threat?'

'No,' Liv sighed. 'It's a desperate plea. We both have to do better, aren't we on the same side, after all? I'm not such a bad person, you know. At least I try to be a good person, and I try to be a good mother. You have to stop judging me, Mum. Please.'

'It's not that I don't think you're a good mother,' Joy retorted. 'Of course you are. You're the boss at work, you have twin boys that you're raising mostly on your own, a house to run . . . For goodness sakes, they call you a "super woman" these days, don't they?'

Then it hit Liv, clearer than ever before. This generation of working mothers must really get up the noses of all the mothers who came before them, the women whose entire lives had revolved around childrearing and housework. And then these little upstarts come along and treat all that like it's nothing but a side act to the main event. No wonder Liv's efforts were never good enough – if they were, that would make her mother's life look rather small and meaningless.

'I'm no super woman,' said Liv. 'Nowhere near it. For one thing, I couldn't do any of it without your help. Dylan and Lachie adore you, we're all lucky to have you.'

Liv wasn't sure, but she thought her mother's eyes may have moistened, ever so slightly. Joy cleared her throat. 'You've done a very good job with those boys, and you mustn't think otherwise. You've always been too sensitive, Olive.'

Liv suppressed a smile. 'Okay, that's a start. Next time try it without the sting in the tail, eh, Mum?'

Joy pursed her lips, but at least she didn't attempt a comeback.

'I really have to go,' said Liv, planting a kiss on her cheek. 'I'll call you later.'

9.30 am

'Mad? Maddie? *Madeleine*! Come on, you have to get up.'

'Go away.'

'Nope, not going to do that. I'm not Mum, I'm no pushover.'

Suddenly the pillow covering her head was whipped away and Madeleine squinted, blinking, dazed and confused. Fragments of a dream were still whirling around in her mind – Aiden smearing wedding cake all over her on the kitchen bench, Henry sitting with a tray on his lap watching sitcoms with his mother, Henry yelling that he couldn't look at her, as he pushed her off a yacht in the Barrier Reef . . .

'*Madeleine!*'

Was that Genevieve? For real, or was she still living in that dream hellscape?

'Where am I?' she asked.

'You're at Mum's.'

'What are you doing here?'

'She was worried about you,' said Genevieve, 'and she couldn't get you to wake up. So she called me.'

Madeleine swallowed. Her mouth was so dry. 'And you came?'

'What's it look like? Now come on, sit yourself up. I brought you some water.'

Thank God, she'd sit up for that. Genevieve passed her a glass of water and she took it gratefully, gulping down half of it.

'Are you hung-over?' asked Genevieve.

Madeleine shook her head. 'I haven't had a drink since . . .' She squeezed her eyes closed, thinking. '. . . Friday.'

'Then what's going on?' said Genevieve. 'Mum's really rattled. She said you showed up here last night, virtually incoherent, bawling your eyes out, but you wouldn't tell her anything, you just wanted to go to bed.'

Madeleine let out a deep sigh. 'Is she okay? I should go talk to her.'

'No, she's with Archie, they're watching *Play School*,' said Genevieve. 'Leave them be, he'll be totally engrossed for half an hour. Now, tell me what's going on.'

This was the first time she was going to say it out loud. 'Henry and I . . . um . . . the thing is, the wedding's off.'

'What?' said Genevieve. 'You can't be serious?'

'You think I'd joke about that?'

'But what could have happened between yesterday, when you were happily picking out your wedding cake, and last night? It can't have been enough to call off the whole thing.'

'It didn't start yesterday,' Madeleine said wearily. She was still so tired, no matter how much she slept. 'You might recall I wasn't exactly happy picking out the cake.'

Genevieve frowned. 'But that was just cold feet.'

'No, that was your theory.'

'I'm still not getting it. Are you the one calling it off?'

'Not exactly.'

'So it was a mutual decision?'

Madeleine wasn't sure how to describe it. 'Henry doesn't want to marry me anymore . . .'

'It's Henry?' Genevieve looked genuinely shocked. 'I can't believe he'd do this to you. I mean, it's as good as leaving you at the altar, this close –'

'No, listen to me,' Madeleine broke in. 'It wasn't Henry, it was me. I did something, something very bad, and . . . well, it's unforgivable. I can't expect Henry to forgive me, so the wedding's off.'

Genevieve looked squarely at her. 'You cheated on him.'

Madeleine blinked. 'How did you know?'

'Come on, that's the only thing in the unforgivable category, pre-wedding. Unless you murdered someone, I suppose. So what, is this something that happened ages ago that you felt the need to purge before the wedding? Seriously, Mad, sometimes it's better to let sleeping dogs lie.'

Madeleine shook her head. 'No, it happened Friday night.'

'That's when you had your impromptu hens' party,' said Genevieve, piecing it together. 'Oh God, did you get drunk and pick up some random guy? Mad, that's just . . . tacky, not to mention stupid. I hope you used protection?'

Madeleine hadn't even thought about that. She was on the pill, but God knows what she might have picked up from Aiden.

'Surely Henry realises it was a stupid mistake?' Genevieve was saying. 'A really awful one, granted, but calling the whole thing off because of a drunken one-night stand? For an affair, maybe . . .'

Madeleine didn't say anything.

'You're not having an affair?' Genevieve asked suspiciously.

'No, but it wasn't some random guy at a bar, either.'

'Who was it?'

Oh boy, here goes. 'It was Aiden.'

Genevieve's eyes nearly popped out of her head and her jaw dropped. Madeleine almost expected wacky sound effects.

'Oh Maddie . . . Maddie, Maddie . . .' Genevieve shook her head sadly. 'What on earth were you thinking?'

'Well, obviously I wasn't . . . that's the whole problem.'

'So,' Genevieve said, 'is this a thing, are you two together now?'

'God no!'

'Because, you know, I get it, Aiden's very –'

'*Gen!*'

'Sorry, sorry!'

'Aiden is an opportunistic fraud who betrayed his best friend,' Madeleine said, putting it into perspective for her. 'He's really not the person we thought he was, he had us all blindsided. Not that that's any excuse for my behaviour.'

'Jeez, poor Henry,' said Genevieve.

'Tell me about it. I hate myself for doing this to him, for hurting him like this.'

'And you're sure he won't forgive you?'

'He said quite plainly that he can't be around me, he can't even look at me.'

'But that's just the anger talking. He'll calm down, Henry's not an unreasonable person.'

'He's not being unreasonable.'

'Yeah, I guess.' Genevieve seemed to be thinking about it. 'But Henry's like . . . you know, he's a cut above.'

'What do you mean by that?'

'Well, he's not like a regular bloke.'

'Don't make fun of him, Gen. He doesn't deserve that –'

'I meant it in a good way,' Genevieve said loudly. 'It was supposed to be a compliment.'

Madeleine frowned. 'You don't even like Henry.'

'Of course I like Henry. What's not to like, seriously?'

'But –'

'Mad, I'm jealous, okay? There, I said it. You're my little sister, you landed an intelligent, kind, handsome man who worships the ground you walk on, moves halfway across the world for you, leaving a New York apartment *and* a house in the Hamptons, then buys *you* a house . . . What else? Oh, and he's a children's author, for crying out loud, *he writes books for children*! You couldn't make this up, no one would believe you.'

Madeleine stared at her, tears pricking her eyes.

'My husband doesn't come home from one month to the next,' Genevieve went on, her voice subdued now. 'He barely knows his own children, and on one of his recent trips back, he said he regretted that we'd never drawn up a pre-nup.' She paused. 'I'm pretty sure he's having an affair.'

Madeleine inhaled sharply. 'Oh Gen, why haven't you told me this before?'

'You've been too busy with the wedding and everything. It wasn't the right time to be dumping it on you.'

Madeleine could feel a lump in her throat. She took hold of her sister's hands. 'Well, I'm here for you now.'

Genevieve raised an eyebrow. 'Are you kidding? You're a mess. You're not going to be good for anything until you get this sorted out with Henry.'

'There's nothing to sort out,' Madeleine said. 'Except to start cancelling all the arrangements for the wedding.'

'Hold your horses,' said Genevieve. 'My advice, such as it is, is to give Henry a few days to calm down – give him the rest of the week. Then go to him on the weekend, throw everything you've got at him, plead, beg him to take you back. He loves you too much not to be swayed.'

'I don't know . . .'

'Just promise me you won't do anything rash before then,' Genevieve said firmly, resuming her teacher/mother mode. 'If it doesn't work out, I'll personally sit down with you next week and we'll make the calls together.'

'You'll do that?'

'I'm your matron of honour, it's my job.' She slapped her hands on her thighs. 'And now I've got to go, or we'll be late for Kindergym.'

'Thanks, Gen,' said Madeleine, grabbing her sister in a hug before she could get up.

Genevieve hugged her back, just a brief, intense burst, before releasing her again. 'And apparently you're needed at work. Mum said your phone has been ringing "off the hook". Her expression.'

Madeleine looked around either side of the bed. 'Where is it?'

'Mum's got it. You left it in your bag out there, but she didn't know how to answer it or what to do, so she just left it.'

Madeleine got up and saw Genevieve and Archie off out the front with her mum. When they came inside again Margaret gave her back her phone, but Madeleine resisted looking at it as she followed her out to the kitchen. She owed her mother at least ten minutes of her time first. Whatever new crisis was going on at work, it was just going to have to wait a little longer.

'I've made a fresh pot of tea,' said Margaret. 'I'll get you a cup.'

'Thanks, Mum.'

'How are you feeling?'

'I'm all right. I'm so sorry I showed up like that last night. I had nowhere else to go.'

'Now, now,' Margaret said. 'You have here, Maddie, this is your home. It will always be your home.'

Madeleine nodded faintly. She'd thought her home would be with Henry from now on.

'You didn't want to talk about it last night,' Margaret said. 'And you don't have to talk about it now, if you don't want to. I know your sister's helped. I'm just worried about you, darling.'

'Oh Mum, I'm sorry. I didn't mean to worry you.'

'That doesn't matter, dear,' Margaret assured her. 'I worry about you all the time. That's my job.'

Madeleine attempted a weak smile while her mother poured the tea and then passed her a cup.

'Anyway, like I said, you don't have to talk about it.'

Madeleine couldn't tell her mother what she'd done; it was just too degrading. She wouldn't be able to bear the look on her face. She took a breath. 'It's okay, Mum, I just had a bad night last night.'

'Well, Maddie, I might be a little slow these days, but I gathered that much.'

That made Madeleine smile properly. She did owe her mother an explanation, something, but it was going to have to be heavily censored. 'Henry and I have been having a few . . . issues,' she began. 'I decided to spend the night at the apartment, but Aiden was there, and he was . . . entertaining someone.'

She saw a faint blush creep into her mother's cheeks. 'Oh, I see.'

'I just needed to go to sleep, Mum. I couldn't drive all the way back up to Pittwater.'

'No, of course not.' She picked up her cup of tea. 'Is everything going to be all right with you and Henry?' she asked, trying to sound offhand.

Madeleine was about to give her an automatic response to reassure her, but she realised she couldn't, because there was a giant lump stuck in her throat. Her face crumpled.

'Oh, darling girl, it's all right,' Margaret soothed, coming around the bench and putting her arms around her.

Madeleine rested her head on her mother's shoulder while she patted her back like she was a baby. After a while Madeleine drew back, wiping her eyes. 'I'm sorry, Mum.'

'You have to stop saying you're sorry,' Margaret said. 'If you can't cry on your own mother's shoulder, well, I don't know what.'

She studied Madeleine's face intently. 'Now I'm not as smart as your father, or Genevieve –'

'No, Mum, that's not true.'

Margaret held up a hand. 'It's all right. I know I don't exactly have the reputation of being the wise one. Your father got to be that, and so he should, he earned it, that should be his legacy.' She thought for a moment. 'You know, Maddie, I like to read biographies, they're always about these amazing people who've done amazing things. Often their children speak about them, they say what inspiring figures they were in their lives, that they wouldn't be who they are without them. It's quite wonderful. Sometimes when I'm reading them, I wonder how I'll be remembered.'

Madeleine covered her hand. 'I think you're loving, and kind, and very, very sweet. And if I was ever to write your biography, that's how I would describe you.'

Margaret's eyes were glistening. 'Thank you, darling girl. You were always the kind one. You got that from your father.'

'No, I think I got it from you.'

Margaret gave a modest shrug. 'Well, maybe you did.'

'You know, Mum, when everything went wrong last night, I just wanted you, I just wanted my mum.'

'Well . . .' She seemed overcome for a moment. 'And I was here. So that's good.' She dabbed at her eyes with a tissue. 'The thing I was going to say, is that I hope you can work it out with Henry. I think he's a good man, I've always liked him. I know your father would have liked him, very much. I don't know if I've ever said this to you, but he actually reminds me of your dad.'

'He does?' said Madeleine. 'I've always felt that too.'

Margaret nodded. 'He has manners, and he's kind. And you know, I imagine Henry would be very forgiving . . . if he was given the chance.'

Madeleine stared at her.

'Now, you better check your phone,' she said. 'I'll make you some breakfast.'

She started to bustle around the kitchen and Madeleine remained watching her for a moment longer.

'Mum?'

She turned around.

'I think you might be pretty wise as well.'

Margaret gave a little tip of her head in response. 'Now off you go and make your calls.'

Madeleine wandered back up the hall, scrolling down the screen of her phone. There were three, no, four missed calls from Liv – she'd better ring her straightaway rather than sift through the voicemails.

Liv picked up immediately. 'Where are you?'

'Sorry, I'm really sorry, Liv.'

'Look, I know you're going through some stuff right now –'

'It's no excuse.'

'Well, it's kind of an excuse, but I need you to come in as soon as you can. Natalie showed up this morning, and, well, she's drawing you into this, saying that she refuses to explain herself until you get here.'

'You're kidding,' Madeleine groaned.

'Do you have any idea what that's about?'

'I had to go back to the flat last night –'

'So I take it things didn't go well with Henry?'

'As well as could be expected,' Madeleine said, quoting Liv's line back at her. Now wasn't the time to get into it. 'Anyway, when I got there, I walked in on Aiden and Nat.'

'Oh fuck.'

'That about describes it.'

'Did you actually catch them in the act?' Liv asked.

'Not quite. Aiden must have literally leapt out of bed when he heard my key in the door – he was still pulling on his pants when I walked in. He tried to keep me out of the bedroom, but . . . Anyway, there she was. Sitting up in my bed like she had all the right in the world to be there.'

Liv breathed out. 'What did you say to her?'

'Not much. I did tell her that she better show up to work today.'

'Did she give you any excuse?'

'Just that she hadn't had a chance to call you.'

'Too busy screwing the best man.'

'He's not the best man anymore.'

'That's beside the point,' said Liv. 'She's been trying to pull some line that her mother was sick, and I wasn't having it. At least now I know for sure it was a lie. But I don't know why she's so keen to have you in the room when she knows that you know what you know, you know?'

'Who knows? But we'll soon find out. I'm at Mum's but I've got my car. I'll be there as soon as I can.'

'Okay.'

Madeleine hung up, and then glanced through her messages. Bloody Aiden had sent a couple overnight. She deleted them without even looking at them, she wasn't interested in anything he had to say. Her heart lurched as she almost scrolled past one from Henry. It had been sent last night as well, late.

Please just let me know you're ok.

Madeleine felt a pang. She didn't want Henry to think that she'd ignored him, on top of everything. She quickly typed a reply. *Sorry, phone was off o'nite. I'm ok. At Mum's.*

He'd been worried about her – he must still love her, like Genevieve had said.

Well, of course he still loved her. You couldn't just drop out of love overnight. She had no doubt she would love Henry for the rest of her life, even if she never laid eyes on him again.

Amblin Press

When Madeleine arrived at work, she walked straight across to Liv's office, tapped on the door and then opened it. She didn't want to risk bumping into Natalie first. Liv was on the phone, and waved her in. Madeleine took a seat while Liv finished her call.

She hung up the phone a moment later with a curious glance at Madeleine. 'I've never seen you in that colour. Is that a new top?'

'New for me. It's Mum's. I didn't have a change of clothes with me, so I had to borrow something.'

Whereas Genevieve was tall like their dad, Madeleine had inherited her mother's short, petite build. So even though Margaret had developed a middle-aged spread, as it was not so politely termed, she had a couple of blouses that Madeleine had thought would look okay with her jeans. That morning she'd chosen a peasant-style top, which was somewhere between being a little groovy for her mum and a little daggy for her. It was a paisley print in shades of pink – not a colour she usually wore – but it would do. Fortunately, given that she'd run out of the house in her bedsocks, they had the same size feet too, so Madeleine had also borrowed a pair of nondescript flats that would do as well. It wasn't her proudest sartorial moment, but it was certainly no worse than yesterday.

Liv gave her a sympathetic look. 'You had a bit of a night of it, didn't you? So how did Henry take it?'

Tears crept into Madeleine's eyes, and she blinked furiously. 'He was angry, very angry. And hurt, and betrayed.' She swallowed.

'His exact words were "I can't look at you, I can't be around you",' she said, her voice breaking.

'Oh Mad.'

She brushed a tear away from the corner of her eye. 'Well, can't say I didn't expect it. Or deserve it.'

Liv passed her a box of tissues. 'Give yourself a minute before I call Natalie in.'

Madeleine sighed. 'I could really do without this.'

'Sorry.'

'It's not your fault.'

'So, how are you going to work things out with Henry?'

Madeleine cleared her throat. 'Liv, if I talk about Henry, I'm just going to keep crying and I'll never be ready to face Natalie.'

'Okay, got it.'

'Tell me how Dylan's going,' said Madeleine.

'Well, he's home –'

'Already?'

'Yep. Kids, they bounce back.'

'So who's at home with him?'

'My mother, full of righteous indignation,' said Liv. 'Though we did share a moment of rare honesty this morning,' she added. 'Don't know if it'll have any effect in the long term. Guess I'll have to wait and see.'

'You should go home when we're done with Natalie.'

'Can't,' Liv said. 'I have to clean up the rest of Natalie's mess.'

'Of course, Anne Reynolds.' Madeleine nodded. 'How are you going to handle her?'

'We're going to disarm her with the truth.'

'How's that?'

'Jane took the whole thing in her stride when I went to see her yesterday. She said we have nothing to hide, that this is an opportunity for a good discussion about the state of the industry, the whims of the public, and the fact that traditional publishers still give their authors more support and protection than they can get out on the great big world wide web.'

'Wow, that's great. And it's true.'

'I know,' Liv agreed. 'She's a smart cookie, that Jane. There's a reason she sits in that office. Oh, and another thing, it's going to give us a chance to talk up all the books involved, using your brilliant press releases. Jane took copies home last night to study up.'

'She's going to sit in on the interview as well?'

'We're both taking Anne out to lunch today.'

Madeleine smiled. 'I'd wish you luck, but somehow I think you're going to have it all over her.'

Liv returned the smile. 'Okay, are you ready for this?'

Madeleine nodded.

Liv picked up the phone and pressed a button. 'Hey, Stace, would you tell Natalie to come into my office, please?'

Stacey's voice came through the speaker on the phone. 'Sure thing.'

Madeleine swapped to the chair furthest from the door, turning it sideways against the wall. She blotted her face with a tissue, composing herself. The door opened and Natalie strolled in, looking very sure of herself. Again Madeleine had the urge to slap her.

'Close the door, please,' Liv said. 'And take a seat.'

Natalie did as she was told, and slumped into the chair.

'Natalie,' Liv began, 'Madeleine's here now, so please explain yourself. Failing to turn up for work without informing anyone is a serious matter, and I am well within my rights to put you on probation if you don't provide a reasonable excuse.'

'I told you I had a family emergency,' Natalie said airily.

Liv glanced at Madeleine. 'And I told you I didn't believe you. And now I have a witness.'

Madeleine could feel herself cringing inside.

'We know you were with Aiden, so stop lying,' said Liv.

Natalie sneered at Madeleine. 'I knew this would happen,' she said smugly.

'Just cut the crap, Natalie,' Liv continued. 'You were seen with Aiden, there was no family emergency.'

Strangely, Natalie didn't look at all perturbed. 'Yes, I was with Aiden. But here's the thing – when Madeleine discovered us together, she said I'd lose my job because of it. And frankly, ladies,' she turned her head to glance at them both, 'I don't think she's allowed to say that.'

'That's not what I said,' Madeleine insisted.

'My recollection is that that was *exactly* what you said.' Natalie's tone was so smarmy. She was enjoying this. 'And don't forget, I have a witness too.'

Madeleine was gobsmacked. She was actually going to drag Aiden into this? And worse, he was going to back her up?

'From where I'm sitting, this is starting to look really bad,' Natalie went on. 'Here's the way it went down. Madeleine discovered me sleeping with her best man, and she was understandably outraged. After all, only a few nights before, she'd come onto him pretty strong.'

Madeleine drew in a sharp breath.

'But sadly for her, he rejected her outright,' said Natalie. 'After all, the groom is his best friend. You can imagine how awkward it was for him, to put it mildly. But she wouldn't give up, she came looking for him, desperately hoping to talk him around, and was devastated to find him with a coworker. So she threatened that coworker with dismissal, and then tattled to her best friend – the one with the power to do just that.'

Madeleine really wanted to smack her now. No, she wanted to strangle her.

Liv spoke up before she could do either. 'Natalie, those allegations have yet to be proven. The thing that is inexcusable, however, and certainly grounds for a warning, is the verifiable fact that you sent emails to two of our authors before informing members of the media who were involved, resulting in an embarrassing and potentially disastrous situation for the company, not to mention considerable distress to one of the authors. The director has been informed, and has agreed that this constitutes the basis of your warning. You're now officially on probation. A letter to this effect has gone on record and will be forwarded to you forthwith.'

Natalie just sat there. She clearly had no comeback to that.

'You can close the door on your way out,' Liv added.

Natalie stood with an audible huff and left the room, closing the door behind her.

Liv turned to Madeleine. 'What on earth did you say to her when you found her with Aiden?'

Madeleine's head was spinning. 'I, um . . . oh God, I can't remember exactly.'

'Well, you have to remember, exactly,' said Liv. 'Look, I understand how you must have felt, but if you threatened her like that, we're screwed. We can't touch her.'

Madeleine rubbed her eyes as she trawled through her brain. 'I barely spoke to her,' she said finally, opening her eyes. 'But then, just before I left, I went back and asked her if she'd answered any of your calls. She said she hadn't had a chance.' Madeleine looked directly at Liv. 'Then I said she better call you, or come in today, or else . . .'

'Or else what?'

'I didn't think she'd have a job for much longer.'

'And there it is,' Liv sighed.

'I'm so sorry,' said Madeleine. 'But I wasn't threatening her on the basis that she slept with Aiden, only because she hadn't contacted you.'

'I get that,' said Liv. 'I just don't know that a tribunal would.'

'You think she'd take it that far?'

'Who knows. The way she acted in here today I wouldn't put it past her. The little . . . ugh, there are so many words I want to call her, but I don't like to call female coworkers any of them.'

'I'm sorry,' Madeleine said again.

'It's not your fault,' said Liv. 'You obviously had no idea what you were up against. She's certainly never seemed that clever around here before.'

Madeleine was frowning. 'She said that Aiden rejected me – that must be what he told her. Why would he be talking to her about it anyway?'

'She could have made it up.'

'I don't know,' Madeleine said. 'I'm getting the impression that Aiden will say whatever he has to to save his own arse.'

'And you think now he's prepared to lie to save Natalie's?' Liv said. 'Why would he get himself involved?'

'I don't know, but I've had enough of this.' Madeleine picked up her handbag and took out her phone. 'I'm going to give him a call, and a piece of my mind.' She looked over at Liv. 'Oh, do you mind if I do it in here? There might be shouting involved.'

'No, but I might leave you to it,' Liv said, getting up.

'Are you sure? I don't want to force you out of your own office.'

'It's fine,' Liv said. 'I'll go down and get us a coffee, okay?'

Madeleine gave her a grateful smile. 'Thank you.'

Liv closed the door as Madeleine tapped the screen to call Aiden. He picked up almost immediately. 'Maddie, I'm so glad you called. You got my messages?'

'Yes, but I didn't read them.'

There was a pause. 'Oh . . . Well, I was hoping we could meet.'

'That's not going to happen, Aiden.'

'But I want to see you one more time before I go.'

'You're leaving then?'

'I will be, just as soon as I've seen you.'

'I'm not going to see you, Aiden,' Madeleine said squarely. 'Don't you understand? I don't want to have anything to do with you.'

Another pause. 'Then why are you calling me?' he said eventually, his tone becoming terse.

'Because I want to know why you told Natalie that I threw myself at you.'

'What?' He sounded shocked. 'I didn't say that. Honestly, Maddie, I wouldn't say that.'

'I'm afraid honesty means something different to you than it does to me, Aiden.'

'Maddie, I don't know how to make you believe me, but I swear I didn't say that to Natalie.'

'You must have told her something.'

He breathed out. 'I had too much to drink, I ended up telling her that we had a . . . a moment, because I was feeling so bad about everything. I never said you threw yourself at me.'

Madeleine didn't know whether she entirely believed him, but she could believe that Natalie might make more out of whatever he'd said. It didn't matter anyway. Except for one thing. 'Well, she expects you to be her witness that I threatened her job.'

'That's never going to happen.'

'She seems to think it is.'

'On my word, it's not.'

'You really should stop using expressions like that, Aiden. Your word doesn't actually mean a whole lot.'

'I never lied to you, Maddie.'

'Oh really? What about the whole Gillian story?'

'Why are you bringing up Gillian?'

'Because Henry told me what really happened,' said Madeleine.

'I think he and I might have a different take on that.'

'Stop it,' she said. 'I believe Henry, and that's all there is to it. You lied back then, and you're still lying about it now. Do you even know what the truth is?'

Madeleine heard a loud sigh. 'Maybe I don't,' he said finally.

She thought about something Henry had said. 'You know, Aiden, for someone who has so much going for him, you don't seem very happy.'

'Why should I be?' he said, his tone bitter. 'What have I got compared to Henry? And look at the way he treated you. He doesn't deserve someone like you, he doesn't appreciate you.'

'So you thought you'd take me away from him? Or at least ruin it for both of us.'

'It's not like I planned it, Maddie. It just happened.'

What was the point of going over it? 'I don't know why we're even talking about this. I have to go.'

'Maddie, wait,' said Aiden. 'Henry will get over it, you know.'

'I'm not so sure.'

'He'd be a damned fool to let you go.'

'I have to hang up now,' she said.

'Goodbye, Madeleine Pepper. It was nice knowing you.'

She wished she could say the same about him.

2.30 pm

Liv and Jane stood on the kerb after the taxi had pulled away, taking Anne Reynolds with it.

'So, how do you think that went?' Liv asked.

'Who knows? It's out of our hands now,' said Jane. 'You can't have any control over what a journalist does with what you tell them, more's the pity.' They started to walk up the street in the direction of their office building.

'Well, anyway, I'm sorry about everything, Jane,' Liv said.

'You don't have to apologise, you're not responsible.'

'Where my staff are concerned, the buck stops with me.'

'And you're my staff, so that would mean the buck ultimately stops with me,' said Jane. 'I might be responsible for cleaning up the messes, but I'm certainly not responsible for every stupid mistake that gets made. God, I could never live with that.'

'I suppose you're right.'

'Oh, I know I'm right. I'm the boss. And as the boss, I'm advising you to give yourself an early mark. You haven't taken any time off in lieu for your last tour yet, have you?'

No, she hadn't. Where had that time gone?

'And your son's in the hospital, right?' Jane asked.

'Not anymore, he was discharged yesterday. My mother's at home with him today.'

'You should go home and be with him,' said Jane. 'Take a couple of days, they're owed to you. But don't spend the whole time being a nursemaid. Have a break. Are you seeing anyone at the moment?'

Liv suddenly realised that for the first time ever, she could say yes. 'Actually, I am.'

Jane looked at her. 'Someone's very pleased with herself.'

Liv suspected she was sporting a particularly goofy grin right now. 'I guess I am.'

'So, I take it things are going well? Good for you.'

Truth was, things weren't really going at all. She needed to do something about that.

When they made it back to the building, Liv went directly down to the basement carpark, at Jane's insistence. If she went back up to the office, she'd only get caught up for another hour or more on nothing of any consequence. Jane said she'd let Madeleine know she'd left the for the day. Liv felt a little mean abandoning poor Mad, but she'd make a point of calling her later to see how she was doing.

But right now she realised she had a couple of hours up her sleeve. Her mother wasn't expecting her for a while yet. She thought about David, recalling the last time she'd seen him. She wanted to let him know that she was still interested. Very interested. No more excuses, no more hesitation. She was ready to give this thing a go. After all, she had her ex's blessing, what was she waiting for?

Liv headed straight for the hospital. She wanted to try to park closer to the cardio ward, so she drove right around the opposite side to where Dylan had been admitted. The hospital was huge, Liv had never realised, with numerous buildings covering several blocks. She came across another multi-storey carpark and found a space, then entered the closest building. It was still like finding her way through a maze, but at this time of day there were plenty of people around she could ask for directions. Eventually she arrived at the glassed-in bridge, and she knew her way from there.

As she approached the nurses' station, she saw a woman filling out charts.

'Excuse me,' Liv said.

'Yes, can I help you? Are you looking for a patient?'

'No, not a patient. I was wondering if David Lessing is around today?'

The woman removed her glasses. 'You're a friend of his?'

'Yes, yes I am.'

'Sorry, David's not on today. He was on night duty last night, so he won't be in now for a couple of days.'

'Oh, okay, thanks for that.'

Liv wandered back down the corridor, feeling a little silly. And disappointed. She realised how much she'd been looking forward to seeing him.

She found her way back to her car and drove off towards home. But as she headed up King Georges Road, she had a thought, and it wouldn't go away. She pulled over, and brought up the White Pages on her phone. And there he was – D Lessing in Hurstville Grove. She clicked on *View Map*, and there was his house, literally minutes away from where she was stopped right now. It was so easy to be a stalker these days.

She pressed *Route*, and then *Start*.

'*At the next intersection, turn left,*' the robotic voice began.

And she was off, her heart beating wildly in her chest. Would he think she was crazy? She drove on regardless, following the directions until she heard, '*In twenty metres, on your right, you have come to your destination.*'

Liv pulled over and stopped the car, cutting the engine. She had parked just short of his house, in case he happened to be looking out the window or something. She still had a chance to make a quick getaway. His house was a neat brick bungalow, and there was a car parked in the drive. That was a very strong indicator that he was there . . . But maybe he was asleep? He'd been on night shift, perhaps he'd come home and gone straight to bed.

For crying out loud, she was here now, just get it over with.

Liv got out of the car and walked across the road and up the path to his front door. She took a deep breath and knocked. After a moment she heard footsteps approaching, then the door opened and a young woman was standing there, smiling at her expectantly. She looked just like her father. That was his smile. His blue-grey eyes.

'Scarlett?' Liv said.

'Yes . . .' Scarlett looked a little taken aback, not surprisingly. 'Sorry, do I know you?'

'No, you don't. I should apologise,' said Liv. 'It's just that you look so much like your father, I assumed –'

Scarlett's eyebrows shot up. 'Are you Liv?'

Okay, now it was her turn to be surprised. It was one thing for David to talk about his daughter to her, but to talk about her to his daughter . . . She could feel herself blushing.

'Who's there?' That was David now, coming into the hallway. Scarlett stepped back from the doorway, and the look on his face when he saw it was her . . . well, it was flattering, to say the least.

'Hello, Liv,' he said, ambling up to the door. He was wearing a faded grey T-shirt and old jeans. His hair was ruffled, and he had stubble on his chin. Liv knew on the spot that this was a man she could have sex with. Not right now, but one day. Soon.

'So you've met Scarlett?' he was saying.

She stirred. 'Yes, briefly.'

He really did look pleased to see her, and it was giving Liv the flutters. She hadn't had the flutters in a very long time. And it wasn't half bad.

'Would you like to come in?' he asked her.

'No, it's all right. I can't stay.'

'Well, it was nice meeting you, Liv,' Scarlett said, taking the chance to slip away.

'Sorry,' David said, rubbing his chin, 'I'm a bit of a scruff. I've been on night shift, I only got up a little while ago.'

'It's fine. You look fine.' *You look fricking great.*

'So, what can I do for you?'

'Sorry, this must seem strange.'

'It doesn't have to be.'

Don't blush again. 'Scarlett's lovely,' she said, redirecting the conversation.

He glanced back over his shoulder. 'I think so.'

'I thought she was in Melbourne?'

'She was, but she's all done now. She got back a few days ago. This is only temporary, until she finds her own place.'

Liv nodded. 'Anyway, I don't want to keep you. I have to get back, Dylan's home.'

'How's he doing?'

'Really well, they discharged him yesterday.'

'I know, I checked,' he said. 'Nosy nurse syndrome.'

She smiled. 'Anyway, he's with my mother – you know, the short, scary one you met the other day.'

'She didn't scare me. She seemed to scare you though.'

Liv winced. 'I'm sorry about that. I think I might have been rude to you.'

'No, I wasn't offended,' he said. 'Just a little disappointed.'

'Well, that's why I dropped by,' said Liv. 'I was hoping that maybe we could see each other again?'

'You're not going to be too busy . . . ?'

'Only until Dylan's on his feet. But not forever.'

He gave her a slow nod, and the way he was looking at her was a little unnerving. In a good way.

'I just didn't want you to give up on me,' said Liv.

'Oh I had no intention of giving up on you,' he said plainly.

'You didn't?'

'Course not. I'd never waste such a great "how did you meet?" story. People are going to love it, we could dine out on it for ages. I think it's worth giving this thing a shot, for that reason alone.'

Liv was grinning. 'I agree. So I'll call you as soon as things are back in a routine and I know what I'm doing.'

'Great.'

'Great,' she echoed. They stood there, looking at each other, smiling, until Liv realised she was the one who had to make a move. 'Well, bye, David.' She turned and stepped down off the porch.

'Oh, Liv?'

She turned around again. He had followed her off the porch, and he was right there, close enough to touch.

'Thanks for dropping by.' He leaned in and cupped her face with one hand, giving her a sweet, lingering kiss. Oh, she could definitely have sex with this man.

He drew back, smiling at her. 'I'll look forward to hearing from you.'

4 pm

Madeleine had attempted to get on with her work for the remainder of the day, but she kept catching herself staring in a daze at the computer screen, and then wondering how long she must have been sitting there, slack-jawed and bug-eyed, doing absolutely nothing. A couple of times she had a fair idea, because she was roused by the screensaver, flashing and twirling around in its psychedelic pattern. This was getting ridiculous – she'd barely done a solid jot of work lately. At this rate she hardly had a right to be criticising Natalie's performance.

Her mobile started playing the rumba. Hopefully it was something that would jolt her out of this ennui. She checked the screen. It was Lucy from Trousseau.

'Hi, Lucy,' said Madeleine. 'How's things?'

'Things are all done,' she chirped. 'Your dress awaits you, my dear.'

Madeleine should have felt excited, but instead she felt as though she'd just been kicked in the guts. 'Oh.'

'Well, I have had better reactions.'

'Sorry,' said Madeleine. 'I'm just in the middle of work.'

'Then I won't keep you. I just wanted to let you know that your wedding dress is all packed up and ready for you to collect.'

That was about the last thing she felt like doing – it was only going to make her even more depressed. But she couldn't just leave it. Lucy had been so good to her, and it wasn't as if

Madeleine would have to tell her anything. In fact, it occurred to her that Lucy was probably one of the few people closely involved in the wedding whom she wouldn't have to cancel on or give an explanation to, thank goodness. So she might as well get this bit over with.

'How late do you stay open, Lucy?' Madeleine asked. 'I can come this afternoon, after I leave work.'

'Excellent,' said Lucy. 'I'll be here for hours yet. I'll see you when you get here.'

*

An oversized white box wrapped with a silver bow was resting on the counter when Lucy showed Madeleine into the salon.

'Here it is,' she announced.

'Oh,' said Madeleine. 'I thought it would be hanging up.'

'No.' Lucy shook her head. 'It could get damaged too easily in transit that way. It's all wrapped in acid-free tissue, and arranged carefully inside the box, where it can't get dirty, or scrape along the pavement, or get caught in car doors.'

Made sense.

'And when you get home, it's a lot of fun to unwrap it,' Lucy enthused. 'You should hang it up straightaway, though. There's a silk-padded hanger inside the box, and the dress has loops so that you don't have to hang it by the sleeves, they're too delicate. And you must leave it to air – do not cover it in plastic, no matter what. Depending on the humidity levels, it can discolour the silk.'

'Okay then.'

'I packed up the veil as well,' said Lucy.

'Thank you, that's sweet,' said Madeleine, though she knew she wouldn't be wearing it. She sighed inwardly. She wouldn't be wearing any of it.

'And your shoes are in their box, inside here.' Lucy held up a large carry bag.

'I can't thank you enough, Lucy.'

'It was my pleasure,' she said. 'I loved working on your dress, I think it's really special. I only wish I could see you in it on the day.

But that's the catch-22 of this job – Saturday is my busiest day, so I never get to see my brides. I have to wait for the photos.'

Madeleine gave her a weak smile. Damn, she would have to tell Lucy eventually. All that work for nothing.

Lucy carried the box out to the car, and Madeleine opened the back door so she could slide it in across the seat. 'Drive safe,' Lucy said. 'That's precious cargo you've got on board!'

She waved as Madeleine pulled away from the kerb. It was only a short drive to the flat. She realised when she got there that she wasn't going to be able to manage the box and the bag with the shoes at the same time. She would have to remember to bring the shoes up later.

She did manage to swipe herself into the elevator while juggling the box, but she had to put it down on the floor while she unlocked the door to the flat. As the door swung open she had a momentary feeling of dread – what if Aiden was here? Surely he wouldn't dare show his face? She could not have made it any clearer that she didn't want to see him. She picked up the box and stepped warily into the flat.

'Hello?' she called. But all she could hear was the muffled sound of traffic from the street below. That was a relief. She carried the box into the bedroom and set it down on the bed. The place was immaculate, even the bedding had been changed. At least he'd had the decency to clean up after himself.

But she wasn't going to think about Aiden now. Or hopefully ever again. She wondered what she should do about the dress. She wished she could just leave it in the box and not have to think about it, but Lucy said she had to hang it up to air it, something like that. She'd better do it – she didn't want to ruin the dress, even if she didn't know what on earth she was going to do with it. She doubted she was going to want to keep it, it would only make her sad.

Madeleine went into the bathroom and washed and dried her hands thoroughly. She kicked off her mum's shoes and stepped tentatively over to the bed. She pulled on the ribbon around the box and it unfurled perfectly, just like in a movie. But it wasn't fun like Lucy said, it was a little heartbreaking. She lifted off the lid and put it aside. The coathanger Lucy had mentioned lay across the top.

Madeleine picked it up and placed it on the bed. She moved aside the layers of tissue paper to reveal the bodice of her dress. It was so beautiful. She reached her hand down to touch the delicate beading, her fingers tracing the lines of the *H* and *M* entwined around each other at the centre. She leaned closer, tears pricking at her eyes, and before she could stop it, a single tear had dropped onto the embroidered letters.

'Oh no . . .' She grabbed a tissue from the bedside table and tried to blot it up, but it had already soaked in. Perhaps that was appropriate, poetic even. She stepped back, dabbing at her eyes. Calm yourself. She picked up the hanger and hooked it over the door of her wardrobe, then turned back to the dress. Okay, carefully now. She took hold of the bodice under the arms and slowly lifted as it unfolded, shedding more layers of tissue. She held it up high before her, the light from the window catching it so the fabric seemed to shimmer. Madeleine carried the dress to the hanger. She wasn't to let it hang by the sleeves, Lucy had said. She felt for the silken ribbons, looping her fingers through them and sliding them onto the hanger, over two notches, which were actually tiny rosettes sewn into place for the purpose. Lucy had a remarkable attention to detail. Madeleine drew the sleeves up to hang loosely off the ends of the hanger. There. She stepped back and stood, gazing at it. She saw herself walking up the aisle, hand in hand with her mother. She saw Henry standing at the end, watching her, one of those shy smiles on his face. But she was never going to get to see that in real life.

Madeleine sighed deeply, and caught sight of herself in the mirror in the pink paisley top. She pulled it off over her head and tossed it aside. As she stood there, gazing at the dress, she started to wonder . . . No, she couldn't try it on, definitely not. That would be pathetic. But Lucy had put so much work into it, she owed it to her to wear it once, finished. To be able to report – when she had to break it to her that there were no photos, that there had been no wedding – that the dress had fitted perfectly.

Madeleine was decided. She stripped off and opened her underwear drawer, rummaging around until she came across the bra wrapped in tissue paper, the one she'd kept aside especially to wear on her wedding day. She unwrapped the tissue and put it on. She had three pairs of the seamless pants – nothing like being prepared. She slipped on a pair, and walked back over to the dress. She picked up the hanger and turned it around. Oh damn, the buttons, she'd forgotten. Only the top one was fastened, obviously to avoid stretching and pulling at the tiny loops more than was absolutely necessary. They were only meant to be done up once more, on the day of her wedding, when she'd have someone to help. Not when she was alone, trying on the wedding dress she was never going to wear walking down the aisle, like some sad Miss Havisham figure. Oh God, maybe she shouldn't bother . . .

Or maybe she should just get over herself. It'd be all right, she didn't need to do all the buttons up, she'd get the effect well enough.

Madeleine undid the top button, being careful not to pull at the loop too much. She slipped the sleeves off the edge of the hanger, and then the ribbons over the rosettes. She lifted the dress from under the arms, as before, and the ribbon loops fell away. Madeleine lowered the dress in front of her so she could step into it, carefully positioning her feet so that she wasn't standing on the fabric. Then, slowly, she drew it up around herself, until the bodice was in place. But it wasn't going to stay there without the buttons done up. She gingerly wriggled one arm at a time into the sleeves. Okay, now it was staying up, though it was gaping a little. She twisted her hands back behind her, in various contortions, trying to reach the buttons, but it was no use. She couldn't do this on her own, she realised, and the realisation, the loss, was suddenly overwhelming.

'Madeleine?'

She swung around, her heart pounding. Henry was standing in the doorway, watching her.

'Henry,' she breathed. 'I didn't hear you . . .'

'The front door was wide open.'

She must have been distracted carrying the box and forgot to close it. 'But what are you doing here?'

'Looking for you, of course. They said you'd already left work, and I thought I'd try here first before I went to your mother's. I didn't want to upset her.'

'Oh.'

'Besides,' he said, shoving his hands into his pockets, 'Aiden was coming to pick up the rest of his things and I didn't want to see him, I thought I might do something I'd regret. I already lost it on the phone, but in person . . . He'd probably beat me in a fight, so, better safe . . .'

Madeleine couldn't speak. She still didn't understand what he was doing here. Had he come to have it out with her, once and for all? She didn't think she could take it, not that she didn't deserve everything he could throw at her. It was only fair, she had to at least allow him that much.

'Do you want me to do that up for you?' Henry asked. 'You looked like you were having some trouble.'

Why would he want to do that? But Madeleine just nodded, turning around, still unable to speak. Maybe she was in shock? Henry came up behind her. She shivered as she felt his fingers graze the skin on her back when he took hold of the dress. She could see his face above hers in the mirror, frowning in concentration as he fastened one button after the next. Madeleine so loved that face. She closed her eyes for a moment, imagining that everything was all right, that this was their wedding night, that he was helping her out of the dress, not helping her into it . . .

'There,' he said finally, his hands briefly resting on her bare shoulders. 'Turn around.'

She did, slowly, as he stepped back to take in the full effect. The expression on his face brought tears to her eyes. At least she had got to see that.

'You look . . . very beautiful, Madeleine.'

'Thank you,' she managed to say.

'But this isn't right, is it?'

Her heart plummeted. Of course it wasn't right. It was a charade, she was playing dress-ups, kidding herself.

'I'm not supposed to see you in your dress,' Henry added.

What? 'Well . . . it hardly matters anymore.'

He frowned a little. 'Why not?'

'Um, because . . . there's not going to be a wedding.'

'You don't want to go through with it?' he asked, his frown deepening.

She blinked. 'You do?'

'Well,' he said, 'I don't think you get to . . . to do what you did, and dump me as well. That doesn't seem fair.'

'Henry, I would never dump you,' she exclaimed. 'But after everything, after what I did . . .' She started to shake her head. 'You can't still want to marry me.'

He released a heavy sigh. 'I thought maybe I didn't, or rather, that I couldn't.' He sat down on the end of the bed, leaning his elbows on his knees and clasping his hands together. 'You see, I was worried that I wouldn't be able to look at you without imagining you with Aiden.'

Madeleine winced.

'But then I realised that would mean never being able to look at you,' he went on, 'never seeing you again, and that's something I can't even conceive.'

'Henry . . .' Madeleine dropped to her knees on the floor in front of where he sat, her dress falling in a swirl around her.

'I should have been more wary of Aiden,' he said. 'I assumed he'd have grown out of it by now, after all this time. But I should have warned you about him, at least given you some background.'

'Henry, none of this is your fault.'

'That's not entirely true,' he said. 'You were having doubts, feeling neglected –'

'That's no excuse for –'

'No it isn't,' he said firmly. 'But then again, you don't sleep with someone else if everything's okay in a relationship.'

Aiden had said something like that. But Madeleine wasn't going to let Henry take any of the responsibility for this. 'No,' she said. 'You stupidly sleep with someone when you're too drunk to think straight. I've got no one to blame but myself. Not even Aiden.'

Henry met her gaze directly. 'But I don't believe you would have slept with someone else if Aiden wasn't there. Do you?'

'I don't know . . . I don't want to believe that, but I've done it before.'

'Madeleine, you brought that up last night. I don't know why. We weren't officially in a relationship back then, we weren't even living in the same country. I told you at the time to put it behind you. I did . . . I have.'

'That's very gracious, Henry, but how many times can I expect that of you?' said Madeleine. 'I don't want to hurt you again, I couldn't bear it.'

'I'm glad you feel that way.'

'I can't put you through it anymore. Look what it did to your mother.'

'What?' he said. 'It's not the same. My mother stayed with a man her whole life, a man who habitually abused her and eventually destroyed her.'

'And I don't want to destroy you.'

'You're not like my father, Madeleine.'

'Maybe I am.' She took a deep breath. 'Truth is, I think I might be an alcoholic, Henry, and I have to do something about it. I'm going to do something about it.'

'Okay,' he said squarely. 'And I'll be right there beside you.'

'I have to fix myself,' she said. 'It's not your job to fix me.'

'But it is my job to stand by you while you do . . . Till death do us part.'

She was stunned, literally stunned. He was such a good man. He was too good for her. 'I don't deserve you.'

'Madeleine, you have to stop talking like that,' he said, getting to his feet. 'I don't want to hear it anymore.' He turned away to pace the floor, dragging a hand through his hair. 'You're always claiming that I saved you, but don't you know you saved me too?' He turned to look at her again. 'God, if anything, I'm more like my father, shutting myself off from people, from the world. I would have been alone, maybe for the rest of my life, if it wasn't for you.' He paused. 'I'll never forget what you said at the airport that time . . . you were worried you didn't come across well, that you grated on me. You had no idea . . .' He shook his head. 'Maybe I haven't loved you enough, or reassured you enough, that you are the best thing that ever happened to me.'

Madeleine's eyes filled with tears.

'Come here,' he said gently, reaching down to take her hands and helping her up to stand. 'Do you know why it's been so hard for me to write those vows?'

She shook her head.

'Because I've never felt the way I do about you, about anyone in my life before, and I honestly don't know how to describe it. I write children's books, full of simple ideas, but the way I feel about you, what you mean to me . . . that can't be contained in a few phrases. I just don't think words can do it justice.'

Madeleine's heart was so full she thought she might burst out of the dress.

'So I guess we'll have the traditional vows then,' she said in a small, tentative voice.

His face relaxed into a smile as he drew her into his arms. 'I think that's a very good idea.'

'And you know, I'm going to call that place and change the order to fruitcake.'

'I like fruitcake.'

'I know you do.'

He pressed his forehead against hers. 'Only one thing,' he said. 'I don't have a best man.'

'Oh, but I do,' said Madeleine.

The next day

Voicemail left at 3.30 pm.

'Hi, David, it's Liv. Um, look, I know this is kind of late notice, with your rosters and all, I don't know how easy it is for you to change shifts. But anyway, I was wondering if you'd like to come to a wedding with me? Next Saturday? The bride, she's probably my closest friend, and, well, for a moment there, it was on shaky ground – there's a whole story, but anyway, it doesn't matter now, everything's back on, and I think it's going to be a really wonderful day. I'm not asking you because I need a plus one or anything, but, well, I'd really love you to meet them . . . I'd love them to meet you . . .

'So anyway, think about it. Call me. Best finish before the –'

Beep.

Acknowledgements

It's been a long time between drinks. Actually, not that long at all between drinks, but too long between books. However, life gets in the way sometimes, and unfortunately writing is an occupation without sick leave or special leave for moving house. When you come back to your desk, no one has filled in for you and kept everything up to date, so that you can step back in as though you'd never been away.

I have many people to thank for helping me get back on track. I was going to give up, I really was, I thought the well had finally dried up. Then I had the spark of an idea, characters bounced into life and a vague journey came to mind. But I had no time to wait and see where it would go. I had to be efficient. I had to plan! Fortunately for me, Pat Naoum and Olivia A. Fay came to my rescue. I supplied soup and red wine, and we sat around a table until the wee small hours, plotting out the story on big sheets of paper with thick felt markers and sticky notes. Their enthusiasm energised me, and I don't know if I would have completed that first draft without them.

Thanks to my publisher, Cate Paterson, whose insight never fails to inspire me. She took that first draft, and along with my tireless and very patient editor, Jo Lyons, gave me wonderful direction and the space and support to make it bigger and better. Thanks also to Clara Finlay for a scrupulous copy-edit. Sometimes it takes a village to write a novel, and I'm so grateful to you all.

And now I must add a disclaimer: Characters in this book who happen to be publicists in a publishing house are fictitious and any resemblance to anyone from the Pan Macmillan publicity department is entirely coincidental – except for the exceptionally lovely characters! Which reminds me, congratulations to Tracey Cheetham – Her Eminence, Grand Duchess of Publicity and Marketing – on her well-deserved promotion.

Thanks always to my immediate family, Pat, Dane, Joel and Anna, for their love and support and for bringing the joy, but special thanks has to go to Zac, who had to shoulder more than his fair share of my angst. That's what you get for being the youngest and the last to leave home.

Thanks to fellow authors Liane Moriarty and Ber Carroll, and Tony Park, for the laughs and the drinks and the camaraderie. Heartfelt thanks to all of my extended family and cherished friends – there are too many of you to list here, but I can never *not* mention Diane Stubbings, because my debt to her is perpetual. And because I've never mentioned them before, I want to thank Zoey Berinati and Nikola Stubbs for being the best listeners in the 'burgh, and for managing to make me laugh when I didn't have a lot to laugh about.

In loving memory of Anne Murphy

More Titles from Dianne Blacklock

About Call Waiting

Of course Meg was a success: she planned, she set goals, she made lists. Ally never made lists.

Ally Tasker is trapped in a dead-end teaching job and a relationship that's going nowhere. Her college friend Meg has a fabulous job in advertising, a doting husband and a gorgeous baby boy. Why did Ally's life seem to be permanently on hold?

When her grandfather and sole relative dies, Ally has to return to the Southern Highlands. As she sets to restoring the rundown home of her childhood, the past unravels, and Ally realises the choice to be happy has been in her hands all along.

Meanwhile Meg's life is not as idyllic as Ally imagines. She longs to inject more passion and spontaneity into her life, but at what cost to her career, and more importantly, to the people she loves most in the world?

Sometimes you have to risk all you have to realise what is worth saving.

Find out more at: books2read.com/callwaiting

About Wife for Hire

When she was a little girl, all Samantha Driscoll ever wanted was to be somebody's wife. She would marry a man called Tod or Brad and she would have two perfect children. But instead she married a Jeff and he's just confessed to having an affair.

Desperate times indeed. Sam has to find a way to support her kids and keep her dream house, but she has no qualifications, having given up any career aspirations she might have had to become the consummate wife. So much for that. Then she finds the job she was born for: Wife for Hire - a service offering everything from domestic help to personal shopping to planning social events for people who don't have the time - people who need a wife.

Surrounded by a gaggle of girlfriends, an eccentric sister, a mother who brings whole new meaning to the word 'demanding', and two teenagers discovering their dad has hormones too, Sam successfully manages a cast of clients from the sublime to the ridiculous, including American businessman Hal Buchanan, who insists he doesn't need her services even if they are part of his executive package. If that's the case, why does he keep hanging around?

Sam may be a born organiser, but there are some things in life that do not go to schedule.

Find out more at: books2read.com/wifeforhire

About Almost Perfect

It's no big deal to love someone who's perfect ... The trick is to love someone despite the fact they're not.

With a beautiful house in an upscale Sydney suburb and two successful careers, anyone would think that Mac and Anna have the perfect life. But their marriage is cracking under the strain of infertility. Consumed by her dream of having a child, Anna cannot see how her pain and disappointment are driving Mac away.

Close by, in a beachside suburb, Georgie Reading and her sister-in-law have made their bookstore, The Reading Rooms, an unqualified success - unlike Georgie's love life. In her thirties, with a deadbeat roommate and no romantic prospects in sight, her beloved brother Nick suggests that maybe she's waiting for someone she was never going to find - the mythical perfect man.

Then Liam walks into the bookstore, and Georgie thinks she has finally found just that. Well, he's perfect for her, anyway. ... At the same time Mac and Anna reach breaking point, putting Mac on a path that will have unforeseen consequences for them all.

Find out more at: books2read.com/almostperfectblacklock

About False Advertising

Helen and Gemma, two women who couldn't be more different, are thrown together when their lives take an unexpected turn.

Helen always tries to be a good person - she recycles, she is even polite to telemarketers. As a mother, wife, daughter and nurse, Helen is used to putting everyone's needs before her own. But it only takes one momentary lapse of concentration to shatter her life forever.

There was no such momentary lapse for Gemma, she had never done anything by halves, and she had certainly never been quiet about it. So when she barges unceremoniously into Helen's life - pregnant, alone, estranged from her family, with a once-promising career in advertising in tatters - things will never be the same again for either of them.

FALSE ADVERTISING is about loss and grief and second chances, it's about knowing when to hang on, and knowing when to move on. And it's about realising that when life falls short of our expectations, it was all just false advertising anyway.

Find out more at: books2read.com/falseadvertising

About Crossing Paths

Jo had learned the hard way that life was not mystical, or magical; it was hard and grey and cold most of the time. Much better to see it for what it is than to be perennially disappointed.

It's not as though Jo Liddell never had dreams. She was going to be a journalist and travel the world, but life had a way of stealing her dreams right out from under her. Okay, she had her column, but heaven forbid she had an opinion about anything that mattered. And now that she's saddled herself with a hefty mortgage, Jo has resigned herself to living a less-than-perfect life.

That is, until she crosses paths with Joe Bannister - a celebrated foreign correspondent, returning home to care for his dying father, take the pressure off his long-suffering sister and maybe pull his recalcitrant brother into line. He did not expect to find himself falling for a headstrong woman who seems to resent him.

But after devastating news, Joe is forced to make an impossible choice, and Jo must fight hard for everything she never believed in - success, self-acceptance, and above all, real love.

Find out more at: books2read.com/crossingpaths

About Three's a Crowd

'Well, we're different, we lead such different lives. I'm not sure how we'll go now without Annie. She was like Carrie, you know, in Sex and the City. Annie was our Carrie.'

Without Annie, friends Catherine, Lexie and Rachel are lost. How will they fill the void? Will their friendship survive?

Catherine is characteristically unfazed, forging ahead in her high-flying career while struggling to connect to her unfathomable teenage daughter. But secrets from the past emerge to shatter her carefully constructed image, and threaten all the relationships she holds dear.

Meanwhile Lexie is juggling the demands of her young family and the ego of her hardworking husband, while taking the first tentative steps to achieving her own dreams. She just wished Annie was around to talk to - Catherine is so bossy, and Rachel ... well, her head seems be more in the clouds now than ever.

Rachel knows what her friends think of her - but what they don't know is that she's currently in the thrall of a new relationship. And she doesn't want them to know, because when the truth comes out, fragile friendships will be put to the test all over again ...

Find out more at: books2read.com/threesacrowd

About The Right Time

The Beckett sisters need to shake things up.

Emma has been planning her dream wedding even since she was a little girl, and she's determined to get her happy ending. Just as soon as her boyfriend Blake gets around to proposing …

Liz is a well respected and successful doctor and supposedly the brains of the family, yet she still believes her married colleague will leave his wife for her, one day …

Evie is cheerfully married to Craig, but after three children, things have stagnated. When Craig suggests a way to spice up their relationship, Evie is horrified - but she always tries so desperately to please …

And Ellen, the eldest sister and the anchor of the family, is dealing with the end of her marriage and getting back into the dating game. But she wonders if she'll ever be able to get naked in front of another man, let alone open her heart to love again.

When their parents drop a bombshell that affects them all, and one sister must make a life-changing decision, it's the right time for the Beckett sisters to band together and face the challenges head-on.

Find out more at: books2read.com/therighttime

About The Secret Ingredient

'Taste was such an evocative sense; Andie had closed her eyes, with the scone melting in her mouth, and been transported back to her grandmother's kitchen …'

Nourishment is nurture. That's what Andie learned from her grandmother and what she's always believed, but somehow, since marrying Ross, she's allowed her love of cooking to take a back seat and given up her dream of becoming a chef.

Lately she's been craving more. And as her marriage implodes, deception, betrayal and tragedy lead Andie all the way back to what really matters to her. The new Andie is ready for anything, even a bad-tempered chef who makes it clear he won't tolerate mistakes.

With help from the unlikeliest of allies, Andie uncovers the secret ingredient for a new life, and shows that no matter how many false starts, if you hold on to your passion and your dreams, anything is possible.

Find out more at: books2read.com/thesecretingredient

www.ingramcontent.com/pod-product-compliance
Lightning Source LLC
Chambersburg PA
CBHW032200180726
48284CB00001B/118